EUGENIA DMITRIEVA
VASILY MAHANENKO

A SONG OF SHADOW

*Books are the lives
we don't have
time to live,

Vasily Mahanenko*

THE BARD FROM BARLIONA
BOOK 2

MAGIC DOME BOOKS

A Song of Shadow
The Bard from Barliona, Book # 2
Copyright © E. Dmitrieva, V. Mahanenko 2018
Cover Art © Timur Kvasov 2018
Translator © Boris Smirnov 2018
Published by Magic Dome Books, 2018
All Rights Reserved
ISBN: 978-80-7619-005-4

TABLE OF CONTENTS:

CHAPTER ONE

R E-ENTERING BARLIONA turned out harder than I imagined. My fingers trembled as they reached for the capsule's sensors. My memory unkindly replayed the terrible agony I'd experienced during the changing of my alignment. It wasn't right. Who came up with the idea of torturing players like that? Or was this supposed to be a particular 'penalty' for switching to the dark side? A tacit punishment for choosing the faction of the gameworld's villains? And if so, what would I face later?

As soon as I slid into the capsule, the first thing I did was carefully double-check the sensory filter settings. Everything was as before—a pain threshold of 10%. After a couple seconds' hesitation, I turned this down to five percent. Realism is good and all, but I think I've had enough. More than enough.

Welcome to Barliona!

An updated Lorelei the Captivating looked at me reproachfully from the game's loading screen. There hadn't really been anything captivating about her before, aside from her epithet. Now, new, small and sharp thorns protruded from her aquamarine epidermis, their arrangement forming whimsical patterns in some places and completely chaotic ones in others. The epidermis itself was streaked with little black veins which contributed to the ornament's eeriness. The veins reminded me of the kind that frequently appear in holofilms as a symptom of some plague spreading through the victim's circulatory system. However, instead of the branching of vessels, these veins formed something like a runic script on my Blighted Biota. Perhaps this creative tattoo meant something in one of Barliona's languages. The only question was whom to ask for assistance in decoding it: a botanist, a dermatologist or a linguist.

My avatar's eyes had changed too: A regular green glow had consumed the iris and pupil. Strange—in the video from the web, the shaman's eyes had seeped with fog during the transformation. Was this a racial trait? Or was my scenario different? It didn't do any good to guess—I was better off entering the game and figuring things out on location.

I don't know what I expected—fanfare and an achievement like 'You have become the first player of Shadow' or maybe heaps of presents from the renegades, moved to the bottom of their hearts by my selfless deed—but whatever it was, nothing happened. Nothing at all.

I was even upset for a second: That Shaman Mahan got an epic sacrifice from the top players, trips to the ancient past, a unicorn on a leash, but little old me...all I got was a camp full of renegade vegetables. No fortifications, major facilities, haunted castles or even ordinary old houses. The place looked less like the headquarters of sinister conspirators, and more like a temporary camp for some tourists to spend a few days. Even the Sixth's 'throne room' was little but a simple meadow, albeit covered in blight. Although, I have to admit that the conspirators' tents were kind of pretty: Instead of the players' typical tents and huts, these were large cup-shaped flowers, whose stalks grew normally and then doubled over at about half-height so that the actual flower would cup a plot of ground.

Renegades from both races were running to and fro between the tents, individually and in units. Sentries in polished armor stood about; cauldrons boiled over bonfires under the watchful eyes of pirqs, awaiting troops returning from their missions. The ones about to set out were checking their weapons and equipment, going over their orders; a little off to the side, at a safe distance, some mages and bowmen were practicing.

All of this stood in contrast with the scenario I had seen in which Geranika recruited an apprentice, thus putting me on the thought that my plot line would be somewhat different.

"You've spent a long time coming to your senses, my new ally," a voice said so unexpectedly that I started and turned quickly.

Elegantly-attired, as if he'd just returned from a soiree, Geranika stood in the meadow smiling. It's odd to smile like that. Like a cat that was deliberating whether to eat the mouse now or play with it some more.

"The process turned out to be a fairly...painful."

The mere memory of it made me start.

"You had to be reborn, Lorelei. And birth is always a painful process. For a human, for an idea, for a new world order..."

As Geranika went on speaking, I tried to understand what the great villain wanted from me. I doubt he's about to pull out a celebratory cake with a burning candle and suggest I make a wish.

"A new empire is being born, Lorelei," Geranika went on. "An Empire of Shadow. A great war is coming and like any emperor, I will need useful people. Companions, strong and faithful. You are a special free citizen, Lorelei. You were unafraid to join the side of the renegades. You accepted Shadow, despite the loathing of those who live in Malabar and Kartoss. I find you interesting."

I listened in silence.

"But interest on its own is insufficient," he went on. "You are still too weak and I doubt you will be useful to my empire."

I perked up my ears. I doubt I'd survive another 'trial' like the last one. To hell with that. I'd rather delete my avatar and start again than go through that again.

"I can help you become stronger." Fog whirled in Geranika's open palm. "But first you must prove to me that you can be useful, Lorelei. Prove to me that I should expend my time and effort on you."

Quest available: *Impress the Lord of Shadow*.

Description: The Lord of Shadow seeks allies, but it's no simple task to join their number. Do something that will earn Geranika's consideration.

Quest type: Unique chain. Reward for completion: Variable, next quest in the chain. Penalty for declining the quest: -20 Attractiveness with Geranika.

So the rumors are true. Ever since Kartoss became a playable empire, the fora have been rumbling about a new Shadow faction. The wildest flame wars raged about the question of whether players would be able to play for Shadow. It looks like I now know the answer to that.

"I will do this," I promised and noticed Geranika's lip jerk just barely before he vanished.

I was left alone in the middle of the camp. Neither the Sixth nor her bodyguard were around. A short stroll around the encampment didn't afford me anything apart from the esthetic pleasure derived from the exotic flora-architecture, some observations of army life in the field, and the benefit of breathing some fresh air. The typical gaming infrastructure I was accustomed to, was entirely absent here. There were neither signs, nor barkers nor the barest indicator of where to go or what to do. Nothing but rows of flower huts, some sentries loitering beside them and the odd messenger hurrying past with a leather satchel. And that's it. An ordinary guerrilla outfit, with a touch of the local, floral flavor. And how was I supposed to level up my character? How was I supposed to make scratch here? Where could I find the gear I needed?

The answer to the last question popped up on its own. Using the scientific method of poking around aimlessly, I came across the local quartermaster, hiding out in one of the flower huts. This biota was sitting so still that I initially assumed he was part of the decor, and I would have moved on if he hadn't spoken up.

"I've never seen you before, Lorelei," the renegade said flatly. He was ensconced in the same plate armor I had observed on all the guards in the city. The same combination of wood and metal, only the wooden parts of it were black. He had a whimsical name too—Palisandro.

"It was only recently that I..." I hesitated, trying to find the right word. Switched? Became blighted?

Turned?

"Joined Astilba," Palisandro came to my aid. He smiled compassionately. "I know that the first days are the hardest. The life you were used to has ended. Difficult trials in the name of our brothers and sisters who cannot yet even fathom our motives lie ahead of you. I remember how shocked I was at first. Do you know what helped me?"

"What?"

"Work. Occupy yourself with whatever it is that brought you here. Move toward your goal and your doubts will waft away like dried chaff."

"Work..." I echoed. "I can't even imagine where to start and who to ask..."

Palisandro's thorny brows rose with surprise.

"Are you saying that no one has briefed you? Given you a quest? Assigned you to some task?"

I coughed with some confusion, recalling what an offline player looks like to an NPC. It's like sleep, but I suppose you could call it a deep coma too.

"No. After my transformation, I lost consciousness and came to only recently."

"It is a painful procedure," Palisandro agreed. "At least now you get to experience a new power. Our strength has grown so much among these shadowy lands that there are no unwanted guests that would dare visit us."

He had a point here. Whereas before the transformation the blighted ground would saddle me with a debuff, now it worked in the other direction:

Blighted Strength. +50% to all stats. +1% HP for every minute spent on blighted ground.

"Are there many unwanted guests that try to come here?" I asked.

"There will be quite a few soon enough," Palisandro squinted unkindly. "So don't waste time and prepare yourself properly. Choose the equipment you need and locate Yavar. He is personally in charge of the preparations."

The equipment was available without any restrictions, unless you take level requirements into account. There was no required reputation status—friendship sufficed. However, the quartermaster's inventory was hardly impressive. The same old assortment of vegetable, leather and metallic gear with the typical 'Shadow' skin and a modest +2 to various stats. Strictly speaking, some of my items weren't any worse, but I dispensed with modesty and picked out a full set of blighted gear. At this point, another not-so-unimportant detail occurred to me: The 'weight' of the armor affected stamina cost as well as my spellcasting time. Wearing the lightest gear available, which consisted mostly of the leaves and stalks of mysterious plants, I could cast spells at my full capacity. Leather armor would penalize my stamina slightly. Chain mail had a serious effect on my stamina and a little one on my casting time, while plate armor really encumbered both. A quick search of the fora brought me to a thread full of complicated formulas, from which I surmised only that as long as my Strength and Constitution stats remained below certain thresholds, heavy equipment was not for me. If I were a pirq bard, for instance, I could calmly jingle jangle around in my heavy plate armor all day long.

I couldn't help but recall the drawing I had seen on the forum: A pirq in what looked like knight armor (as it is depicted in historical films) with drums of skulls hanging on his chest. It looked impressive, but...As Pasha-Chip would say, it's not for me. Which is too bad...I could imagine it now: I step out all dramatic like the heroine of a mega-blockbuster about elves, jingling my plate armor and lute and the enemies just collapse all around me...in laughter. After all Pasha and Sasha would surely be right behind me, making stupid faces and just generally clowning around in their uniforms.

On the other hand, this fact didn't upset me in the least. The new gear looked quite solid—I was ready to step out on the stage of some goth festival. I wonder if I try to cosplay all this out in meatspace, whether I could wear this gear for a long time? I doubt it, considering the cute accessories like the belt and the bracelet of thorny rose and, even prettier, a necklace of the flowering branches of black bramble. The vaguely BDSM style was completed by a small, sheathed dagger hanging on my belt. It's not like I really needed it, but the renegades were giving me the equipment for free, so why not grab the dagger too? There was no concrete calculation here on my part—I just figured it'd be nice to have a knife if I went out into the wild.

When I had finished, I surrendered to my vanity for a second and stepped up to the large mirror and turned on my camera in order to take a memorable selfie-hologram. Recalling my assignment to shoot footage for our video, I didn't bother turning it off. The guys and I could select the more effective footage later and put together a nice clip.

"If you've satiated your narcissism," Palisandro taunted me kindly, "you should go see Legate Yavar and get to work."

Thanking the quartermaster, I set out to find the legate, relishing the creativity of the devs along my way. As Chip, my personal know-it-all, had explained to me, Barliona featured a mixture of old languages and cultural traditions of all the different races and peoples of our real, human history. At this point, Sasha set off on a wide tangent, comparing tattoos and writing, but Pasha stopped him in time, begging the lecturer to go make tea in the kitchen. Otherwise our excursion into comparative anthropology could have cost us a few hours at least.

I located the legate at one of the countless huts that housed the renegades. I was expecting to see something like a yurt of the peoples of the north, but approaching closer realized that I had made a mistake. The hut was constructed of enormous leaves, three times my height. They were bound in a clever manner by means of some kind of sticky substance, to which small litter had managed to stick before it had dried.

Legate Yavar was a stocky pirq with a leopard's markings, sealed in coal-black plate armor that sumptuously harmonized with his fur. The typical alterations caused by Shadow only made this NPC appear more vivid. The sword hanging from his side looked more like a mutated sickle with a long handle. And it was on this handle that he drummed with his fingers as he spoke with two other pirq officers also outfitted in black plate armor. Noticing me, Yavar dismissed his companions with a gesture and concentrated on my person.

"Ah, a recruit," he rumbled in a throaty baritone, and looked me over from head to toe, paused at my lute and shook his head disapprovingly. "And what am I supposed to do with a little booger like you?"

I made a mental note to cut this phrase out of my video, otherwise, I could just sense that this 'little booger' would stick to me—courtesy of my idiot friends.

"Any ideas, centurion?" The legate glanced over at the colossal, jet black pirq standing beside us with a Zweihander.

The pirq growled grimly, raised his upper lip, baring a row of sharp teeth and grumbled with displeasure:

"What could you possibly do with her? The best she could do is be a buccinator, but then she'd have to swap her lute for a buccina. And yet this piece of brushwood wouldn't even be able to lift the horn and were she to attempt to blow it, she'd fall apart to leaves…Better send her over to Altaik's turma, I say."

Listening to this exchange, I was silently grateful that I hadn't decided to play for the pirqs. It looked like this race had a militaristic society with a touch of ancient history about it. No wonder Pasha chose them.

"To the velites?" the legate asked. "You think I should send her beyond the blighted ground at her level?" He squinted. "It's too high a risk."

"She's a free citizen," the centurion reminded him. "It's easier for her: The free citizens can return from the Gray Lands."

The legate twiddled his whiskers, weighing the pros and cons, as I tried to understand what they were even talking about. Well, I mean, in general I had understood that my formidable Level 7 made it difficult to find me a suitable quest, yet the details of their conversation escaped me.

At the same time, Yavar glanced at me and asked with some doubt in his voice:

"We need to think…You can't summon an army

of phantoms with your music like your Tenth, can you Lorelei?"

"No..."

"Then it's decided," the pirq stuck his paw into a huge bowl carved of wood, pulled out someone's charred rib and began gnawing on it with a pensive look on his face.

"To the velites," he declared. "Seek the scarlet banner with the lightning bolt emblem on it. You will report to Centurion Altaik."

Quest available: *Help the Renegades.*

Description: The Renegades of the Hidden Forest have committed themselves to preventing an alliance with Kartoss. Locate Centurion Altaik and offer your assistance. Quest type: Rare scenario. Reward for completion: +50 Reputation with the Renegades of the Hidden Forest; +100 XP. Penalty for failing or refusing the quest: -50 Reputation with the Renegades of the Hidden Forest.

Naturally, I accepted the quest and leaving the hut began peering around for a scarlet standard. It was nowhere to be seen, but at least my old friend Vex appeared on the horizon. And I still had questions for that book thief.

"Vex, hang on!" I called, hurrying after my fellow bard.

"Ah, Lorelei," he waved and stopped. "Are you feeling better?" he inquired when I approached.

"Yes, quite a bit! I have some business to discuss with you."

"Is it urgent?"

"Not very," I confessed, "but it won't take long."

Vex looked away somewhere to the right, in the direction of the enormous tree whose roots formed the seat of Astilba's throne and answered unhurriedly: "Go on then, but do so quickly."

"Did you take a part of the songbook from the Tree library?" I asked without wasting any time.

The renegade looked at me a little oddly and nodded.

"I did. How do you know this?"

"Back at the Tree, I was trying to decipher the songbook and discovered that it was incomplete. The librarian recalled that you were the last one to work with the scroll."

All of Vex's hurry vanished instantly. He turned to face me, squinted his eyes and asked tensely: "You know how to decipher the songbook?"

"Well, yeah," I said with some surprise. "Weren't you doing the same thing?"

"Not at all. I'm a poet, not a musician. I was merely copying the scroll at Astilba's request, but I didn't manage to finish my work and was forced to...extract the last fragment from the library."

"What does Astilba want with the songbook?

She's definitely not a bard."

The renegade nodded, sighed deeply and waved his hand, offering me to have a seat in the shade of a sprawling thorn bush. It did not seem like he was in a hurry any longer.

"As you know, a bard's spells are learned in conjunction with the spells of other classes. Astilba is trying to divine the structure of Cypro's spell and recreate it on her own."

"What kind of a spell is it?"

Vex hesitated and then replied barely audibly:

"Cypro knew how to summon the souls of heroes who had passed to the Gray Lands. Astilba cleaves to the hope that she can return the Fifth. She asked me to find all mention of this spell and my search brought me to this scroll. The writing in it is some kind of cypher, so I was simply copying the scroll to give it to the Sixth. Unfortunately we have no bards who specialize in music and so we had no luck deciphering the scroll. But if what you say is true...Perhaps Astilba will accomplish what she's sought all this time."

"Perhaps," I echoed, though I had my doubts.

As far as I understand the info in the Barliona FAQs, the dead could only return as mindless undead or members of the zombie race. In order to have an NPC return to the world in his right mind and sense, some kind of magic seal would be required. It followed that the Fifth didn't have this seal...and a zombie lover would please only some fan of stupid pseudo-romantic movies, not Astilba.

"Notes are written in it," I explained to the excited biota. "I already deciphered the part in the library, so if I get the rest of it, it won't take me long to recreate the songbook."

Vex jumped lightly to his feet and announced decisively:

"I will speak to the Sixth and if she grants her permission, I will bring you the missing fragment. Wait for me."

"Hang on," I stopped the renegade from rushing off. "I've been sent to Centurion Altaik. Tell me where I can find him and we can just meet there."

"Altaik?" the bard ruminated. "Follow that there brook downstream and you'll come upon his turma. But wait for me to return and if anyone orders you otherwise, tell them that you're waiting for orders from the Sixth. Understand?"

"Yes. Do I have to wait long?"

"Not long," Vex insisted and dashed toward Astilba's meadow residence.

I decided to pass the time productively—by filling in my map. To my surprise, Chip's drills paid dividends and I managed to chart a part of my route from my former place of imprisonment to the renegades' camp. It wasn't very precise, but there were definitely less white space on the map when I finished. If things go on this way, the cartographer's mysterious prize is as good as ours. Chip just has to copy my map and complete the quest. There was just one issue...If we did this, Eben would get his hands on the map with its vague, yet discernable, location of the renegades' camp. And then who knows what the spymaster would do? No. First I have to find out how the Sixth's attempts to resurrect her lover will turn out and only then move on to the map quest.

At last Vex returned. He looked very worried and was all but dancing from impatience.

"The songbook!" He waved a small scroll in front of me. "Here is the missing portion. You have to decipher all of it. This instant!"

Quest available: *Decipher the Songbook.*

Description: Vex wants you to restore and decipher Cypro's songbook this instant. Quest type: Unique, class-based. Restrictions: You must begin the quest on the spot and perform it until it is complete.

Reward for completion: +1,000 Reputation with the Renegades of the Hidden Forest, +14,000 XP. Penalty for failing or refusing the quest: -1,000 Reputation with the Renegades of the Hidden Forest.

"Erm..." I mumbled, a little at a loss as I read the quest description. "I guess I'll just do this now then."

I looked around, found myself a spot near the

roots of a tree where a stranger wouldn't run into me, sat down and leaning against the trunk unfurled the remainder of the scroll. This was definitely it—the same babble about the sun, the Milky Way and the seven planets. There was no surface suited for writing on, so per habit, I arranged the parchment on the body of my lute. Someone else might find this uncomfortable, but my guitar synth had served me as a desk, as an umbrella and even a club in its day.

The experience I already had in deciphering the scroll did its part and my work went quickly. The only irritation was Vex who stood over me and drilled the scroll with his eyes to the point that I was afraid he really was going to burn a hole through it.

"Are you going to stand there all day?"

Instead of replying, Vex nodded curtly and pointed at the unfurled piece of scroll impatiently. No one has any patience these days. Although, hell, neither do I. I do want to know what spell the Tenth used to summon the army in my vision.

Just over two hours had passed and the work was done. A lean stack of sheets covered in notes was lying before me, and still nothing happened. No fanfare, no system notifications about a completed quest...Nothing but Vex's impatient and inquisitive look. There was nothing left but to shrug in reply and start reviewing the notes. Maybe I had made some mistake? A single inaccuracy could throw off the harmony of the composition. Of course, there was a simple way to check the thing.

Having no music stand, I placed the sheet music right before me, picked up my lute and recreated my uneven row of marks with sound. The melody was a pretty one but clearly unsuited to a lute. The sound was missing something. As harmonious and complete as the music was, there was something inadequate about it. Still, I sensed no mistake in it.

As soon as the final chord had rung, the sheets with the deciphered notes began to glow. My yearned-for fanfare sounded from somewhere and the parchment vanished, leaving behind a songbook shimmering in a pearl glow.

Congratulations! You have recovered Cypro's legendary songbook!

Your deciphering of the songbook has taught you a new spell: 'Bonds of Memory.'

Since times of yore, bards were the keepers of memory about the feats and tragedies of Barliona's heroes and villains. Thanks to the bards, tales of the past remain in the memories of the races, creating an imperceptible bond between the present and the past, the living and the dead. This bond permits certain bards to use their songs to summon the souls of the heroes of yore. To be resurrected, the souls require a portion of the Bard's vitality and their strength depends on the strength of their summoner.

Casting time: Perform a composition about the summoned soul from beginning to end. Cost of performance: 50% of the Bard's max HP. Maximum level of the summoned soul: (Bard's Level + Composition) Maximum number of the summoned soul's skills and spells: (Soul Level ÷ 10 + Composition). Maximum number of souls summoned at once: (1 + Composition) Duration of summoned soul's stay in Barliona: (Intellect ÷ 10 + Composition) hours until the soul exhausts its vitality. Cooldown: 72 hours.

Skill increase:
+3 to Bardic Inspiration. Total: 14.
+3 to Fame. Total: 14.

Quest complete: *Recover the Songbook.*
+500 Reputation with the Biota. Current status: Hatred.
+10 to Fame. Total: 21.
Speak with the Tree's Librarian to receive the rest of your reward.

Quest complete: *Decipher the Scroll.*
+1,000 Reputation with the Renegades of the Hidden Forest. Current status: Friendship.

Experience earned: +14,000 XP.
Level gained!

...

Level gained!

Current Level: 18.

Unallocated stat points: 90.

Training points remaining: 6.

Achievement unlocked:

'Legendary Hit I' (Four learned or created songbooks remaining until next rank).

Achievement reward: +1% chance to receive a quest that leads you to a legendary songbook.

The pure glory of the notification made my eyes ripple, while the golden flashes that accompanied the new levels only aggravated the situation, and I spent a long time blinking dumbly and rereading the system messages. My entire rich lexicon failed me, leaving a single unprintable but ecstatic exclamation in my head. Now this is the way to complete a quest!

"It worked," Vex whispered in shock. "You did it, Lorelei! Quick! Give me the songbook so I may bring it to Astilba!"

The songbook, which had managed to appear in my palm, was shining enticingly.

Cypro's songbook. Songbook type: Legendary. Contains the 'Bonds of Memory' spell.

Attention! To reproduce this song, you must have a rare musical instrument.

Attention! Your spellbook already contains 'Bonds of Memory.'
Attention! This songbook may not be copied.
Attention! This songbook may not be traded.

I was holding a scroll with a unique spell. I wonder, purely theoretically, how much I could ask Astilba for, for a spell she wanted so badly. As far as I know, NPCs in this game cannot take a player's property outside of very rare scenarios. Theoretically I could haggle and refuse to hand over the songbook for free.

Eh. I'm not much of a businesswoman and lucre's just lucre.

"Here you go."

I handed the songbook to Vex without further thought. It's much more interesting to find out how the Sixth's experiments will work out than to get my hands on a heap of gold.

"Tell Astilba I wish her luck. I hope everything will work out for her."

The renegade clenched the scroll tightly in his hand and smiled warmly. My Attractiveness with him surged to 55 points.

"I will relay your words to her. Thank you, sister."

And Vex rushed off like a whirlwind in the direction of the Sixth's residence.

"Think nothing of it," I called in his wake, forcing

him to look back.

It was always like this: Either a torrent of new events or solitude and indecisiveness. If you discount the new levels I had gained, nothing had changed for me at all. I couldn't even use my new spell—I had no rare instrument. And no way of finding one. The local quartermaster didn't seem to have any, and the craftsmen around here weren't exactly master luthiers. Maybe I could ask Chip? And yet, even if we pooled our resources we wouldn't have enough for one of Pirus' pieces. All right, we'll talk it over out in meatspace. Only, before exiting the game, it wouldn't be bad to find out what quest I'm supposed to get from the mysterious centurion.

The camp, meanwhile, had gone on with its own life. You could hear the growling of the pirq teams, the clangor of arms, the coming and going of small bands of warriors. Those who had returned were eating ravenously outside of their quarters and then immediately collapsing and falling asleep in their bunks without taking off anything apart from their footwear and armor. It's much easier for the players in that sense—we could sleep in our armor without experiencing the least bit of discomfort.

Centurion Altaik turned out to be a light-ginger, almost blond, pirq. At the moment of my visit this glorious warrior was occupied with five tasks at once. He was hungrily consuming his bowl of gruel and meat, drinking milk, kicking his boots off his feet, glaring into a map and bitterly arguing with one of my cousins, a biota.

"What'd you need?" Altaik growled, generously bespattering my new cape with his spittle and bits of gruel. Uncultured bastard...

"Legate Yavar has sent me to you," I rattled off, carefully brushing off my cape.

My answer forced the two quarrelers to fall quiet. Then again, the centurion used this interlude productively, taking the moment to stuff more grub in his maw. Smacking, he began to inspect my person. My cousin, Immortal Biota, also fell to looking me over and for a while the silence in the hut was punctuated only by the centurion's smacking and chewing. Having finally finished his meal, Altaik purred with contentment, licked his spoon, placed it on the table and deigned to interact with me.

"Well and then what does he want?"

I definitely didn't expect this question. The transition from legendary events to 'what'd you want?' was a little too swift.

"Erm..." I declaimed profoundly. "He wants you to give me some quest."

"Recruit," the pirq barked at his companion.

Only now did I notice how closely the two resembled each other—the pirq and the biota. Not in appearance but...in their expressions, their eyes. They were filled with an old weariness mixed with some kind of grim, doomed decisiveness and confidence, which did not gel with their intentionally-careless demeanor.

Altaik slid the empty bowl aside and asked: "Do you know how to read a map?"

Receiving my nod as an answer, he went on: "Look. We're here right now." The centurion's finger poked a green triangle in the middle of a forest shaded with black. "Our turma's objective is to extend the fortifications up to this location..." Altaik picked up a lead pencil and marked a series of dots indicating a route. "We haven't any time to spare, so everyone has to work. Right now, you will go to Signifier Lotos, receive equipment and instructions and then get to work. Any questions?"

A short dotted line between the forest and the foothills indicated where my future work lay.

"Where can I find Signa-uh-fier...Lotos?"

"He's in the third bulb-tent downstream from here."

Signifier Lotos turned out to be a sickly-gaunt biota of a reddish hue, which I couldn't help but associate with the color of spoiled meat. Having heard my explanation, he quietly issued me two linen bags filled with black seeds, large and small, a piece of parchment with something that reminded me of a rat maze charted on it, made a mark in his giant book and dismissed me with a gesture.

Quest complete: *Help the Renegades.*

+50 Reputation with the Renegades of the Hidden Forest. Current status: Friendship.
Experience earned: +100 XP.

Items acquired: Shadow Seeds.

Quest available: *Help the Renegades. Step 2.*
Description: Sow the Shadow Seeds. Quest type: Rare scenario. Reward for completion: variable reputation increase with the Renegades of the Hidden Forest, variable XP gain. Penalty for failing or refusing the quest: -500 Reputation with the Renegades of the Hidden Forest.

Boy, I sure am lucky: First the garrulous legate and centurion, and now this dumb plant who doesn't even deem it necessary to explain what it is they want me to do.

"Erm...And where am I supposed to sow them?" I asked when it became clear that further instructions would not be forthcoming.

Lotos glanced over me gloomily, sighed barely noticeably as if he was sorry to have to speak the words and replied: "Sow them based on the pattern—the locations have been marked on your map."

And he stuck his thumb in the direction of the exit.

Quest updated: *Help the Renegades. Step 2.*

Description: Sow the Shadow Seeds in the locations indicated on your map.

Once I was outside of the tent of the unfriendly biota I opened the map and studied the locations to be sowed. At least there was a bit of luck there: the quest area was practically abutting the Arras. This means that the time had come to coordinate with everyone who wanted to cross it.

It was time to exit Barliona.

CHAPTER TWO

OUR FURTHER GAMING PLANS became subject to wide-ranging discussion. In addition to Sasha, Sloe's guildmates also wanted to cross the Arras and at this point Sloe announced that he would act as the scout. The plan was elegant in its simplicity. Sasha hit on the idea of selling his contacts in the Dark Legion the opportunity to enter a closed location. By way of payment he was going to ask the Legion to teleport his avatar to the Arras as well as protect him from the hostile mobs in the area.

"Under no conditions can we let third parties in on this! Let alone the Dark Legion," Sloe objected on the conference call. He looked like he was about thirty, tall, gaunt, with a pocked, narrow face. "My clan will handle teleportation and security. We'll sweeten the deal with some gear for you, useful scrolls and whatnot—whatever your noob soul desires. But no Dark Legion or anyone else!"

"What do you care whether you lot get in there alone or with someone else?" Chip asked, surprised by his reaction. "The more, the merrier—and the higher the chance of victory."

"Why there's a whole forest of local scenarios here!" Sloe brushed him off. "And they're there for those like me who started playing as pirqs or biota. The new location has to have a new dungeon. Whoever completes it first, will earn incredibly useful bonuses for his guild. There's nothing dumber than sharing an advantage like that with your competitors. Got it?"

"Not really," my warriors shook their heads in sync, and Sasha elaborated:

"The hell do you need to get into the game so much? It's like you people are losing your minds in there..." At this point Sasha trailed off and began to snuffle the air with his long nose. In the next instant he yelled, "The burgers are burning!"

And Snegov jumped from his seat and dashed into the kitchen.

Sloe's sigh of despair sounded in the comm, while Reed, who had stayed silent this entire time, remarked bashfully: "For some people this isn't a game but a means of survival. For people like that, having an advantage is important."

Reed's appearance matched his voice. He was an ordinary-looking guy my age with a potato-shaped nose and a shock of reddish hair. His mussed hairdo reminded me of the Scarecrow from that ancient kids' movie. All he lacked was a straw hat.

"We won't ever understand that," Pasha confessed, opening a box with the model of some ancient vessel named SS *Great Eastern*. I don't know why this five-funneled steamship was famous, but both soldiers had danced a shamanic dance over the kit's box when it was delivered and were now planning on spending all evening assembling it. They had a generally unhealthy, in my view, obsession with various models of historical and speculative-historical machinery. Pasha's room, for instance, was decked out with shelves full of all kinds of junk: From an ancient T-34 tank to a small Death Star. On the other hand, this hobby helped Pasha train his fine motor skills which were lacking following his accident.

"I don't want you to understand, I want you to keep in mind," Sloe explained patiently. "Don't you care who it is that helps your friend reach the Hidden Forest?"

"Not one bit," Pasha replied laconically, using a precision knife to separate the parts from the rest of the plastic cast. "The goal is the most important thing...Everything else doesn't matter. Hah!" He triumphantly raised half of the hull and held it out to us like he had just dug up a nugget of gold.

"Excellent," Sloe smiled with satisfaction. "I will coordinate the party and conduct the negotiations. Now, explain to me please exactly what you're planning on doing. As I understood, we won't be leveling up with Lori anymore, but we now have the opportunity to provide the Seventh with information about the renegades. I imagine we can use this to squeeze out something interesting."

"You can decide this among yourselves. I'm curious to see what's going on among the local villains. You can figure out how to use this information on your own. I'll tell you everything I see without any problems."

"What are your plans, Chip? Are you going to switch too or will you go on fighting on the side of good?" Sloe asked Pasha.

"We'll have to wait and see," the pilot replied vaguely, concentrating on some unruly piece of the model.

"Uh-huh," Sasha backed him up, returning from the kitchen. "You can rest easy my fine friends—I have saved our dinner!" He sat down beside his friend, and arming himself with some pliers began to separate the tiny pieces of plastic.

"Good, evil..." the ranger smirked, "It's all nonsense. As they used to say: What's good for one is death to another. Like for instance, who decided that Bastilda or whatever her name is, is evil?"

"Astilba," Sloe corrected him fastidiously. "Well it's just an example. Anyway, why do you want to go to that location? The pirqs and biota won't exactly welcome you—crossing the Arras will immediately give you a negative rep with them. The renegades won't be happy to see you either. They're like Nazis or whatever—they're opposed to alliances with other races. And what are you going to do there at your

Level 30?"

"See the sights, hear the sounds, smell the smells," Sasha shrugged. "Maybe dig some holes..."

"Tourism, in other words," Sloe concluded.

"I'm a tourist in general," giggled the ranger. "Where haven't I been! I've even gamboled on the surface of the moon! And all on the taxpayers' dime."

Sloe waved his hand grimly and turned to the most taciturn member of our party.

"Reed, do you have any plans?"

"Not in particular," Reed shrugged his shoulders. "I'm reading the forums bit by bit, considering how I'll make money and leveling up. Only..." He blushed deeply, coughed bashfully and with a little difficulty added: "I uh...I'm in a party. With Kate...I mean Brouhaha. We're leveling up together."

At the mention of Brouhaha, Pasha twitched a cheek, which led me to conclude that he hadn't forgotten her insult. Like a little child, I swear...Sasha merely smiled to himself, and Sloe calculated something to himself and then looked over at Reed doubtfully.

"Once you leave the starting location, I'll ask my people whether they need a bard for their party. All right, let's get in touch later. I'm going to arrange the raiding party for crossing the Arras."

"I'm going to return to the game too," Reed announced, concluding our slightly muddled deliberations.

The burgers in the kitchen sure smelled good.

"Time to eat," Snegov ordered, intercepting my look and sliding aside his tools. "Pasha, set the altar of sacrifice."

To my amazement, the burgers tasted much better than the ones the autocook would make. The guys discoursed about man's superiority over technology, while I couldn't help contemplate a small paradox of life. All of my guy friends proudly claimed that cooking wasn't a man's job, but a woman's—that they were humans, not kitchen appliances. And as a result it worked out that in the minds of most of my generation, cooking became an unworthy activity, a lowly one and entirely non-masculine. And here were two grown men, who had seen things that I hadn't even seen in the movies, cooking their hearts out without for a second imagining that this was somehow to the detriment of their masculinity. To the contrary: What kind of a man would you be if, far from civilization, you died shamefully as a result of your own inability to provide food and shelter for yourself? You can't argue with that. Eh, something strange and perverse is happening in our society if helplessness has become a synonym of civilization and progress.

"But really," once I'd satiated my hunger, I returned to the topic of Barliona, "what are you really going to do in the Hidden Forest?"

Still munching on his burger with gusto, Sasha

flashed me a sardonic look.

"You'll laugh," he said. "I just want to get out."

"No, I get that part. But—how? Everyone you meet is going to try to kill you. The biota for crossing the border, the renegades for being an alien. Dying again and again seems to me a bit suspect as a form of entertainment."

"They'll have to find me first," the ranger waved his hand. "I've got a good handle on camouflage and I've had a decent cloak made. Once we meet up with Pasha, we'll figure out what to do next."

"Are you asking me out?" The pilot formed a little gable with his recently-regrown eyebrows. Considering how the rest of him looked, the ensuing face was simultaneously comical and terrifying. "Oh you monster!"

"What of it?" the ranger spread his arms akimbo. "A romantic stroll through the woods. A bonfire of ents, a bouquet of biota skulls..."

"You don't say," Chip agreed. "You, Snegov, should be writing novels instead of wasting your time in the army. Novels about love among psychos."

"You forgot a muff of pirq hide," I couldn't keep myself from contributing my own banter to this idyllic scenario.

"And you should be his coauthor," Pasha chimed in. "A perfect partnership."

In response, Sasha stuck out his tongue and shuffled closer to me, saying:

"Keep your jealous envy to yourself, you pirq muff. You better hope we won't come skin your hide for its fleas! Right, Lori?"

"Aren't you forgetting something?" Pasha squinted slyly.

"Like what?"

"Well..." The pilot propped himself up against his chair's armrest with an expression of triumph on his face. "Your numb skull has forgotten how Lori likes to treat her allies!"

Sasha made a grimace of terror, stole a piece of the burger from my plate and jumped away, almost losing his balance and rolling out of the kitchen on his stool in the process.

"I rescind my offer!" he yelled, stuffing the stolen piece into his gob.

"Eh, where has my knight in shining armor gone?" I sighed with all the pathos I could summon. "All you men are alike! You only think about one thing—how to get some more grub!"

"Thass uss alright..." The ranger agreed through his stuffed mouth and spread his arms helplessly.

After dinner, Sasha went home. As we understood from his vague explanations—he had to get ready for a 'romantic stroll through the Hidden Forest.' Pasha and I chatted some more and then went to our rooms. He went to bed, and I entered Barliona. I wanted to go over the quest I'd received and see what it entailed.

I traveled the not-so-short distance to the location indicated on my map without any problems. The blighted beasts didn't bother me and the mysterious sentries of the Hidden Forest didn't enter blighted ground. The tall thickets of thorns and brambles, like the one that fenced the Sixth's meadow, kept them from shadowing me. If this were all happening out in reality, the thick thorns would have long since tattered my leafy cloak to pieces, as well as my dark blue dress and thin fringe.

In general, these thickets were all over the place and they didn't grow randomly as much as according to some sort of system. I tried my best to fill them in on my map, but I didn't bother checking everything out either, so my 'doodles' looked a bit like the intestines of some mysterious animal. I don't even want to imagine what I would be in this simile.

The difficulties began once I'd reached the border of the blighted ground. My path wound its way through, but there was an overgrown ent with a very unpleasant appearance standing in the fog. A Level 300 Forest Sentry. So there's the catch in this seemingly simple, at first glance, quest. Go ahead and try to get past a guard like this.

"Okaaaay..." I remarked to myself, staring into the monster's smoldering, red eyes.

I wonder whether he's a sentient relative of the biota or something like a nature elemental.

"Greetings, my dear fellow!" I called as politely as

I could from a respectful distance.

No reply. No reaction whatsoever. He kept staring at me from the edge of the blighted ground as before.

"I mean you no ill!" I reassured the creature without much enthusiasm. "I would simply like to pass on my way!"

Zero emotion. The dull log! Standing there, guarding the border. Hmm...why that's an idea...

Knowing ahead of time that this idea was actually a dubious one, I got out my lute and played the Hendrix lick...

Machine gun
Tearing my body all apart
Machine gun
Tearing my body all apart...

Three magic missiles went flying at the wooden giant and one after the other slammed into the monster. Fail. The Forest Sentry shifted his weight with a displeased look, but there was no other discernible reaction. That's what you call, 'not even tickled.'

Right. Even if the sentry can step onto the blighted ground, it would take me two months to kill him, no less. If I can even hit them, given our level difference. This means I have to find another way. The tactic of moving in camouflage had worked earlier, maybe it'll work now too?

I activated my natural camouflage and began

creeping along the border. The sentry followed me with a stern look. Oh come on...Okay. What are my other options? I looked over the wooden colossus critically: He had short legs. This Pinocchio might not be much of a sprinter. In theory I could simply run away from the sentry, reach the location indicated on my map, toss out some seeds and then book it to the next patch. I wonder where I'll respawn if things go awry? The Tree with its Branch of Oblivion was closed to me and according to the lore that was where we biota received our new bodies. Although, surely there was a mechanic for biota players to respawn in the wider world? In that case there should be a respawn point here too. The only question was how far it would be from my current position. I didn't want to check, but my options were fairly scant.

Okay, what else do I have in my arsenal? Buffs won't help, debuffs...Weakening spells wouldn't do me any good and I didn't have any slowing debuffs. Song of Confusion? A debuff to perception might allow me to creep by camouflaged, but I'm afraid that playing the lute will give away my location, and that spell was channeled—the target had to hear the music. It wouldn't work.

Vengeful Flame. Here I had to pause for thought. In theory, this spell would allow me to kill the sentry even at my level. That is if he will maintain his distance and doesn't have any ranged spells to take me out with first. He might throw some pine cone grenade or something, who knows. But even if things went perfectly according to plan, the spell would destroy us both. If I stop at 1% HP for the two of us and heal myself...Practice had just shown that it would take me hours to finish off the ent, and that wasn't taking into account any regeneration that he was capable of, or self-healing etc. Meanwhile, Vengeful Flame's cooldown was 24 hours. Nothing doing.

Therefore, the only useful spell was Shadow Haze. What's the deal with its range and effect duration?

Shadow Haze: Target area is covered with a haze of impenetrable Shadow in which only creatures who have adopted Shadow can see. Even a divine gaze would have trouble piercing the haze of Shadow.

Negative effect: -40% to efficacy of divine magic.

Negative effect: Blocks all communication.

Effect duration: Until spell ends. This spell is channeled. Confusion or some other form of control over the character interrupts the spell. Casting time: Instant. Cost of performance: (Spell radius) MP per second. Maximum radius: (Intellect ÷ 4) meters.

Cooldown: 1 hour.

Hmm. Purely theoretically, I can cast the haze, dart in the direction I need and gain a decent head start before the sentry realizes what's going on, leaves the area of effect and finds me again. The question is whether he uses sight to orient himself or some other sense. I wish I knew whether I had the mana pool and stamina to make this work. All right. My mana regeneration was 2 MP per second, which wasn't great. Either way, I'd never know if I didn't give it a shot.

For the lulz, I waved farewell at the sentry and returned to the thicket of black brambles where he couldn't see me. It's dumb to hope, but it's dumber not to try—what if losing sight of me, the sentry will simply go about his business? I'll study the pattern that Lotos gave me in the meantime, compare it to the lay of the land and visualize where I have to sow the seeds. It's better than trying to figure all that out while on the run.

The Forest Sentry didn't go anywhere. Either the jerk sensed that I'd be back or that was his typical post. For the sake of curiosity, I returned to the brambles where the sentry couldn't see me and left the blighted ground at a tangent to the path I needed to take, skirting the watchful ent. It's much easier to loop around the dangerous area than perform dubious experiments.

The first few minutes it seemed to me that I had tricked the system and that my ruse had worked. My minute of patting myself on the back was interrupted by the sentry's thunderous footsteps. He was ponderously moving to intercept me, returning my intellectual benchmark to its previous position—average. Of course. The Forest Sentry had sensed a threat to his dominion, otherwise, what kind of sentry would he be? I didn't much feel like checking what means of intercepting me he had at his disposal, and so as quickly as I could, I dashed for the area I was supposed to sow with the seeds. According to my guesstimates it was near a plant that resembled a giant gladiolus. The sentry added speed but was still moving much slower than me. The forest echoed with my triumphant laughter. That's how we do it! First you have to catch me, you slow stump you!

And then the stump caught me.

A tangle of roots burst from the earth, two of them coiling around my legs, binding them with the force of steel shackles. I went down and kissed the ground at full sprint, earning a 'full kisser' (as Sasha liked to say) worth of leaves and humus, which, unexpectedly, tasted pretty good! Still, I began spitting and sputtering reflexively and cast Shadow Haze.

The world went gray but didn't lose its definition, while the sentry slowed his pace and began looking around in confusion. So his sight is important to him after all. It's too bad only that it isn't vital. This driftwood was no dummy, and he continued to lumber in my direction where, in his educated guess, I should be fettered by the roots. And, damn it all, there was some logic to this.

I quickly tried to get up on my feet, fell down, sat up awkwardly, grabbed my lute and cast Song of Cleansing, really, really hoping that the roots wrapped around my legs were classified as a 'negative magic effect.' There was no result. And for good reason— there was no debuff to dispel. What to do? Scorch everything around me with Vengeful Flame? Or should I start casting magic missiles at the roots one at a time. My mana would evaporate in a moment...

The approaching sentry wasn't helping my thought process. The ground beneath me kept shaking from each footfall. Damn, damn! I'll try to destroy my fetters. I quickly selected a wooden noose wrapped around one leg and was about to blast it with a magic missile when I noticed that the root was subject to a coveted buff: 'Magic Control.'

Song of Cleansing—on the root this time!

This freed my right leg, the root holding it slithering back under ground where it should've stayed all along. Now the other leg...

I jumped up and dashed away from the approaching guard. He had just reached the spot where I had been trapped. He tarried there without finding anything and again stomped his bark-covered paw.

Once again roots burst from the ground, and

again I faceplanted into the earth, but this time I managed to free myself much faster. Even if belatedly, but I recalled that I can spread my spells across several targets at once. It's too bad only that I didn't gain any more knowledge or mana in the process. The sentry turned his terrible face in the direction of my lute and thumped in my direction. I gave myself a knock on the head: If I only had a brain! I needed to use Canopy of Silence immediately!

I cast the canopy with the smallest radius possible—one meter—but I didn't dare start running again. Another faceplant was guaranteed, the spell's channeling would be interrupted, and the sound of the faceplant and its attendant jingling would clearly be heard by the monster. My mana wouldn't hold out for too long, so I should use the time left to me to study my opponent and work out a sensible strategy.

I forced myself to calm my beating heart and walk carefully backwards, away from the Forest Sentry, playing my lute and maintaining the canopy. Damn, my hands were occupied and I couldn't drink a mana potion or even some water!

The log had just now reached the site of my second fall. He stamped in place pensively and then began stomping, telegraphing the roots' appearance. This time I stopped ahead of time and avoided faceplanting. Moreover, my brains finally woke up and began to analyze what was going on. Another Song of Cleansing made a deep hole in my mana reserves, so I had to dispel the canopy of silence and drink a mana potion.

Due to your racial trait, a minor mana potion restores 100 MP.

Drinking the potion doubles your mana regeneration for 10 seconds. Current mana regeneration: 4 MP per second.
Current mana: 293/760 MP.

Life goes on! It's too bad only that my reserve of a dozen mana potions seemed a bit meager at the moment. On the other hand, I began to discern a pattern to the sentry's actions. The roots were popping up only within 100 meters of the thumping log. They would pop up and if they missed their mark, they'd disappear again underground. And what if I tried jumping in place at the exact moment that the sentry stomped?

I didn't have to wait long to find out. The next blow that shook the ground followed about ten seconds after the previous one. I didn't try to run and merely waited for the log to lift its paw and then jumped as high as I could. I have to say that in meatspace, my jumps weren't so impressive—here I flew up by a good one to two meters and watched with pleasure as the roots that erupted from the earth retreated empty-uh-handed.

Current mana: 133/760 MP.

A second potion of mana.

Current mana: 233/760 MP.

This time the Forest Sentry didn't leave. He tossed his hoary head left and right, trying to hear the trespasser. I, in turn, tried my best not to make any noise. After ten seconds a new stomp came. A jump, the roots flailed in the air futilely and retreated underground. It looks like it takes ten seconds for his spell to cool down. The radius remained unchanged, about a hundred meters.

Current mana: 73/760 MP.

I drank seven potions in a row and looked sadly at the remaining three bottles. Finding a timer in my interface, I waited for the next 'stomp,' jumped and as soon as I landed, sprinted away from the sentry.

Current mana: 701/760 MP.

Never in my life have I run so fast. By the next appearance of the roots, I had managed to leave the haze's AoE and cover a quarter of the distance left, when the timer reminded me that it was time to jump again. The roots popping from the ground didn't get me, but they did indicate that the sentry's spell range was close by: About five meters ahead of me, the vegetation was behaving itself as it should without any writhing roots to be seen. Without slowing down I ran for my yearned for gladiolus.

You are tired. Current stamina: 35/100.

Without breaking my stride, I whipped out my flask, sipped some water and happily read a notification about my fully-restored stamina and temporarily increased mana regeneration.

Current mana: 305/760 MP.

I was nearing the gladiolus, while my timer counted down until the next stomp. Two, one...Jump! And nothing. Landing, I looked around in midstride. The sentry far behind me was slowly trudging toward the border of the Shadow Haze, the presence of which had no effect on my own vision. It just looked like a portion of the forest landscape had been filmed in black and white. And in this monochrome scene, a solitary ent was slowly trudging to the land of Technicolor.

Current mana: 241/760 MP.

I only needed time to plant at least one seed

before he gets out of there and my mana goes to zero and the haze is dispelled. As I approached my flower objective I slowed to a fast pace and opened my map. I need to head north a little and skirt that small hill...Uh-huh! Right there!

Current mana: 81/760 MP.

I couldn't see the sentry for the hill and I hoped that stupid stump couldn't see me either. My mana was almost out and I needed to save the remaining potions for an emergency. As for now, it was time to sow some seeds.

There was no explanation for the big and small dots in the pattern, but I figured that these designated the spots to sow the large and little seeds respectively. The earth shuddered beneath my feet, reminding me of the Forest Sentry's implacable approach. I quickly took a large seed from my bag and examined it. It seeped black fog in my hand. How was I supposed to sow it? Simply stick it into the ground? Which way was up and which was down? And how deep did it have to be planted? The earth shuddered once more. The hell with the details! Taking out my dagger (I guess it turned out useful after all), I feverishly dug a shallow hole, stuck in the seed and covered it with the loose earth.

Quest updated: *Help the Renegades. Step 2.*

1 of 14 large seeds planted.

13 large seeds and 57 small ones remaining.

Achievement unlocked! 'Grim Sower I' (Sow 9 more Shadow Seeds to earn the next rank).

Achievement reward: +1% to Blight spread.

As I was about to run for the next waypoint, my old friend, the Forest Sentry, appeared from behind the hill. I still did not have much mana and there was a good hour left on Shadow Haze's cooldown, so I had to act quickly and accurately. Wait for the root spell, jump into the air, reset the timer and keep running!

As the log caught sight of me, he roared triumphantly and raised a stumpy paw. I jumped as the roots erupted all around me.

Hang on. Not all around me!

The spot of earth immediately under me was growing black, the grass withering and sprouting thorns. As soon as I landed, the system greeted me with a welcome buff.

Blighted Strength: +50% to all stats. +1% HP for every minute spent on blighted ground.

A safe space! The large seeds blight the earth and create a refuge for me! It was too bad that the blight spread slower than the sentry's approach. Something tells me that he won't have to step onto the actual blighted ground in order to get at me with his big old paw. And this means I have to keep running. In theory, the problem isn't a complicated one: Maintain a respectful distance, jump once every ten seconds and wait until the blight spreads and creates a refuge. At that point, 'I'm back on base!'

In actual fact everything worked out differently. The sentry chased after me with all the grace of a galloping elephant, and I tore in a wide arc, dutifully hopping according to my timer. After the third seed, though, the sentry no longer 'stomped' to send the roots after me. He stopped, looked up at the sky and glowing emerald will o' wisps began to circle his ample trunk.

A bad feeling rose in my gut and I took off as fast as I could for the slowly-spreading spot of blighted ground...I didn't make it.

Whirling in a spiral, the swarm of fireflies beelined after me...

Damage taken. -230 HP.
HP Remaining: 0/230.
Attention! Respawn Penalty: -30% XP.

The launch screen and a familiar notification:

You have died. Enter Barliona again in 12 hours.

Sheer pedantry compelled me to open the battle

log. I'm curious after all just how hard the stump had let me have it. What I saw was impressive: 100,000 damage from a spell with the telling name 'Sylvyn's Wrath.' I expect it'll take me another couple hundred levels to be able to survive that kind of attack. Like I give damn though. I was pleased with myself: Despite the sad conclusion of today's adventure, I had found a way to complete this quest. Maybe not at my first attempt and maybe not even the second, but with practice I definitely would manage it. And that means that I'll be able to reach the Arras and lead Sloe's clan through it, then get my hands on all kinds of nice gear and have an easier time of this game. But that's all later. Right now, I needed to sleep.

CHAPTER THREE

I SLEPT IN RIGHT THROUGH THE MORNING. I'd forgotten to set the alarm, the apartment was dead silent, and so I only woke up to a cautious knocking on my door around noon.

"Kiera..." The door cracked open and Pasha's snout appeared in the opening. "Do you feel like having some breakfast?"

"Mmm?" I muttered and tore my head from the pillow. I glanced at my comm lying on the ottoman, made out the time and muttered something by way of confirmation. The door shut and the room turned into a mini-zombie-apocalypse complete with the awkward shuffling, incoherent mumbling and generally undead appearance of the main heroine. It was only once I'd come to in the shower that I mentally reproached myself. Some assistant I was, sleeping in until the patient had to call me to breakfast and not the other way around.

I made up for it by doing the daily cartridge swap. I had already mastered this procedure: Take out the empty cartridges, put them into the sterilizer, insert the new ones until they click and make sure that the regenerators are working. Pasha would blush and huff and puff like an ancient steam engine every time I performed this procedure. In order to distract from his clearly awkward thoughts, he began to rattle off his morning's virtual adventures with an exaggerated bravado.

"After I respawned, I found myself back at the training ground," he said, making an effort to look away from the sterilizer, which I was loading with used cartridges. "It's all messed up in there, worse than you see in the post-apocalyptic horror flicks. That weird touch-me-not, the botanic Krampus was there. He jumped on me as soon as he saw me; almost pulled out my whiskers in his excitement."

"Touch-who-what?" I inquired about yet another one of Pasha's verbal pearls.

Used to this, he explained:

"Like a prude. You know, one of those who won't abide any jokes in their direction and immediately adopt the pose of a Spanish cavalier ready for a duel. Old Eben in other words."

"I'm afraid to ask how you came up with that one. And so what did this, uh, prude want from you?"

"Eh...He wanted to know what the hell happened at the training ground and who was responsible for the damage to state property at his secret facility. I explained to him in simple terms—I mean that piece of oak really has trouble understanding simple speech—what was what, so he grabbed me by the gills and dragged me to the local jail. I had to explain to him that you were really getting into your Mata Hari act and that I was like your tracer agent."

"Tracer agent?"

"Come on, Kiera, you've been living with us how long?" Pasha seemed outraged by my lack of knowledge. "And you still haven't mastered ordinary human speech! A tracer agent is like a messenger for other secret agents. That's it...I'm putting Snegov on notice for his neglect of your military intelligence education. Although never mind..." Pasha caught himself, "we're dealing with a ranger here. They're too sensitive for punishment. Reproach them once and they'll soil the slippers the same morning."

"I think I can even guess whose," I chortled. "So what about Eben? Did he give you some new quest? A medal perhaps? Tell me he gave you a cookie at least!"

"Yeah right. I'd have to wait till kingdom come before that cactus would offer me a baked good," Pasha snorted and twitched a little as I inserted another cartridge and the alimentary liquid once again flowed through the regenerator's tubes, growing the tissue. "He deigned to grant me four levels. And it wouldn't be a big deal but that I went in there as a Level 9 druid so that now I guess I'll have to be a druid forever. That's all she wrote, the ship has sailed and we will all die now: You can't change your class at Level 13. That herbarium cheapskate, mmm...yeah...He's worse than my old master sergeant at the academy. In exchange, he heaped me with a ton of orders—not shy that one." Pasha giggled: "He wants a breakdown of their resources and the location of the HQ and their future plans and he wants it all nice and chewed up like fodder for a chick's beak...or for his roots...how do those plants eat anyway? But basically, he wants it all on a plate."

"And half a kingdom as a reward, I hope?"

"If only...He's just offering some magic junk from the local warehouses. I didn't delve into the details, but I wouldn't get my hopes up if I were you. These penny pinchers are watching every tax copper. So it's good if they don't punish us, and the whole reward thing is a different matter altogether."

"What are we going to do then? I've already marked the camp on the map, but I don't know anything about their plans yet. And what if Eben & Co. decide to act all of a sudden? I still haven't learned the renegades' history."

"Dang, Kiera!" Pasha howled like a hero of Greek tragedy and grabbed onto his head for dramatic effect. "I keep teaching you and teaching you...We're going to inflate our valuation on our own. You'll feed some info to that damn root and he'll give you some trifles in exchange and heap praise and titles on you, after which everyone will set out to do battle against the rebel barons. Just make sure to plug up their throats: Our whiskers are our own and we won't be led about by them. So we draw out the fun, hike the payoff amount and when we reach the maximum, we'll deliver the goods. In the meantime, make sure to avoid taking any initiative that may affect our family budget."

"Already family?" I asked, surprised by such a turn.

"Uh what? Are interracial marriages banned in there? Discrimination," Pasha sighed. "But all right, in that case we'll call it the company budget—which is even more important."

"And how are we going to increase our valuation as you say?" I asked just in case. "Relay news from the field like, 'I've died once again in an attempt to infiltrate the citadel of evil?'"

"Leave that to me," Pasha said soulfully, pressing his hand to his heart. "An old warrior is a wise warrior. When it comes to telling tall tales, only our long-nosed friend could outdo me. I promise you: You're going to be number one in the botanic spy rankings by the end of the week. They'll even present you with a gilded spike."

"Why a spike?" I asked, baffled.

"So you can poke a hole again after they kiss your butt closed," Pasha explained.

"The poet in you has died," I replied to such a lyrical turn of phrase. I was even envious.

"Well I'm an old soldier and I don't know anything about words of love..." Pasha sighed pitifully and added: "And yet I know many other shorter but very effective words! This old lieutenant colonel will make a human of you yet!"

"Listen, maybe you should give it up? The army, I mean. You could be our band's manager. With your cunning, we'll be touring the world within a month."

"No, no, no!" Pasha shook his head, frightened. "It's me who's going to end up doing a tour—in prison for murder. Or at the cemetery from a heart attack: Edilberto alone is worth a squad of greenhorns, and that's not mentioning the hordes of civilians at your concerts!"

"Well, you've torn out my career at its root," I feigned sorrow. "Actually, about careers. What are we going to do with your character? You was going to be a warrior. How is a pirq going to play as a caster?"

"I imagine I'll get by one way or another," Pasha shrugged.

I really had found my way into odd company. Pasha didn't care about his character's future, Sasha only ever repeated that it was just a game, and I had borked my own character for the sake of a plot twist. When Pasha climbs into his capsule, he groans like a centenarian, but when Sasha offered him the box with the steamship, he hopped up and down like a 10-year-old and almost sent his regenerators flying to the floor.

"Honestly, this whole thing is kind of whatever to me," Pasha went on in the meantime. "When I get

better, ain't no one ever going to see me in that
Barliona again. Oh, by the way! You were asleep!
Listen up: We've hatched a sly and artful plan!"
Propping himself up on one arm, Pasha lowered his
voice conspiratorially.

"'We' as in you and the biota, you and Snegov—
or you and your schizophrenia?" I asked suspiciously.

"Well, persons two and three in your list are
actually just the same individual," the pilot corrected
me. "My plan with the biota isn't artful, it's merely
racy—more so than OG Kush. Anyway, they're going
to remove that thing from my jaw today and then
tomorrow we can go and do a barbecue! What do you
say?" He gave me a look like he'd just gotten tickets to
Iron Maiden undead at the Albert Hall.

"I'm up for anything, apart from a hunger strike.
I'll have to reschedule band practice with the guys
though and wrap up some business in Barliona.
Ideally, I'd like to reach the Arras, so don't wait for me
too long. I imagine I'll be eating dinner inside the
capsule tonight."

* * *

I RESPAWNED close to the renegades' camp, in the
center of a circle of mossy boulders. It wasn't exactly
Stonehenge, but it looked solid all the same. I wonder
how the game lore justifies being respawned in this
spot. And whether any of the NPCs know it...Then

again, now isn't the time for idle curiosity. I have a lot of work ahead of me.

First I need to increase the time I can channel the Shadow Haze. Should I invest some points into Intellect? Then I'd be able to increase the AoE of the haze and get a big leg-up. It's too bad but it looks like I won't be able to avoid doing this. I'll invest a few unallocated stat points before my next attempt and try to grind Intellect in the meantime. First I'll heal myself until my mana's gone, then take a sip from the flask, a small yet welcome increase in my mana regen, after that more healing and so on and so forth.

Mana potions are vital too. I had the alchemist trait and even a small collections of herbs, but those would be but a drop in the old mana pool. I hadn't seen any chemists around here and, anyway, most of my cash was in the bank. I'll have to ask Chip to pick up some potions for me. The important thing is to choose some place that won't be too difficult to rendezvous at.

This is where the difficulties began: The renegades were obviously trying to blight the entire forest and I didn't know the areas already blighted and more importantly the paths connecting them. Should Chip and I simply beeline for one another, or should we check out the renegades' territory? I'd guess the second. I have to know where I can move safely.

The next item on the day's agenda was traits. I

spent a long time ruminating why unlike that Mahan, I didn't get any of those shadow spells I'd seen in the videos. Every class in that quest got new skills and powers, but not me. And, I believe, I stumbled on the answer. I could simply learn whatever powers I wanted from the renegades' classes. And in that case I should figure out what I can spend my training points on as well as what I'll need for my upcoming battle to sow those seeds. In other words, the time had come to chat up some folks.

I didn't have many acquaintances in the camp: Vex, Palisandro the quartermaster and the not-so-friendly legates, centurions and all those other velites. I didn't bother adding Geranika or the Sixth to this list for obvious reasons. Those two weren't about to teach me for nothing. Heck, I couldn't even have much of a conversation with them. Although...Aren't I on good terms with the Sixth now or something? Should I try my luck? And yet how exactly is a necromancer going to help me kite the Forest Sentry? Either way, I should talk to her last. Vex, on the other hand, was someone who could surely help my cause with some sensible advice.

As it turned out, I wasn't destined to talk to Vex just then. As soon as one of the armored pirqs saw me, he waved an enormous paw.

"Lorelei!" he barked so bombastically that I jumped in place. "Astilba wishes to see you!"

"W-why?" I was so stunned by the bellowing of

my name, I even got the hiccups. Had this been meatspace, I would've outrun my own squeal.

"The details of the matter aren't my concern. My orders are to deliver the Sixth's summons and bring you to her."

It all sounded so emphatic that I didn't even bother arguing. My only connection to the Sixth aside from our mutual faction was the Cypro songbook quest. It's reasonable to assume that I was about to discover the next episode in this chain.

We headed for the familiar meadow but contrary to my expectations, I didn't find Astilba sitting on her throne. In fact she wasn't around at all. The pirq didn't seem bothered. He stomped confidently past the giant wolves following us with their eyes and approached the spot where the roots webbed together. He had barely entered the dusk cast by the immense tree's shadow when I finally noticed that which lay hidden from the prying eyes of anyone straying into the camp's closed area. An entrance to a dungeon stood darkly within the tree's roots, cloaked with a shimmering film. A dungeon! The very one that our dear Otolaryngologist and his buddies were looking for, and the same one Sloe wanted to find. Yeah. Given the renegades' level, none of the above would be finding this dungeon any time soon. I think Chip was having his effect on me because my next thought was to sell the location's coordinates. Not now, of course, but once the scenario was done. I wonder how much I could get for this info...?

As soon as I stepped through a barely glowing area of the meadow, a system notification appeared before me:

Message for the player! A new dungeon has been discovered: Headquarters of the Renegades of the Hidden Forest. +50% chance an enemy drops a valuable item. +20% XP earned.

Yup. Really valuable information. Hell, I could turn this entire place, the Sixth and all, into a loot-rich source of XP mixed with compost. As for unlocking new areas, that was as useful to me as a saddle on a cow.

My contemplation of the meta ended barely having begun. No sooner had we entered the dark passageway, which smelled of humid earth and withered leaves, than we found ourselves in a curious facility. A system of tunnels running among several spacious halls was built into the tree's roots. The floor, the walls, if these terms still applied here, were covered with barely glowing moss which created a mysterious gloom and lightened the otherwise grim ambience. Here and there hung clumps of some kind of blighted plant. I could swear that when I passed, some part of them moved.

We went through about seven halls but I only managed to glance into one and even then briefly. I saw an imposing biota in beautiful, intricately-ornamented, wooden armor explaining something to a ginger, furry pirq. I recalled both the pirq and the biota from my vision of the Schism. This was the Second—the eldest warrior of the biota—and one of the pirq chiefs that I was seeing with my own two eyes. Does this mean that these boys were going to be the bosses in this dungeon? And so Astilba too? The thought alone made me feel a bit queasy. This means that the scenario's outcome was predetermined and the renegades would become XP fodder for the players coming from Kartoss. Shall good triumph or shall evil conquer? Who cares? The game was all that mattered. It would be an ignominious end to an interesting story.

As I reflected on all this, we reached the end of our brief journey. I would call this place a laboratory, even though there weren't any workbenches with alembics, vials, crucibles and all that other fluff that typically decked out labs in the movies. In exchange, there was one very ominous-looking altar and shimmering pentagrams etched into the very even and for some reason stone floor. There were hexagrams too and a couple other-grams. The Level 400 demon standing in the center of one of these etchings did not seem like an ornament that the Sixth had chosen for her interior. And indeed Astilba herself looked different from last time: Her traditional biota dress of flower petals, as well as her vermillion mantle, were decorated with various characters. A small scabbard hung from a belt fashioned of the same petals and a necklace of a dozen softly glowing stones was clasped around Astilba's neck. It all looked like items from the 'Dream of the Necromancer Set,' no less.

"I have no answer to your question," the demon standing on the other side of the magical barrier growled to Astilba. "That which you wish for is impossible!"

"You err," the Sixth replied in a deceptively soft voice—an indomitable flame blazing in her eyes. In one deft flick she whipped out a strange looking knife, squatted down smoothly and with one swipe etched a new line, changing the image. The glowing lines flared up for a moment then faded and the demon vanished in a puff of red smoke.

"Greetings, oh Sixth," the pirq escorting me bowed reverently and I hurried to follow him. This NPC gave me the shivers. I don't know who programs the game imitators—or how—but they definitely know what they're doing. A single glance at Astilba was enough for me to sense her presence with my own skin: Hers was not the kindest vibe, but it was definitely vivid.

The Sixth straightened out, put the dagger away, raised her head and fixed me with a dour, trying look.

"Thank you, Borofos. Leave us now."

Without a trace of obsequy, the pirq bowed his head and retired, leaving me one on one with the local dungeon boss.

"Lorelei," Astilba said with an odd intonation, either greeting me in this manner or acknowledging the fact of my existence. I glimpsed at the level of my Attractiveness with this NPC: 32 points and that was taking into account both the quest I completed for her and my Charisma. Not bad at all. In any case, she wasn't about to sacrifice me.

"Sixth," I replied unable to think of anything better and bowed in response.

The necromancer approached the altar and picked up a scroll lying there. A very familiar scroll. Cypro's legendary songbook.

"You are very young, Lorelei," Astilba went on. "And yet you managed not only to decipher my old friend's songbook but master the spell that it contained. The question, however, is—will you manage to use your music to summon a soul from the Gray Lands?"

"I think I could." I didn't bother offering anything further because I hadn't even tried using my newly-learned spell yet. Who knows, maybe there's a snag there, some secret requirement? "However, my poor lute is too crude and common to perform such a summons."

"I shall procure for you a worthy instrument," the Sixth promised, "but I need you to summon the soul in my presence. Bardic magic is compatible with other forms of conjuring, and yet I was unable to understand the structure of this spell on my own. The best I can do is observe the channeling of power, study the magic that you wield and then recreate the same incantation in a spell of my own. As a reward, I'll teach you one of my spells. Are you willing to help me, Lorelei?"

Quest available: *Summons from the Gray Lands.*

Description: Astilba wants you to summon a soul from the Gray Lands in her presence. Quest type: Unique, class-based. Reward for completion: +1,000 Reputation with the Renegades of the Hidden Forest, +15,000 XP, and one of Astilba's spells. Penalty for failing or refusing the quest: -1,000 Reputation with the Renegades of the Hidden Forest, -30 Attractiveness with Astilba.

There wasn't anything to consider really.

"Of course, oh Sixth, I will be happy to help you."

The necromancer nodded as if my answer had never been in doubt.

"Excellent. Let's move on to the instrument now. Our camp lacks a suitable luthier and purchasing it through our brothers who remained on the Tree would take some time. But it just so happens, that I have held onto an instrument for an old friend. If you manage to get the eid to produce a sound, we won't have to await a delivery from master Pirus' store."

Quest available: *Taming the Eid.*

Description: Make the eid—one of Cypro's legendary instruments—produce a sound. Quest type: Unique, class-based. Reward for completion: Hidden. Penalty for failing or refusing the quest: None.

Everything seemed to be working out suspiciously well. That's a hell of a reward for casting a single spell, and it comes with the opportunity to play a legendary instrument that used to belong to the oldest bard of the Hidden Forest...And what's the difficulty? What's this taming deal? The eid isn't some bull or mustang to need taming. More than likely it's some exotic hurdy-gurdy that takes 'a few drinks to figure out' as Beast liked to say about any instrument that had more (or, for that matter less) than his four string Ibanez. All right. In any case, I won't risk anything if I fail this quest.

"I have never seen an eid, but I can try to...uh...tame him."

The Sixth hummed to herself for some reason but didn't say anything more. She gestured me to wait and left the hall. I fought my desire to touch the altar, walk around the etched symbols and stick my curious nose in all the nooks and crannies. This isn't meatspace of course, where (were it even possible) poking around the palaces of power would end in tears, yet still, I didn't feel like risking Astilba's good graces. Who likes having a guest wander around rummaging in their cupboards when they're out of the room? As a result, all I could do was look around, recording everything on my camera.

I didn't have to wait long. The Sixth returned with a large vegetable cocoon in her hands. Not a bad case for this eid, it catches the eye. All that remained was to figure out what the eid actually was. Astilba dispensed with any further drama and suspense. The necromancer recited a spell, touched the cocoon with her hand and it opened, revealing its contents.

It's not like my knowledge of acoustic instruments was exhaustive, but it was ample enough to understand that if *this thing* can produce music, then it's entirely due to magic. A body of leaves without the slightest hint of a sound hole, the fretboard's heel growing right out of the body, a smallish growth where the bridge is supposed to be and as for the strings themselves...they were neither steel nor nylon and not even the sinew of some legendary dragon. More than anything else, they reminded me of the whiskers of some coiling plant, stretched taut. The pegs were made from pine (or perhaps cyprus, I'm not much for wood) cones.

Mmm...yeah....It's not much of a surprise that not just anyone can play this strange invention of the devs. I too feel a bit at a loss. But okay. There are plenty of players who run around this place armed with swords that are larger than they are—why can't I jam out on some botanical Stratocaster. What's so complicated about it? Pick it up and play—that's the extent of it. Thinking such happy thoughts I picked up the instrument.

You meet a hidden requirement of this quest: Master of String Instruments.

Please confirm that you wish to enter the 'Intermundis' location.

What's this Intermundis place?
Confirmed.

CHAPTER FOUR

THE FIRST THOUGHT I HAD upon entering the new location was that there had been some glitch in the game. I was surrounded by a white blaze that roiled in constant motion. A milky ether whirled and tumbled all around me, triggering nausea and dizziness. Thankfully the game's interface remained motionless, a single island of clarity and regularity in the constantly changing world around me. I shut my eyes and breathed in and out several times. I felt a little better. My nausea ebbed and I regained the ability to think a bit.

And so. I am in some kind of quest-based location. A strange location. What I can do here aside from throwing up what I'd eaten wasn't clear. But logic suggested that since this quest was connected with the eid, who remained in my arms, then I should focus on the instrument. After all, I still need to learn to play it. So what does it matter where I do this—in the forest or in this vomit comet.

I was forced to open my eyes after all: It's very difficult to play an instrument you're unfamiliar with without being able to see it. I tried to look only at the eid, ignoring the white vortex, and gradually I ceased to notice it entirely. A close examination of the instrument did not enlighten me about the bridling procedure. What am I supposed to tame here, when I'm holding what amounts to the weirdest guitar in the world. Recalling a phrase from an ancient joke— 'there's no time to think, you have to jump!'—I placed the fingers of my left hand on the fretboard and strummed the strings with my right, fretting several chords. The eid produced a strikingly deep and clear sound and out of the corner of my eyes, I saw the white vortex twitch.

I halted my experiments and, taking ahold of myself, looked at where I had seen the odd motion. Alas everything remained as before: a dizzying vertigo. I concentrated once more on the eid and promised myself that I would hold off from enjoying the local landscape. I'd be happy to rip off the hands of the jerk that thought up this Intermundis—right down to his knees. Perhaps someone wasn't well after an intense drinking binge and decided to recreate his feelings in VR. Fifty shades of nausea, or something like that.

I brainstormed a dozen or so stinging epithets for the dev in question and, having blown off some steam, turned back to the eid. On the whole, the problem wasn't such a complicated one. The fretboard was a bit too long and there were twelve strings like a concert guitar, but nothing radically new. A little practice and my fingers were soon finding the right frets. So what's the taming part all about?

If Master of String Instruments was a hidden requirement, then I suppose I have to do better than finger some chords and play a cogent piece too. I didn't attempt anything fancy and decided to try one of the fantasy songs I had learned especially for the gaming audience, one composed by some musician larpers. Their oeuvre was all over the web but I downloaded several greatest hits albums in this genre and chose the songs that would sound best on lute.

I liked this song. It had that special, elusive magic which took its listener to the nonexistent world of fairy tales. Perhaps a sad one, but beautiful and magical. In addition to this, the very name of this place, Intermundis, forced me to recall a song about the intersection of worlds.

The beautiful ballad of love and separation, of traveling between worlds, was captivating. Every musician tries the song on himself, for a short time living as the protagonist, living the song, believing in it. You can't instill true passion or sincere feelings into your performance without this. If you don't believe in what you're singing, the listener won't believe it either. So I too transformed into a wandering minstrel, suffering from the many separations in his life.

The last chords sounded, I lowered my trembling hand and inhaled the fresh forest air, tinged with a hint of smoke. Some people really know how to compose...To invest an entire world and an entire destiny into four couplets...

The epiphany came with a bright flash. A forest? Smoke? I looked up from the eid and around in astonishment. The milky white nauseating ether was gone. I was surrounded by a warm, summer night; a full moon filled the meadow with a silvery light and the fading embers of a bonfire pulsed at my feet.

Where had all this come from? How?

"Beautiful..." said a voice behind my back blissfully.

I jumped from surprise and managed to turn while in midair in violation of all the laws of physics, which I guess isn't surprising considering how they'd just been violated anyway. Before me stood a knight decked in heavy plate armor which glowed dimly in the moonlight. A long white cape draped over the stranger's shoulders revealed a sword in its scabbard and a shield's rim peeking from his back. His helm's beaver was down, covering the knight's face.

"Who are you?" I blurted out, a bit shocked at what was going on.

"Me?" The knight seemed surprised at my question. "I am Eid. Or rather, I am the spirit of the eid."

I suppose my astonished expression led him to the conclusion that I was a bit dumb because the knight pointed at the instrument in my hands.

"The great master craftsmen channel a part of

their souls into their best works," the knight explained languidly, clearly relishing the chance to chat. "Thus, I am a part of my luthier's soul in addition to my own unique soul—and still the largest part of me is determined by the musician who makes me sing. My nature is transitory and I change in order to better represent whatever image the bard expresses through me with her music. Today you have created me in this form. I find it pleasing. Both myself and this place. It is beautiful."

I shook my head, crudely trying to clear my thoughts. It didn't work very well. I remembered only that I was in a game where anything was possible and that helped me calm down. I had merely found my way into a unique scenario—and it looks like I'm making progress. Here's that Eid. I need to tame him. Only, he doesn't look untamed. He is calm, courteous and quite pleased with life.

For curiosity's sake, I tried to look at the soul's attributes.

Eid. Attributes hidden.

Who could've guessed?

"This place," I asked. "Where did he come from?"

"You don't know?"

The knight seemed surprised yet again, and so sincerely that I involuntarily felt like a student who had forgotten the answer to two plus two.

"This is the Intermundis. The place between worlds, if that helps you understand. There are many worlds and planes, which exist side by side without intersecting. The space between them is called the Intermundis. Although, this is more of a state of being than a place. A potential. An unrealized idea, containing all possibilities within itself. Through your music, you have temporarily given structure to a part of the Intermundis. You have in effect selected one of its possible forms and brought it to life through your power. You don't have much of it, so this place will soon vanish. But there were beings in the past who had the power to create entire worlds. You call them gods."

I took a fresh look at the world around me. The song had barely described it, but I could see the familiar characteristics: The oaks rustling in the breeze, the black shadows of birds flitting in the moonlight, the four roads leading in the cardinal directions. Even Eid's cape bore a Templar cross. Neither blind fate nor death was anywhere to be seen, but perhaps the song wasn't recreated literally?

"Why am I here then?" I had many questions, but this one seemed the most relevant. "To meet you?"

"Among other things," the ghostly head nodded its heavy helm. "But above all you are here for your trial."

"Trial of what?"

"Your ability to summon the requisite soul from the Gray Lands—without letting the others out."

I hiked my eyebrows, giving my face a shocked-idiotic expression. This seemed enough to apprise Eid about my knowledge in this area.

"Come with me. You have already created a suitable road. Along the way I will tell you about what happens to Barliona's creatures after they die."

I didn't say no to this and we set out along one of the roads that wound its way into the oaks' dense shadows.

"Every creature," Eid began, "essentially consists of three parts. The body, the spirit and the soul."

"What's the difference between the spirit and the soul?" I interrupted.

"The soul is your bodiless essence. It is something akin to your unconscious and conscious memory of the world and at the same time, the world's memory of you. Your spirit, or your 'vitus,' as it is called, is that which generates your vital force or vitality. It's a bit like an animal spirit. The vitus fills your body with life, allows it to breathe, move and perform various actions without your input. More importantly, the vitus does so by generating vitality. Thus it is your vitus that regenerates your health and magic. In most languages, the concepts of soul and spirit have blended, becoming synonymous, so for the sake of clarity, I will simply refer to the spirit as the vitus. It is the vitus that allows living creatures to derive energy from the world through alimentation and a series of other less obvious actions. This makes creatures that are full of vitality desirable prey for those who lack vitus or whose vitus is distorted. Vampires and the majority of the undead are the examples here."

As I listened to Eid, I contemplated the ensuing conception of Barliona's world. No doubt all of this is self-evident to some necromancer that spends his time manipulating souls, vituses and other non-material forms of being, but for me it was entirely new.

"I, for example," Eid went on in the meantime, "have a soul and a body incarnate, but I have no vitus. Thus my body generates no vitality. Some animals have a body and have a vitus but lack a soul. Non-sentient zombies have a body and a perverted vitus but lack a soul. Sentient zombies have a soul and a body but their vitus is absent or perverted. The overwhelming majority of beings are triune. Death violates this unity. Stripped of its vitus, the body ossifies and dies. When that happens, the soul sets off for the Gray Lands, where Erebus calls it to itself. If a soul lacks the strength to resist the call—it will eventually make its way to the gates of Erebus where Chaos will consume it."

We came around a bend in the road and discovered that the road ended. In the most literal sense possible. The concrete, pleasant world ended like an etching that had been ripped out of a book. The milky haze moiled beyond the precipice, gradating into a gray fog towards the horizon. The gust of wind that struck our backs tore off onwards, reached the fog and scattered it momentarily, and I beheld countless streams of ashen shades plodding along thousands upon thousands of cobblestone paths. No doubt the magical nature of the place, or perhaps Eid's assistance, allowed me to perfectly make out the tiny figures at this great distance.

Several seconds passed and the leaden fog and the milky haze refilled the vista.

"That is Erebus, the border region of the Gray Lands. Never approach it. You risk losing your vitus."

Hm. Aren't I player? What could happen to me? Character deletion? Or would my race change to 'zombie' or 'bodiless spirit?'

My companion touched my shoulder and nodded in the other direction, suggesting we return. I had expected something special from his touch, but it turned out entirely ordinary. Neither goosebumps nor shaking in my knees—a simple touch. I was even a little miffed.

Casting a farewell glance at where the milky haze had occluded Erebus, I followed after Eid.

"In the absence of a vitus, the soul grows weak and begins to evaporate, vanishing forever," he went on. "But there are others as well. Souls that have been preserved in the memories of the living. The more frequently that the living remember them, the more vivid the emotions that come with the recollections, the more energy the souls receive in the Gray Lands. Some barely have enough to resist the call and delay their last journey to the gates of Erebus. But others accumulate quite a bit of power. And all of them want to return. Not for long, but return all the same."

He fell silent and I suddenly began to consider what had happened to the instrument's soul while he was gathering dust in Astilba's coffers. Was he in the Gray Lands? Did he languish in the Intermundis? Or was he dispersed and unconscious? I'll have to make sure to ask him about it.

"Through their songs, bards preserve the memory of the souls," Eid began again. "Frequently, this is the strongest memory there is. Songs of heroic deeds and passionate love are sung for centuries. Thousands upon thousands of the living preserve the memories through songs. A famous song can become a substantial and direct path between the Gray Lands and the world of the living. I was created by my luthier in order to help one bard summon such souls. And I know the perils that lie along the way well. Rare is a hero's feat that doesn't involve some villain. And as a result, the songs also involuntarily preserve the memories of great villains, traitors and scoundrels. They too are nourished by the memories of the living, they too seek to see the world again and the bard's songs pave their way for them."

Listening to this, I couldn't help but be impressed by the inventiveness of the game designers. They had arranged things quite neatly. This lore worked well with the natural human tendency to preserve the memories of their ancestors, as well as be remembered in song and thus leave a trace in history. This was just the souls' desire to survive death. Yet the thought that I could summon some villain of yore instead of the hero I needed, worried me.

"And how does one avoid this outcome?" I asked.

"There are several ways, but at the moment you have access to only two of them. The first is to perform or compose songs which mention the villain as little as possible. Songs that mention no names and only a general outline, as a rule, leave the villain out of people's memory."

"And the second?"

"You can return from the Gray Lands and therefore can go there on your own and bring back the soul you need to the world of the living. With time you will learn how to properly direct energy at the Mindful, those who remember. You will learn to close the way to evil but this knowledge won't come right away."

Should I go to the Gray Lands and retrieve a soul? It'd be cool to roleplay Orpheus, who went down to Hades to retrieve Eurydice. But how does this work in the game? Do I have to die for each summons? Doesn't sound very enticing.

In the course of our conversation we reached the place we had first met. With the steel toe of his boot, Eid nudged the ash, uncovering the glowing embers in the fire pit, and sending scarlet flashes coursing along his armor. The knight raised his helm's beaver and I saw the same milky white haze where his face was supposed to be. The sight forced me to start and Eid, noticing my reaction, spread his arms akimbo.

"When you sang your song, you didn't imagine my face. My corporeality is an expression of your will and fantasy. Just as pretty much everything that you see around us. The Intermundis is infinite possibility, an idea awaiting embodiment."

I now saw the white haze, the constituent matter of this place, differently. If I recall my physics correctly, sunlight contains all the colors. A potential rainbow as long as you know how to select the colors of the world. An infinity of possibilities...I couldn't help but recall the classic series of novels by Roger Zelazny. The will that created a world from the magical primordial soup. That or tiny fragments of various worlds, ephemeral day flies when compared to real worlds. I'd be ready to give quite a bit for such an experience, even if it was only in-game. I mean, this was awesome after all! A form of creation that literally and immediately changed the world!

An impatient excitement flared to life inside of

me, calling me to start experimenting with this unique opportunity. Who knows whether I'll ever be able to find my way back to this wondrous place?

Glancing at the white haze moiling in the knight's beaver, I touched the eid's strings without any further doubts. I'm sure there are other ways to create here, but I like the idea of creating a world through music too much to try anything else.

His eyes are subterranean lakes,
Abandoned, royal chambers...

Lev Gumilyov's immortal verses, depicting a portrait of a man, caused the white haze within Eid's helm to transform into a handsome, proud and somewhat melancholy male face. Hazel, almost black eyes, a light satin skin, lips pressed in a smile. He was a bit too cute for my taste, but this was entirely lost in the euphoria that filled me from the very fact of creation. I had created him! Who knows why, but I had done it!

"Thank you. This is a little more comfortable," Eid bowed picturesquely, removed his helm and scratched his neck. "I've been dreaming of doing that forever, but uh, well I didn't have a nape before," he explained in reply to my inquiring glance. "A nape is a pretty rare occurrence in this world."

"Pudding—Alice: Alice—Pudding," I quoted another classic.

"What?" Eid echoed, surprised.

"Nothing, I'm just babbling," I shrugged, considering what else I should create.

All sorts of nonsense was popping into my head and I couldn't help recall the alien rabbit from the ancient cartoon. He created a materializing cream and sold it to people, but they only had enough imagination to use it to create watermelons.

The Intermundis reminded me of the White Book. A hefty, leather-bound volume issued on art paper and containing not a single letter. A tiny mirror occupied the spot where the author's name was supposed to go and all of the pages were virgin blank. SNOW press, which published this book, had preceded the release with a large-scale ad campaign in which it advertised the countless number of stories that could occupy the White Book's pages. Every reader could read something entirely original and unbelievable. The book immediately became extremely fashionable, taking up its position on the shelves of collectors. Several hundred people discovered their talents for writing, but the overwhelming majority saw only blank pages, in the best cases, scrawled with the expletives that one may typically find on fences and the walls of underpasses.

"Tell me," I turned to Eid, who had remained watching me, "since the Intermundis is like a connective tissue between worlds, then can I use it to reach any world I wish?"

"In theory, yes," the knight replied after a little hesitation. "But you can't reach all of them. Some of these worlds are inaccessible to the living—and others to the dead. Many of the worlds are guarded by guards. Besides, as soon as you pave your way to some world, its inhabitants will be able to use it to get out. And not all of them are friendly."

This tidbit forced me to think some more. At my newbie level, any encounter with aggressive monsters would end predictably—with my premature demise. I should consider that in that case I would die and have to leave the gameworld for twelve hours. As a result, I would fail the quest. Then again how important is this quest? Especially since I still don't understand what exactly it entails. If I can't play Eid, I'll wait until I get a rare instrument from Pirus and then continue the Sixth's quest. But here...Here I can experience what it's like to be the Creator!

"Tell me," I decided to iron out the details right away. "What will happen to me if I die upon meeting one of these creatures?"

"Like everyone else, you will go to the Gray Lands and then be reborn in Barliona."

"Will I be able to reach the Intermundis again?"

"Maybe one day you will find a way. I don't know this."

I gathered from Eid's vague reply that I wouldn't get a second chance in this quest, but that I could still theoretically find another way here. And yet it wasn't a given that I would ever succeed. And in that case—I might as well burn it all to the ground!

As soon as I made my decision, I felt a lot better. It was as if I had sprouted wings on my back. I cracked my fingers and shifted the eid in my hands.

"Well then, how would you like to take a stroll through some worlds?" I asked the instrument's soul incarnate.

"Do you realize how dangerous and reckless it could be?" the knight inquired, yet I thought I saw his eyes flash for a moment.

"And do you realize that you're getting the chance to relax and adventure a bit in...FSM knows how many years?" I replied to his question with my own.

Eid hummed vaguely but didn't offer any further objections.

The road leading to Erebus did not appeal to me. And it wasn't even the risk of losing my enigmatic vitus. A grim and dour place. What's to catch there? Three more roads were left, so without hesitating I set out along the next one before me. I wonder where it'll lead me.

I didn't have to wait long to find out. After several bends and turns, we reached the edge of our miniscule world. The white haze and its limits faded before me, illuminated by scarlet flashes from somewhere below. To see their source, I had to approach the very edge and look down, but here an irrational terror enveloped me. My imagination rendered a dizzying height, a long, plummeting flight and a painful stop below. The thought that this was just a game didn't do anything for me. I'd rather climb into the maw of a terrible monster than fall. The first at least resembles reality.

Gathering my wits, I forced myself to approach the edge and squatted down. As Eid looked on mockingly I carefully crawled up to it on my knees. Far, far away, at the very edge of the visible, I could make out a darkness cracking with fire-red thunderbolts. The sight reminded me of a video of volcanic eruption at night—a grim and terrifying beauty.

The Fire of Tartarus burns not for mortal sight.
None of the Dark Gods wish to protect you!
You have been damned for your temerity!

A debuff called 'Curse of Tartarus' appeared in the corner of my vision. +100% vulnerability to dark magic. How lovely. I wonder whether the curse will expire when I leave the Intermundis or die? Or will my character carry it forever?

One way or another, I hadn't any desire to receive a tourist visa to Tartarus. I don't think I was much welcome there. At least I don't have to go on sitting at the edge of this cliff! As I backtracked carefully, I happened to glance upward. A light as thick as melted gold struck my eyes, blinding me with its majesty.

The Divine Chambers glow not for mortal sight.
None of the Holy Gods wishes to protect you.
You have been damned for your temerity!
The Holy light blinds you!

The blinding light gave way to pitch darkness, disturbed only by a list of debuffs. Blindness for a day. 'Curse of Eluna': +100% vulnerability to holy magic.

'See the world,' they said...But what really upset me wasn't the curses so much as the blindness. Does this mean that I have to hang out here for a full day before I can go on with my exploration? Or should I figure out a way out to the larger gameworld and look for healing? Although...It'd be a good idea to take care of this on my own.

Blindly, I felt my way away from the edge, got to my feet and felt around until I found the eid. After some practice I managed to produce a clear chord, activating the Song of Cleansing. There was no effect.

"You're an odd creature," Eid's voice sounded in the darkness around me. "You have something within you that is clearly reviled by both Light and Darkness."

These words set off a whole chain of associations. Omar Khayyam's immortal verses floated up to my mind:

The hypocrites say, "Heaven and hell are in the sky."
Glancing within myself, I was sure this is a lie:
Heaven and hell are not spheres of the world's creation.
Heaven and hell are two halves of the soul.

But the concepts of heaven and hell did not exist here, so these verses didn't apply. On the other hand, there was one old song called "Forbidden Reality" which fit perfectly. It was too bad only that I didn't have my guitar synth or at least an ancient Telecaster...

I imagined how fitting a guitar synth would sound in this setting with its ability to produce practically any sounds. I could play something with organ and electric guitar—that would be some concert! On a whim, I strummed the strings and to my astonishment heard the familiar sound. A triumphant organ filled the infinity of the Intermundis. On the eid, every note sounded exactly as it would on my syntar in reality! At the same time, the realization of how deeply Barliona's technology had penetrated into my mind didn't scare me so much as made me ecstatic.

Okay. So how do I switch to electric guitar? There weren't any controls and I wasn't aware of any voice commands. Then again, how did I produce the organ to begin with? I simply imagined the sound I wanted.

My imagination immediately recreated the riffs of a heavy metal guitar and the strings at my fingers sang with a new voice—a mighty roar that caused every cell in my body to shiver. All I need now is a mic!

Several minutes of practice later, a harmonious duet of organ and electric guitar thundered around me. Let the Chambers of Tartarus and Eluna file all the noise complaints they want! It felt like my voice, also amplified by some unknown method, had flooded the Intermundis and every world it bordered.

The song about the thin, vanishing line between light and darkness, good and evil, thundered in the very tissue of the Intermundis. The icons of my 'Curse' debuffs began to tremble, left their ordinary place and began to twirl in the darkness before me. But that didn't matter. I was drunk from the eid's new sound and the power of my own voice.

The debuff icons hurled like mad comets at one another and smashing together, created a bright flash. A moment later the darkness faded, returning the familiar landscape at the edge of the world.

The milky white haze stitched together the figure of a woman. Blurry, barely recognizable with empty eye sockets in a motionless face, as in my song's verses. The woman raised a transparent hand which pointed at me. Yet I looked upon her without fear. She was just another being created by the music. My music!

The song poured from me, telling of a merciless fate and a friend's betrayal—a blow to the back. In the next instant, true pain pierced my body and a sword tip appeared from my breast. Eid's sword.

"You cannot escape Fate," roared the eyeless woman and the world went dark, leaving a system notification in its wake:

You have died and gone to the Gray Lands.
You will automatically leave this location in 12 hours.

CHAPTER FIVE

DARKNESS, MY HEAVY BREATHING and the echo of fading pain. My heart was beating like a hectic metronome, my fingers clenched the eid's fretboard. What was that?

"Forgive me," a familiar voice sounded next to me. "There's no arguing with Fate, and you yourself sang of dying from my hand. You are destined to complete the trial in the Gray Lands. You cannot escape Fate."

Only now did I realize why it was dark—I had reflexively shut my eyes from the pain, as little as there was due to my filter settings. Opening my eyes, I took in the dour, gray landscape. It was like all color had drained from the world, transforming its vibrancy into grayscale. The grass, the stones, the trees, even the sky—everything was faded and somehow unreal. No trace of the sun. No trace of shadow. A monotonous, oppressive grayness.

Eid had changed too. Now he was little more than a blurry silhouette, a vague trace of his former incarnation. I couldn't make out the expression on his face since he didn't have a face, but for some reason I imagined that he was sincerely remorseful for what had happened.

"Don't worry about it," I shrugged after a little bit more thought. "They say that everything comes back in this life. That's what I get for offing Chip."

"Doing what to whom?" Eid didn't understand.

"If you behave, I'll introduce you two," I promised. "I don't know whether you'll get along but you won't be bored. Speaking of boredom. Why do you look like Hamlet's father all of a sudden?"

"My previous incarnation was a part of the world we left, and you haven't given me a new form yet."

"Hmm..." I muttered with some curiosity. "So I can make you look however I like?"

"Something like that," Eid replied carefully, perhaps anticipating something bad.

"Well aren't you lucky!" I tried to clap Eid's silhouette on the shoulder but my hand passed straight through him.

"Why is that?" the spirit wanted to know.

"If Beast had stumbled upon you, you'd be a chesty sex doll. He always said that the bass was his one true love. You'd present him with the chance to make this sentiment a reality."

Did I imagine it or did the spirit backtrack slightly?

"Relax buddy," I guffawed, reassuring Eid's anxiety. "Spiritophilia isn't one of my fetishes. Ours is a professional relationship exclusively. Although it'd make a heck of a love song."

"I seem to have grown unaccustomed to you mortals' humor."

"What, Cypro didn't crack jokes like that?" I wondered, only now realizing that I was speaking to an authority on all things Tenth.

"By the time I was created, he was over a hundred years old already and his humor was a bit more...mature," Eid explained delicately.

"And who taught you to be so polite?" I said a bit disheartened, wary that I was about to travel with a humorless companion.

"This character trait, I believe, I inherited from my luthier," Eid replied in a dignified tone.

Meanwhile, I was contemplating what form to give him. Chatting with an incorporeal spirit wasn't exactly pleasant. And at the same time, for whatever reason, nothing occurred to me.

"Any requests?" I asked my companion hopefully.

"I liked my last form," he replied. "I was handsome and it fit my sound. So how about something masculine and heroic?"

I tried to run through the relevant songs in my head but all that came were dumb jokes. I wonder what would happen if I sing some malarkey like 'her legs never ended, her teeth reflected the moon?' Would the system dutifully recreate such a bit of surrealism? Or would it be Lobachevsky time? An introduction to non-Euclidean geometry?

Luckily for Eid, I didn't bother experimenting and played what I felt like: Led Zeppelin's "The Battle of Evermore."

This time, as I played, I watched his transformation carefully, unwilling to miss such a strange sight. Eid changed with every word I sang. The smoke that the spirit consisted of swirled, waxed, thickened and took on the form of a black knight on a raven-black steed. For whatever reason, I imagined his warhorse this way. It's also worth mentioning that Eid now resembled a Ringwraith from *The Lord of the Rings*. I guess this is the failure of my impoverished imagination, but this is what I associated with a black knight who had taken thousands of souls. By the way…On the topic of taking souls…Was it a waste to use the verses on someone who'd already sent me to the Gray Lands? Although, where else would I go? I'm here already. As Sasha liked to say—they can't send you further than the frontline.

The world around me hadn't changed one bit. There were no fires in the distance, though the gray dust was still there. And here and everywhere else. Either the song didn't fit or in the Gray Lands I couldn't change reality as I wished.

Eid's steed snorted impatiently and stomped his hoof, while the Black Rider atop him looked down on me.

"Happy?"

"More than happy, thank you," the spirit nodded majestically.

He dismounted and patted his horse on the withers. Oddly, Eid wasn't as gray as everything else around us. And I too still had my 'basic' coloring. I suppose that was because he and I belonged to a different world. But I wonder why. After all, technically, I'm dead...Eid had killed me, hadn't he?

Dead!

The thought pierced me quicker than Eid's sword. What did that creature in the mirror tell me? "These writings are open only to the dead." And I couldn't be deader! I'm standing in the middle of the Gray Lands!

My fingers trembling with excitement, I got Cypro's notes from my bag. Opening the tattered cover, I found uneven lines, written in a small script.

You were curious enough to find all the sigils around the Tree and reach the repository. Since you chose the unassuming travel journal, stories attract you more than artifacts, magic armor and the secrets of craftsmen. You are not prepared to sacrifice others to reach your goals, and your music is capable of touching others' souls. Besides this, you are sufficiently acute to find a way to reach the Gray Lands and read these lines.

Whoever you are, you and I are alike. The road is

our fate and it seems to me that one day it will allow us to meet.

Every traveler can use a guide. And you need a very special guide for the roads of the Gray Lands. A guide that belongs to two worlds at once. Finding someone like that, is a great stroke of luck. But luck is not a trustworthy companion. You should not rely on such a fickle lady. I will teach you how to create such a guide—a cicerone for the land of the dead.

The text ended at this point, giving way to a system notification right there on the journal's page.

Quest chain available: *Creating a Cicerone*. Do you Accept? Yes/No

As soon as I accepted, the rest of the page filled with handwriting.

The nature of the Gray Lands is complex and not fully known to any creature I am aware of. At times, it seems to me that this place is not at all the way it appears to us mortals. For example, why do I sometimes encounter the souls of animals? Are there really so many sentients that preserve memories of them? I sense that this is somehow related to certain tribes venerating totem animals.

Either way, you have to locate one of these souls and bind it to yourself. Good luck to you, my mysterious friend.

The quest changed, specifying the object of my search—an animal soul. But there was no hint where I should even look for this soul. The journal's other pages remained blank.

"Listen Eid," I turned to the spirit watching me with curiosity. "Where do you think I can find an animal soul around here? And how can I bind it to myself? I don't suppose I'd need a lasso like a cowgirl..."

"Have you forgotten that you must complete a trial?" Eid answered my question with one of his own.

"Why should I forget it? But tell me what I have to do to complete it."

The phantom knight assumed a pose and announced triumphantly:

"You must select a soul and lead it from the Gray Lands to Barliona."

"And that's it?" I asked, a little surprised.

"You think that's simple to do?" Eid smirked.

"Well, it doesn't sound very difficult," I admitted. "Tell me about the souls of animals. Could I perhaps lead an animal soul out?"

"Not very difficult?" echoed the instrument's soul. "In that case you should be able to handle this quest without any problems. As well as all the other ones."

Having said this, Eid fell silent, clearly unwilling

to provide any further instructions. Well he can go to cold pasta hell then, this moody knight. I'll figure it out on my own.

Now that my vision had adjusted to the monochrome palette of the world beyond the grave, I could take a proper look around. A strange landscape. Paradoxically, the first thing that stood out was the awful visibility. There weren't really any dust clouds, fog or other natural phenomena, and yet about a hundred meters ahead of me everything kind of melded together as if I were looking at a smudged pencil sketch.

But even within the limits of the visible there were plenty curiosities to examine. Buildings of diverse dimensions and styles were arranged all around without any discernible order. Some of them seemed clear and rendered in detail, while others were no more than vague outlines. Approaching one of these buildings, I could study the viscous substance it was built from. Fluid and yet dense like mercury, it was in constant motion, changing the edifice past recognition. A bas relief depicting some arachnoid creatures appeared and gave way to a dimpled wall of some unpolished stone, and then another bas relief but this time depicting a sacrificial ritual. It was like the building couldn't make up its mind what form it should take.

I turned to Eid as the local expert on traveling through the Gray Lands.

"What's wrong with this wall? And where'd these buildings come from anyway? I thought this was the place souls go to, not a construction site. Or do you think that the souls need places to live too?"

"All of these are like me—the works of great master craftsmen," the spirit explained. Or should I say, 'soul,' since he still had his spirit/vitus...? But that sounded a bit awkward and not quite right so I decided to keep thinking of Eid as a spirit.

"Creations that acquired a soul thanks to their creators' efforts. Legendary objects that lost their material incarnation but remained preserved in memory. Ruined temples and palaces, sculptures and paintings, armor and arms. Their souls too reach the Gray Lands."

I took a renewed look at the gray world around me. The cemetery of legends. A museum of memories from a myriad generations that had lived in Barliona. And perhaps, not just Barliona? If the Intermundis is the space between worlds, then maybe the souls that come here are collected from many worlds too?

Unfortunately, try as I might, I could see nothing that either confirmed or refuted this theory. Eid and I passed many objects and buildings but I couldn't tell if a single one belonged to some other world.

I turned my head left and right like a country bumpkin at her first visit to the capital. The Gray Lands amazed me with their impossible blend of the lifeless and the changing. A completely stunning impression...

"Why are some objects static while others are constantly changing?" I asked after watching the transformation of a tree that grew right in the middle of our road. "You had no form at all, and when you acquired one, you remained unchanged."

"Some items were described accurately and their images were preserved," Eid nodded at a sculpture of a winged woman who reminded me a bit of Nike from Greek mythology. "Only contradictory legends survive about others and each person who remembers them imagines them differently."

My eye caught something vaguely familiar and I stopped to get a better look. A chess set stood on a pedestal that kept changing from a stone altar to an immense table to a simple, crude hunk of rock. Some of the pieces were missing, and those that were there kept changing constantly. The board on the other hand remained distinct: The light and dark squares were a sufficiently classic image. Everyone imagined them the same way, unlike the constantly changing finish.

I tried to determine what the pieces on the board were. The squares where the pawns were supposed to be were vacant. The knights were rendered as classic animals in elaborate metal armor as well as the local variety of mountable lizards. The pieces 'drifted,' changing form, but remained recognizable on the whole. The rooks were present only for one of the sides: The two pieces towered over the others and yet changed so quickly that my eyes didn't have time to process their various guises. The bishops were less ephemeral: One pair possessed the body composition and pointy ears common to elves. The bishops on the other side boasted the fanged maws characteristic of trolls.

The queens proudly occupied their proper squares on d1 and d8. One of them wore a strange hat with deer antlers and was covered in melted wax, making it impossible to determine its race or gender. The only difference with the other queen was that I could discern a staff in its hand.

On the other hand, the kings were a bit more definite. One was clearly an orc. Time and again, a wolfskin appeared on its shoulders, the sword in its hand transformed to an axe, a spear and sometimes even a scimitar. The other chess king was clearly a human, though its apparel and weapon kept changing from a sword to a staff and back.

Chess, chess...Something about chess kept spinning in my mind. That's right! The Legendary Chess Set of Karmadont...Or was is Kardamon? I couldn't remember exactly but it was something like that. The Barliona fora had been erupting at the news that some unknown jeweler had begun to recreate the legendary chess set. It followed that the souls of the recreated pieces had been reincarnated in the world and I was seeing the ones that were next.

I wonder whether all the other buildings, sculptures, suits of armor and weapons were also awaiting some craftsman to start recreating their ancient legend. Was it possible for me to reincarnate the soul of an item in Barliona at least temporarily too?

I was seriously considering conducting some experiments when a motion drew my eye. Not the mere transformation of one image into another but one that was self-contained, autonomous. Among the changing silhouettes of items, a person was plodding along the dusty ground. His bowed head, drooped shoulders, hunched back and scuffling gait was at odds with the impressive plate armor he was wearing.

The dead man's cuirass boasted a masterful engraving of a lizard, clearly visible even under the layer of gray dust. His ash gray head was crowned with a metallic circlet and his shoulders were wrapped in a long cape, pinned with a fibula in the shape of the same lizard. His limp hand gripped his long sword, dragging it along the ground behind its long-dead owner.

Looking closer, I noticed that his armor was fairly ragged and his sword was nicked and chipped from many blows. Some king who had fallen in a legendary battle? Judging by the state of this soul, his ancestors had forgotten much of that ancient story.

The spirit paid no attention to Eid and me. He simply plodded along, periodically skirting some chance obstacle. I looked around with curiosity trying to see any other denizens of this afterworld. In the distance, at the very edge of visibility, I made out an enormous figure creeping across the horizon, but the intervening gloom concealed its details, making it impossible to examine the colossus. Who was it? A titan? A dragon? A fallen deity?

My feet carried me after the receding figure of their own volition, but the giant's stride was so long that he quickly dissolved beyond the indefinite horizon of this world. In exchange, a tall, stately figure of a woman stepped out from behind a majestic maple tree. Maybe there was some legend associated with this tree or this was the spirit of some dryad...She held her chin raised proudly, her shoulders back, and she stepped with a smooth yet confident step. Even ignoring her sumptuous dress, I could guess that this wasn't some poor, recently-deceased girl.

Unlike the dead king, the lady noticed me. She stopped for a few seconds, appraised me with an exacting glance and crumpled her face in derision. It was as if she had encountered some horse dung amid the pretty path that had been laid for her personally. Having expressed her contempt, the lady continued along the way only known to her through the dust of the world of the dead.

I shut my mouth, which I had opened to greet her. My desire to chat up this sour-faced dame about returning to the world of the living evaporated just like that. No big deal. I still had an entire king in reserve. By the way, where'd he go?

Luckily, catching up to the slowly shuffling man in a crown turned out to be as simple as pie. Alas, it was the last piece of pie. How was I supposed to bring him back?

"Hey...your Highness!" I ventured without much confidence.

He didn't react in any way, plodding onward to a goal that remained unknown to me. Although, why do I say that? Eid had told me that the souls that no longer had the strength to resist Chaos's call would wander toward the Gates of Erebus. I guess this soul's hour had come.

Just to make sure, I tried touching the soul, waving in front of his eyes, stepping through it and even trying to prod it with the eid, which earned me a look of disapproval from the instrument's soul. None of this had any effect. The plodding phantom did not react to my efforts in the least.

Call me callous, but I thought the whole thing was funny. What an interesting quest the game had assigned me. I wouldn't call it common at any rate: It was certainly far afield from the typical 'kill ten rats and harvest their hides and tails' fare. This one required thought.

I circled the blindly plodding spirit and contemplated what I should do. Call me callous (again), but the ghost's pitiful sight did not elicit much compassion in me. I wasn't familiar with this NPCs history, so the nameless king was nothing but a faceless bit of code for me. He did however interest me as a lab rat of sorts. I'd be curious to know what power I had over the souls and in this place in general. The only hitch was that I really didn't know his story. In fact, I didn't know the history of a single local ruler, fallen in battle. And in that case, how could I sing about him?

I trailed the king unhurriedly as I considered the situation. I sure am lucky today with my companions. It's all knights and kings like in the popular romance novels. Though, unlike in those novels, the local knight had already stabbed me today. And I mean that literally—not figuratively-erotically. And now this nameless king was ignoring my illustrious person.

The nameless king....That reminds of something...

I stopped and rubbed my face with my palms, trying to catch the elusive song. The tune dodged and avoided my consciousness for a bit but finally gave up and dredged up a memory of a fantasy song I'd heard recently. It was in the collection of fantasy songs I had downloaded when doing research for the game. A classic of prog. I hadn't ended up learning it, but I remembered the first chords and I tend to memorize the lyrics the first time I hear them. And if there's something I don't recall, I can always improvise. As long as the foundation is there, filling in the gaps presents no problem. And so Em9 to Em9 with a flat sixth, I believe...

Eid followed behind me, leading his horse by its bridle, and observing with interest as I muttered the song's verses under my nose and fingered various chords, trying to weave the sounds into a melody. It was clear that he wasn't about to help. When I had finally remembered the lyrics and found the one chord that kept eluding me (F#m7b5, ugh!), I sprinted ahead of the ghost and sat down in the middle of his way so that he would hear me play as he passed.

For the first time since we met, the ghost reacted. Hearing the singing, he started and slowed his already turtle's pace. I rejoiced to myself. There's a sign! He can hear me. Or see me. Either way, we have contact.

The ballad of a witch arriving to a royal court that whirls with revels, tournaments, and puppet plays resonated with the soul. He stopped and raised his head with noticeable difficulty. The look in his eyes was terrifying. Empty and senseless, it gave rise to an otherworldly horror in me. Living people never look like that. Or at least I hope they don't.

As I sang, the soul of the nameless king approached me. The man straightened out to his full height and looked me in the eyes. A look of comprehension appeared on the ghost's face. He was listening.

When the ballad's last notes faded, the phantom was still staring at me. Suddenly a fire flared in his eyes, scorching the dusty grayness of the land of the dead. The world filled with color and smells, changing everything entirely.

Like barbed wire cutting at it, the scent of ashes parches my throat and the acrid smoke stings my eyes and squeezes forth tears. I cannot move in the slightest—I cannot control what is happening—I am only a bystander, an observer.

A crescendo of ringing steel sounds amid the roar of raging fires. Through the tongues of flame, I can see a wave of steel-clad cavalry rushing towards me. The surging fear forces me to start back, but my back encounters an obstacle and someone's hand pushes me forward.

"Not a step back, carrion! Either you consign the souls of these filthy beasts to the Lords or they will consume yours!"

I still the trembling in my hands and notice in passing that my skin is a vivid green. I grip the spear's haft tighter like a piece of rope that will save me from drowning. I am much more afraid of the Lords than the oncoming foe.

"To battle!"

Obeying the command, I take a knee and stick the spear's heel into the ground, pointing the tip in the direction of the avalanche coming toward me.

The infantry bristles with two ranks of spears, awaiting contact with the cavalry. The mages conjure a wall of flame not five meters before us. My armor heats noticeably from its heat. Even trained warhorses would not rush through such fire, I tell myself. They will buck their riders and all we will have to do is finish off the unlucky ones, allowing the Lords to devour their souls. Their souls—not ours. But the cavalry does not stop. They have mages too and the tall wall of flame wanes to a harmless barrier no higher than my shoulder.

And then the riders fall upon us.

Time slows. I can clearly see the first rank of mounted knights. Among them, I discern a rider with a crimson lizard on his breastplate. My heart, feverishly beating in my chest, goes still from terror and skips several beats. It is he—the Salamander King—the one who dared challenge the Lords and rebelled against the Tarantulas!

The earth rocks and falls from my feet. Weakened by the enemies' spells, the ground yawns beneath us and the even row of spears collapses, allowing the cavalry to break through our ranks. Something heavy slams into my helmet and the light fades in my eyes.

I open them again when the battle's already ended. Corpses strew the field before the castle; the Lords step languidly among them. The spiders' immense bodies halt over their fallen foes, the terrible fangs plunge and a barely noticeable mist seeps from *the fallen bodies into the Tarantulas' maws. The Lords harvest their crop.*

One of them approaches me and I overcome my pain and get to one knee.

"Lord..." I whisper hoarsely, hoping that the plentiful food has been enough and the same terrible fate will pass me by.

The enormous spider hangs over me. I stop breathing. No, not me. I fought for you. You promised to spare our souls. The moment which lasts an eternity passes and the Tarantula moves on. The feast continues.

Stumbling over the earth, rutted by spears and spells, I head for the castle. My people are there—there are healers there. The Lords are not there right now. Two ogres drag a moaning, wounded person past me. He has crimson hair and the familiar lizard on his breastplate. Yours is a sad fate, oh Salamander King. You shall serve as an example to everyone unhappy with the Lords' rule. A terrifying example.

I do not rejoice at his fate, I pity him. If I had believed in his rebellion even for an instant, I would have joined him. But I did not believe. And I was right. We are too weak, too insignificant to oppose the Lords. And yet, may the Abyss take me, how I yearned for your victory...

The world wavered before me and the first vision gave way to the next.

I am standing sentry outside of the dungeon and listening to the screams of agony. They have been sounding for many days now—all throughout the fortress of the Crooked Tusk. The Lizard King, as the minions of the Lords called him, had swapped his throne for the rack, yet remained king. The Tarantulas' torturers knew their craft, yet Salamander did not give up. The blood froze from his screams, but the captive refused to recognize the Lords. The Tarantulas could naturally devour his soul, but first they wanted the leader of the rebellion to publicly recognize their hegemony. To this day, they had not gotten their wish.

Another soul-freezing scream, forcing my body to tremble, cuts off abruptly. I hope that Salamander has finally said farewell to his life, but the torturers emerging from the chamber curse, discussing new methods for breaking the prisoner. That means he merely fainted. A pity.

The torturers depart, leaving me to guard the chained and powerless prisoner. As if he can escape. Escape...

An unbearably outrageous thought appears in my mind. Flight. A desperate flight from the Lords' domain. Not a single one is in the castle at the moment, which means they would not be able to catch me. The thought of freedom makes me drunk, granting me a careless courage, and I hurry to the chamber, worried that my decisiveness will evaporate. I lock the chamber from the inside and with great effort scoot the now-vacant *rack to prop the door shut. The wounded man hangs limply in the stocks. The sight of his twisted joints and lesion-covered body no longer affects me. None of this is important. We will be able to escape.*

The Salamander King opens his eyes, as if sensing something. His eyes stop on me. I do not know how but he has understood it all. He grins toothlessly. And I plunge the dagger home.

Go with peace, Salamander King. They will not have your soul. By the time they realize what has happened and call the Lords, we will be in the Gray Lands. They cannot reach you there. Neither you nor me.

Now I will plunge the dagger, its blade soaked in Salamander's blood, up to its hilt into my own throat. My lips strain to form a grin. I am free.

The darkness that veiled my eyes gave way to dull grayness. I was sitting in the dust, staring dumbly at my trembling hands and trying to understand which world I was in. My eyes tickled but there were no tears. Players can't cry in Barliona—this is a place of entertainment and diversion, not tears. The screams of the tortured man lingered in my ears, and my mind refused to comprehend the system notification that had appeared.

Attention! Through your Bardic Inspiration you have recovered lost lore about the Salamander

King.

You have used song to bind yourself to the soul of the Salamander King. From now on, you may summon this soul from the Gray Lands by performing this song.

Attention! Binding a song to a being that is not directly mentioned in the song can only be accomplished in person in the presence of the being in the Gray Lands.

Attention! This song does not mention the Salamander King directly and its performance will not nurture this being in the Gray Lands.

Stats, bindings, performances and other game mechanics simply didn't gel in my shocked consciousness. I was looking at the soul of the Salamander King and it was looking at me.

"Who are you?" The spirit spoke slowly as if with great effort.

"I'm a bard," I replied, looking up at him. It seemed that Salamander didn't care about names so much as what was going on. "I have traveled to the Gray Lands from Barliona to conduct a departed soul back to the world of the living. But only temporarily," I added, noticing Salamander's eyes flare with fire.

"Barliona..." the king said pensively. "What is it like right now? Have the Tarantulas been defeated?"

"To be perfectly honest, I'd never even heard of them until now."

"Haven't even heard..." Salamander gaped.

His sword fell to the ground with a dull thud, his legs wavered and he collapsed awkwardly to the ashy earth. Salamander was staring ahead somewhere into a nearby sky and smiling. Tears of joy streamed down his cheeks.

"They have fallen...They have fallen and been forgotten..."

I watched him silently as thoughts about the contradictory nature of human behavior flowed through my mind. Sometimes we laugh in moments of peril and cry in moments of happiness.

Eid didn't say anything, preferring to remain a detached observer. I wonder if he cares about what's going on even a little. After all, I think of him in ordinary human terms, yet when you consider it, he's not one bit human. What does a musical instrument—even one that's been imbued with life by its creator—care about our joys and sorrows? As if he had sensed something, Eid looked over at me but didn't say anything. Meanwhile, the Salamander King finally processed the good news from the larger world and returned to his dull reality, picked up his sword, swept the dust from its blade and slid it back in its scabbard.

"If even the Tarantulas have been forgotten, it is no wonder that I am barely remembered," he said with humility and resignation in his voice. "It has been a long time since I've heard anything, aside from the call of Erebus. Your music managed to drown it out, but it hasn't grown any weaker. And I haven't the strength to resist it any longer."

My reply came of its own volition:

"I will remember you, Salamander."

The rebel king smiled bitterly, yet bowed his head gratefully.

"Thank you, bard. But I am afraid that your memory won't be enough to save me from the call. And there isn't much sense in it anymore. The Tarantulas have fallen and I can dissolve in Erebus peacefully now."

"Don't!" I blurted out.

I looked pretty dumb I bet. A player begging a long-dead NPC to cleave to life. Not so much as live, as 'be.' However, the visions I had lived through made this person and his history real. To me, at least. And the thought that in exchange for his deeds he would only receive oblivion and utter dissolution, forced me to protest. His life and death deserved a reward. Even if only a small one. Even if it was no more than several hours in the world of the living. That was all I could grant him.

Or was it?

"I will write a song about you," I promised the spirit. "A good song. It will spread among those who want to remember and you will regain your strength."

Salamander smiled and shook his head.

"That is the most generous offer I have heard

since my death. Thank you. But spare yourself the futile labor. Look around. The Gray Lands are not the place where one would want to spend eternity. And even if time passes differently here, I see no reason to cling to this kind of existence. The Tarantulas are gone and my debt has been paid. I can depart with peace in my soul."

As bitter as it was to admit it, his words made a lot of sense. I don't know who came up with the afterlife in Barliona, but whoever it was, was clearly a sadist. You wouldn't wish an eternity in this dull place on your worst enemy.

"Maybe you'd like to see Barliona one more time?" I asked after a little hesitation.

The hell with the Fifth. He'd waited so many centuries that he could wait a little more. I'd be willing to bet that Astilba's might, as well as her maniacal obsession with her departed lover would suffice to maintain an entire army of spirits. Meanwhile, Salamander did not have long left, and this was his last chance to look upon the world he had fought to defend in his time.

"Lay eyes upon Barliona?" the spirit echoed. "Is that possible?"

"In theory. This would be the first time I summon a soul from the Gray Lands to the world of the living," I confessed.

Salamander got up to his feet, bowed ceremoniously and offered me his hand, helping me up in turn:

"In that case, it would be an honor to accept your offer. And don't worry about failing. You can't make my situation any worse."

"You sure know how to cheer a girl up," I quipped, and by sheer reflex grabbed his hand to pull myself up.

Stop. Grabbed his hand? Didn't I walk through him just a second ago?

"Hey Eid, why is it that I can touch him all of a sudden?" I asked the instrument's soul.

"You have promised to lead him from the Gray Lands, and he has taken his first step on the Way that you are to pave for him. He no longer belongs to this place, temporarily, like you and I."

I looked at the Salamander King again, noting the changes taking place. It was like a layer of dust had been blown from the ghost. The grayness of this world was melting from him like the snow on a spring meadow. It was like the setting sun had illuminated his hair, his circlet began to glint with dull gold, and the lizard on his breastplate flushed with crimson. The colors were dull, like on a tapestry that had faded with time, but they already stood out vividly in the colorless world around us.

"And what must we do now in order to return to Barliona?" I asked Eid without much expectation of an answer.

This morose instrument is about to tell me that

this is what my trial consists of and I have to figure it out on my own...

"The Gray Lands have several Gates," Eid began to explain in spite of my misgivings. "Each Gate has its own Gatekeeper whose duty it is to guard the border between the worlds of the living and the dead. You must find the Gate, deal with the Gatekeeper, reach the Intermundis and pave a way back to Barliona."

Such clear instructions lifted my spirits, though the many gaps in them, dampened my mood at the same time.

"And how am I supposed to find the Gate?"

"You are a Bard," Eid reminded me. "Think of a suitable way."

Music, in other words. I could've figured that out on my own. I'm doing a class-based quest and am in an area that is accessible only to bards. Although...Don't shamans and necromancers also work with souls and spirits? I wonder whether they drop in here as well?

But away with these unrelated thoughts. I need a guiding song. I looked around, trying to find some hint in the landscape around me. A dull grayness and an oppressive silence. I need to shake up this musty place!

As soon as my fingers touched the eid's strings, I recalled a fitting song from the same immortal album as before—*Forbidden Reality*. Maybe it didn't fit as perfectly as I wanted it, but for the moment it would be enough. More life! More roar!

Deafening guitar riffs erupted in the silence of the Gray Lands. The Salamander King started from surprise, whipped out his sword and began spinning in place looking for the source of the clamor. Eid jumped up into the saddle of his steed, which had begun to stomp nervously, and burst into mirthful laughter. He clearly enjoyed the new noise.

The musty, stale air of the Gray Lands suddenly began to spin in a twister, carrying the dust up to the leaden skies and with a powerful burst struck me in the back. The black steed bucked and reared up on his hind legs, Eid's black cape began flapping like a pair of wings and I, carried by the wind, couldn't help but take a step, then another and another until I was hurrying in the direction nature wished me to go.

I sang of the wind of travels and the wind led us along the lifeless world. Although, I guess it wasn't quite so lifeless. Souls began to gather around us. Some of them, like the Salamander King earlier, could lift their heads only with great difficulty; others looked quite lively—if this word even applies to bodiless spirits. Humans, trolls, minotaurs, elves, sirens...Dozens, then hundreds of souls drifted to the source of the sound and followed in our steps. The wind, tearing at our capes, tussling our hair, pushing at our backs, passed through the ghosts surrounding us. Not a single burst bothered the shades of the departed.

When the last sounds of my song had ended, the earlier silence did not return. The wind howled frantically and desperately like some living creature. Perhaps it too was locked in this place like the other souls? There are natural spirits too after all. Perhaps this wind was one of them? It roves about, desperately trying to break out to the world of the living...

Whatever it was, the wind stubbornly pushed us along a course known to it alone. We walked, no, we almost ran past transparent castles and cities, ruined masterpieces. And the host of souls followed behind us. The sight was both impressive and slightly creepy. Eid's words about how many of the souls yearn to escape the Gray Lands along the ways that bards open for them, surfaced in my mind. It follows that as soon as I open the Gate, all the souls will try to burst through it?

These troubling thoughts hounded me until the moment we reached the Gate. Though to be honest, I didn't see any Gate at all at first. All of my attention had been fixed on the mountain. That's right. A true mountain, about one and a half kilometers tall, complete with wooded slopes and a plateau where its peak would have been. Its majestic silhouette came gradually into focus as we approached and we soon found ourselves at the foot of this colossus. The wind gave me one last shove in my back as if saying goodbye, rustled the leaves and fell still.

I stood with my head tipped back looking up and starting to suspect that the mysterious Gate was right there on top of that plateau. Am I really going to have to climb up there? The very thought of climbing that high made me forget all about the retinue of hundreds of souls following our party. They, however, did not forget about me.

"Take me with you..." said some suspicious lady quietly and mournfully. Her long hair dragged along the gray ground behind her like a forgotten bridal gown.

Something about her appearance suggested pernicious witchcraft. Considering that in Barliona, the NPC's appearance almost always corresponded to their character, I was reluctant to take on a companion like this. She'd boil me in a cauldron the first chance she got and then have a nice vegetable broth for supper.

"You must lead me to Barliona!" demanded an opulent man in a mighty, impatient voice that brooked no objections. With his sable cape and overwrought crown, this one would make Sauron weep in envy. "Lead me from this place and I shall tell you where my riches are buried!"

Quest available: *Return of a King.*

Description: The soul of a deceased ruler wishes you to lead it from the Gray Lands and to Barliona. Quest type: Unique. Reward for

completion: Hidden.

"What do you need riches for when I can offer you secret wisdom!" interrupted a gaunt, sharp-nosed spirit in a long cloak. The winding staff in his bony fingers was crowned with a crystal—in which a face, distorted from suffering, flashed for an instant. The instant passed and the crystal's surface regained its pristine stillness, yet the icy hand of fear had gripped my heart.

"Help me pass the Gate," the warlock went on smoothly, "and I shall teach you a spell of unimaginable power!"

Quest available: *Unlocking the Warlock.*
Description: The warlock's soul wishes to pass through the Gate from the Gray Lands. Quest type: Unique. Reward for completion: Hidden.

"Don't listen to them!" popped up a mighty knight in plate armor. For whatever reason, I realized instantly that I was looking at a paladin. "These are dark creatures who wish to feast on the living, stripping their vitality. If you revere the Blessed Eluna, hallowed be her visage, help her true defender leave this place for a little while to complete a duty I have been charged with. My enemy has not been vanquished and that means the commoners are in peril!"

Quest available: *A Soul's Debt.*

Description: The paladin's soul wants you to lead it from the Gray Lands to Barliona to help it complete a task. Quest type: Unique. Reward for completion: Hidden.

"Save me!"

"Take me!"

"No, me!"

There were so many voices that they merged into one general clamor. Pleas, threats, promises, orders, exhortations—my head was simply cracking from this din. Kings, emperors, counts and dukes, heroes, villains, saviors and traitors—human memory turned out to be very inventive indeed. I couldn't see a single peasant or laborer among this crowd. They're not frequently the subjects of ballads.

Quest available: ...

Quest available: ...

Quest available: ...

Hah! At this rate, I could start a soul delivery service in Barliona. I'd have it all: treasures, rare spells, ancient wisdoms. I could even start to hold auctions...

This last reverie was dispelled by the weeping voice of a child that pierced the crowd's babble.

"Take me to my mother..."

The little voice sounded so pitiful that I couldn't help but start. A girl of about six was smearing her tears down her cheeks with her knuckles.

"I want to see my mommy! This place is terrible and someone scary keeps calling my name..."

My heart sank from pity. I told myself that this was only an NPC, a simple script, but the face of the bawling, lost child suppressed every thought. Had I the opportunity, I would stick the dev who'd come up with this scenario here and forced him to listen to this child's crying all eternity. What kind of sadist places a child's soul in a place like this?

"Come here, little one," I called her, not entirely sure what I had to do.

The girl approached me haltingly. She looked neither like a princess nor a heroine of legend. She wore simple clothes and had ribbons tied around the little ponytails that stuck out from her hair. Her feet were bare. Most likely she was a peasant child that died recently and was languishing in this place on the strength of her loved ones' memories. I reached out my hands to hug and console the poor girl, but they merely passed through her ghostly body. What a bunch of bastards, those devs!

"Will you take me from here? To my mommy?" the girl asked. I could only look at her at a loss.

What do I say? That I already made a promise to another? That even if I lead her out of this place, it'll be temporarily? That I doubt I'd be able to locate her mother?

"Of course she will, darling," the Salamander King interrupted my futile brainstorm. He squatted down next to the girl and flashed her an encouraging smile. "We can't leave a little one like you without some kind of supervision. And I just remembered that I have some very important business to take care of here."

I watched Salamander silently, understanding that neither one of us could permit ourselves another course of action. I would have started crying, yet Barliona doesn't have that feature for players. And this amounts to perversity on the part of the developers: The souls of children wander the land of the dead, but a player can't express her sadness.

I could kill those devs...

The soul of the Salamander King looked on me with an approving smile. I think he was even happy to do this kind deed.

"I'll take you with me, little one," I promised, paying no attention to the displeased murmur of the rest of the souls gathered around us. "But I doubt I can bring you to your mother right away. I live very far from her."

I could say that again. Without even trying to guess which continent the girl's mom lived on, I could confidently assume that she wasn't in the Hidden Forest. And even if I ever make it out beyond the Arras, human settlements are off limits to me. Those who've aligned themselves with Shadow have a negative rep with all of the other Empires. They'd kill me before I could explain what I wanted. I wonder what happens to a soul I've summoned in that case...

"Where do you live, lady?" the girl looked up at me with her little, gray, tear-streaked face. Although, it was already not as gray as before. Like the Salamander King, she was regaining her faded colors.

"In a magical forest," I smiled, deciding to stay quiet about the blighted beasts, Geranika's Shadow and the further wonders of our lovely biome. Not right now.

Now I could even embrace the girl. It was a strange feeling—like touching a hollow plastic doll. A little elastic and pliant, not cold and not warm. Not living. The plague take those devs.

"Oh, you're so warm." The girl shut her eyes blissfully and pressed herself to me tighter. "It's like I'm back home, asleep in my warm bed."

This memory caused her to start weeping again quietly, while I again cursed the sadist who'd come up with this scenario. I'll never set foot in the Gray Lands again, or I'll end up spending my entire gaming life pointlessly rescuing little ones from this purgatory. And the system will just generate new ones and new ones...

Salamander sat beside the girl quietly, stroking her hair in silence. It seemed that Eid was the only one entirely unaffected by what was happening. The instrument soul stood apart, holding his steed and observing the unfolding events with the impassiveness of a theater director who had seen the scene before him hundreds of times. Then again, what else can you expect from a 12-string guitar?

The other spirits, meanwhile, refused to calm down: some were appealing to my pity, some were talking about the legions of orphans wandering Barliona, others were promising all the world's riches, and I barely managed to keep up with all the quests I kept having to decline. The reward always remained hidden, so even if the Salamander King and the little girl hadn't been here, it would've been worth it to think well before agreeing to any of these offers.

"I hope you will be able to make it out without any problems," said Salamander, ignoring the pleas of the spirits around us. "Let me know if I can be of help somehow. Maybe, I will be able to perform one last good deed."

"I'm sorry," I said mutely, mouthing the words.

But Salamander understood and smiled happily in reply.

"I would not have it any other way!"

Eid snorted contemptuously.

"You are making a very foolish decision, bard. Giving up the presents, powers and knowledge offered you in order to help some snot-nosed orphan? What kind of help is it anyway? You won't bring her back to life, Lorelei. That's not within your power. She will be nothing but a soul, rejected by Barliona, and she will exist solely as a parasite to your own powers. What use is she to you? She cannot help you in battle. She won't teach you anything. She won't even be able to reward you for your service."

My mind agreed with Eid's callous but reasonable words. Instead of taking a risk and choosing one of the souls that had offered me something enticing, I was about to play babysitter to an ordinary NPC who was a dime a dozen in any rural village. I could at least write a song about the Salamander King, but what could I do with the little one? No one cares about some banal 'tearful' tale about a dead peasant girl—doesn't matter how you dress it up. There'd be no profit in it.

The girl began to shift in my arms, she looked up at me with her bright eyes and gave me a look of such limitless trust that all my rationalization dissolved into nothing but a litany of empty arguments. My heart stubbornly repeated that I had to live according to my conscience instead of for gain. If I wanted profit, I'd be better off playing in the stock market instead of a virtual world.

"I'll speak with Astilba. I believe she is close to inventing a ritual that returns a soul to its body..."

"The Sixth won't waste time and energy on some human child!" Eid cut me off sternly. The Nazgûl guise I had created for him really fit him to a T at the moment. "This girl is no one. Dust under our feet. An empty waste of talent and effort. You have potential, Lorelei. You can achieve great things. You feel music and you know how to weave magic with it. You could reach the heights of Cypro one day, if you had the ambition. But you are throwing it all away for this little girl!"

The spirit shamelessly jabbed his finger in the direction of the quiet child.

"You have no heart!" the Salamander King roared, jumping to his feet.

"I do not," Eid agreed. "And I never did. My luthier created me perfectly, without any of the weaknesses that afflict you lot. I am created for true grandeur, not for languishing in the company of the wretched who are unable to realize and nurture their potential. I want you to know, Lorelei, that if you decide to follow the path of pointless pity, then at the end of this journey you won't be able to pull a single note out of me."

I paused to think here. And I thought hard. It would be stupid to decline a legendary instrument. And stupider still to decline the equivalent of my guitar synth, which I so missed here in Barliona. And on top of it all I would throw it all away for a social quest which I probably wouldn't even be able to complete.

I cast a long look at the girl and sighed heavily. I've lived a fool's life so I guess I'll die a fool's death too.

"In that case, you'll just have to go on gathering dust in Astilba's closet. Master Pirus makes wonderful instruments. I imagine I'll be able to find something to my liking when I get out of here."

Eid's smirk gave way to utter disappointment. Well...who cares. At least the Salamander King looked at me with evident approval. But of course— senselessly heroic deeds are just his thing. I guess he decided that he's found a kindred soul in me. How does that proverb go? A fool knows a fool from afar. Or was it something else...?

My ruminations were interrupted by the hiss of Salamander's sword leaving its scabbard. I followed the spirit's eyes—and was struck numb.

The cause of this hostile and threatening act by Salamander was the appearance of a new individual. Then again, I'm not sure that the eight eyes crowning the thorax of this creature qualified it for the term individual. Due to the nature of the local atmosphere, which permitted the eye to see only up to a certain point, the tarantula's immense silhouette came into focus only gradually. It was about ten meters tall and just as gray as the surrounding world, yet I could discern a slightly darker pattern on its belly and paws. Spiders have never scared me. One time I'd even held a large bird spider in my hand. But seeing a creature the size of a small townhouse, I experienced an intense spasm of xenophobia mixed with arachnophobia.

"It looks like someone in Barliona still remembers the Tarantulas," Salamander seethed through his teeth.

The fallen king stepped forward, screening the child and holding his sword *en garde*. What he was about to do remained a mystery—the spirit's weapon looked like a toothpick relative to the impressive spider torso.

Seeing the tarantula, the rest of the souls around us scattered every which way. I wonder what one spirit can do to another? Why are they so afraid of this creature? Or was this merely their vestigial memory of living under the yoke of the Arachnid Lords? And yet there were some who didn't take fright at the sight of the giant spider. My paladin friend also unsheathed his sword and stepped shoulder to shoulder with the Salamander King, while the gaunt warlock examined the Tarantula with naked interest, but without fear—like an equal.

"Art thou here still, Lizard King?" the sounds emanating from the spider were odd, full of clicks and chirrs. But the voice pierced me to the core. The girl squealed in terror and hid herself under my cape. "Do some weak minds still recall thy senseless rebellion, thy just suppression?"

"It wasn't quite so senseless if you're here instead of in Barliona," the rebel king parried.

I couldn't discern any emotions on the Tarantula's terrifying visage, but its tone oozed condescension.

"'Twas maugre all thine efforts, worm. Thy life, as thy death, were naught but a fleeting hindrance. No matter—I have come to speak with *thou*, oh nullity."

All eight of the spider's eyes fixed on me, kindling a strong urge to exit the game. However, the trembling girl clutching my leg and the intrepid king's spirit before me—prepared to fall once again to save another—forced me to suppress my terror.

"Let me guess, you want me to lead you through the Gate as well?" I asked with a challenge—even as I repeated silently to myself: 'it's just a game, this isn't real.'

The spider wiggled its tentacles revoltingly, and began to chirr and gurgle. It took me a moment to realize that this sound was its version of laughter.

"I haven't spent millennia accumulating my powers in order to re-enter the world for a brief space as some insubstantial spirit. Nay, I seek not thy conduct to the Gate."

These unexpected words caused Salamander and me to exchange glances.

"What do you want then?" I couldn't help but ask.

"There are still creatures in Barliona who have maintained their fealty to their lawful Lords," the Tarantula replied with evident pleasure. "I shall tell thou where thou may'st find my trusty servants.

Obeying my word, they shall welcome thou and perform the orders I relay with thee. Following the cataclysm, caused by a certain cretin, there are only a handful of my kind in Barliona. Feral and insensate, they have hidden themselves. Only I know where. All thou must do is bring one of my servants to them. They shall accumulate energy that will permit them to summon me into the world of the living in my full might and power. The rest shall be my care. I shall possess the body of an insignificant descendent and the world shall once more shiver beneath the Tarantulas' myriad heels! My servants shall reward thee with ancient, powerful artifacts and thou shalt assume a noble station in the restored chain of being."

Quest available: *Tarantella Reprise*.

Description: Locate the Tarantella Cult in the Free Lands and relay to them the commands of their Lord. Help the cultists perform the summoning ritual with the Tarantula's spirit and his living descendant. Quest type: Unique scenario.

Reward for completion: Exalted status with the Tarantella Cult.

Respect status with the Tarantula Lords.

— THE BARD FROM BARLIONA —

Hatred status with all other Barliona factions.

Three artifacts from the treasure vaults of the Tarantella Cult. An official title and property.

Penalty for failing or refusing the quest: Hatred status with the Tarantella Cult.

"You're wasting your time," the Salamander King laughed. "She would never accept your offer. No one aside from some madmen wishes to see the return of your hegemony."

I have to admit that such sincere faith in my character, warmed my heart. The sadder it was to disappoint this person.

"Four artifacts and we have a deal!"

Salamander turned slowly, clearly unable to believe his own ears. The puzzlement in his eyes gave way to such a deep disappointment that I felt unbearably ashamed. Eid, meanwhile, burst out into loud and triumphant laughter.

"I see you have seen reason, Lorelei."

"Don't do this, bard!" the paladin spoke up. "No treasure in the world is worth dealing with such a monstrous villain! All of the gods of Barliona will curse you!"

"They're not too happy with me as things stand," I informed the indignant spirit and then turned back to the Tarantula: "So what do you say? Four artifacts, or do you prefer to dwell here another hundred years before some other bard finds a way into the Gray Lands?"

"Thy disposition pleases me," the Tarantula chirred contentedly. "One must care for one's interest, snatching the boons from Fortune's hand at every chance. Thou hast my consent. Four artifacts it shall be!"

Quest updated: *Tarantella Reprise*.

"I will do what you ask," I said, accepting the quest. "Tell me where I am to seek your servants and descendants."

The immense spider body quivered in seeming ecstasy. Although, I haven't the tiniest idea about arachnid body language.

"Thy map has been marked, bard," the Tarantula clicked happily. "And now 'tis time I depart. I must contact my servants. Let them prepare for the ritual..."

Twitching his furry fangs and emitting the odd click, the Tarantula Lord crawled off languidly. This one had it made. He could communicate with the world of the living and he had some cult that kept him remembered. It looks like even in death, the mighty creatures have it easier than everyone else.

"How wrong I was about you, bard!" the Salamander King spat in my face. He looked enraged:

his eyes fierce, his hands trembling from barely contained wrath. "Maybe the Tarantula was right. In vain I fought for my descendants—who with their own hands pave the way back to Barliona for this greatest of all evils!"

"I am not one for excessive theatrics," remarked the warlock, whom I'd already forgotten about entirely, "but you are treating with powers that you could not even imagine."

"Do you want to help that scary spider monster?" the girl backpedaled from me. "Are you going to send that nightmare to my mommy?"

The paladin, meanwhile, didn't mince words or moralize. Getting a better grip on his claymore, he raised it overhead and brought it crashing down onto me. I jumped reflexively but the blade passed through my body without any pain.

"By the Light of Eluna's Blessed Visage!" the holy knight cursed and took another swipe at me perhaps to make up for this latest transgression. Also without any effect, but I appreciated the gesture. A man of action. I can respect that.

Eid was the only one enjoying the situation. The instrument's soul was giggling like a madman. In general he behaved a little oddly. Back in the Intermundis he was quite the polite spirit. He had even apologized when he killed me. Now however he was acting like the Dark Lord. Had his new Nazgul guise gone to his head?

"I suggest that everyone calms down," I tried to assuage the spirits' righteous wrath. "We need to find the Gate."

"And you think that I'll go on helping you?" Salamander seemed stunned by this new audacity.

"Don't you want me to rescue the little one's spirit from here?" I appealed to the rebel king's soft spot.

He ground his teeth and forced himself to nod:

"Only for the sake of this child shall I help you, oh false-faced abomination!"

"Your assistance, noble paladin, would be welcome too," I said to the paladin, insolently. "If you care for this poor, innocent child, you will help me find the Gate that leads out of the Gray Lands."

The paladin glanced from me at the clammed up girl and then at the irate Salamander. The rebel king returned his look heavily and then, after a moment's hesitation, nodded.

"All right," the holy knight agreed. "I don't understand entirely how I am to help, but for this child's sake I shall escort you. However, if Eluna can still hear me, she will curse you as soon as you return to Barliona, bard."

"I am sure she will," I assured him. "But at the moment, I need to find the Gate."

The mysterious warlock didn't try to join our company. He merely repeated, "Remember my offer, bard" as a farewell and went off on his business.

No one said anything else after that. Salamander and the paladin cast me immolating looks, the girl (whose name I still hadn't bothered asking) preferred to hold onto the deceased king, and Eid, as per usual, walked apart, enjoying the show in the company of his mount.

CHAPTER SIX

THE DENSE FOREST GROWING OVER THE FOOT of the mountain sparked an intense curiosity in me. How come there are trees growing in the world of the dead anyway? Is the mountain a part of the Gray Lands or another ghostly memory of some mythical mountain that once stood in Barliona? A mountain destroyed by some irate deity? Was this some magical forest that had burned to ashes as a result of some terrible firestorm?

Eid ignored my questions on this topic and my spirit companions made a show of wandering off in various directions, seeking to find the Gate and get away from the treacherous bard. The girl preferred to stay with Salamander. I guess I no longer radiate trust and compassion, what can you do...

I was left to stroll through the ghostly trees in Eid's company. The place's strangeness fit him pretty well. What kind of a forest is this? There's no brushwood, nor bushes, nor grass, nor even a trickling brook. With the toe of my boot, I dug into the omnipresent dust and revealed bedrock—out of which grew a tree. 'Curiouser and curiouser!' cried Alice.

I squatted and touched the stony surface with my fingers. It was cool to the touch—the first change in temperature I'd encountered since arriving in the Gray Lands (a curious and useless discovery). I was about to stand up when I noticed something unusual in a hollow beneath the tree's roots. More than anything, it resembled a shallow hole, the bottom of which was carpeted with some kind of vegetation.

I could see these details only thanks to my racial night vision trait. For an ordinary player, the hollow would appear as a dark hole between the roots and no more. Intrigued by such an unexpected sight, I crawled up to the hollow on all fours and peered in. Under closer inspection, the matting turned out to be made of grass. I wonder where it comes from if there's no grass here? And, just as importantly, whose lair is this? Does it belong to one of those animals Cypro had mentioned? But in that case where is the creature itself and how can I bind it to me?

I suppose I should stick my hand in there and rummage around, but an irrational fear kept me from doing so. Every horror story I knew that involved something like this ended with a bitten off hand, in the best case. Imagine that—it's scarier to feel around in a dark hole in the ground than take a dagger or fireball to the back.

Sighing deeply, I told myself several times that this is just a game. It didn't help much. The chill along my spine abated but I still didn't want to surrender my fingers to the local fauna.

"Eid, I need someone to feel around in this hole here," I said to the instrument soul.

He looked at me with an academic's interest, like an entomologist examining an interesting bug.

This annoyed me.

"What is it, too difficult for you or something? If you lose a hand, I'll sing you a new one, better than the last. I'll even throw in an extra finger. Ladies love scars and extra fingers."

"Fascinating!" the spirit deigned to answer me at last. "You were not afraid of treating with an ancient Tarantula and you are prepared to allow an unimaginable evil enter Barliona, yet you are terrified of being bitten by a small critter?"

Even Eid's horse snorted contemptuously and flicked its tail, aghast at the immensity of my cowardice. Oh a cold pasta hell with the lot of them!

I exhaled deeply and stuck my hand into the hole. Contrary to my paranoia, no one chomped at my delicate fingers. Instead, they encountered something interesting among the grass. Something familiar...Carefully closing my fingers, I grabbed my find and pulled it from the hollow. A tiny egg, half a pinkie finger in size, lay in my hand.

Ghostly Egg: This item's attributes are hidden.

There you have it. I can wrap my mind around animals remembered through legends, but an egg...If it were some Grand Easter Egg of Omnipotence, it would surely be on some pedestal or in a temple. But this one's just lying around in a hole in the ground. Why is that? Birds nest in trees, turtles in sand and lizards...Do lizards lay eggs? I should ask Sasha for a relevant lecture.

Whichever way it is, I was holding a potential guide in the land of the dead. If it hatches that is. And if not? Maybe the egg will just roll ahead of me, showing me the way like in a fairy tale...Where can I find a specialist on fantastical creatures and the places they inhabit when I need one?

"Eid..." I called the spirit over and showed him my find. "What is this thing?"

"An egg," the spirit replied seriously. "I think that's obvious."

"Whose? For what? What do I have to do to get it to hatch?" I refused to surrender.

"I am not an expert on avian obstetrics," Eid replied with a bit of mockery in his voice, forcing me to wave my hand. He doesn't want to help so I have to figure it out on my own.

What was it that Cypro wrote in his journal? I have to bind an animal to me. But there is no animal, just this egg. Or could I bind it with a song too? What a bunch of nonsense. I don't know any damn songs about any damn eggs. If they exist, then it's just as commercial ditties.

Unable to come up with anything better, I stuck the egg into my inventory and returned to my search for the mysterious gate.

At least here there was progress. It seemed that it would not be necessary to ascend to the summit after all. A heap of enormous boulders appeared among the trees growing around the foot of the mountain. It looked like the boulders had rolled down the slope at some point. I could see no scar on the mountain—if the avalanche had left one, then the gash had already closed and been covered with the forest. Then again, a heap of boulders could also serve as a monumental if awkward residence of some giant. Two enormous stones, meeting at their tops, had formed a triangular passage into the innards of this construction.

Yet there was no residence within. A spacious corridor, wide enough to allow three horsemen to ride abreast along it, receded straight into the depths of the mountain. I couldn't help but look for traces of artisans' hands on the walls around me—nature seldom created such orthogonal lines. But I could find nothing and not at all due to the darkness that grew thicker as we passed deeper into the mountain. Despite the lack of visible light sources, the corridor was still filled with the same omnipresent grayness which smudged everything outside. They're not called the Gray Lands for nothing, I suppose. The developers had put in some overtime to justify the name.

My companions, having returned and gathered together again, looked over the uneven stone vaults overhead with a subdued air. You'd think that since every one of them was already dead, the fear of being buried under enormous stones wouldn't occur to them, but I could see anxiety in everyone's face, apart from Eid's.

"Break time," I announced and sat down on the stone floor.

My companions stared at me like I was crazy but I ignored them, picked up the eid and began to strum 'Sound of Silence.' A Canopy of Silence descended upon us.

"Now we can have a chat," I began, "without eavesdroppers."

"We have nothing to speak of," the Salamander King interrupted me as the paladin nodded in agreement.

"I don't see it that way," I objected. "I don't know about you lot, but I see nothing shameful about deceiving an enemy. I don't have any intention of summoning the Tarantulas into Barliona. I simply wanted to find out where the Tarantulas' minions were hiding, as well as the refuge of the Lords' dependents. Barliona is full of creatures who would fight the return of an ancient tyranny, to say the least. They will be jump at the chance to reunite the cultists with their spider lords down here in the Gray

Lands. And there are plenty of hunters who would relish the opportunity to stalk some Tarantula descendants. I will tell them where the monster may be found and they will decorate their halls with its hide."

There was still mistrust in Salamander's eyes, but his face mellowed a little and his tension gave way to pensiveness.

"In that case why did you haggle for a greater reward?" he asked.

"So there wouldn't be any doubts that I was ruled by greed. Only someone who has no intention of holding up their end of the bargain would not bargain."

"And how do we know that you aren't lying to us now?" asked the paladin's spirit with some doubt.

"What would be the point?" I asked, a little surprised. "No offense, but what do I need your trust for? I don't belong to this place. No one who exists here can do me any harm. Nor have you two promised me mounds of gold or ancient secrets. I even managed to locate the Gate without your help. I just wanted to tell you all this and I didn't want to do it while one of the other spirits could eavesdrop on us and then relay to the Tarantula that I'd betrayed him."

"What about me?" Eid spoke up. "I still believe that it is stupid to refuse the help that's been promised you. I could go find the Tarantula and tell it all about your betrayal."

"As far as I recall, you are still subject to my will," I smirked to the difficult spirit. "I get to decide what form you take on. If you decide to go against my wishes, I'll sing that Billy Idol classic about eyes without a face."

In response to the knights' surprised expressions I explained without a hint of a smile.

"I can compose songs. All kinds of songs. I can also toss a priceless instrument into the fire and spend a long time watching the dying embers."

I guess something in the way I said that forced Eid to believe this threat and there were no further remarks from him. The king and the paladin also stayed silent for a while, weighing the pros and cons. The girl didn't say anything either, watching us with her enormous eyes.

"And why did you tell us all this?" Salamander asked at last. "As you pointed out, we're of no use to you."

"Not everything in life has to be useful," I shrugged and out of the corner of my eye noted my gradually depleting mana. It should hold out until the end of the conversation. "There are some things we do for the sake of our souls, excuse the pun. I promised you a trip to Barliona and I'd like you to wait around until I can do that for you, instead of setting off to Erebus disheartened by everything. And you," I turned to the paladin, "wanted to complete some task. I am going to try to bind your spirit with a song. If it works, I will be able to summon you to Barliona at a later date. If not, you can tell me your story right now and I will be able to compose a song about you and summon you that way."

The paladin's gray face lightened a little and he nodded approvingly. For his part, the Salamander King looked away in embarrassment.

"You said that you can write a song about me," he began uncertainly. "Now that I know that there is a chance that the Tarantulas might return to Barliona, I do not wish to go to Erebus. No earlier than the last one of them goes there. I will need strength. And...if you sally forth with those who go to vanquish the minions and progeny of these beasts, I wish to be by your side in that battle."

Attention! You have received the Salamander King's consent to be summoned. +50% to damage done by this companion.

"I will compose a song and perform it to anyone who cares to listen," I promised and discerned gratitude in the eyes of the taciturn spirit. "Now, please resume your morose expressions. Who knows what powers that overgrown spider has. What if he is watching us even now?"

"You needn't worry," Salamander assured me. "The Tarantulas never learned how to interpret facial expressions."

"Let's not risk it," I decided to be extra safe just in case. "I need several minutes to restore my mana and come up with a somewhat fitting song.

The paladin and Salamander nodded silently and fanned out to cover the possible approaches to our party. Eid stroked his horse on the crupper with a sour expression on his face. What a strange creature: He feels no compassion for a child, but a horse occupies all his care. Maybe that's because he was created by the biota, who have no children among them? Or is it because the horse is actually just another part of Eid's incarnation?

The girl, who was surprisingly quiet for her age, sat down across from me and watched me with wonder. The shimmering canopy faded and I sipped some water from my flask to increase my mana regen. Shutting my eyes, I recalled another song from the collection I had studied. Once I get back to meatspace, I'll download an entire omnibus of prog songs to my visor. Practice shows that a bard in Barliona better have the widest repertoire possible.

It took me some more time to compose a melody for the chord progression, but my companions waited patiently and didn't hurry me either with gesture or word. Finally, I completed my preparations, cast the Canopy of Silence and broke into a ballad about a sad paladin who was in love with death.

You have bound a song to the soul of the

Paladin General. From now on, you may summon this soul from the Gray Lands by performing this song.

Attention! Binding a song to a being that is not directly mentioned in the song can only be accomplished in person with the being in the Gray Lands.

Attention! This song does not mention the Paladin General directly and its performance will not sustain this being in the Gray Lands.

The canopy's shimmer faded, yet silence reigned in the stone corridor for a while still.

"An odd song," the spirit of the so-called Paladin General interrupted our silence. "Is it possible to love death?"

Uh-huh. In other words, I haven't hit upon the paladin's backstory. But the binding has taken place anyway. Is this like a bonus for those who go into the Gray Lands to find souls? Can I bind a spirit to a song that has nothing to do with it or does there have to be some minimal relevance like sharing the same race or class?

"I don't know," I replied honestly. "They say that love knows no limits. But the important thing has been done—there is now a bond between your soul and the song and I will be able to summon you to Barliona. I won't promise that I'll do so soon, but I will definitely do it."

"Thank you, bard," the paladin's spirit nodded curtly in recognition. "I now have hope that I will complete what I have begun."

I smiled at the holy warrior and concentrated on the last soul that wasn't bound. I didn't know any songs fit for this child. It was rare that we sang anything about kids. Or was it just that I never listen to such songs? Whatever it was, the time had come to conduct a field experiment. Without overthinking it, I selected the child's soul and played 'Octupus's Garden' without singing the words.

You have bound a tune to a creature's soul. From now on, you may summon this soul from the Gray Lands by performing this tune.

Attention! This song does not mention Anica directly and its performance will not sustain this being in the Gray Lands.

Aha! So I can bind souls to whatever I like as long as I'm there to do it in person in the Gray Lands. I wonder how a tune without vocals can be bound to a soul? Unless it's the soul of the tune's composer...

Okay. And what if I do the same thing with this here egg? My attempt was a failure. The system refused to bind anything to an object. Damn. It was all going so well...

"Onwards! To the Gate!" I ordered, getting to my feet. "The time has come to meet the being that guards it!"

As we moved further along the corridor, I began to discern some kind of noise, which was odd in and of itself: Until now, the only sound in this dreary place had been produced by me or the souls speaking with me. The noise grew as we approached and soon I began to make it out in more detail. And I liked these details less and less. A quiet, monotone howling gave way to impenetrable mumbling, then rose into a scream. Try as I might, I couldn't discern anything concrete among it all. It seemed that the local environment limited not only visibility but hearing too.

Salamander raised his hand, halting our party, and approached the girl. He squatted down so that she wouldn't have to gape up at him and asked softly:

"What is your name, child?"

"Anica," the girl's soul replied. "And what's your name, mister?"

"Azur," Salamander replied in turn and smiled at the sight of the girl's lips repeating his name silently. "We are going to play a game. As soon as I, uncle paladin there and auntie bard tell you to do something, you will do whatever it is we told you to. And if *he* tells you something," Salamander pointed at Eid who was casting them a condescending look, "or some stranger, you have to stick your tongue out at them. Understand?"

"Uh-huh," the girl nodded a little uncertainly. "It

doesn't sound like a very fun game."

"This is just the beginning," the Salamander King assured her. "Later it'll be your turn to tell us what to do. But that's later. Okay?"

"All right!" Anica nodded happily.

"In that case, let us begin," Salamander announced, getting up. "Anica, stay behind uncle paladin and don't step out from behind him."

The girl quickly hid behind the paladin's massive figure and for some reason stuck out her tongue at Eid. Salamander nodded approvingly and looked back at me. Indeed, he still has some things to teach. I personally have never known how to deal with children. My lack of practice showed.

Another soul-rending howl forced me back to more mundane matters. How can there be any matter at all in the Gray Lands? Per the nascent tradition, the Salamander King and the paladin bared their weapons. Eid meanwhile cast me a suspiciously sly look, as if he knew something we did not. What a ghoul he was. Soon as we get out of here, I'll sing him a new guise...and I'll be sure to use my entire arsenal of cheesy lines: 'Her brows bobbed under the sign of the moon,' and 'the breeze set her lips aflutter,' and 'her eyes were like two three-carat diamonds.' Oh and that's right, I wanted to experiment with 'her legs never ended, her teeth reflected the moon.' I'd make a woman out of him. One that you'd need a good stiff drink to even look at. Acting the way he was, he certainly had not earned a noble and courageous appearance, the jerk.

The Salamander King still looked at me expectantly, and so I postponed my fantasies of petty vengeance until calmer times. We had to decide what to do next. Since I didn't understand what was going on any better than the others and since I was never a brilliant strategist (or tactician), I simply waved my hand and headed to the source of the sound. This quest is for bards, not great generals, after all, so I will complete it according to the tradition of musicians—by listening to my heart.

The tunnel led us into a vast cave. The veins of some luminous ore gently gleamed amid the walls. Looking closely, I read the properties:

A vein of spectral ore.

Were I a bard miner, I'd have a field day here. But I was more interested in the creature rushing about the cave. It was about three meters in height, astonishingly curvy and rounded to such an extent that it reminded me of a ball of dough that had put on extra curves in preparation for hibernation. The impression was spoiled only by four small paws that from time to time darted from the thick fur. Unlike the other inhabitants of the Gray Lands, this creature had a traditional inscription with a name above his head: Ha'art the Gatekeeper (Level 440). And it turned out that the Gate he was keeping was a completely ordinary Barliona portal.

"A-ah-*ah!*" Ha'art ended his scream on a high note, grabbed his head and rolled on the floor, continuing to scream. "Oooh! I hate it! I haaate it!"

I have to admit that his screams scared me quite a bit. While the earlier Tarantula, despite its impressive dimensions and repulsive appearance, came across as a fictional being, this Ha'art fellow screamed very naturally. The image of a drug addict from a neighboring building instantly popped into my mind. A particularly bad experience with some bath salts had forced him to the roof of his apartment block and his poor relatives saved him only by having him hospitalized. The inhuman, mindless screams as the sturdy orderlies dragged him away, still seemed to me some of the most revolting sounds I'd ever heard. Ha'art's cries sounded strikingly similar.

"Ya-ya-ya," the shaggy ball hollered and looked up at me with red eyes. "Argh!"

I assumed a defensive posture, but the monster did not attack. It took me a few seconds to realize that his eyes were not shining, they were simply inflamed—like a student's the night before finals.

"The Liviiing!" Ha'art howled as loud as he could and in two hops bounced over to me.

Now I could discern his face. It resembled a grotesque caricature of a human one: ample bags under inflamed red eyes, a large nose curved to the lips and a wide mouth spanning ear to ear.

"It's all youuu!" the gatekeeper yelled at me with his gaping and impressive mouth. Fortunately, there were no smells here, so I was spared knowing what he'd eaten for breakfast.

"Youuu are tooo blaaame!" Ha'art raged and flopped before me.

"For what?" I could not stand these unfounded accusations. I'd never seen this guy and did not recall having offended anyone like this creature before. "I just want to go to the Gate, nothing more."

"So gooo!" the gatekeeper acquiesced unexpectedly. "Get out of heeere!"

I had no desire to look a gift horse in the mouth, and given that I'd already been forced to see Ha'art's teeth up close, I didn't object. I waved at my companions and went straight to the portal.

"Nooo!" crazy old Ha'art rushed forward and blocked the souls' progress. "Only the liviiing. This is no place for the liviiing! Souls can't leeeaaave!" he howled.

Well here we are then. It turns out that the gatekeeper only keeps the souls of the dead from leaving. I can leave without any problems, only by myself. I wonder if this applies to Eid too? He's, like, not a local either. I glanced at the soul of the instrument. Judging by his grin, the gatekeeper won't keep him either.

Okay. What are my options? Judging by the

traditional indicators like name, level and his ample HP, we didn't stand a chance against Ha'art. Maybe if I had a comparable level and a raiding party behind my back, it'd be different, but given the context and the location, it is unlikely that such a straightforward solution would do. So, I guess I should chat him into submission.

"Oh, they're not going anywhere," I told Ha'art as sincerely as I could. "We would only like to get to the portal. They just came to see me off. Well, you know, say good-bye, wish me good luck, pass on some greetings to the other side. They're just going to wave me goodbye and go about their business. Right boys?"

Salamander nodded eagerly, but the paladin's answer was unexpected:

"That is a lie."

Apparently my face expressed my surprise eloquently enough, since the paladin explained without waiting for the question:

"I cannot tell a lie. My vows to Eluna prohibit me from distorting the truth."

Oh come on. I will have to remember this detail when I summon this goody-two-shoes to Barliona. A companion like that will ruin quests left and right— and spill every sin and misdemeanor he witnesses along the way. Why he might even insist on a tribunal right there on the spot.

"Words! False words! Too many wooords!" Ha'art howled again, grabbed his matted locks and began rolling around the cave in a mad, furry fury. He moved so quickly that there was simply no chance to slip past him and into the portal. "You speak unnecessary words and you keep the important ones to yourseeelf!"

What are the important words? A password? I do not know any password. The Salamander King's and Paladin General's puzzled looks told me that they didn't know either.

"Will you please explain what the matter is?" I couldn't help but exclaim. My head was beginning to ache from his all his hollering. I could see no debuffs, so the effect was purely psychosomatic. "What are these unnecessary and important words?"

Without ceasing to roll around the cave, Ha'art began to chatter madly:

"Words spinning in my head...Unfinished verses...Unsung songs...The wind of the Intermundis carries them to me. They clamor in my head! Oooh!" he howled. "They're driving me crazyyy! I haaate them! I just waaant to sleeep! But they won't let meee!"

It was not simple to discern the message among Ha'art's delirium and I was not sure that I understood correctly.

"How can unsung songs keep you from sleeping?" I barely managed to inject the question into the gatekeeper's renewed mumbling.

"I can heeear them..." Ha'art's voice fell to a barely audible whisper. "What the living composed, but never performed! The dead wind sings me dead songs and doesn't let me sleep. Yeeears... Centurieees... Eeeons.... Oooh..."

With a crazed wail, Ha'art orbited the cave like a furry comet, leaving me completely at a loss. If I understood correctly, this NPC hears something like the ghosts of compositions? The stillborn poems and songs, swarms of which dwell in the minds of people. Is this just a developer's fantasy or has Barliona penetrated so deeply into our consciousness that the corporation can really read ideas and intentions? After all, isn't creation in the Intermundis a reading of images directly from my brain? If so, I would give a lot to dig around in Ha'art's overflowing head. The next moment, the insane gatekeeper uttered such a pitiful, high-pitched moan that I felt ashamed. The poor fellow is in this dreary place and he hasn't slept in years, and I'm thinking about how to steal something interesting from him. Okay. I'll try to help him somehow.

Without paying any attention to his incessant muttering, I sat down on the floor of the cave, arranged the eid on my lap, remembered one folk lullaby and began to play. The furball slowed down, rolled closer, looked at me with longing in his bloodshot eyes and began plaintively wailing an octave lower. Damn, do I sing that poorly? To clear my conscience, I played another lullaby, but there was no result. Ha'art did not fall asleep.

So, the solution to the problem lies in a different plane. If there are unsung songs in his head, maybe if I finish one of my drafts right here and now, he'll find some relief? Although how would a single silenced melody help when there were hundreds of thousands in his head? I had no other ideas, so I might as well try it. I just have to decide what that'll be...

My eyes stopped on the Salamander King. Yeah, it would be ideal to immediately create a ballad about the rebel king but I had to face the truth: It's not that simple to just cook up a good ballad on the spot. Even a burst of inspiration would only allow me to write a passable sketch, which would then require many painstaking hours of honing the rhymes and polishing the melody. Sitting around here for several days with interruptions to exit to meatspace in order to sleep and maintain the capsule did not appeal to me, so it's necessary to work with something I already had. I'd been grappling with a ballad about the Lord of Shadow for several days already, but it still hadn't come together. I had a bunch of couplets and phrases, but they didn't yet resemble a unified whole. I knew too little about Geranika to connect what I had in a single thread, a narrative. Instead, what I had pertained to Shadow in general and even then it was more the result of a fantasy based on what I had seen in the clip about the failed shaman student and my own observations. Hmm. Or maybe this was just what I needed? Forget for a while about Geranika and write about Shadow?

Having fished out my cartographer's kit from the inventory, I began to scribble over the sheets, bringing what I had already written in line with the new idea. Geranika can have a ballad, this will be hymn—a hymn to Shadow! Powerful, awesome. My imagination painstakingly sketched in Mordor's gloomy expanses, the formidable legions marching from horizon to horizon, and the cave we were in resounded with heavy guitar riffs punctuated by the majestic sounds of the organ. A little woodwinds, some drums and percussion...Eh. Wish the guys were here to help me. The guitar synth, of course, allowed me to produce whatever sounds I wanted, but I wasn't much of a one-girl band. Nor were there any editing or production features here, so I couldn't overlay pre-recorded tracks. No big deal. I'll sketch out the score and we will play it all together at practice. Straus can add his special effects as he sees fit.

To be honest, I forgot about Ha'art and why we'd come here in about five minutes. Finally I managed to latch onto the right idea. As soon as I stopped bothering about Geranika, my earlier scribbles quickly came together into a hymn to Shadow, and the music literally poured into my ears. It even occurred to me that the dead wind tearing around this place was whispering me one of the melodies that wanted to be played. No more than four hours later, the work was completed. It was still a draft, of course, but it sounded like a hymn. The guys and I could tinker with the arrangement at our next band practice and flesh out the melody, but even here and now it should sound good!

In anticipation, I touched the strings of the eid and froze, enjoying the sweet moment. I live for just these kinds of moments. The idea, which originated somewhere in my head, had encountered the music from my heart and was about to enter the world. Is this not bliss? Is this not the act of creating a new world in the human imagination?

A dark melody, full of strength and menace, filled the cave. The rhythm of the percussion and deafening bass was palpably lacking, but the sounds of the hymn made the body tremble with a sense of hidden power. The score laid out before me glimmered and disappeared like Cypro's songbook had earlier, leaving a songbook shimmering in soft pearl light on the gray stones before me.

You have created a new song: 'Hymn to Shadow.'

Description: Shadow is the power that lurks on the wrong side of the world, equally opposing Light and Darkness. Those who accept Shadow gain a source of incredible power, but at the same time become outcasts for the rest of the world. Spurned by gods and mortals alike, creatures of Shadow do not seek pity and indulgence. Their

goal is to seek power and find their own way at any cost.

The Hymn to Shadow strengthens all minions of Shadow:

+ (Composition + 20)% to all base stats for (5 + Composition) hours.

– (Composition + 10)% to debuff efficacy for (5 + Composition) hours.

Simultaneously dispels all active debuffs in the first seconds of the performance of the hymn. During the performance of the hymn, creatures of Shadow gain immunity to some debuffs.

Casting time: The entire hymn must be performed.

Casting cost: 100% MP.

Area of effect: Affects all creatures of Shadow within hearing distance.

Cooldown: 10 hours.

If the hymn's performance is interrupted, all Shadow creatures that have heard it receive debuffs proportional to the buffs they would have received if the hymn had been completed.

Skill increase:

+1 to Composition. Total: 2.

+10 to Fame. Total: 31.

The sense of satisfaction from the created spell was no match for the triumph of the composed hymn.

Spells, characteristics—who cares! I had written a great song! And, among other things, Ha'art had fallen asleep. A buff called 'The Composer's Gift' hovered over the slumbering ball of fur, its description explaining that due to the completed song, not a single soul would be able to enter the cave of the gatekeeper for the next three days and he himself wouldn't hear songs or poems for that duration. And indeed the entrance to the cave was really covered with a flickering shroud like those that covered dungeon entrances.

"You are singing a hymn to a force that is opposed to all that is good!" the Paladin General's angry exclamation interrupted my thoughts, ruining the sweet aftertaste of my achievement. "Your verses shall poison hearts and minds, warding them away from the Blessed Visage of Eluna!"

Ugh. Talk about a holier than thou attitude! Way to spoil a great moment...I glanced at the indignant holy warrior and seriously thought about whether it was worth trying to reason with him. Did I really need to? There are thousands of souls who can tell interesting stories in here, and I'm sure many of them did not care about my belonging to Shadow. And this moralist can easily attack me as soon as I summon him. If he had been here alone, I would have simply ignored his righteous anger, but Salamander also looked at me somehow suspiciously. I guess I'll have to explain my spy mission for the benefit of my evergreen homeland.

A brief account of my, no doubt, heroic act of self-sacrifice took a little time, but caused a volatile reaction. Both the paladin and the Salamander King had lived long before the emergence of a new faction and now experienced mixed feelings. But if the rebel king was on the whole happy to hear that the holy and dark empires had united against their common foe, the paladin general deemed such an alliance unnatural and the Shadow faction 'apostate.' Eid meanwhile looked at me so intently that I sincerely hoped he couldn't tell Astilba what he had just heard. Oh, and a lot of interesting things he can tell her...

One way or another, my composition of the hymn had been dealt with for the time being and we turned our attention to the portal from the Gray Lands.

"Well, it's time to say goodbye." The Salamander King's smile seemed a bit melancholy. "Anica, behave yourself and obey your aunt."

The girl sniffed, ran to Azur, hugged his leg and sobbed loudly. The paladin looked at her graciously, though when it came to me, his look was still full of suspicion. The eid's malicious spirit was shifting from foot to foot at the portal, indicating his desire to hurry to the Intermundis. No big deal. He can wait. If I can't take Salamander with me, then at least I should say goodbye to him normally. I just have to wait my turn to speak to this crimson-haired nanny...

I did not have time to consider what would happen once my turn came. I guess there isn't that much useful space in that skull of mine because the sudden hint that popped into it displaced everything else. Crimson-haired! Salamander's hair was still crimson! And he can touch me and Anica. So, my promise is still in force, despite the fact that I had promised to take only the girl's soul to the world of the living.

Opening my spellbook as quickly as I could, I found the 'Bonds of Memory' spell and carefully read over the text. Maximum number of souls summoned at once: (1 + Composition). And I had just leveled my Composition up to 2, and that meant that I could take up to three souls with me at once! Yes! There's no need for Salamander to stay here and wait for a later summons!

My joy quickly gave way to healthy pragmatism. Sure, I can bring all three with me, but now the paladin with his pathological love of truth and fanaticism will blow my cover with the renegades. I can't take him with me. Not this time. The right way to do it is to bring the Fifth with me—since this entire venture was his fault—but the cave is closed to all souls for the next three days. There was, of course, the option of leaving through the cave entrance, calling the Fifth with my song and finding another gate, but then Anica and Salamander couldn't return to Barliona. They would have to remain in this cave.

Theoretically, they could go through the portal on their own, but what will they do in the Intermundis? Hang around that nauseating whiteness for an eternity? It seemed like old Portulac would have to wait a few more days.

"Enough with the tears already!" I interrupted the touching farewell scene. "Plan's changed. I can summon both of you."

The joyous surprise on the face of the Salamander King paled in comparison with Anica's pure ecstasy.

"Really? Really really?" She began bouncing up and down as energetically as she had been sobbing a second before. "And uncle paladin? Will he come with us, too?"

"Not this time," I answered vaguely, and, not wanting to continue the awkward conversation, waved at the portal. "Let's not waste time."

The men shook each other's hands curtly, Anica limited herself to waving vigorously at 'uncle paladin,' and I made do with a brief, "See ya, pal." To everyone's surprise, Eid briefly inclined his head and cheerfully exclaimed "We'll be back!" and dived into the portal immediately after me.

The familiar white jelly of the Intermundis was obscured by a system notification:

Quest complete: *Taming the Eid*.
You have passed the test and have proven

yourself worthy of playing Cypro's legendary instrument. From now on, you can not only create spells with the help of the eid, but also call on its spirit to help you.

You have unlocked the 'Summon Instrument Soul' ability.

Experience earned: +5,000 XP.

Level gained!

Level gained!

Current Level: 20.

778 XP remaining until next level.

Unallocated stat points: 100.

Training points remaining: 7.

'Summon Instrument Soul.'

A true master puts his soul into his creations, but a true bard can awaken this soul and acquire a devoted companion.

Requirements: Must own an instrument type Rare or higher.

Occupied with something else entirely, I did not read any further. How could I have completed this quest? Eid, after all, had clearly expressed his position regarding my prospects of achieving something in this life. I had no bright future ahead of me and this overstrung balalaika does not want to waste his best years on me.

"Oh!" Anica's frightened squeak caused me to

postpone the mystery of the unexpected completion of my quest.

The girl clutched Salamander's hand convulsively and squeezed her eyes tightly shut. The king himself looked somewhat dumbfounded. It was understandable. Even for a player like me, this place was pretty impressive. What is there to say about NPCs? For a peasant girl, the Intermundis must be some nightmare.

I looked around for some inspiration, a suitable song to transform the particles of the Intermundis. The place was full of the same impenetrable, milky maelstrom. I could see neither Eid nor his steed. I guess he's hovering around somewhere nearby, awaiting his next guise. Everything in good time. First I'll change the surrounding curds and whey to something easier on the eye, and then I'll have a soul to soul with Eid. I'm just brimming with puns today, aren't I?

The child's sobbing did not help me think, so I performed the first thing that popped into my head— the song about golden town that had pissed off Chip so much. The solution turned out to be suitable: The white morass obediently transformed into an idyllic landscape full of meadows, flowers and other animals mentioned in the lyrics. After years spent performing this song, my imagination had filled in such a detailed and beautiful picture that I never for a moment doubted the world it would embody.

"You can open your eyes, Anica," I told the girl.

"It's scary out here!" The girl's soul shook its head and refused to open her eyes.

"Not any more it isn't. Look," Salamander suggested to her.

Anica carefully opened one eye, froze, squeaked enthusiastically and flapped both eyes wide open. The white stone walls with a golden finish were almost lost among the riot of greenery and flowers. Never before had I thought why in my imagination the golden city was not made of precious metal, but mostly of white marble. There was plenty of gold of course, but the majority of it was stone. A touch of fantasy, I guess.

"Is this the forest where you live?" Anica rattled, hopping in place. "And this is your city? Can I pet the bull? Can I feed it grass? Can I ride it?"

I did not get the chance to reply, as Anica uprooted a bunch of local greenery and thrust it into the muzzle of the ox who seemed uncomfortable from such sudden, intense attention. The picture was so comical that my lips involuntarily curved into a silly smile.

"This is not Barliona, is it?" Salamander asked in a low voice, approaching me. "None of this was here until you started singing."

"Not yet," I confirmed his hunch. "But it's very close to Barliona."

All that remained was to figure out how we could get home. And that problem came with some fine print. Obviously, I should choose some suitable song and use it to travel to the main game world. Under closer examination, however, things weren't so simple. Let's say I sang some song about Anhurs—would I thereby lay the way to the actual city or just recreate Anhurs here in the Intermundis? And it's not like I even need to go to the imperial capital. I needed to travel to the Hidden Forest, back to Astilba. Would I have to compose a new guiding song? It would be nice, but it's not as easy as baking cookies—an hour isn't enough. And anyway, if I really had to compose, then I'd rather it be something universal about a guide to the Intermundis. Although...I already have a certain experienced musical blockhead in mind. And it would be nice to figure out the issue of the completed quest.

"Eid, are you here?" I asked just in case.

The only response came from the ox, who lowed melancholically. Oh really? I looked at the pachyderm chewing his cud, and he looked back at me with large, sad eyes. Did I accidentally embody the instrument's soul in this form? The ox finished chewing its cud and lowed again sadly. Damn! Can he even talk?

"Good little cow," Anica said enthusiastically, shoving a bouquet of flowers fearlessly into the animal's maw. Personally, I would not get so close to a beast that large in meatspace. Either the girl understood that she was already dead and she had nothing to lose, or, for a peasant child, this was an entirely ordinary situation. "After the cow eats its lunch, we can go for a ride."

Why there's an idea! Even if Eid can't speak at the moment, he can still show us the way. Last time he just moved me from Barliona to the Intermundis, maybe he can perform the same trick in reverse this time?

A soft but deep roar sounded from somewhere behind the white stone walls. Salamander and I both turned around: I in shock, the king on guard.

"My guess is that's a lion," I finally guessed. "I don't think he's dangerous, but just in case, let's look around."

The Salamander King nodded in agreement, and feeling very foolish, I went to the ox and with a certain apprehension held out my hand. Such are the tricks of the mind. I wouldn't be afraid of entering a forest full of mobs. That situation was clear beforehand. A mob is a mob so it can attack you. Here on the other hand, I was dealing with what seemed like an herbivore, a peaceful creature—yet my fear refused to leave me. Well, what if he bites my hand? When all is said and done, I am a vegetable creature and would make a decent meal for this herbivore.

"Eid, can you take us to Barliona? Or at least tell me, which way we need to go?"

The ox raised his head, looked at me with big sad eyes and again lowed sadly.

"I think it's time for you to take a rest, Lorelei," a

strange, screechy voice came from somewhere above. "You seem to be talking to witless beasts."

A large eagle with golden plumage was perched on the branch of a tree. And he was speaking to me.

"Did you really think that out of all the essences suggested in the song, I would choose this unwieldy ruminant for my next incarnation?" The eagle cocked its head in a typical avian manner and looked at me reproachfully.

"Eid?" I inquired a bit dumbly.

"No, the goblin queen in her finest evening gown," grunted the eagle, then gracefully hopped off the branch and landed on the grass next to me. This was one huge bird. He stood up to my waist and his wingspan was more than four meters. I immediately wanted to quip something about 'Freebird' but restrained the dumb urge. "Of course I'm Eid!"

"Do goblins have queens?" Salamander popped in with a tangential question.

"Are you assuming that goblins are incapable of organizing themselves politically?" The eagle turned his head sideways, spotted Anica sneaking up behind him, hastily flapped his wings and returned to his previous perch. The girl followed him with a disappointed look, sighed and went back to feeding the ox.

"We can find a queen for our king sometime later," I quickly intercepted the attempt to steer the conversation aside. "We have more pressing matters to deal with at the moment."

Salamander blushed for some reason and muttered something unintelligible about pure curiosity. However, at the moment I was more interested in Eid than interracial dynastic marriages.

"To begin with, explain why I was credited with completing the quest associated with you," I demanded. "Didn't you swear that you wouldn't concern yourself with me any longer?"

"I was just testing you," Eid confessed. "My creator did not want his creation to serve an evil or self-serving sentient, ready to be tempted by generous promises and let monsters, like the Tarantula Lords, enter Barliona. You rejected the tempting offers in order to grant a few hours of happiness to the child's soul without any reward. Even the threat of losing a unique instrument did not make you change your mind. This deserves respect. And so, you are the second person after Cypro whom I am prepared to serve in your travels around Barliona or beyond."

Attention! You have been granted permission to use the eid beyond the scope of this scenario.

My heart warmed. It was not even a matter of receiving this fine instrument as a reward. It was merely nice to realize that Eid was not the selfish creature he had seemed like so recently. At least in this game, the sentients turn out to be better than I had imagined.

"And right now, I could really use your help. Tell me, how do I return to Barliona? Preferably to the same place we left from?"

"There are several ways, but right now only one is available. You have to find the right song to approach the border with Barliona, and then I'll help you get back to where you started your journey."

Doesn't sound too difficult on the whole. As far as I understand, the song should evoke Barliona or a similar place in my mind. It doesn't even have to include keywords like Hidden Forest or Kartoss. A few minutes of contemplation and I can be on my way. But...I did not want to leave the Intermundis. When will I get another chance to be a god of creation? To make fantasy a reality, albeit virtually?

"Tell me, Eid, will I ever be able to return to the Intermundis?"

"I do not know, Lorelei. There are such places where the boundaries of the worlds become blurred and some beings and objects like me can cross them."

"Like you?" I seized upon this idea. "And can you send me to the Intermundis at any time?"

"No. It takes a lot of energy to cross the boundary. I can absorb it from the world, collecting it, but it takes a long time to accumulate enough of it."

"We won't rush it then. I want to enjoy the Intermundis while I have the chance."

"The Intermundis is full of frightening creatures,

Lorelei. Remember your first trip. Are you willing to imperil the souls who have placed their trust in you for the sake of entertainment? And they do not have much time left. In the Gray Lands they were nurtured by the memories of the living. In Barliona, they will draw from your vitality. Here, however, they have no source of energy and you do not yet know how to share yours voluntarily. Soon the souls will begin to weaken. Eventually they will disappear altogether."

Dumbfounded by this news, I looked at the properties of the Salamander King. Indeed, the soul carried the 'Waning Vitality' debuff with a timer that indicated he had an hour and a half left. Anica barely had forty minutes, even if her ecstatic face betrayed no sign of weakness.

I guess our excursion in the Intermundis will have to be canceled.

"Anica, say farewell to the ox. It is time to go."

"Let's take him with us!" the girl looked at me with that same look that turns a nice profit in toy stores the world over.

"That's not possible," I said, not entirely sure that this was the case. I wonder if it's possible to get something out of the Intermundis into Barliona? Then I could, for instance, conjure up some Trusty Vorpal Blade of a Thousand Snicker-Snacks—and sell it for mega bucks at auction...

"Have you chosen a song, Lorelei?" Eid prodded me along. "Remember, if you interrupt your performance, we will stray from the path. The souls following behind you can get lost among the worlds."

A song...Under the eagle's gaze, I sat down on the grass and strummed the strings with perplexity. Various tunes popped into my head, but some of them suggested a fairly thorny journey, while others dealt with modernity and probably wouldn't suit the gameworld's fantastic nature. The minutes counting off Anica's life were ticking away one after another and I began to grow nervous. I mean, I know hundreds of stupid songs, so how am I having so much trouble finding the right one? I'll have to risk it and play 'Goldentown' again. I wouldn't want to pass through suffering and pain, risking the souls following in my wake, but I have no choice. Yet as soon as I made that decision, my anxiety left me, my mind cleared, I glanced at the eagle watching me and another song immediately popped into my mind. I did not have the sheet music at hand, but the chord progression was simple enough and it took me five minutes to recall the parts. Maybe it's different from the original, but this isn't a cover contest.

I got to my feet, adjusted the eid in my hands and checked the debuff's timer. Anica had nine minutes left in the Intermundis.

"Get ready, we're heading out."

"Should we be ready for something in particular?" asked Salamander and took Anica, who had gone quiet suddenly, by the hand.

"If I only knew," I sighed and began to sing. Am to E7: "*On a dark desert highway, cool wind in my hair...*"

The subtle story of a wandering soul returning to a home it no longer recognized transformed the fabric of the Intermundis, embodying the images of the ballad.

G to D: "*Warm smell of colitas, rising up through the air,*" and F to C: "*Up ahead in the distance, I saw a shimmering light...*"

The world around us shook and rippled. Eid was changing again, his plumage growing gold and his body growing. He spread his wings and grew several-fold in size. The shaky reality around him was thinning, melting and we were once again in the middle of the white abyss of the Intermundis. The eagle shrieked, flapped his wings and ducked under us, turning into a mount for our entire party. Salamander stood firmly on the back of the giant bird, pressing Anica to himself. The girl had hardly moved, watching the metamorphosis that was happening with a mixture of fear and delight. And she wasn't alone. My heart was on the verge of bursting from my chest. How I love this Intermundis place!

And I sang: "*Such a lovely place (such a lovely place), such a lovely face...*"

The chorus melted the surrounding fog, giving birth to the world under the bird's wings. The horizon blossomed with a desert sunrise flaring far away, but the eagle flew confidently into the other direction from the sun, into the cold radiance of the starry night. The spectacle was so magical that I could hardly concentrate on playing.

"How they dance in the courtyard, sweet summer sweat. Some dance to remember, some dance to forget."

A ridge of clouds appeared ahead of us like a mighty wall. Dense but soft even in appearance, their impeccable whiteness was interrupted by the warm radiance of a majestic, Spanish structure. Its white, adobe walls evoked the halls of a desert queen. Its courtyards were festooned with flowers. Light gathered around the alabaster dome into a soft radiant, glow.

In a few sweeps of his mighty wings, Eid brought us to the hotel in the clouds and landed in front of the wide-open gate. The eagle's wing extended in the manner of a ladder, and he himself began to shrink so quickly that we barely managed to disembark our magical aircraft. Without a single doubt about what we had to do, we stepped under the dome. To my surprise, it was neither hot nor cold here. On the contrary, a tender warmth filled my body and even Anica started. Her eyes glowed with delight and an exclaimed sigh escaped her lips.

The eagle suddenly waved his wings, soared to the domed ceiling of glass and shrieked loudly. Gold dust began to shower from his plumage, reflecting a million times and rising into an impenetrable, blinding whirlwind. And when the dust settled, we were back in Barliona...

CHAPTER SEVEN

ASTILBA'S LABORATORY seemed particularly dark and gloomy after such a vivid and rapid trip. Dumbfounded by the insane journey, Salamander and Anica looked around in bewilderment. Eid was nowhere to be seen, but I did not attach importance to this fact. All the impressions had jumbled into a fine mess in my head. I even had to reread the system notifications several times to understand their meaning.

Quest updated: *Creating a Cicerone*. Read Cypro's notes.

You have summoned souls from the Gray Lands at the cost of half of your vitality.

Attention! Summoned souls cannot exist in Barliona without an external supply of vitality. Every 10 minutes, you will lose 20% of your maximum HP for each summoned creature. Current summon upkeep: –40% HP every 10

minutes. The upkeep for summoned creatures ignores all skills and spells of damage absorption or reduction.

In the event of your death, a summoned creature will return to its original plane of existence, unless it finds another source of vitality.

A debuff called 'Leeching Souls' appeared and began counting down until the next time I would have to donate my HP to Anica and Salamander.

Attention! A new trait has become available to your character: Summoner. As your Summoner trait levels up, your summoning skills improve. The effectiveness of spellcasting increases, the power and skill of summoned creatures increases.

Do you accept? Attention, you will not be able to remove an accepted trait!

My thoughts stirred sluggishly to process this seemingly straightforward question. Do I want to play as a summoner? Why not? Each soul is a story that can become a song.

You have unlocked a new trait: Summoner I.

Attention! Your new trait has modified some of your spells:

'**Bonds of Memory.**'

Cost of performance: (50 – Summoner)% of max health.

Maximum level of the summoned soul: (Bard Level + Writing + Summoner).

Maximum number of skills and spells available to summoned soul: (Soul Level ÷ 10 + Composition).

Maximum number of souls summoned at once: (1 + Composition + Summoner).

Duration of summoned soul's stay in Barliona: (Intellect ÷ 10 + Composition) hours until the soul exhausts its vitality.

Cooldown: (72 – Summoner) hours.

Vitality upkeep for summoned souls: (20 – Summoner)% HP per (10 + Writing + Summoner) minutes for each summoned soul.

New achievement earned: 'Summoner I'

+1% damage done by summoned creatures. 19 summons remaining until next rank.

New achievement earned: 'Journey to the Gray Lands I.'

You have made a voluntary journey to the Gray Lands and returned earlier than the standard deadline. –1% to duration of stay in the Gray Lands upon death. Return 19 more times before the standard deadline to earn the next rank.

My overstimulated consciousness needed a break and I was about to exit the game when I noticed Astilba. She walked slowly around her lab, examining our motley company.

"You did it!" The pure green glow of her eyes, devoid of irises and pupils, prevented me from following her gaze, but I felt that they had stopped on me. I guess my break will have to be postponed indefinitely. "Not only did you manage to tame the eid, but you've returned with these souls."

Astilba's hand touched the Salamander King's shoulder. Barely noticeable ripples radiated from the place of contact between the biota and the ghost. The flesh, it seems, had met resistance. The spirit was not bodiless. Salamander himself looked so dumbfounded by his return to the world of the living that he did not even react to such a familiar gesture. He stared at the Sixth intently.

"A magically stabilized corporeality," said the necromancer, paying no attention to the dumbfounded king of antiquity. She went to the table, grabbed the candlestick and hurled it at the ghost. He reflexively caught the flying object and stared at it in shock. I could understand the guy—it'd been centuries since he held so much as a candlestick in his hand.

"He can interact with the physical world," Astilba summarized.

"That lady is scary!" said Anica, pointing at the

Sixth with childish innocence and hiding behind Salamander.

"It's all right, Anica," I tried to make my voice sound soothing. "You're back in Barliona. I'll explain everything to you in a little bit."

"Outward signs that the spirit has retained its individual personality and lifetime emotions," Astilba reacted to the girl's remark in her own detached way. "A parasitic link to the summoner's vitus. The vitality channel is still weak and unreliable, but this is a question of practice. The strength of the summoned soul is limited by the power of the summoner...It looks like you really managed to bring souls from the Gray Lands, Lorelei!" She concluded solemnly and smiled a little eerily.

I shuddered involuntarily. There was something very unsettling about the Sixth at the moment. It was as if some ancient force that had waited in long anticipation was finally gathering itself, ready to break out at last. The primordial fear, turning somewhere deep inside of me, scattered my drowsiness in a flash.

Quest complete: *Summons from the Gray Lands*.

+1,000 Reputation with the Renegades of the Hidden Forest.

Current status: Friendship.

Experience earned: +15,000 XP.

You have gained a level!
You have gained a level!
Current Level: 22.
Unallocated stat points: 110.
Training points remaining: 7.

"You are a bad lady!" Anica told the Sixth but was not allowed to elaborate further. With an imperious flourish of the necromancer's hand, spectral spheres appeared around the summoned souls. Two identical debuffs appeared over the portraits of my ghosts in the game interface: 'Soul Fetters.' Judging from the description, the fetters are a kind of magical trap for disembodied entities like ghosts and spirits. I wonder if all mages have access to this spell or only necromancers...

"Do not worry, Lorelei, they shall be all right," Astilba explained condescendingly. "I do not have much time to spare for empty conversations with useless outisders. I will free them when we finish. Dispose of these souls on your own."

I did not object. The less the souls hear now, the less I will have to explain to them later. Easier for me that way.

"You managed to come to terms with Cypro's eid, Lorelei," Astilba continued. "This is a major achievement for such a young and inexperienced bard. Now I believe that everything will work out. Eid will help you summon the soul of Portulac during the ritual. Until then," the Sixth raised her hand sternly, "the instrument shall return to the vault."

At these words, my heart filled with bitterness and my fingers couldn't help but clench the eid's body. The last thing I wanted was to part with this miraculous instrument. But what could I say? Eid had been given me only within the limits of the quest. I still couldn't even access his attributes. The instrument belonged to someone else and I reluctantly extended it to Astilba. She took it gingerly and put it in its already familiar green cocoon. It seemed to me that a look of approval flashed across her odd eyes. But I couldn't be certain—it's hard to make out emotions amid such a solid green glow.

"I promised to reward you by teaching you one of the spells I know. Unfortunately, you are absolutely not familiar with the schools of warlocks, demonologists and necromancers and therefore unable to learn something truly complex. I can teach you a short-term summons of a minor demon or how to harvest the vitus of mortals after you kill them so that you can later raise a zombie or an undead skeleton. Given that you have become a summoner, this knowledge will be useful to you. Also I may teach you the subtleties of how to direct the flow of vitality. This knowledge will allow you to see the currents of vitality and control them. You will learn how to draw from the enemy's vitus, redirecting the flow to yourself or to your allies. Make your choice now, Lorelei."

I took some time to think it over. Raising the dead did not appeal to me very much. I'm not a fan of zombie apocalypses. As for demons...It's interesting of course, but I can learn to summon them from any old warlock. However, I do not remember ever coming across the manipulation of vitality in guides and FAQs. The warlocks had a vampirism spell, but it only allowed life to be drained from the enemy directly. There had been no mention of transferring vitality to allies. It seems that my channeling it to the summoned souls had unlocked access to a non-standard skill.

"I would like to learn the subtleties of working with vitality."

"You have made your decision."

A flashing glow that resembled the effect that came with a new level engulfed my avatar.

Astilba has taught you a new spell: 'Detect Currents of Vitality I.'

Warning! You do not specialize in necromancer spells and therefore incur the following penalty when using this spell: – (Composition – 30)% to base spell efficacy.

Spent 1 training point. 6 training points remaining.

"You could delve deeper into the spells of this school, Lorelei," Astilba continued. "But to do so you must study the dark magics and avoid being distracted by the skills of other classes."

Attention! You can choose the way of the Singer of Death, forever linking your life with black magic (+100% to all necromancer spells). However, you will lose the ability to learn the spells of other schools. All previously learned spells for other classes will be forgotten.

Do you wish to become a Singer of Death?

No. Absolutely not. I do not want to associate my class with a single school. And we already have a Singer of Death in our party.

"Thank you for your generous offer, Sixth, but I prefer to wander around the world in search of new stories and knowledge. I do not wish to limit my studies to a single school."

My health had ebbed to 36% by now, so without worrying about decorum, I produced my lute and played a Song of Healing. The Sixth watched me quietly and then suddenly remarked:

"You remind me of Cypro. He, too, dreamed of wandering, exploits unsung and ancient wisdoms. I assume you will cross the Arras and leave your native forest as soon as we foil the fatal alliance with Kartoss?"

"Prevent the alliance? Is that possible?" I jumped at the chance to avoid answering the question right then and there. I sensed some ulterior motive in it. And it wouldn't hurt to find out the point of the Schism and the alliance with Geranika. It was already evident that the renegades were plotting something. But I still did not know what exactly they were going to do.

For a while, Astilba was silent, regarding me with her eerie eyes.

"Everything in this world is possible," she said, when I had already decided that an answer wouldn't be forthcoming. "What do you think would happen if the Dark Lord of Kartoss hears that his embassy had been destroyed in our forest? Would he still be eager for an alliance?"

"I doubt it. But he can start a war."

"Now? As Geranika threatens both Empires? No. It would take the combined power of both Emperors as well as all the magisters of Kartoss to breach the Arras. Depleted, they would then be defenseless for more than a week. Neither the biota nor the pirqs ever invaded Kartoss, so the Dark Lord has no reason to embroil himself in this conflict. And if he does decide to do so, Geranika will use the opportunity to strike unexpectedly. An alliance with this shaman is mutually beneficial to us. Geranika gives us the strength to carry out our plans, and we prevent the strengthening of Kartoss at the expense of our people. If they are trying to draw us into the war, then we prefer to fight for our independence instead of against

Geranika. And yet I truly expect to solve this matter with as little blood spilt as possible. The blood of the ambassadors. The Hidden Forest must remain neutral."

It sounded sensible, but one embarrassing question confused me:

"To get through the Arras, you need the help of a local. The embassy will be welcomed by our brothers and sisters. Won't spilling their blood imperil our neutrality as well?"

For a moment, doubt crossed Astilba's face—and vanished a second later without a trace.

"To begin with, we will merely explain to them what our goals are. If we don't succeed in persuading them, I will temporarily disable them with the help of mighty demons. With a bit of luck none of our brethren will suffer."

It all sounded so rosy that I immediately doubted the viability of such a 'bloodless' scenario. Things don't work out that way.

"I answered your question, Lorelei, and now I would like to receive an answer to my question. Are you going to leave the forest and go into the world of the outsiders?"

Thinking this over, I absentmindedly tuned up my lute, then replaced it behind my back. What was the right answer?

Logically, if I confess my desire to leave, I can say goodbye to any more quests from this powerful

NPC. I'd be going to fraternize with the enemy, after all.

But at the moment, I had no desire at all to get involved with special quests. My trip to the Gray Lands had completely exhausted me. I wanted to exit Barliona, take a shower, lie on the couch and put my thoughts in order. Or sit down with Pasha in the kitchen and tell him about the Intermundis.

"Yes, I would like to go wandering." I'm sure I will regret this honest answer tomorrow, but I don't have any strength left for diplomacy. "I want to see the other races, hear their songs and tales. I'm interested in seeing the world beyond the Arras."

The Sixth's face suddenly broke into a smile. For a moment, this trifle altered the frigid necromancer: She looked like the biota that I had seen emerge in my vision. But the moment passed and once again I found the morose mistress of the dead standing before me.

"You really are alike. Perhaps this is a sign..." Astilba said, then looked at me tryingly. "You have little experience and strength, but there is something in you that makes me believe that you will succeed. Tell me, what do you know about Cypro?"

"About the Tenth?" I asked. What an odd question..."He is the first bard of the biota, a member of the Council, one of the Ten. He was able to summon souls from the Gray Lands, and it was thanks to his songbook that I learned this spell. One day Cypro crossed the Arras and never returned. No one knows what happened to him."

"True, although not very accurate. Cypro set out from the forest several times on his voyages, but none of them lasted longer than a hundred years. The Tenth would repeatedly return to our people with new knowledge and songs. He knew how to reconcile us with one another and with ourselves. If Cypro were with us, no doubt the Schism would not have occurred. But he is not here. Following the battle at the Stone Maw, he set out to seek knowledge that would spare our land from further war. It was Cypro who found the ancient spell that made it possible to create the Arras. He helped erect a solid wall around our house. The same wall into which the Council now invites the foe."

Bitterness filled Astilba's voice:

"A little more than a hundred years ago, Cypro set out on a new journey. The breeze used to bring news of his travels, but one day that connection broke. The Tenth disappeared. The last dispatch from him mentioned some ancient ruins in the Free Lands. I believe that it is there that you should look for Cypro's tracks. You are a free citizen, Lorelei. Whatever the outcome of our cause, you will survive and you will be able to perform a task for me. I want you to learn the fate of the Tenth and ask him to return to the Hidden Forest. We could use his wisdom."

Quest available: *In the Footsteps of Cypro.*
**Description: Find the missing member of the Biota
Council. His last known whereabouts are some
ancient ruins in the Free Lands. Quest type: Class
scenario. Reward: Variable. Penalty for
failing/refusing the quest: None.**

"I'll go in search of Cypro as soon as I leave the
Hidden Forest," I replied, accepting the quest.

A new location has been added to your map.

"Before he set out on his last voyage," Astilba
went on, "I asked Cypro to leave the eid with me. I
longed to study this legendary instrument to
understand how it helps summon souls from the Gray
Lands. But the Tenth disappeared, and for a while the
eid was gathering dust in my vault, waiting for its
owner. Now he will help in the search for the Tenth.
You will return the eid to Cypro when you find him."
Astilba's tone was so commanding that it brooked no
objections. The next moment her voice faltered
slightly: "And in the event that Cypro has
perished...the eid will decide whether you are worthy
of becoming its new master."

With these words, Astilba handed me the
familiar green cocoon.

Quest updated: *In the Footsteps of Cypro.*

You have received an item required to complete the quest.

When my initial elation subsided, I opened the vegetal instrument case and checked the eid's attributes. Not that they were important to me, since for the sound alone, I would happily deal with negative ones. I was simply curious.

The Eid. Durability: Unbreakable.
Description: Created by a great luthier for the first bard of the biota, the eid accumulates vitality flowing through the world and helps its owner sustain summoned souls. While equipped: -50% to HP cost of sustaining summoned souls, +25% to casting speed. The soul of the instrument may be summoned.
Item type: Quest item.
Other attributes are hidden and inactive because you are not the true owner of the instrument.

Uh-huh. So, until I became the legal owner of the eid, some of its capabilities will remain locked. Still, the little there was, was more than enough for me.

"Now come with me," Astilba beckoned me with her thorny finger. "We need to make some preparations for Portulac's summoning."

"I will need at least seventy hours to summon another soul," I warned, secretly hoping that the Sixth would postpone her mysterious preparations and I could finally pop out to meatspace.

"It does not matter," the necromancer dashed my dreams. "It takes a long time to prepare a stable channel."

"A stable channel?"

"Follow me and I shall explain everything."

The web of underground passages brought us to another cave that was so immense that I couldn't see its ceiling for the darkness. This cave contained eleven Forest Sentries. These sentries, however, no longer resembled the ones I had encountered in the forest. Five of them were the happy bearers of thorns as well as other marks of Shadow. They were labeled 'Blighted Forest Sentries (Level 300).' Another four were undergoing their transformation it seemed. Their bark was slowly but steadily growing darker and sprouting thorns. The last two hadn't changed at all yet. Standing before them was none other than Geranika.

Hearing our approach, the Lord of Shadow turned leisurely.

"Astilba in the company of the young free citizen," he said pensively. "Why have you brought her?"

"I need her for some important business," the Sixth replied.

"What important business requires a Level 22 free citizen? A bard to boot...You need her to sing a lullaby?" Geranika inquired with a mocking tone, as if he hadn't just recruited me into his empire the other day. Does he want to keep Astilba from knowing that he is poaching her followers?

"I'd be happy to sing one for you," I replied, fixing the Lord of Shadow with a challenging look.

The Lord of Shadow arched an eyebrow, looked me up and down and said, "My time is valuable, but I can always spare some for such vim and vigor. You have my permission. Only, take note Lorelei—if I don't like what I hear, you shall pay dearly."

I barely heard the last words—the cave filled with the sounds of the Hymn I had just composed. With every passing measure, the expression on Geranika's face changed more and more: The skepticism gave way to curiosity which in turn gave way to enjoyment. The Lord of Shadow, the Sixth and the Blighted Sentries seemed to be absorbing power from the music. With the last chord, their eyes flared with a terrible fire, which faded instantly, leaving only a buff that was called 'Might of Shadow.'

The renewed silence was disrupted by Geranika's polite clapping.

"I must admit that I have underestimated the power of music until now," he remarked, clapping one last time. "And entirely to my detriment. Tell me, where did you find this hymn that strengthens

Shadow beings so much?"

"I did not find it. I composed it," I replied.

"Composed?" Curiosity filled Geranika's voice. "One weak free citizen created a spell that can nurture my entire host?"

"Your host?" Astilba asked coldly. "You forget yourself, Geranika. We are your allies, not your host."

"I was merely referring to the non-sentient creatures of Shadow," replied Geranika without a trace of embarrassment. "With a hymn like that, I can increase my faction's strength by orders of magnitude. I am impressed, Lorelei."

Quest complete: *Impress the Lord of Shadow*. Speak to Geranika to receive the next quest in the chain.

"Perhaps my new empire could use such artful minstrels," the future emperor smiled graciously. "What do you say, Lorelei?"

"This is a very gracious offer, Emperor," I bowed my head reverently, "but before I agree, I would like to find out about my future duties? As you so accurately mentioned earlier, my powers are all too insignificant. Moreover, I have not yet discharged my duties to Astilba."

The Sixth nodded approvingly, while a system notification informed me that my Charisma had grown.

Geranika seemed disappointed, so I found the hymn's score in my inventory and offered it to him:

"I wish to present you with this songbook. Even if I am unprepared to join you right this instant, perhaps you can teach one of your other minstrels my creation."

Your reputation status with the Lord of Shadow has changed. New status: Friendship.

Geranika carefully accepted the scroll, examined it for a little while and then looked up at me and shook his head:

"I never thought that I would receive a present from a free citizen of Barliona. And such a valuable present at that. In exchange, accept this gift from me as a sign of my gratitude and a symbol of my protection, which you shall acquire once you become one of my minstrels."

Geranika has taught you a new spell: Shadow Shield.

Shadow Shield: You allow a piece of the surrounding world to enter you and summon materia shades to protect you from incoming damage. The Shades follow in the Bard's footsteps and intercept incoming damage. Damage absorbed by each Shade: (Intellect × 10). After absorbing its maximum level of damage, the Shade vanishes. If

an undamaged materia shade receives damage in excess of its maximum absorption level, excess damage is channeled into the interior world. Maximum number of materia shades: (Composition + 1). Casting time: 5 seconds. Casting cost: (Character Level × 10) MP. Cooldown: 5 minutes.

Geranika's present exceeded all expectations. I was already seriously considering joining his band of minstrels and now I had no further doubts. I would be close to the central character of the latest expansion, and I would have the chance of recording video and songs. And that's saying nothing of spells like this. That's it, then. As soon as I complete the Sixth's scenario, I'll sign up with Geranika.

"New wisdoms are a bard's greatest reward, Emperor," I bowed my head respectfully. "I thank you."

"Emperor...I like the ring of that. We shall speak anon, Lorelei. Let us return to our business for the moment. Astilba, I will introduce particles of Shadow into these sentries, but you know very well that that will not be enough. The Kartossians are planning their invasion. They will bring free citizens with them. Free citizens who are very strong and quite merciless. They will deal with the blighted sentries and then turn on your brothers and sisters. We must bring the local Guardian over to Shadow too. That will guarantee our victory over the embassy's guards and..."

"No!" the Sixth angrily cut off Geranika's speech. "The Hidden Forest needs its Guardian. The Forest Sentries are mere forest golems who lack mind and reason. A Guardian is an ancient and wise being. He was created by Sylvyn at the same time as the Tree. Neither the biota nor the pirqs would dare harm their Guardian. He shall be fettered by the power of your shadows precisely until the point that we destroy the Kartossian embassy. After that, he shall be freed and all the renegades shall surrender themselves to be tried by the Council and the Guardian."

"You do understand that they'll simply execute you, right?" I couldn't figure out what lurked behind Geranika's look, but there was more than simple curiosity in his eyes. It seemed that he really wanted to understand.

"Such is our choice," the Sixth replied stoically.

"Well, if you change your mind, I am at your service," Geranika reminded and approached the uncorrupted sentries. A thick, coiling fog began to pour from his hands, crawling like living snakes toward the suddenly agitated wooden giants. The fog curled around the giants, seeping into their eyes and under their bark, causing it to grow dim and darken.

The Sixth's voice tore me away from this horrid spectacle.

"Approach me and stand there, Lorelei," she commanded, indicating a small but complicated etching on the floor. I did not have the energy to examine this new image. With every passing moment I just wanted to go back to meatspace, so I took up my position and watched the unfolding ritual wearily and in silence. A purple glow enveloped both me and the blighted sentries. Fibrous tendrils began to flash and fade between us, but the details of the entire spectacle escaped my exhausted mind—I had resumed my recording upon our return from the Intermundis, so I could always watch all this some other time.

As soon as several permanent effects called 'Binding Seal' had appeared on my character (the Sixth only needed me long enough for the seals to stabilize), I pushed the exit button.

* * *

THE LIVING ROOM and kitchen were empty. The monotonous hum of a running capsule sounded from Pasha's room, second only to the hum in my head. This was the right time to do something productive and rest my overtaxed mind.

I spent the next hour actively justifying my presence in someone else's house—I kicked the domestic appliances into work mode. The custodial bot beeped its outrage at such barbaric treatment, but went about its business cleaning the place. I stuffed the washing machine with my dirty laundry, inspected the fridge, ordered some produce and programmed the autocook with the upcoming meals.

It's nice to live in a technologically advanced age in which rote domestic labor is reduced to a minimum.

Doing my chores allowed my thoughts to clear up and I was already entirely lucid when I started making tea. With that said, my lucid mind was occupied with trifles instead of Barliona. I was contemplating why Pasha was so categorically opposed to disposable tea bags and automatic services when making the most ordinary cup of tea, even as I watched the agile cleaning robot rush about its work. It was just stretching out a thin, flexible manipulator with a tube on its end to clean the odd dust motes and cobwebs from the ceiling. There must have been some error in its cleaning script, since even now it skirted the corner behind the curtain, the one with the web. Judging by the fat, happy spider in the middle of the web, this error was a recurring one and the rude arachnid had moved in permanently. What a mess...

"To hell with you, descendent of the Tarantula Lords," I swore at the unassuming spider and looked around for something to make good on my threat with.

I didn't feel like messing around with someone's imitator, and all I really had to do was slap it with a towel and no more, so I decided to deal with the spider in the old fashioned way. I twisted the towel into a tight spiral and clambered up on a footstool when I heard Pasha's roar behind me:

"Stop right there! Leave Sarge alone!" Having instantly forgotten all his traumas, the pilot rushed past me as quickly and noisily as his beloved chopper. "Sarge, you poor fellow..." He began rummaging amid some model boxes on the windowsill and produced a jar with a still living fly that had had its wings plucked off. Fishing out the insect, Pasha tossed it onto the cobweb and stepped back, observing the suddenly alert spider rush onto its breakfast. "Sarge is off limits," the pilot warned me curtly.

"I have two questions," I said, my shock dispersing. I got down from the stool and looked closely at my friend. "'How?' and 'What the hell for?'"

"What exactly?" asked my friend, casting the spider a loving look.

"How did you catch the fly in your condition and what the hell do you need a spider for?"

"Why would someone catch a fly?" Pasha asked a little taken aback. "You just pour a couple drops of sweet tea in the jar and they show up on their own. Once they're in there, it's a question of technique. And Sarge, well, he's company."

"Mmm...yeah..." I had to admit. "Snegov and I are really slacking in our duties."

"Oh he showed up before you guys," Pasha jumped to defend his pet. "I had barely started to hobble back then. I couldn't even throw anything at the jerks singing Goldentown under my window."

"Well, I guess if he was here first..." I squinted at

the spider. He seemed haughty and impudent, as if he was well aware that he enjoyed the landlord's protection. "By the way, I have never heard your infamous street singers. Am I to assume you finally threw something hefty at them?"

"Nah…" Pasha said a little awkwardly. "They were just beginning to redeem themselves in my eyes, when some thugs showed up…You know the type—street drunks who chug two Mad Dawg Malt Beverages, decide that they must be Vikings and start assaulting and battering anyone around them? Well, while I was looking for my fragmentation grenades to toss at them…while I was fishing them out…well, the bastards broke the musicians' guitar and violin. Bitches…I haven't felt so bad for a long, long time."

"Yes…that's not fun," I agreed and then, just for fun, suggested: "I propose we make a bunch of gold in Barliona doing our cartography business and buy the poor musicians some new instruments. And then you will have them under your window again singing 'Goldentown.'"

"I don't even know them," sighed Pasha. "But it's not a bad idea."

"Come on…That's no problem," I snorted. "If they were playing here so often, I bet one of them lives right here in this building. Post an ad on the building website and I'll post a few signs around the block just to make sure. Ask them to contact you to discuss a project. Someone will call, if for curiosity's sake."

"I'll try it," Pasha nodded without much certainty in his voice. But my main goal had been achieved—the powerless regret in his eyes gave way to a timid hope.

"Yeah. We just have to make our first million," I giggled, placing two mugs onto the table and pouring the tea. Pasha lowered himself into a chair with a groan, stirred three teaspoons of sugar into his tea, spilled a few drops into the empty jar and replaced the baited fly trap on the window sill.

For a while we just chatted about meaningless nonsense, and then I told Pasha about my latest gaming adventures.

"That's a good business with your new guitar," drawled the pilot, wistfully regarding a still-forbidden cookie. The jaw regenerator was scheduled to come off in bit and Pasha was already counting the hours until he could eat normal food again. "What do you think we should do next? I'm pretty bored of running around and drawing maps."

"Yes, it's time to load up on some potions and head for the Arras." I sat down at the table and outlined my immediate plans. "I already have four letters from Sloe in my inbox. The raiding party wants to know what coordinates they should head to. By the way, will you bring me some mana potions? I need 'em desperately and the renegades don't sell any. Besides, I have no access to my bank account."

"Not even a question. Meet me at the site of your

perfidious betrayal, outside of Eben's playground. That's right at the border of the blighted ground. I'll bring you a medical package."

"And what will you do?"

"The local Getafix ordered me to locate and bring back a sample of that crud your lot is spreading," Pasha took a sip and frowned: The regenerator housing on his lower jaw caused him an incredible itch and I had already noticed him several times scratching it surreptitiously with a paper clip. "So I'll try and dig up this 'revenge weapon,'" he concluded his summary of the quests he was working on.

"Geta-what?" I didn't understand.

"The local druids," Pasha explained. "That's just the name of the druid character from that series about the two Gauls—the whiskered, cunning fellow and the, uh, portly young lad with the menhir and the striped pants. Maybe you've seen it?"

"Doesn't ring a bell," I confessed. "But I think I understand what they want from you. I was instructed to plant some seeds to spread the blight around the land. And it just so happens you need to collect a sample of the same stuff for your Getafix' study. We can team up: I'll sow the seeds and you dig them up after I get my reward. It's just that I have to sow them really far away. I'm not sure you'll make it even if you use your stealth. The monsters out there are a bit bigger and you might run into renegade patrols. I'll just give you a few of the seeds when we meet."

"What about your quest?"

"I'll just get a smaller reward. Not even a thing. And your druids might come up with something more interesting with the seeds. Maybe they'll even find an antidote to clear the forest. I would like to see what Geranika does."

"In that case, let's finish this tea and jump on in?" Pasha proposed, emptied his mug with two more gulps and slid it aside.

"Let's do it," I agreed.

CHAPTER EIGHT

THE CAVE I APPEARED IN had not changed at all. Yet Geranika and the Sixth were nowhere to be seen—a renegade biota glanced at me indifferently and returned to his observation of the Forest Sentries. Now all eleven looked the same, although only five of them bore the 'Binding Seal' buff. Exactly the same one that I had. No descriptions or explanations, no additional effects. For curiosity's sake, I cast the new Detect Currents of Vitality spell on myself. Nothing changed. The world neither blurred around me nor snapped into focus. Everything was the same as before. It was only when I looked closely that I noticed thin, barely discernible, spectral threads tethering me to the sentries that bore the seal. So is this the weak channel that needs time to grow? Cool. Having no further questions, I turned to go and only then noticed two ghostly umbilical cords that had been emanating from my back. The translucent, pale tendrils suddenly flushed with a vivid purple and I lost 10% of my HP. The system helpfully informed me that some vitality had been transferred to my summoned souls. The ghostly cables faded to their earlier dull luster. So now I can look on as my ghost buddies suckle on my vitus. All I have to figure out is what the point of this spectacle is.

One way or another, I need to bring the souls with me and figure out how to control my new companions. The party interface indicated that the souls had about seven hours before they would return to the Gray Lands. It turns out that when I exit the game, the countdown doesn't pause. Too bad. Even worse was the level difference among my companions. Though Salamander was at a respectable Level 23, Anica was still merely at Level 6. I guess her level was pretty low when she was alive, while the Salamander King's level was limited by my summoner trait and then modified by my composition stats.

The king had five abilities: Leadership (a +5% to damage for allies and rage recovery rate), Spider Exterminator (+50% damage to all arachnids) and three attacks which did damage to the enemy. Anica had one ability, but it was a very useful one: Curiosity (+10% to XP earned). I even stopped to consider whether it was worth putting off our foray to the Arras in order to grind a bit in the company of this sweet girl, but in the end I had to drop the idea. The scenario's climax was quickly approaching and I still had not brought the raiding party to the location. Who knows, I might even need the help of high-level players. And I can always summon Anica again later.

The spheres that fettered the souls remained lying in the middle of Astilba's laboratory. Astilba herself was engrossed in some convoluted seal she was etching on the floor with a shimmering lilac-colored liquid. As soon as I opened my mouth to greet her, the Sixth looked up from her work, waved her hand and said: "Go away and take your souls with you. You are disturbing me."

I shut my mouth and beckoned my unfettered companions to follow me. We left the staff headquarters quickly and silently. Even Anica obeyed quietly and followed me with mincing steps. The camp outside headquarters seemed suspiciously empty. Apart from the quartermaster, languishing in his tent hopelessly, we met only a single biota, himself surprised at the sight of ghosts. Well, yes, it's not an ordinary sight. Under different circumstances, I could make some scratch here. Set up a tent and have my ghosts put on a show for passersby. I'll just need to summon some clowns, acrobats and jugglers from the Gray Lands.

"What kind of a creature are you, Lorelei?" Salamander's voice broke through the clinking of gold in my head.

"What do you mean?" I even stopped from my surprise, and Anica, who had not managed to slow down, bumped into my back. Maybe she's a ghost but she sure has a palpable forehead.

"In the Gray Lands, your essence was..." The king hesitated, trying to find the right word. "Blurred. Changeable. Almost foggy. I did not see clearly there in general. People were only silhouettes. There it seemed to me that you were human, but you are a..."

"Thornbush!" Anica popped into our exchange. "You look like a blackthorn we had growing near our field back home. You've been bewitched, right? You're really a princess? Is the prince looking for you?"

I was already growing exhausted by so many questions. Uh-huh, I'm an elven princess; I'm just slightly under the weather at the moment.

"I am a biota," I began to explain, waiting for the girl to run out of questions. "We are something like sentient plants from a magical forest. I'm not a princess, but I am a little bewitched, like this entire part of the forest."

The blighted forest around left no doubt that a curse or two had been cast here.

"We are going to go meet a good friend of mine right now and along the way I will tell you a story..."

We passed the journey to the rendezvous point in conversation. Thanks to the Shadow Ward spell, the blighted beasts did not attack my ghosts and no one disturbed us. A couple of times I glimpsed the silhouettes of renegade biota, but they never hailed us. I related to my companions the events unfolding in the Hidden Forest in the most picturesque, fairy-tale manner I could, omitting anything that could seem objectionable. In the correct light, the situation could be rendered as a tragedy with an open ending and as a result, when I had finished, both souls felt sympathy for all sides in this conflict.

After that, Salamander told us a bit about himself. I did not hear anything fundamentally new, but the story of the rebel king's life would definitely help me in writing the song. Anica's story turned out to be much shorter and simpler. The girl lived in a village with the funny name Cranberries that was situated in the Malabarian frontier, near the border with the Free Lands. The region was a very peaceful one so the children would frequently go to the forest to pick berries and mushrooms on their own. And it was no different on the day of her demise.

"I had just grabbed the mushroom to pick it," Anica said quietly, "when I stepped on something hard. I thought it was a stone. I looked down and saw like a jewelry box, old and partially rotted. It had been in the ground for a long time. Grass and mushrooms had grown over it. Only the corner was sticking out. The lock too had rotted. And inside it there was this pendant. A very beautiful pendant..."

The girl even squinted and smiled, recalling the marvelous find.

"I put the pendant on and everything grew cold, very cold, and then dark too. And I found myself in that terrible place, and a voice was calling me. And my mother is waiting for me at home." The girl sobbed and wiped her nose with her sleeve. "You'll take me to mom, won't you?"

Quest available: *Homecoming.* **Description: Go to Cranberries Village on the border of Malabar, summon Anica's soul and bring her to her mother. Quest type: Unique. Reward: None. Penalty for failing/refusing the quest: Anica's party bonuses will no longer apply.**

"I already said I would," I reminded the girl, accepting the quest. "Only I cannot promise that it will be soon. People like me are not much welcome in Malabar. But I will definitely find a way to take you to your mother."

"Hooray!" Anica exclaimed joyfully and dashed ahead of us.

"Are you really going to fulfill this promise?" Salamander asked quietly.

"Absolutely."

"It is a noble goal," the spirit said after a pause.

He sat down on the tree root sticking out of the ground and stretched out his legs, enjoying the world of the living. Even the ugly, blighted forest failed to dampen his mood. I understood him. Anything that was different from the monotony of the Gray Lands seemed beautiful.

"Azur," I called to my ghostly companion. "Can you help me? I need to read this one text."

"Of course." He seemed happy at the chance to help. "If of course it is written in a language I know."

This gave me pause. Indeed, the ancient king could not know the language of the biota. And yet here he is speaking to me. Is this some feature of summoning the dead? Probably.

"Let's find out."

I pulled Cypro's notes out of my inventory and looked inside just in case. Nothing. Blank pages. Sighing, I handed the journal to Salamander.

"You were curious enough to find all the sigils," he began, but I waved my hand, gesturing him to skip ahead.

Salamander continued to patter through the text until, at the words "Good luck, my unknown friend," I gestured for him to slow down.

"The soul of the animal belongs to the Gray Lands. In order for it to become your guide, it must also become a part of the world of the living. In my travels, I have encountered various solutions to this problem. There are such generous shamans who voluntarily invite the spirits into themselves and thereby become guides into their world. Sorcerers would instill their cicerones into the bodies of animals whose souls had been weakened beforehand. Perhaps someone tried to do the same with sentients. For us, the biota, everything is much simpler. There are special flowers that grow in the druids' grove called vitars. Acquire one of its seeds. With its help, you will be able to summon the soul into the seed and grow a suitable body for your cicerone."

Quest received: *Creating a Cicerone. Step 2.*

"A new body..." Salamander repeated in a fascinated whisper and looked at me curiously. "Is that possible? For ones like us?"

I paused to think here. What would happen if I summon the king's spirit into the seed? Can I grow a biota out of him? Or how about from Anica? Why then doesn't Astilba know about this method? This is a way to respawn NPCs after all...And if he knew all this, why didn't Cypro simply revive the dead using the vitar seeds?

"I imagine it's not so simple," I answered honestly. "But if you like, I can try to summon your soul into the seed."

"And I will return to Barliona?" Salamander asked, doubting his own words. "Will I be like you?"

"Maybe. We will try."

"And Anica?"

"If she wants to—why not? But biota do not grow after spawning. I'm afraid, in this case, she will forever be locked in the body of a child."

Salamander fixed the girl with a stare of mixed feelings as she went running happily across the blighted meadow. In the tree line, Chip's tall, shaggy figure loomed from the brush. Seeing him, Anica stopped, stretched her hand in the direction of the apparition and exclaimed:

"Look! An animal in a costume!"

It so happened that this was the first pirq we had come across on our journey.

"Why look at you, you're a bona fide little anthropologist," Chip said, approaching us.

He stopped in his favorite pose: on one foot, propped up by his halberd, with his left heel tucked into his right inner thigh. A balancing act of fur and steel.

"Good girl," he continued, examining Anica. "That's the right way to think about it. Oh, hello, my rock and roll star!" This was already addressed to me. "Have you taken up the, uh, Ghostbuster profession?"

"It talks!" yelped the girl with a mixture of rapture and fear. "Did you hear? Did you hear?"

Here, Salamander pleasantly surprised me. Instead of whipping out his blade and sallying forth, he glanced at Chip, then at me, then at Anica, mumbled something to himself and...that's it. I guess he had managed to get used to the local flavor and figured that we were looking at a sentient with a strange appearance. Or maybe he was still preoccupied with the chance of getting a new body and the appearance of a giant talking cat didn't interest him.

"You have no idea how much he talks, Anica. Meet my friend Chip. He is very nice, though you wouldn't think so by his appearance. Isn't that right, Chip?" I looked at Chip expressively, prodding him to say something reassuring.

"Eh?" Chip muttered indistinctly.

What's wrong with him? The pirq was gawking at the ghost with a look I couldn't quite read.

"Chip." The furball squatted down slowly before the girl. "And what's your name, young lady?"

Hearing these words, the girl's mood changed entirely. Her fear fled without a trace and a sly smile bloomed on her face. She picked up the hem of her dress and performed a curtsy.

"Lady Anica, sir," the girl said coquettishly.

It was so amusing and cute that I could hardly suppress my laughter, only doing so for fear of offending her.

"Lady Anica," Chip repeated gravely. "A pretty name. And where did the young lady come by..." The shaggy bastard nodded at me and Salamander. "This lovely zoo?"

"Lovely what?" The girl repeated, staring at Chip in fascination.

Honestly, I would not be surprised if she kissed the pirq on the nose, causing him to undergo a magic transformation like in a fairy tale. Only in this case, not into a beautiful prince, but a pink pony.

"The zoo," Chip winked. "That's a kind of place where various animals live so that people can come and watch them. Sometimes, you can even pet them."

I was just wondering what would be a suitable way to get the shaggy jerk back when the karma decided everything without my participation. Anica enthusiastically opened her eyes and asked with childish spontaneity:

"Oh! Is that where you live? At the zoo? And can I pet you too, yes?"

This time I could not restrain myself and began giggling quietly into the palm of my hand.

"I'm from the reserve," Chip said with a self-important air. "That is where the rarest and most priceless animals live."

He bowed his overgrown head, lowering it to the child's hand. Anica immediately began to stroke the pirq's fur while hopping in delight. But the most ridiculous part was that Chip began to...purr! And exactly like any other house cat, only at his proper volume! I wonder if the developers had done this on purpose or I simply don't know something about Pasha's talents?

"It was worth dying and coming back to life to see this," Salamander muttered in astonishment.

I could understand him. It was a hell of a sight. Like Beauty and the Beast with the scenery from Sleepy Hollow.

"Say, you denizen of the goblin reserve, have you brought me those herbs?" I reminded Chip of the business at hand.

"I have brought the package!" the pirq replied.

"What about you, Dr. Strangelove? Have you acquired the Doomsday Device?" He tossed me a new inventory bag with 40 slots practically overflowing with mana potions.

"Would there were something to acquire, my dear Mr. Bond," I took two Shadow Seeds from my bag and offered them to Chip. "One of each caliber."

"Hold up!" The pirq reached into one of his bandoliers and pulled out...

I assume it was a gas mask. In any case, it was sewn from a crude material with round eye sockets that made it look quite a bit like an ancient gas mask. Chip pulled this over his face...and I realized that Chip's passion for stupidity and showmanship was limitless. How else could you explain the time and money he had spent on ordering a craftsman to make this utterly useless item?

"Da-da-da-da-da..." Chip meanwhile began humming the Twilight Zone theme song and stretched out his paw. "Still the trembling in your hands, you'll drop them," he hurried me.

"Chip..." No longer paying attention to the NPCs who as per usual went blank-eyed as soon as players started talking about meatspace. "What the hell is this thing?! Can I call you a doctor?"

"Personal protective equipment!" proudly proclaimed the owner of the cloth muzzle. "Who knows what these prehistoric Mendeleyevs cooked up in their alliance with the medieval Michurins."

"And who made this miracle of engineering for you?"

"Oh, one of those ninnies that hang around this place their entire lives," Chip chuckled. "Though for whatever reason, he decided that it was me who had a few screws loose—can you imagine? When people lose their sense of humor...where does it go?"

"I'll venture to guess that in some heads, it is sometimes replaced by common sense. All right you flea-bitten stalker, take these seeds."

As soon as the foggy seeds fell into Chip's paw, his HP bar began to fall, and I received a notification that I had hurt another player and therefore earned the outlaw status.

"Massaraksh!" Chip hurriedly poured the seeds into a copper phial with a screw cap. "I guess those blessed druids gave me this vial for a reason after all. Lori, I'm sorry..." He nodded guiltily at my avatar's name, glowing outlaw red.

"You're the damn ninny!" I cursed at Chip with all my heart. "If they gave you a vial for the quest, why didn't you get the fu..." I glanced at Anica and caught myself, "...ngible thing out?"

"How was I supposed to know that this crap is really toxic?" Chip spread his paws.

"Okay, forget it," I muttered, calming down. "Grinding won't work, and to the dogs with grinding anyway. I was planning on doing the cicerone quest. By the way! You're about to go see the druids, right?"

Chip nodded, and I rubbed my hands eagerly.

"Bring me a scarlet flower from an enchanted castle, will you, pops?"

"Why don't I just skip the flower and bring you the furry beast for your amorous satisfaction?" Chip chuckled cheerfully.

"Why?" I asked surprised. "I already have one."

I cast the pirq a meaningful look.

"Whoa, whoa, whoa!" he protested emphatically. "I am strictly limited to serving the aesthetic and edifying pleasure of gaze and mind. And I would prefer you to avoid confusing things in this area."

"Well, in that case bring what I'm asking and not whatever you come across. I have this quest. It requires vitar seeds, which the local druids should have. Get me three or more. I think they might be useful."

"Vitar seeds, huh?" Chip thought for a moment. "All right, I think I'll manage. It's not exactly hunting bison."

"Go complete your quest and come back here with those seeds."

I cast Shadow Ward on Chip to keep him safe from the mobs along his way and gave him a copy of my map.

"Ah, by the way," Chip slapped his forehead lightly. "Your buddy Beast owes Sasha two bottles."

"When did he manage to accrue that debt?" I asked surprised.

"Well, I was just about to dive into this place when Sasha called me up," Chip snorted glibly. "Basically a natural situation. You are aware that your bassist bro is good at recruiting followers? So he pulled something that led to an entire percussion ensemble to assemble in his honor. Beast, realizing that he would play the part of the percussion for this ensemble and that it's time to scram, took off into the forest...right to the exact place where Snegov had carefully arranged his dirty little traps. Someone had asked him to ambush someone. So Edilberto came tearing right into this idyll with the crowd on his heels...Can you imagine what happened next?"

"A large-scale excursion to the Gray Lands?" I logically assumed.

"Precisely!" Chip raised a finger. "And the best part is that the prey, the magic piglet, broke through the entire area without a single scratch! Talk about fool's luck, huh? Sasha was howling his head off."

"Uh-huh, I can imagine them now," I giggled. "Red Hulk vs. Green Hulk."

"Yeah, the red one's digging the earth with his toe, guiltily, while the green one is hopping around and screaming so loudly that the birds are falling out of the trees," Chip joked along with me. "Sasha set the reparations at a case of rum to begin with, but Beast was in his element that day. Not only did he manage to figure out that the percussion ensemble was about to beat his ass all on his own, he also performed the role of the starving artist to a T, turned his pockets inside out and managed to talk Sasha down to two bottles."

"Those two should not be hanging around each other." I sighed. "Not only will they drink themselves to death, they'll cause property damage in the process."

"Nah, Snegov's basically sober at the moment. The proctologists got to him," Chip reassured me. "So there's no danger of them drinking themselves dead."

He thought for a second longer and added:

"Can't speak for the property damage though."

"Are you trying to say that two bottles of vodka is sober?"

"That was the base ration!" Chip tapped his forehead with his finger. "We were going to barbecue, remember? So Beast was volunteered to outfit our little expedition with fuel."

"All right, let's get back to virtual reality. I still have to grow my cicerone, the way to the Arras remains untraveled and I haven't made a map yet. By the way, let me copy yours down."

I didn't use the auto-copy feature. Copying by hand leveled up my cartography a little, but it also helped me understand this field better in real life. And, since my abilities left something to be desired, Pasha's guidance here was quite useful. In exchange for my diligence, I not only raised my cartography a bit, but discovered that the druids' grove was nearby.

The blighted ground arced around it, forming a crescent with the druid's lair right in the center. It followed that the druids had some way of fighting off the blight available to them. So why didn't they use it right away to protect the entire forest?

I asked Chip about this.

"Who the hell knows them?" He scratched his head and shrugged his shoulders. "I'll make sure to ask them when...Anica! Don't touch that!"

He dragged the little girl away from a blighted plant.

"This tree is sick. If you touch it, you might catch what it has. Kiera, don't you know to look after a child?" The furball turned on me.

"Pasha, could you look down, please?" I asked the suddenly agitated pirq. "What do you see?"

"Yeah and so what?" Chip stared at the blighted ground beneath our feet. "She's not going to stick her foot in her mouth. Her hands are a different story."

That was some killer logic there, what could I say? You expect to hear this from a mother of four, not an officer with combat experience. Maybe all this lying around at home had affected him or something?

"Pasha, are you okay? This is a game. She's already a ghost. Bacteria aren't dangerous for her."

"Hmm...Yeah you have a point. Sorry..."

Chip wilted a bit, and then squatted down in front of Anica and began to show her a cat's cradle with a string between his fingers, no longer paying attention to Salamander and me. I observed my friend for a short while trying to understand, but in the end had to wave my hand and forget it. It was clear only that the topic of children wasn't a simple one for Chip. I guess his had been a complicated divorce. Or marriage. When I get out of the capsule, I'll ask him about it in more detail.

"Listen," An idea occurred to me. "Maybe you'll take Anica with you? To the druids? I don't like to stray beyond the blighted ground unless it's necessary and the landscape here isn't exactly picturesque. She can take a walk through the woods with you at least. Anica, do you want to go for a stroll with Mister Chip?"

"I do!" the girl instantly lit up. "Will he show me more tricks?"

"Sure, I'll show you," Chip agreed willingly, rising. "As long as you behave well and don't touch anything without permission. Deal?"

"Uh-huh!" Anica quickly agreed and darted forward to catch a large colorful butterfly.

"Hey, but don't take her to the actual druids, just in case. She's supposed to be with me and the locals are against me now. Who knows, maybe they will start aggroing against the spirit. She has about five hours before she has to go back to the Gray Lands. Let her enjoy the woods a bit. If something happens, tell her to hide somewhere while you complete your quest."

"I would not advise them to...how did you put it? Aggro, right?" Chip smiled crookedly.

"At your level, no one is going to ask you anything," I set upon the stubborn pirq. "Just limit your stroll to the ordinary part of the forest—where it's safer."

"We'll see," Chip answered mysteriously and it occurred to me that with his attitude, he could go as far as battling the local guards if they tried to arrest the suspicious ghost.

"You can use me to test how hostile the locals are to ghosts," the Salamander King suddenly offered. "I am accustomed to battles and I can stand up for myself. In the worst case, I will return to the Gray Lands, but at least I will have done some good."

"The voice of reason from the powers that be," Chip agreed. "Come along now. We will conduct some trials. If everything goes okay, I'll be back for the young lady. And if not, your new name will be Nicholas II."

The wait turned out to be a long one, but there was no reason for anxiety. Salamander's frame indicated that His Long-dead Majesty was in rude health, which logically led to the conclusion that the locals' attitude toward summoned souls was not contingent on their attitude toward the summoner. Or maybe it was still contingent, but in some convoluted, subtle manner. Either way, the biota did not attack the spirits.

By the time the experimenters returned, Anica was full of impatience. She kept trying to run after them, but I did not dare let her leave the blighted ground. Here we were in relative safety: the sentries would not come here and my shadow ward kept us safe from the local mobs.

"The trial has been deemed a crushing success," Chip said, nodding toward the glowing Salamander. "The Greenpeace faction jumped for joy: They have long since wanted to chat up a soul returned from the Gray Lands. So they vehemently swore that they would honor and cherish their valuable guests. Pass me your charge and go ahead with your quests. I did not mention that the bard who had summoned them had gone over to the dark side. Who knows, after all. If they change their mind, I'll have a hard time proving that I wasn't trying to destroy druidism in the flower of its youth."

"Good point. Have you brought the seeds?"

"That's a bit more complicated...They have some kind of sacred significance, I didn't find out exactly what. But you can get them by completing a quest chain. I'll try to bargain with them some more. Heck, haven't I brought them a guest from the other world or what? Anyway, I will get the seeds, it's just not clear when that'll be."

"It's a pity," I said sadly. "And what about the Shadow Seeds? Did you hand them over?"

"Uh-huh. Didn't I say that it's like the army in

here? If you complete some task, good job and here's some more work. Which is to say that the druid party immediately assigned me another quest: Someone impudently snatched the body of the local glorious leader from his sacred resting place in the local mausoleum."

"Huh?"

"I'm not sure there's a better way to put it," Chip clarified in an apologetic tone to the ghosts who had gone blank from our exchange. "The local Guardian is gone. He doesn't respond when they summon him and their magical gadgets don't detect him. They've ordered us to look for him using the typical scientific method of poking around."

"That's our boys' work. The renegades, I mean. They've stashed the guardian away so he doesn't interfere when they ambush the embassy," I shared the fresh gossip. "By the way, tell Eben what the renegades have planned," I ordered, and again, briefly, related to Chip the information already known to him: A quirk of the game. To limit cheating, NPCs would only accept information that the player received inside Barliona and not read on the fora or learned in real life.

"Make sure to emphasize that they do not intend on hurting their own," I reminded. "Only the ambassadors. After that, they'll surrender themselves to the mercy of the Council."

"Yeah," Chip scratched his head furiously, as if

he had fleas in there. "Do you happen to know which particular dungeon the Guardian is languishing in?"

"No idea," I confessed, "but I'll let you know as soon as I find out."

We managed to avoid any long farewells. Chip just waved his paw, Salamander saluted with his sword, and Anica simply rushed off to frolic among the greenery, completely forgetting about me. I mean, kids these days!

And yet, despite the ever growing distance between us, I simply could not get those souls out of my mind. Not for excessive sentiment but rather due to the hefty blow to my HP that I was taking every thirteen minutes. Thanks to the eid's attributes, the cut was not too much, a little less than ten percent, but even this bit had to be healed, distracting me from the cartography of the area I was walking on. Wish I had a horse...But mounts cost an unbelievable sum around here. And I don't have access to the bank either. I'll have to ask Sloe whether his guildmates can hook me up with some old nag. It won't do to try and get around solely on my two legs, burning through my poor reserves of stamina.

"A miserable sight," a familiar, resounding voice said suddenly.

Geranika.

The Lord of Shadow stood ankle-deep in swirling fog, observing me. In my head the cartoon donkey of my childhood quipped in a melancholy voice: "Thanks for noticin' me." Ugh. That's memory for you!

"Emperor?" I stopped, respectfully bowed my head and looked inquisitively at Geranika. "What are you talking about?"

"About you, Lorelei," he clarified ruthlessly. "With your talents you could reach unprecedented heights, bard. By my side you could sing of the conquest of Barliona. You could master such powers as most free citizens do not even suspect exist. Power, greatness, might...The empires that so recklessly rejected you shall be washed in blood. But instead you prefer to waste your time serving Astilba. Impoverished, weak, pathetic."

Geranika's voice was full of contempt, yet he failed to make much of an impression on me. I remembered too well that video in which a shaman named Mahan was offered to become a disciple of his. It looked like this entire situation was following a similar script for finding a student. Not exactly risk-averse, this Geranika fellow: As I recall, the previous candidate had almost deprived him of immortality. If I were in Geranika's place, I wouldn't allow any free citizens too close to me, but he didn't seem to care one bit. He keeps trying to recruit me. Cute game going on here.

So let me recall what the shaman had to do in his situation...I believe he had to turn on his race, his teacher, his totem and his friend. Let's see what will happen in my case. I can't really be penalized more than I've already been.

"It was the thirst for true greatness that called me to accept Shadow," without hesitating further I began to pull the wool over Geranika's eyes. "I still lack experience, but I am constantly searching for new knowledge that can make me stronger. Astilba can teach me a lot, but I have to earn the right to learn."

"You are right about that." A pleased smile appeared on Geranika's face. "The right to an apprenticeship should be earned. But you have erred in your choice of teacher. There is no creature in Barliona more powerful than me! No one else will teach you to command the forces of Shadow."

But of course—he's looking for a student. I wonder whether this is a scenario requirement or whether this is just Geranika's imitator stepping on the same rake as before...

"I dare not dream of a teacher like you, Emperor," I said aloud, bowing. I should look up a video on how to curtsey properly. I don't think I'm supposed to bend my back like that. "How may I earn such an unprecedented honor?"

The question clearly pleased the Lord of Shadow. He slowly approached me:

"I have to be sure that you're ready to break with the past. With your race and your people. Compassion and the attachments of the past shall not deter *my* student."

"How can I prove this to you, oh Master?"

The grin on Geranika's face went crooked:

"Kill three dozen biota as a token of your devotion."

Quest available: *Way of the Apprentice*. Step 1.

Description: Geranika is ready to become your mentor, but before you start learning, you need to prove your loyalty to your new teacher. Kill 30 biota. Deadline for completion: 72 hours. Quest type: Unique chain. Reward for accepting quest: Unlock the Shadow Transform ability. Reward for completion: Next quest in chain, +1,000 Reputation with Geranika. Penalty for failing/refusing the quest: Hostile status with Geranika.

I re-read the quest description in perplexity, considering what to do. Killing biota would make enemies of both Astilba and Eben. Yet if I refused, the doors to the new empire would be shut to me forever.

"I will do as you wish, my Lord," I decided.

In the end, I have three days to complete this quest. Or not complete it...

New ability unlocked: 'Shadow Transform.'
You absorb the shadow energy of the world around you and shoot an impact shade at your

target. Casting time: 5 seconds. Cost: (Character Level × 5) MP. Damage dealt: Intellect × 5. Impact shades do Shadow damage and ignore all types of armor. Range: 100 meters.

I must have looked ridiculous at that moment: my eyes bulging in surprise, my lips stretched into an unwitting smile. Range of one hundred meters. One. Hundred. Meters. When the average range of spells is usually twenty meters. Holy Meatballs!

"It's...amazing," I finally managed to find the right words.

"Oh but this is but a trifle compared to what I can teach you in the future," Geranika seemed to be pleased with impression he had made.

"I have a question, Master. You and Astilba are allies, and I was tasked with a quest for the renegades. Will you permit me to finish what I started, or should I forget about her orders?"

The Lord of Shadow blew an invisible speck of dust from the sleeve of his elegant jacket, and casually waved his hand:

"Do it. My interests really do align with Astilba's at the moment. In fact, here is something to help you complete these tedious chores..."

A snap of Geranika's fingers and fog instantly enveloped me.

Buff gained: 'Indefatigable.' +100% to running

speed. –70% to Stamina cost. Immunity from immobilizing and slowing debuffs. As long as 'Indefatigable' is in effect, the character cannot be saddled with the 'Exhausted Nag' debuff.

"Thank you, Master."

"Do not let me down, Lorelei..."

The fog at Geranika's feet surged up, enveloped his figure, and when it receded, it left no trace of my future mentor. I, in turn, sat down on the ground, opened my map and started thinking long and hard.

The Arras wasn't so far from here. About an hour's journey, judging by the map. But this wasn't taking into account the running from the sentries and the sowing I had to do. And once I'm there, I'll be able to usher in the players from outside, gear up and consider how best to go about completing Geranika's quest. Killing biota was the last thing I wanted to do, nor did I want to anger Astilba at the most interesting point in the story.

I sighed deeply, collected myself and decided to get on with it.

Running was surprisingly easy and pleasant. No cramps or stitches, no labored panting. A tremendous feeling. Plus, once I hit a good pace, my agility began to grow as well as (much more slowly) my Constitution. I should take note of this method of grinding my stats. The only downside was that my stamina was dropping really quickly despite

Geranika's buff. I should come up with some method of leveling up my Constitution because otherwise I'll find myself without water and my stamina will run out at an inopportune moment.

As I reached the edge of blighted ground, I slowed down and looked around. There weren't any sentries in sight, but something told me that this was merely temporary. At least the large seed I had planted here earlier had sprouted and the blight had spread further. My safe path now reached further than before. I was forced to tinker a bit with the sowing of the little seeds. The plat I'd been assigned with the quest insisted that I maintain a ratio between the large and small seeds, so I had to spend fifteen minutes checking the distance between the holes and then another ten watching the hedge of thorns grow. So that's where this labyrinth came from! This is not just a decoration, it is being intentionally planted by the renegades.

There was no time to fully appreciate my latest discovery and I moved closer to the border with the untouched part of the forest. The sentry was there as expected. He was wandering along the border of blighted ground as if he knew that I would return to continue my mischief. That's okay. This time I know what to do.

I cast Shadow Shield just to be safe. In addition to a new icon that had appeared in my gaming interface, something else had changed. My shield now generated four materia shades instead of one. My avatar now cast five shades and something about the four newcomers told me they weren't mine. The shades flickered and waxed and waned, sometimes fading until they were barely discernable. For some time I watched them with some apprehension, but there seemed nothing threatening about them either. Nothing more than a fun visual effect for the spell. And if so, it's time to return to the quest.

My flask is full of water and the eid is hanging from my belt, ready to be played. It might get in the way of my running, but at least I can arm myself quickly. The bag with the mana potions is conveniently at hand. The time has come.

A fake start in a false direction, Shadow Haze on the Forest Sentry, and a rabid sprint in the true direction. Roots shot from the ground, forcing my insides to shrink, but the clingy tendrils merely grazed my feet without slowing me down. Thank you, Geranika!

I did not bother turning around. Whether the sentry is listening or not, whether he's headed in the false direction or following in my wake—it doesn't matter. What matters is closing the distance as quickly as possible and reaching the next sowing point. The haze with the bumbling sentry in its midst was behind me now. A potion restored my mana and stamina.

By the time I reached the place I needed, I

couldn't see the sentry. I checked my plat, dug a hole, placed a seed into it and rushed onward without waiting around. Today I don't have the time to wait for Shadow Haze's cooldown, so I have to move as quickly as I can.

The Forest Sentry overtook me as I was sowing my fifth seed. According to my calculations, he should have fallen hopelessly behind and yet...Here he is— the mossy giant, stomping implacably to intercept me. How did he close the distance? Glancing anxiously at the sentry, I hastily covered the seed I'd just sowed. He raised his ugly head, charging up the sadly familiar Sylvyn's Wrath spell. I didn't feel like sticking around for the finale. Finishing with the seed, I sprinted back to the creeping patches of blighted ground.

The air around me blossomed with a swarm of magic fireflies, and a system notification appeared detailing a long formula of damage taken and blocked. The gist of it was that a materia shade had taken an insane amount of damage. Bursting, the shade channeled all the excess damage into some kind of inside-out world, but that part didn't interest me much. What's important is that I'm alive and I still have another two materia shades in reserve.

I did not have a long time to enjoy this fact. One more Forest Sentry was coming to meet me. It turns out that no one had overtaken me after all. I'd just run away from the first and into the second...and now back into the first again! A humble patch of blighted ground about five meters in diameter lay before me. I dashed for it as fast as I could. Another Sylvyn's Wrath took out another shade, but I still managed to get to the patch in time. The sentries gathered for a consultation at the very edge of my refuge and fixed me with unwavering stares that even had a bit of reproach about them. That's right, boys. Life's not fair.

The blight was spreading depressingly slowly and Shadow Haze still had forty minutes of cooldown, so I decided to take a nap. Sleep in VR isn't like the real stuff of course, but it lets you unload a bit and while away the time. It's not like you're going to climb out of the capsule for a half-hour nap. So I set an alarm in the interface and made myself comfortable right there amid the thorns and the sentries' glowering. Thanks to my passive buffs, the yoga-like comfort of my position did not bother me. The human mind is an amazing thing after all. In meatspace, I'd be afraid of sleeping alone in the middle of a forest—to say nothing of tree monsters—but in the game...In the game, my consciousness changed and distorted, allowing me to do the unthinkable, both big and small. By the time I reached this consideration, I was already dreaming.

But I didn't get the chance to enjoy my sleep properly. I was just starting in on an entertaining dream when a vaguely familiar voice crept into it.

"I see dead people..." A voice whispered softly right in my ear.

Unsure what reality I was in, I still managed to break some of the laws of physics and jump from a prone position directly to a standing one. Pasta, meatballs and blessed sauce! How scary that was! Otolaryngologist, who had just been bending over me, straightened out and began to laugh cheerfully.

"You're real jumpy for a killer," announced the biota rogue after he'd done laughing. "Guilty conscience? Wandering all alone so far from the Tree with an outlaw status to your name. Looks like you've managed to sprout some thorns. Out with it—what's your story?"

He sounded more or less friendly but something told me that he wasn't just trying to get to know me as much as ordering me to account for myself.

"What's it to you?" I muttered, coming to my senses.

The last vestige of sleep had already left me, but my mind still needed time to assess the situation. The patch of blighted ground had expanded quite a bit but it hadn't yet merged with its fellow patch. The two sentries were still patiently stomping at the border, waiting for me. It looked like Otolaryngologist was on his own. In any case, I couldn't see anyone else.

"I'm curious," Oto said eagerly. "I'm generally very curious by nature. I wonder where you've been, what you've seen. Maybe you've found something interesting? Let me copy your map, eh?"

I didn't need a PhD in psychology to understand that I was about to be killed in cold blood. The search for the dungeon continues and this guy won't tolerate any competitors. Unless I give him the coordinates of the very dungeon he's looking for...But that's not even an option. And so I can't afford to leave the game for twelve hours right now, yet I don't intend on telling this killer-celery the dungeon coordinates on principle. This is what they call being between a rock and a hard place.

"Maybe you'd like the keys to the safe in the process too?" I asked, trying to buy myself time to think of something sensible.

"Not a bad idea," Oto approved. "But it's better to start with a map and a story about your unhealthy appearance."

"What's in it for me?" I asked, opening my spellbook. It had been oh so long since I had examined my arsenal and considered my PvP meta. It's a good thing Lorelei's eyes don't have any pupils so he can't tell where I'm looking.

"I won't kill you," the brigand promised amicably and twirled one of his daggers expressively.

"Priceless, that," I had to admit. "You've got a deal. I came across an ancient altar about an hour ago and foolishly decided to examine it further. Ended up picking up this nasty curse for my trouble. Now I can freely walk on the blighted ground without any negative effects, but these stupid logs are after me too." I pointed to the silent sentries.

"Cool," Oto replied. "Will you have the debuff for a long time?"

"Until I die. But don't kill me, eh? I want to see if there's anything interesting around here."

"Well..." the rogue said pensively. "Maybe if you take me to that altar..."

"Not a problem! I'll show you where it is! Only, I will need to move quickly to get away from the sentries. The next spot of blight is near here."

"Only no funny business," warned the verdant blackmailer. "My agility is through the roof. I'll catch you no matter what you try. And when I do, that'll be the end of you. And when you respawn, I'll be waiting too. Understand?"

"Uh-huh. Let me just cast this buff on myself and then follow me."

"I'll be watching," Oto warned and activated his camouflage. Damn, this complicates things.

Arming myself with my eid, I cast Song of Inspiration, buffing my damage by 12%. Every little bit will help in this situation. There were about five hundred meters between us and the next patch of blighted ground. This is not reality—with Geranika's buff, I can run 100 meters faster than the top athlete in meatspace. The sentries cast Roots first and after that Wrath. Since they're not doing so at the moment, the spell can't overcome the blight. So I should make it in time. I only wish I knew whether the roots' AoE will trap Otolaryngologist or whether allied biota don't count as targets.

I took off quickly enough to beat the world record. The dumb forest elementals cast Roots in turn, but I didn't waste time turning around to see whether they were appealing to their forest deity to punish my trespassing. I came flying into the fresh patch of blight like an arrow and noticed out of the corner of my eyes as the fireflies fizzed out behind me. That was close. And where is Oto then? Alas, my hopes were in vain. Either the tough roots did not touch the rogue or he had remained on the blighted ground when they were cast. Too bad.

"You sure run fast," a surprised voice sounded from somewhere to my right. "You're a caster...the hell are you grinding agility for?"

"Just kind of turned out that way," I muttered vaguely without the slightest desire to discuss Geranika's buff. "All right. Let's head for the altar. Let me just check my map."

I made a show of unfurling my map and began to move my finger around it. Time. I had to buy a bit more time...

"Give me a copy of your map while you're at it," the unseen voice demanded.

"Yeah right. And then you'll off me. The altar is on the map."

"What's stopping me from offing you at the

altar?" the rogue asked reasonably.

"Have you heard of Scheherazade? Maybe I'll find a way to buy off your persistent attention to my person..."

"Come now, come now...Crap!" the rogue cursed, reappearing.

Aha! He'd spent a minute on blighted ground and taken damage. I started a timer in my interface and carelessly waved my hand:

"Forget about it. Once the altar curses you, you won't have to deal with this crap."

A notification appeared that I had transferred another part of my life to my summoned spirits. I even jumped in surprise—at first, I'd thought that the rogue had attacked me.

"Oh!" he said with surprise. "What'd you just take damage from?" He had noticed my HP drop.

"The curse on me is hilarious," I said. "Every two hours it takes a chunk of life. By the way, I can show you where I picked up this crud."

"I'd rather you shake a leg and get on with it," muttered Oto and vanished again from my sight.

From the moment the seeds were planted, the blight spread out quite cheerfully along the ground and the areas that I had sowed had almost merged already—forming a kind of safe path for the renegades. The modest patch of green no more than a hundred meters in diameter, didn't bother me. One sprint and the sentries won't even have time to cast a single spell.

"I'm about to run again," I warned Oto who was moving invisibly somewhere beside me. I turned to look at the sentries stomping behind me and glanced at my spell panel. I still needed to buy more time...

"Well, are you going to be long?" asked the irritated rogue, who had again taken damage from the blight and lost his camouflage.

"It's a few more minutes from here," I said, again demonstratively checking the map. "Look, do you mind explaining why you're picking on me? Am I bothering you somehow?"

"You were told that you weren't allowed to be here," the rogue snapped. He didn't bother camouflaging himself again, apparently realizing that doing so on the blighted ground was not particularly effective. "Noobs need to keep out of the adults' area."

"Come on," I answered. "Who am I bothering?"

"My guild," said Oto.

"But you don't have a guild," I said, surprised. "There aren't any guilds here at all. You need five thousand gold to register a guild. I read that. No one has money like that here."

"You're a fool. My main is in a guild, just like two thirds of the players running around here. The corporation allows us to suspend our main avatars while we try out this hardcore area. Accordingly, all the guilds have people here trying out the new location. And no doubt you too have created a new character and are here trying to win something for your guild. You're just playing stupid. Women like that kind of thing."

"Oh absolutely," I agreed, assessing the situation. We had managed to delve deeply into the blighted lands. Great. If he's so sure that women are so dumb, let that at least bring me some benefit beside the customary irritation.

"Enough of this nonsense," Oto blurted out. "Where is the altar?"

"I'm a decent girl," I said, arranging my fingers on the eid's strings. "I'm not going to the altar with the first guy I come across."

Machine gun
Tearing my body all apart
Machine gun
Tearing my body all apart...

The Shadow Haze, which had cooled down ten seconds ago, triggered instantly, and three seconds later the first of the three magic missiles flew from my strings. Oto cursed and activated his camo, but his HP was already in the red. Like any other biota, his Constitution wasn't great and the blighted ground hit his stats for 50%, while boosting mine. My Intellect alone was up to 132 here. In effect our levels were equal around here, even though because of the actual level difference, my spells would miss sometimes. As a result, whoever dealt the first blow gained the initiative. The vital thing now was that he tries to finish me off instead of retreating to assess the situation.

"So what's up, dickhead? Are you having fun yet?" I yelled as glibly and loudly as I could, giving out my location with my voice. As I did so, I recast Shadow Shield.

He won't run away as long as he thinks there's a chance of getting me. And I only have enough health for one hit. Or so he thinks.

I quietly shifted over a few steps, drank a potion to restore the mana I had just spent and again took up the eid. The first thing to do is cast Canopy of Silence, followed by Vengeful Flame. The roaring tongues of fire fluttered in all directions, flooding the forest within a radius of nine meters with a devouring flame. I took damage from my own spell, but the rogue sneaking in the direction of my last location found himself amid the flames as well. He came out of camo and as he did so, I stopped channeling Flame and again cast Magic Missiles. Alas, while Oto had been hidden, he had managed to drink a health potion and raise his health. On top of that two of the three missiles simply whiffed. The rogue not only survived, but again disappeared with health in the yellow. I wonder how many potions he has left.

The timer counted down the seconds dispassionately. Four. Three. Two. One. The damage from the blighted ground hit the rogue making him visible again. Despite his full health bar, he didn't risk it and immediately disappeared again, without giving me the opportunity to shoot my missiles at him. I didn't have any more AoE spells so there was no way to make him reappear.

After the first time he'd killed us, Chip spent a long time asking Sloe about the rogue's skillset and I recalled that they were especially afraid of taking hits while they were camoed. And that in battle he could only use his camo three times. After that, a long cooldown set in. Oto had already used his camo twice, so the question was whether he could find me in complete darkness before the blighted ground damages him again. Given all this, the smart move was to retreat. I cannot let him do that.

"Run along now, noob!" I shouted cheerfully, canceling the Shadow Haze. The world once again regained its customary colors, while I took a potion out of the bag and restored my mana as if everything was peachy. I won't have much time soon.

Damage taken: – 0 HP. {640 damage (critical hit: backstab) – 640 damage blocked (Shadow Shield). HP remaining: 320/320. Attacker: Otolaryngologist the Grassy (Level 43)}

"What the...?" cursed the rogue, but I already strummed my strings, casting the magic missiles.

With the buff from the Song of Courage, a 50% increase to my stats from the blighted ground and a bonus to damage from the natural environment trait, one salvo of the magic missiles (one of which missed yet again), I took off almost all of Oto's HP. He quaffed another potion to restore his HP, while I cast another salvo...The battle ended a half minute later. It seems he had less than ten potions with him. He managed to take out two of my three materia shades before I sent him to respawn. Oto never stood a chance. And I didn't even have to resort to Geranika's last present: I didn't feel like showing all my cards.

The rogue turned into a wisp of half transparent smoke and disappeared, a little heap of gold jingling to the grass where my missile had found into him.

Achievement unlocked:

'Duelist I' (19 player kills until the next rank).

Achievement reward: +1% to damage done to other players.

Quest updated: _Way of the Apprentice. Step 1._

1 of 30 biota killed.

Woohooo! I was jumping and dancing from the surge of adrenaline. I had won! And my PvP kills count toward my quest! Life is great!

Only when the euphoria subsided did I notice how much my hands were trembling. It may be just a game and all, but it sure does make your nerves sing. I'll need to ask Sloe or Chip to spar PvP with me so I can get used to it. I'm not always going to be so lucky. After all, I'm not a calculating, rational PKer, but a lucky noob. My unexpected victory had made me completely lose my mind.

And there was something to think about. First of all, I have a quest with a deadline and need to hurry. Secondly, I had used my Shadow Haze again and wouldn't be able to move on to sowing those stupid seeds for another hour. Thirdly, Oto wasn't alone in this location and I'm sure he's already ringing his buddies out in meatspace, telling them where to find me. I won't be so lucky next time, especially since I don't know a thing about the tactics used by other classes in this game. I never had a particular reason to find out about them. My only hope was the new spell from Geranika.

The more I considered the situation, the sadder I got. It looks like one way or another I'm screwed. Sooner or later. If I get out today, they'll get me tomorrow. And leaving the game for a day or two to lie low wasn't an option either. So, I need to take a risk and finish what I started, before Oto's buddies make their move.

I picked up the coins, richer by two dozen gold, adjusted my settings to receive the minimum possible info while in combat and got on with my quest. The sowing of seeds for the future labyrinth went by without incident so I spent the time remaining on my Shadow Haze cooldown studying my spellbook. My eyes alighted on the spell for summoning the instrument's soul:

Summon Instrument Soul.

Description: A true master puts his soul into his creations, but a true bard can awaken this soul and acquire a devoted companion.

Requirements: Instrument of type Rare or higher.

Casting cost: (Bard Level × 2) MP.

Casting time: Instant. You must perform something on the instrument whose soul is to be summoned. If you change instruments, the inactive instrument's soul is dispelled.

Level of summoned soul: (Instrument Level + Summoner).

Spell Duration: Until spell is canceled or the summoner dies.

Number of skills and spells available to Summoned Soul: (Instrument Level ÷ 10 + Writing + Summoner).

It turns out that Eid will become my companion as he is my active instrument. And he will have some skills. That could be useful. I cast the spell, but instead of the familiar soul, a swirling amorphous ghostly blob appeared in front of me.

Attention! You have summoned the soul of Cypro's legendary instrument for the first time. You assign the role that Eid will play in your party: Tank, Healer, Physical DPS, Magical DPS, or Support.

Attention! Once you make a choice, you can no longer change the role the summoned soul plays in your party.

Ho-hum. Not only do I get a companion, but I can even choose what his job will be? Great. Tank all the way. I really need a good tank...

Selection accepted.

The shapeless blob began to swirl, increased in size and thickened, forming a ghostly figure. Eid looked like the first time we met: the same looming figure ensconced in plate armor, though even a little more looming without his cape. And the shield on his back was larger than the previous one too. I could easily hide myself behind a fellow this big—even my pony-tail will be tucked away. Another ghostly companion. Chip was right, I'm like a damn Ghostbuster.

"Well met, fair Lorelei," Eid said in his rich,

bassy voice.

"My friend, you have no idea how glad I am to see you!" I confessed sincerely and even hugged the dumbfounded spirit from the excess of emotion filling me. He was quite solid to the touch—I even banged my forehead against his breastplate. Eid's temperature, however, was exactly as the temperature around us.

"I'm afraid to even imagine what has caused such a torrid outpouring of joy," a slight note of mockery sounded in the spirit's voice.

"They want to kill me here," I replied. "And here you are riding in on your dark stallion. Life is getting better!"

"Oh, well, that explains everything," Eid chuckled and then asked, "And who dares imperil the life of my musical accompaniment?"

"Yo!" I even forgot about my potential pursuers from indignation. "If you're going to insult me, I'll start to sing show tunes and dirty ditties. Maybe then you will learn the difference between a musician and 'musical accompaniment.'"

"Alright, alright!" Eid waved his hands in a conciliatory manner. "Let's compromise on 'troubadour proprietor.'"

"Deal," I agreed after a little hesitation. "And now let's see what you can do. I can't see your innards, so spill the beans..."

"Spill the beans?" The spirit asked, surprised.

"But I haven't any beans on me..." he continued uneasily.

Well, I'll be...I must be more careful with the slang. Eid is a resident of a fairy-tale medieval world after all. He's a bit behind the times, you could say.

"Forget it, I used the wrong word. Tell me what level you are. I can't see your attributes."

"That's because I do not belong to you," Eid explained. "I cannot wield my full power with you. My level is limited by yours and can only slightly exceed it due to your Summoner trait. At the moment I'm Level 23."

Okay. So he's one of those peculiar scaling quest items I'd read about. His levels grow with mine and his stats jump instantly when they do. On the other hand, the level of my newly-minted tank will grow and this is enough for me. So, what kind of abilities does he have?

In the group interface, Eid's portrait appeared next to Salamander's and Anica's. It's a good thing that I did not take them with me. They would have died either from the sentries' fireflies or from Oto's malice. This way, I'm sure they're sitting on the grass somewhere with the local druids, admiring the natural wonders of the Hidden Forest. But I'm getting off topic.

Eid had five abilities, just like the spirit of the Salamander King: A 'Taunt' spell which was traditional for tanks and which caused enemies to aggro him; a 'Shield Bash' that would interrupt enemies' spells and abilities; a 'Knockdown' attack that was self-explanatory; and 'Soul Link,' which allowed Eid to take half the damage I received for ten seconds. His last skill was passive and was called 'Metamorphosis.' It was this 'Metamorphosis' spell that seemed impossible to understand without first having a few stiff pints, as Beast liked to say.

Eid's soul had two kinds of stats: native ones and bonus ones, which he received from me. As I gathered from the description, my main stats were distributed between all of Eid's stats in the following proportion: 50% went to Constitution, 25% to Strength, 15% to Agility, and 10% to armor bonus and magic resistance. Apparently this was to compensate for the impossibility of equipping the spirit. The damage that he did and the chance of his shield block also somehow depended on my stats, but there were no additional explanations and formulas and I didn't feel like delving into this issue. I will explore the details later when things are a bit more relaxed. At the moment, I was more interested in something else:

"Tell me, what happens if you die?"

"I cannot be killed as long as the instrument is intact," the spirit explained. "When my incarnated body is destroyed, I return to the eid. It collects the vitality flowing through the world and stores it, allowing me to reincarnate in a corporeal likeness."

"And how long does this process take?" I asked.

"Depends on many factors, but on average—twelve hours. If the eid is located in a nexus of vitality or it is filled with vitality by someone who wields such spells, I will return much sooner. The reverse is also true—in lifeless places, my reincarnation will take longer."

"And if I want you to disappear for a while? Will you return to the eid?"

"All you have to do is say so. But bear in mind that with disincarnation, not all of the vitality returns to the instrument with me. A new incarnation will take some time. Not much," the spirit added, foreseeing my question. "An average of about thirty minutes."

"Uh-huh," I concluded profoundly.

It's great and interesting and all, but I'm not sure what I'm supposed to with all of it. The tank is not particularly useful against other players: they will simply ignore him and focus me. If the attackers have a pirq with them, then there is no option at all—a strong and hardy fighter will take me out using his natural resistance to magic. Although...

A plan developed in my head over a couple of minutes. An unreliable one, with yawning gaps, but there was simply no other.

By the time the Shadow Haze cooldown had expired, no one had come to have a word with me. Either Oto's friends were out in meatspace and it took time to mobilize, or for some reason they could not reach our location quickly enough. One way or another, I was faced with a decision: Save the miracle-spell for a future battle, or cast it again and continue planting the seeds. After hesitating a bit, I chose the second option. Time is valuable, and Oto might have so many friends that even a perfect execution of my plan would do no good.

Running from the sentries according to the worked out scheme brought me even closer to the Arras. If my calculations are correct, there were only two areas remaining. And while the blight spread, I remembered Sasha's tales and prepared an ambush of my own on the branches of a gnarled tree. Although my racial trait was supposed to hide me from any unwanted guests, I still couldn't help but feel nervous.

I could see Eid quite clearly. He stood nearby, in the very center of the patch of blight. His sword in its scabbard, the shield behind the back, a tranquil expression on his face and his attributes still hidden. He was skeptical about my idea but he helped with the preparation with such gusto that he gave himself away to me: The eid's soul was that of an adventurer.

After an hour, I was almost certain that no one would come—when a biota hunter named Cunning Fig stepped out from behind the trees. I wonder whether the fig is supposed to be the fruit or something else. Fig was escorted by the strangest beast I had ever seen. The phrase 'of the canine family' didn't quite do it justice, since the animal was clearly of vegetable origin. Instead of fur, it had a thick covering of leaves, and its teeth and claws were of a bark-like material. Do these creatures grow on the Tree too? It wasn't a small dog either, about a meter at the whithers.

At the sight of Eid, Fig readied his bow, but the spirit stopped him, saying:

"Greetings, traveler! Stay awhile and listen..."

The hunter blinked in surprise, lowered the bow, for some reason looked around and hesitantly moved closer to the patiently waiting spirit. I understood Fig's doubts. He had gone to hunt an impudent player and came across an NPC-ghost loitering in the middle of the forest, obviously ready to issue a quest. On the one hand the player had a job to do, and on the other, here was this quest that it would be silly to pass up. What if this was the very NPC that would lead him to the new dungeon?

The hunter decided to listen to Eid, who began to regale him with a sad story I had cooked up about his death at the paws of a terrible monster. The instrument's soul showed considerable inventiveness in the process and even embellished the legend I had spitballed a little while ago. This is what it means to work in a creative profession!

"I cannot find peace while the creature is alive," Eid finished sadly. "But you are too weak for me to entrust this quest to you. There was a biota bard here before you. She was accompanied by a pirq. I too sent them to the monster's den and they have not yet returned. Since I still have not left Barliona, either they did not dare to fight the monster in battle or the have failed."

"Where? Where did they go?" the hunter instantly perked up.

"No one else should die in an unfair battle," Eid said firmly. "Bring at least two companions with you and I will point the way to the monster's den."

The hunter scratched his head pensively, looked back, and then said:

"Was the bard's name Lorelei by any chance?"

"Yes," Eid nodded sagely. "Have you two met?"

"In passing," Fig muttered through his teeth and waved his hand. A pair of biota appeared at the edge of blighted ground: A priest named Satanic Ladan and a necromancer with the odd name Aching Molar. Both of them were Level 40. It's too bad, I was counting on more rogues, hoping to shoot everyone from my sniper's perch up in the tree.

"Well?" Fig asked, when his companions approached Eid. "Are there enough of us now?"

The spirit did not have time to reply: I cast Canopy of Silence and sent the impact shade Geranika had given me flying at the priest. As this was the first time I had resorted to shadow magic in order to hurt someone, I half-expected a bolt from the blue, a curse from the gods and an avalanche of system notifications about how I had betrayed all that is decent and good in Barliona—but nothing of the sort happened. In my hands, the eid roared an overdriven A5/E chord followed by a pinch harmonic, and an ominous-looking shadow hurled itself implacably in Ladan's direction. His shield absorbed some of the damage, so the priest survived, but his health dropped into the red. The healer's hands immediately began to glow—he began to conjure a healing spell. His companions also did not tarry: They turned in the direction where my power chord had sounded and peered into the thorn bushes, looking for me. At the same time, Eid treacherously bashed the unsuspecting priest with his shield, interrupting the spell he was about to cast. Dumbfounded by such a turn of events, the priest hesitated and my second impact shade sealed the deal before Ladan could quaff the potion in his hand.

Quest updated: *Way of the Apprentice*. Step 1.

2 of 30 biota killed.

His friends, occupied with trying to trace my spell's trail noticed Eid's sneak attack too late. Eid turned on the hunter and I switched to the same target. Biota are very squishy creatures in general, so by focusing one enemy and forcing him to heal, we will quickly extinguish the dps they could normally hurl our way. Alas, it was not so simple. A wave of frost erupted from the mage, expanding in all directions. Eid froze to the ground and the hunter leaped wildly away from the spirit. His wolf leaped onto Eid with a snarl, while Fig and Molar focused their fire on me. If it weren't for Geranika's wonder shield and the buffs from the blighted ground, I'd be done in a second. Yet I simply cast another shade which ignored the difference in our levels, armor and resistances at the hunter. One shot, one kill.

Quest updated: *Way of the Apprentice. Step 1.*

3 of 30 biota killed.

By this time, the mage had practically removed all of my materia shades and, seeing the sad fate of his comrades, instantly teleported about twenty meters from me, beyond the range of spells. Ordinary spells.

Another impact shade flew from my strings and the quest counter ticked once again, reckoning the fourth victim. Hah! Easy as pie! Watch out, a cereal killer stalks these woods! I wonder what name the press would give me? I would gladly take something like 'the Grim Minstrel.'

I jumped off the branch and mechanically glanced at my hands. They were trembling again, although the battle had not been that difficult. Well at least I can count on myself to fight on autopilot even in stressful situations. I couldn't say the same for concerts and corporate events. People would throw all kinds of crap onto our stage: from sweaty t-shirts and plush toys to bottles and shoes. On top of that, they would with depressing regularity try to break through to the mic to sing drunkenly. One day someone even shot off a gun—fortunately, only into the air. You couldn't really compare PvP to all that. But I still needed the practice.

The next two hours passed without incident, although I jerked at every rustle around me. I sowed my remaining seeds according to the chart I'd been given. All but the two that I'd given to Chip. I had to think a bit about which area I would skip in my sowing. As a result, the unlucky patch was a side path in the direction of the Arras. It probably had some strategic significance, but personally I did not need it. I will simply tell Lotos that I lost a couple of seeds while running from the free citizens who had ambushed me, and he can decide for himself whether he wants to assign me further quests.

* * *

AT LAST the moment came when I first laid eyes on the Arras. To tell you the truth, I had been looking at it for a long time already. My imagination had drawn pretty pictures from Stephen King's immortal work *Under the Dome*, but the forest looked quite ordinary around here and there was nothing obscuring the sky overhead. I even began to doubt whether my calculations had been correct, when the air ten meters away wavered noticeably as on a very hot day. A step and another, a third, and I beheld the Arras.

Inconspicuous, almost transparent, it resembled a soap bubble, with rainbows playing barely noticeably on its walls. But it was the size of the bubble that was really astonishing. It reached way up high and out, marked by the faintly shimmering air. By the almost inconspicuous curvature of the visible area, I could get a sense of the Arras' circumference, and I couldn't help but whistle. It's like the pyramids: You know about them in theory, you see holograms, but as soon as you're there in front of them, all your prior notions evaporate, leaving only admiration. The Arras truly was a monumental spell.

Curiosity prodded me to touch the faintly iridescent wall, but I restrained myself. Who knows, maybe there is a warning system or like border guards or something...They will catch me and send me to the local jail. No, I'd rather experiment once my raiding party arrives. They'll be able to help me fight off any law enforcement if anything. After taking this prudent decision, I dispelled Eid, exited the game and contacted Sloe. Fortunately, he was not in the capsule, so he answered right away.

"What's up? Did you make it to the Arras?"

"Uh-huh."

"Send me the coordinates. The raid will assemble in an hour. It's hard to say how many of them will break through to you. You'll have to wait."

"I'll wait in real life. I want to get some sleep. When they get close, call me on my visor and I'll enter the game."

"Great! Do you need anything else from the outside world?"

"You know better than me what'll come in handy at my level. The main thing is to bring the amulets of communication so we can talk without leaving the game. And some kind of mount would be nice."

"I'll take care of it," Sloe reassured me. "Have you learned the language of Kartoss?"

"No," I confessed. "I was thrown out of the library, and reading books in a foreign language has not yet produced any results. And is it really that necessary? If it is, we can call each other in meatspace and talk things over."

"That won't do," Sloe said. "It's too slow. Okay, we'll buy you a language pack. Just make sure to accept the present in-game."

"Well, thanks."

"Talk to you soon."

CHAPTER NINE

WHEN THE HOUR STRUCK, I was sitting at the foot of the Arras, drowsy and glum. I couldn't see any raid party, but there were flashes and sparks glinting on the other side of the magical barrier, so I assume the battle was in full swing. I didn't even consider trying to break through to help out. It'd be stupid. The party was composed of high-level players and my assignment was a simple one—sit tight so I can lead them through the Arras once they break through. So I activated the Kartossian language pack, camouflaged and sat down on the grass. Yawning periodically, I drowsily examined the minor changes in the game interface.

Anica's and Salamander's frames had vanished—their time in the world of the living had expired and they had returned to the Gray Lands. By way of farewell, the two left a new bookmark in my quest journal with timers that counted down the time left before the souls would plunge into Erebus. Anica had just over ten days left, while Salamander had an entire three weeks. Damn, I need to start thinking about the quest for the girl like now...or compose a song to sustain her...I had no doubt that the story of the rebellious king would make a great ballad. It was stunning stuff. As for Anica...A medallion that brought a mysterious death is something of course, but it inspires me to solve the quest rather than compose a song.

My eyes again came to rest on the faintly visible barrier. The blight that had sprouted from the seeds I'd sown crept up to the Arras as to the foot of a wall. It was as if a blade had chopped the black earth off. I guess the spell protecting the Hidden Forest prevented not only living beings, but also magical phenomena from crossing its perimeter. Curious.

Meanwhile, the flashes had subsided and a picturesque group of players appeared from among the trees. It was my first time seeing a raiding party in Barliona, and the spectacle was impressive indeed. The average level of the raiders was 280. The band, consisting of members of all kinds of races and classes moved with an evident, yet mysterious purpose. The leader was a hulking creature clad in plate armor with a pavise in his paw. A tauren, one of Barliona's animal-inspired classes. His name was short and simple—Pops. The party's flanks were guarded by two other heavy classes: A human paladin named Thoughtful Fro and a gaunt drow with a huge two-handed axe at the ready. But it was the drow's name that was the true killer: Sylvan Darkness. It's like he knew ahead of time what kind of adventure he was signing up for.

A zombie priest named Dickery Dirk stepped out from behind the tauren and regarded the Arras thoughtfully.

"Ah, there she is," said a drow rogue named Murderous Angel, pointing in my direction.

I started, came out of camo and waved my hand in greeting.

Dirk waved back, cast a magic shield on himself and gingerly touched the Arras with his hand. Nothing happened. The priest ran his hand over the scarcely noticeable barrier, knocked on it with his staff and clearly wanted to do something else, but was rudely interrupted:

"Why don't you test it on your tooth while you're at it?" asked a suspiciously familiar voice.

That's right—Sasha, whose in-game name turned out to be Bogart the Base, stood leaning against his crossbow. An immense cat with protruding fangs sat at his feet, as if it had just stepped from the cover of a book on paleontology. It was the size of a leopard, ginger colored, with a powerful chest, and fangs as long as my palm. The name of this wonder was Merlin Monroe. Bogart scratched his darling on the scruff, drawing a purr of pleasure from Merlin, and went on, "Or headbutt it or something. On second thought, you might want El Toro there to take a crack at it. Isn't that right, Toro?"

He winked playfully at the tauren.

"Keep talking and you'll be picking your teeth out of that shit coming out of your mouth," Pops promised laconically, without however taking any aggressive action.

Next to the mighty tauren, clad in full plate armor, Sasha's Bogart the Base looked like a bum who had been crashing in a three-legged rocking chair behind a dumpster. Heavy-set, muscular, green, covered with tattoos, Bogart the orc looked quite different from the human playing him. Of course, their personalities were completely identical...

"Come to think of it, I could use some dental work," said Bogart.

"You'll be sneezing them through your nose," the tauren added phlegmatically. "But later."

"Oh! You do rhinoplasty too?" the orc said, puzzled. "Merlin, were you aware of this?" He patted his pet on the withers.

The sabretooth, obviously accustomed to its master's jests, hardly blinked an eye.

"Kiera," he called to me. "What's that all about?" A green finger with a gnawed fingernail pointed to my outlaw status. Turning back to the raiding party, he continued, "Make no mistake, fellows, her blood thirst knows no bounds. In the midst of one of her moods, you will be lucky indeed if ye save yer skins. If she doesn't kill once a day, she starts getting these withdrawals, loses her mind and turns on her own friends. I tried to muzzle her once but she gnawed it all to hell."

"I'm about to gnaw someone's nose off," I threatened the joker.

"There, you see?" Bogart sighed contritely. "But no worries, you needn't be afraid—I am with you and I will bear the brunt of the first blow!"

Bogart struck his chest with hollow sound. What an alpha gorilla...only balder and greener. He must have had a painful childhood. You've really got it coming now, Snegov...When we get back to meatspace, I'll serve you a good turn. The object of my musings could not even imagine the barbs prepared for him once he would leave the game, and in the meanwhile he switched to more pressing matters:

"Tell me, my dear turnip, what are we waiting for?"

"We're waiting for my brain to warm up after my nap," I said dryly, pushing away my revenge fantasies. I approached the Arras with a bit of apprehension.

My imagination was painting a variety of pictures: From making a hole in the protective spell to being turned into a heap of ash for crossing the border without authorization. But everything turned out quite a bit more ordinary. When I touched the Arras, it flared brightly and began to shimmer with iridescence. Bogart yelled, "Bonzai!" and hurled himself against the altered section of the Arras— striking it pitifully with his head and collapsing shamefully on his ass.

"Semper Fi!" he groaned, crossing his eyes and feeling the bridge of his nose.

His Merlin sat down next to him and sympathetically rubbed her face, purring something comforting.

"Let's try another way," I muttered, and held out my hand to Bogart.

My flimsy biota palm vanished into his giant paw. I wonder why he's decided to play as this musclehead? Is this how he imagines the orc race? Or is this his Napoleonic complex manifested in VR? Although...I examined the dark orc's hypertrophied body mass one more time. This looks more like a complex of complexes...

As soon as our hands touched, the iridescent radiance spread to the orc and his pet and they crossed the magical barrier without any difficulty.

"I hereby claim," Bogart let go of his She-Ra's ear, which he had used to drag her across the Arras, and assumed a triumphant pose, raising his battle axe to the sky, "this land for the Spanish Crown!"

He stuck the point into the earth between his feet.

"Ain't I as cool as a Columbus?" he asked his audience.

Pops clapped his paw to his face and silently shook his head. It seemed that Bogart had managed to really get under the tauren's skin during their journey to the Arras.

"Let's not waste time," Dirk ordered. "Line up in two ranks, touch Lorelei's hand and step through the Arras. Tanks, healers, keep your eyes peeled. Who knows what might be waiting for us on the other side?"

I spent the next couple of minutes feeling like a turnstile in the subway. Though, instead of loose change, crumpled bills or transit cards, here, a handshake sufficed.

"Well this blows," Fro concluded, as he stepped onto the blighted ground. "Is it far from here to the grass that doesn't give you a debuff?"

"Not particularly, but there are a couple of Forest Sentries waiting for me there," I replied honestly. "They can't step onto blighted ground. However, the renegades might find us here."

"Let's get to work then," Bogart said in an unusually serious voice.

With a sour expression, the orc fumbled with a shaggy green cloak.

"The devil take it," he snorted with annoyance. "It doesn't fit..."

"All right," Dirk snapped at him, "let's make a deal. If you are going to keep traveling with us, which I recommend from the bottom of my heart, then no more improvisation. You do what the raid leader says. That would be me. If you do not agree, it's your business. But something tells me that you'll be dead in the next 10–15 minutes. And I have no idea where you'll respawn. Make your decision!"

Bogart the Base silently rolled up his shaggy cloak and stuck it back in his bag, then he looked around the party with a look of equal parts amusement and contempt.

"So what are you standing there for? Are we waiting for someone?" he finally inquired.

"We are waiting for our raid leader's orders," said Pops, laconically.

"Elk, Soul," Dirk commanded, "scout ahead."

The two rogues nodded and disappeared from sight.

"Cranton," the priest turned to the colorful troll with a huge bow over his shoulder. "Bogart's with you. You will explain the basics to him. His orders are not to die."

"Got it," Cranton nodded and beckoned to Bogart with his blue paw. "Follow me, brother, I'll tell you where to stand and what to do."

Bogart waved at me and followed his new partner, while Fro came up to me and began to take out a variety of junk from his backpack—some gear fit for a Level 20, a few satchels with fifty inventory slots, one of which I immediately passed to Bogart and another to Fro. There was also a small set of alchemical potions for my level and a few scrolls with spells. But the most valuable gift was the horse. Thanks to the game mechanics, the paladin did not

THE BARD FROM BARLIONA

have to drag the animal with him literally. He simply handed me a bridle, which when activated caused the animal to appear next to me: a small, sturdy black horse with a cute forelock, which made it look like a little cartoon horse, and a long, plush tail.

"Kiera, your new name is going to be Kiera Khan," giggled Bogart, looking at my new mount. "A real steed of the steppes."

He stretched out his paw and stroked the animal on its muzzle. Merlin, evidently growing envious, didn't let him go any further and wheezing unhappily pulled her owner away from my pony.

"Do I have to feed her or wash her?" I clarified just in case, admiring my new mount.

"Nothing of the kind," Fro reassured me. "Summon, ride and dispel. Elementary."

"Uh-huh," I nodded. "Thanks."

"Think nothing of it," said the paladin. "You helped us, we helped you. Everyone is happy."

"What about Sloe and Chip?"

"We'll meet with them later and give them some gear," Fro reassured me. "What are you going to do? Are you coming with us or heading out on your own?"

"Depends on which direction you go."

"We're going to meet up with Sloe and start combing the forest."

At this point, I felt a pang of conscience. After all, I know the dungeon's location and I could tell them, and yet...Who knows whether the guild players will honor my request to remain uninvolved until the end of the scenario. They might break in and start killing the renegades...Or the renegades will start killing them and then begin investigating who ushered in the outsiders. And at that point I could kiss the grand finale goodbye.

No. I'd rather tell them when it's all over.

"Try to stay off the blighted ground as long as you can," I requested. "I have some ongoing quests there and you might spoil things."

"We will take your wishes into consideration."

Well. There's an answer for you. I won't promise anything, but I'll take your wish into consideration. On the other hand, it was silly to expect anything else.

I asked them to transfer a couple of my amulets to Sloe and Chip, said goodbye to my new acquaintances and began to study my new stats.

The rare items pleased me with their noticeable boost to my stats. After my basic gear, the growth of my stats from equipping the rare items seemed fantastic: +158 to Intellect, +56 to Constitution. The latter, unfortunately, was capped by my racial penalty, so that the final figures in the stats turned out to be more modest: I now had 246 Intelligence and 58 Constitution (the racial penalty cap kicked in here). At least, this did not factor in the buffs from being on blighted ground.

After hesitating a bit, I dumped all my

unallocated stat points into Intellect. With my racial bonus I ended up with 528 base Intelligence, or 720 Int when you factored in all the gear and profession bonuses.

I cast my Shadow Shield and admired the new numbers. A new monster killer stalked the unsuspecting newbies of the Hidden Forest. How many scalps had Geranika asked for? Thirty? Easy as pie!

And on top of all this, I now had a mount to ride. I activated the bridle and summoned my mare. Or stallion...In the world of Barliona, all animals had the anatomy of a Ken doll and the determination of the creature's sex was frequently left to the imagination. And still, my new pet needed a name, so I started to think. Of short stature, with fluffy forelocks and a lush tail, I associated her more with a girl. And if so, she would be a mare.

Now the name...A ringing silence immediately filled my head. Not a single thought on the topic. I always have problems inventing names. And then a character from a legendary book series surfaced in my memory. He too always had a hard time coming up with names for his horses so that finally he decided to solve the issue in the simplest and most elegant manner possible:

"Your name is Roach," I told the black horse.

She snorted and shook her head, which I interpreted as consent. Done and done. I will deal with the accusations of plagiarism later.

Having decided on the name of my horse, I climbed up into the saddle with some caution. Sloe had told me that horsemanship was a special skill in Barliona that players had to learn. And it wasn't just a matter of pushing a button—you really needed a few days' training with an NPC instructor. Otherwise, the horse would buck, bite and kick her rider. The exception was several easymode breeds like my Roach. Calm, ponderous and plodding, they obeyed even unskilled riders, provided that they have some riding skills from meatspace. Or, as in my case— experience from other games and VR trainers.

In real life, I had had a chance to ride twice around the park on a quiet pony intended for tourists, but I had logged about a week in the equestrian VR simulator. Now, in theory, not only did I know how to ride a little, but I also knew how to take care of the animal. The simulator was realistic, so you had to do everything, up to cleaning the stall. I might not win a race against some cavalry, but neither will I go flying from the saddle of my trotting filly.

The horse moved slowly across rough terrain and through the ubiquitous thorns of the blighted ground, snorting time to time and twirling her ears at the sight of blighted predators. But they simply ignored her, deceived by my shadow ward. Meanwhile, I smiled blissfully, feeling like a fabulous minstrel, driven by the search for adventure.

And soon enough adventure found me. A fireball flew straight into my face, immediately taking out a fifth of my now-ample Shadow Shield.

"There she is!" yelled a biota mage coming out of camo and already kindling his next spell in his hand.

I didn't get a chance to look at his name, occupied as I was with my exciting flight out of the saddle: Frightened by the fire, Roach kicked and reared. As I sank into the grass, I watched gnarled roots emerge from the ground and slip off my body helplessly. Geranika's buff once again had saved my life. Meanwhile, there were about a dozen hostile players already running in my direction, with two pirqs in their midst. Those couldn't care less about my stats—with their magic immunity they would frag me as soon as they reached me.

My marathon for survival began with a low start and some slipping. In the process, several more bardic-scalp seekers joined the pursuers, but there was no time to count thoroughly. I ran ahead of my own squealing, helplessly watching as fire and ice spells, arrows and throwing axes swiftly devoured another materia shade. Shadow Shield had already cooled down, but given the dps I was taking, casting it again would only buy me a few minutes at best. The only chance of salvation was to reach my goal in time. I didn't bother shooting back with my impact shades—all it would take is one slip and I wouldn't have a chance to get up again.

I let go of the flask of water in my hand just long enough to jangle another Shadow Shield on my eid. I wouldn't live to see its cooldown. Heck, I wouldn't have lived this long if it weren't for the Indefatigable buff which gave me enough stamina to stay ahead of the melee fighters chasing my priceless hide.

"Snegov!" I hollered into the amulet of communication. "Where are you?"

"Not far. We've just taken care of the sentries," sounded Bogart's worried voice. "Where are you? What happened?"

"Street goons," I blurted the two words that would explain the entire situation to Snegov.

"Head a few clicks to the...damn. To the east, to the east," he ordered and disconnected.

To the east, so to the east. I don't care where I die. And I had no doubt that I was about to do just that. The materia shades were dissolving one after another and my HP wasn't much even with the new gear.

My defeatist mood had not yet had time to take root when something large and hard swept past me at a frenzied speed and a dark-blue barrier flickered to life around me.

I slowed down long enough to see Bogart and Merlin come tearing in the wake of the unidentified object at my pursuers, hollering "Vaaagh!" as he did so. And it seems, this time he really was angry...Strange, he's a hunter, why would he run into melee range?

As if he'd read my mind, Bogart cut away to the side, removing the crossbow from his back. He raised it, took a knee, gestured for the cat to go gnaw some poor sap's face, and began to focus down the ugliest (in his eyes) of my pursuers.

"Lipo will deal with your buddy shortly," a zombie priest named Qupip said implacably, riding up to me.

His horse was well-suited to its rider: Beneath the sumptuous horsecloth, I could make out the skeleton of a dead nag, its eyes burning with a magical lilac fire.

Lipo turned out to be a Level 264 orc warrior. Along with Merlin, he was hooting cheerfully and chasing after the four surviving players of the first attack, obviously amused at their attempts to escape their fate. Still, they were fairly agile and quick, so Bogart summoned his mount and began galloping after them, furiously shooting his crossbow as he rode and yelling something like "Stop dodging so much and let me aim properly, you bastards!" In turn, I picked up the eid and began to play the theme of the chase from the remake of the popular comic show, shooting impact shades at the runners. A guitar is no yakety sax of course but the melody was clear enough to Qupip who began to laugh cheerfully and contagiously.

"Good one," he flashed me a thumbs up. "Only,

this is no place for you any longer."

"Why is that?" I asked surprised. Out of the corner of my eye, I noticed the kill count record the fifth victim. "The forest is big, let them look long and hard when they respawn."

"Because these kids are from the Dark Legion—the Seconds, we call them in honor of their eternal second place behind Ehkiller's guild. The Seconds went over to Kartoss with a positive reputation with the Dark Lord, so they are the leading candidates to escort the embassy. In a few days there will be a mob of high-level players here legally, so to speak. The local sentries won't slow them down and they'll comb this forest every which way and leave no pebble unturned. And your camo at this level means absolutely zilch. Their trackers will locate you quickly, so you have to get out of here. We won't be much help—we'll be occupied with keeping our own skins alive."

"Well crap," I summarized.

"Yah," the priest agreed. "So wrap up your business here and start thinking about your next move."

Why where would I go? I have hatred status with both empires, the monsters beyond the Arras won't let me take a step out there, and at my level there's nothing for me in the Free Lands. It looks like my only way forward lies with Geranika. And this means that I need to start upping my biota kill count as quickly as possible.

Lipo and Bogart, meanwhile, completed their sweep of the battlefield and approached us.

"Clear," Bogart reported. "How are you? Are you all right?"

"I'm alive, so everything's fine," I said and pulled out Roach's bridle.

Activating the item did nothing.

Simple Steppe Horse Bridle. Durability: 0 / 200.

Uh-huh. So they killed my Roach after all. The upside is that it isn't forever. All I have to do is find a stable master, pay him some gold and he'll fix my bridle, resurrecting my horsey. The downside is basically that I have no idea where to find a stable master. The Tree is off limits to me and there are no other options. Although...I could give the bridle to Chip and have him take it to the stables.

"They killed my Roach," I complained to Bogart.

"That's what you get for stealing him from Geralt. And anyway," he nodded in the direction of the battlefield, "who are those goons? Your fan club? Why don't they ask Pasha and me for permission to interact with you privately? A young lady from a decent Southern family shouldn't be out gallivanting without her governess, coquetting with random Yankees—they are not bona fide!"

"Well those guys never asked me anything," I sighed. "They're buddies of our old friend Otolaryngologist. Pasha and I told you about him. And, it seems, they're all from the Dark Legion."

"So Yankees all the same..." Bogart grunted and grinned unkindly.

He had his own reasons to dislike the Dark Legion and these reasons struck me as odd. So they bet on his dying in game against a high-level PKer...and so what? Didn't it just help even the playing field in the process? But no, their wagering had annoyed Sasha enough that now he was jumping at the chance to spoil things for them even a little.

"Where are they going to start their search from?" Bogart confirmed my suspicions, looking around the area with an unpleasant squint.

"I do not know about them, but the Forest Sentries will kill you as soon as you stray from the raid party," I reminded. "You're an illegal alien in these parts. The locals will all aggro you and your Level 45 won't scare them away."

"You're like my grandmother, Kiera," Bogart replied. "Next thing I know, you'll be swatting at me with a towel and yelling at me to come inside to eat. You think this is my first disco? That I don't have a head of my own? I only wanted to leave a couple surprises lying around. It'd be rude not to. Just show up, slay some stuff and not even say goodbye...Let me just dig this little hole and set up some spikes down in its bottom—like a bona fide Southern gentleman. Then we can move on."

"Ten minutes, no more," Qupip declared with finality. "Long enough for the scouts to look around and my mana to regenerate."

"In ten minutes, we'll be legging it trippingly for the Canadian border," Bogart reassured him.

"I can help," Lipo offered. "I'm curious!"

"In that case, start breaking the branches from that bush over there," said Bogart and whistling a cheerful tune, began digging the earth as briskly as a mole.

I didn't feel like poking around in others' business. If Bogart wants to dig holes, let him dig them himself. Everyone plays however he likes. Especially since they won't get in the way. I need to get 25 more frags to make Geranika happy and take me on as his court minstrel.

"Listen up, prickle pear," Qupip interrupted my thoughts. "Sloe said that you are a cartographer. How much would you sell your map for? I'd rather not poke around here blind."

"Oh, you can have a copy for free," I said, shrugging and unfurling my map. "You've helped me out a great deal as it is."

There was just a small problem—in a lapse of judgment, I had marked the dungeon on the map. Although, why am I so worried? I can always erase it too...It took me a second to change the name of the dungeon—labeled automatically by the system to 'Renegade HQ.' I glanced over at the orcs, already up to their ears in the ground and quickly sketched in my recent path, skipping Pasha's beloved details like altitude and keeping only what the players needed most.

"Here," I handed the copied map to the priest. "Just stay away from the renegades. I really want to see how the scenario plays out."

"We won't go there without good reason," Qupip assured me. "The debuff from the blight is bad enough."

"Eh, it's too bad there's no good manure heap around here," I heard Bogart say in a voice full of sincere regret. He was in the process of driving sharpened stakes into the bottom of the pit, taking them from his partner.

"Otherwise, I'd be happy to fertilize this a bit..." Bogart went on muttering. "It'd grow and flower better that way."

I looked at him askance with mixed feelings. On the one hand, he was a good person but at the same time—what a nutcase. After all, it's not like he'd invented this in game—he had brought these tricks here from meatspace. There sure were some sinister screws loose in his head—I don't even want to guess exactly what they were all about. As long as he didn't lose the plot out in real life.

"Let's head out!" Dirk ordered and the raiders

saddled their mounts.

"Kiera—make sure to stay out of trouble, okay?" Bogart said in an unexpectedly serious tone as he mounted his shaggy wolf. "Because, who knows...what if we don't make it?"

"Relax, Sasha," I replied. "It's just a game."

"Yeah, sure, a game," he spat. "A gentle, happy, game. You know, Kiera Khan, I'd better stick around. For the sake of peace of mind and propriety. Who knows if one of these psycho fans decides to go to one of your concerts."

"Are you like her husband?" asked Qupip.

"Give me a bit more credit," Bogart replied with dignity. "I'm her impresario!"

"If there is anything I value about you, my green friend," Pops clapped him on the shoulder, "it's your knack for buzzing so pretty. You weren't an English major by any chance? You sure do know a lot of words."

"Nah—what happened was, there was this hefty tome that fell on my head when I was a kid," Bogart dug at the ground with a toe bashfully as the other raiders giggled. "I didn't know how to read back then, but I assume it must have been a dictionary because I've been suffering from all these words in my head ever since that day."

"All right, you poor thing you," Qupip laughed. "Until we meet again."

"Adios, amigo," Bogart replied.

The raiding party moved on to conquer the Hidden Forest, while the green phenomenon and I stayed behind to guard the thorns. To make sure they weren't stolen, Bogart explained.

"By the way, I'm a veritable Monstrichello now," I bragged, sharing my character's properties with Bogart.

Despite all the grumbling about the stupid game mechanics, Bogart was so carried away by the hunt for the players that he himself did not notice how he acquired a thorough knowledge of the mechanics of Barliona. And now, at the sight of my stats, he—as he liked to say—'twisted his face in amazement' and whistled:

"You're a real Hit-Girl…Listen, Bride of Frankenstein, at this rate you'll become the chief baobab in this place. The shamans will be conjuring all around you, making bloody sacrifices. Will you become the head honcho? With your *droit du seigneur* and all?"

I pretended that I was thinking:

"Does the sight of plants excite you so much? Or are you more of a hefty and furry pirq kind of orc? What are pirq females called anyway? 'Pirquettes?'"

"The hussars were a sullen lot and they banged everything that moved. Things that didn't move, they'd kick and if they moved then, they'd bang them on the spot," the orc recited an ancient joke. "The court jester knows what the pirqs call their females.

But we should find out just in case...Should we whip up a bonfire? We're sitting here like two shepherds in a pastoral painting. All we're missing are some sheep and cows..." and, without waiting for an answer, Bogart set off to gather kindling.

"Listen! Maybe that's why the biota corpses don't disappear?" I shared my hunch. "They just dry up and become brushwood? You haven't encountered a wooden skull anywhere, have you?"

"Nah. I was just about to show you something else though, maybe you'll recognize it?"

The orc dumped the collected brushwood on the spot chosen for the fire. Shaking off his hands—an empty gesture in the game because there was no dirt here—Bogart untied his bag and pulled out of it...a ukulele.

"Here you go."

In the huge green paw, the funny little guitar looked like a toy.

"Thanks. Where did you dig it up?" I asked with surprise, looking at the properties of the instrument.

A type Rare, with the standard +25% to casting time and a bonus to earning Attractiveness with NPCs.

"I took it off a corpse. I am an orc, after all," Bogart winked.

"Mmm..." I smiled bloodthirstily and wiped the non-existent blood stain from the ukulele. "I wouldn't have it any other way."

"A girl after my own heart," smiled Bogart, stacking the firewood. "Play something to lighten up the mood."

The eid resumed its place in my satchel and my fingers slid along the ukulele, getting used to the unusual size of the little fretboard. I bet I look pretty funny holding this thing in my gloomy and edgy getup of thorns and veins.

A simple motif cheerfully fluttered through the forest, causing the bald orc to break into a broad grin. He lit the fire and hummed along to the simple cartoon song. I had already observed that both vets for some reason preferred cartoons to movies.

As soon as the flames flared up, Bogart pulled out his battle axe, which he had nicknamed 'Croaker' and galloped off, like an epileptic, imitating the dances of Native Americans in ancient Hollywood Westerns. Although, in his version, it looked like the dancer was suffering a series of electric shocks.

"Listen! This is a rare instrument!"

"Yeah, it belonged to none other than Israel Kamakawiwo'ole himself," nodded the orc without interrupting his frenetic dance. "He used it to record the soundtrack to the old Bourne movie. And so what?"

"I can summon his soul! Want to try? Because otherwise, I've only seen Eid."

"All right!" Bogart immediately sat down beside me. "Commence the ritual."

To my surprise, instead of a clump of fog and a prompt offering me to choose the role of my new companion, I was confronted with a notification warning me that I could be exposed to 'adult content'...Well, I must say, the warning intrigued me more than the summons.

As soon as I confirmed that I had read the notification and was okay with the consequences of my actions, a ghostly fop with a sleek face, a sly grin and an insolent glance appeared before me.

You have summoned the soul of the ukulele (Level 20 Rogue).

"Mmm..." he crooned, looking me over from head to toe. "Well this is something new...I've never been touched by someone like you before..."

I almost choked—I had thought that this kind of thing was impossible in Barliona.

"What, are you accustomed to—big, hairy, man-hands?" The orc asked sympathetically. "You poor darling." He blew a fanfare with his nose for comic effect.

The ukulele's spirit measured him with a contemptuous glance and, it seems, decided simply to ignore him. Instead, he sat boldly down beside me, embraced me around the waist and whispered suggestively:

"I like it so much when you strum my strings..."

"Listen here, you Casanova," Bogart flared up predictably. "I'm about to loop those strings around your scrotum and hang you from that there branch. And then we'll see what tears first: the scrotum, the string, or your vocal cords!"

His voice was so convincing that the spirit of the ukulele immediately removed his hands from my person and slid away a respectful distance.

"Oh," I was even a little miffed. "And I was about to ask you to blow the fire higher so that I could burn a dumb log."

"Nah. He's educated, can't you see?" the orc tossed more brushwood into the fire. "We'll teach him the statutes and make a human out of him. Do you hear, Uke...what's your name anyway?"

"Whatever you want it to be, you big hunk you..." the spirit replied in a different voice: a female one. The ghostly figure rippled and began transforming, turning into an attractive woman in nothing but a necklace of flowers and a tube dress.

"*Hic*," Bogart hiccupped and dropped his jaw. Having mastered his surprise, he asked: "How about just bare-ass naked? Is that too much to ask?"

"Weren't you saying that VR is boring and meatspace is fun?" I burst out laughing, looking at the orc's engrossed expression.

"It's not too much to ask at all," the ghostly babe winked at him. "But first we'd have to step aside..."

"You can cut my tongue out, so long as I can

keep my eyes," I said. "I want to see all of it!"

"I'll hold you to that," Bogart immediately responded. "No, but why not? There is something to see here indeed! She reminds me of one of my stripper friends."

Encouraged, the ukulele spirit winked at the orc and arranged herself in his lap.

"Send me the video, we'll make a clip out of it," I told Bogart, whose eyes were already rolling back into his skull.

He somehow regained control of his face and even tried to use his fingers to unroll his eyes.

"Rather than a clip, use it for a drama," he finally corrected my proposal. "One that'll make Shakespeare jealous..."

"So I should throw her in the fire after all?"

I brought the ukulele up to the fire with a very serious face, observing carefully the transformations on the faces of Bogart and his new girlfriend.

"There's burning jealousy for you," the orc remarked and winked at me. "Kiera Khan, say the word and I'll be faithful to you all my life. And, you metamorph, don't panic," he counseled Ukulele who had frozen in horror, "Auntie Kiera is joking. She doesn't harm the defenseless. Well, if they behave well."

Bogart clapped his hands behind his head and lay back on the sun-warmed earth. With Ukulele still sitting on his lap, the picture turned out to be a vulgar one and I was just about to remark on it when I was interrupted...

You have been stunned for 5 seconds!

A biota rogue appeared out of nowhere and a torrent of system notifications about incoming damage to my materia shades began pouring past my eyes. During the seconds that I was stunned, another rogue took out the ukulele spirit and shanked Bogart who was still in stun too. The orc saved himself at the last instant, somersaulting backwards out of his supine position. As he did so, he managed to quaff a healing potion and then jumped back a good ten meters. The fireball that slammed into Bogart elicited a flurry of polished swearing. Merlin appeared out of nowhere and darted at the mage who had overplayed his hand.

I counted about a dozen attackers and to Bogart's luck, eight of them poured everything they had into me. Geranika's shield creaked and groaned under the colossal dps as I frantically jangled on the ukulele, sending the first impact shade at the rogue. Four seconds and a one-shot. I even noticed the face of a mage contort in surprise, before the next shadow sent him to rest in meatspace. A fireball crit almost wiped out my second materia shade, but Bogart's well-aimed dart punished the insolent, depriving my spell of its next target.

"I got the right one!" I shouted to Bogart, summoning another impact shade into the world.

I have a fairly uniform spell rotation. Practically one-button, not counting the upcoming Shadow Shield recast.

"Ten-four!" barked the orc and focused the priest, whom I had somehow lost track of. Merlin on the other hand had not: Having finished chewing what was left of Bogart's first attacker, the tigress happily sank her fangs into a new victim.

The battle ended in less than a minute. A hectic minute, but still a minute. The penalty from the blighted ground and my buffed damage didn't give the attackers a chance. When all is said and done, Shadow players are a terrible, ugly kind of OP. But whatever. I now had 13 of my 30 biota kills.

"That's that," said Bogart, looking around the battlefield. "Our little ghostly temptress has fallen! We must say something fitting for the occasion..."

He looked around, found the place where he had been at the beginning of the battle and collapsed to his knees raising his hands to heaven.

"Noooooooo!" the orc's howl resounded through the forest.

Startled birds scrambled from the treetops, and Bogart, listening to the echo, grunted with satisfaction and got to his feet.

"I declare this civil funeral service complete," he said, concluding the battle, and wiped off his pants.

"Here Merlin! Ah, good, good kitty..." and, still scratching the tigress behind his ears, he asked: "Look here, you Floral Terminator, you sure did a number on those guys: You had eight wise men pouring all their wisdom into you and you were hardly bothered. Does everyone in your faction get that kind of firepower or did you earn it yourself?"

"Geranika has designated me as his favorite wife," I stuck my tongue out at the orc. "Do you remember how I told you about the defensive spell that he gave me for composing the Hymn to Shadow? Well, its protection is determined by Int and I just dumped all my stat points into Int. Until those murderous fan clubs start equipping gear with +150% to their stats, they won't be able to touch me. Well, and then there's another recent acquisition—the impact shades. I summon a shade from the wrong side of the world and it turns my enemies inside out. It ignore defense, and doesn't give a crap about level difference. Oh and they never miss."

"A straight up Wunderwaffle," Bogart scratched his head first, and then, carefully wiping his hand on his trousers, scratched Merlin. "I would even say, revenge weapons, a villain's dream from movies about special agents and superheroes."

"That's me I guess," I scarfed a foot and bowed to my meager audience. "Okay, I don't think I need to gank anyone for the next twelve hours, so I'm going to run and see if there are any quests from the renegades and then take a break out in meatspace."

"Are you talking about a quest to the kitchen for tea?" the green jerk immediately gibed.

"Are we doomed to such a monotonous existence?"

"Well, we can have some ice cream at that ice cream shop near the tourist tram," Bogart offered, after a moment's thought. "They got these little meat-filled pastries there, so I won't starve either. Better yet, we can wander around the park. Go up to the singing gazebo. Well, if you're in the mood for a walk that is."

"Oh," I said with excitement. "What's that singing gazebo like?"

Bogart looked mournfully at the skies. The heavens responded with a migrating flock of bird-lizards, which were abundant in these parts.

"Where do these barbarians come from anyway?" the orc complained to no one in particular. "Kiera Khan, child of the northern climes, how can you not know about the singing gazebo of the glorious city of Pyatigorsk, eh? It's decided: We will visit the singing gazebo. As they say, it is better to hear it once than listen to others talk about a hundred times."

* * *

THE 'SINGING GAZEBO' turned out to be an antique building at the summit of the highest of the hills at the base of Mount Mashuk.

The dome, supported by seven columns and crowned with a weathervane, as Pasha and Sasha explained to me during our ascent, was actually called an 'Aeolian harp'—in honor of the ancient keeper of the winds in the *Odyssey*, and was built more than two centuries ago. It was the citizens themselves that had christened it the 'singing gazebo,' due to the harp installed inside: strings that were connected to the weathervane and which ran from the roof to the floor, changing direction and sound as the wind changed. The view of the city from here caused a whole barrage of emotions, warmed by the string symphony of nature itself—a simple, and simultaneously complex, majestic melody, living its own life, beyond the touch of man.

Naturally, this wonder could not leave any intelligent creature indifferent. Therefore, the site was constantly crowded—from couples who came for the romance of the place to artists and sculptors earning their money from the streams of tourists.

Perhaps, our trio did not attract much attention thanks to this. Only some elderly lady looked at Pasha with puzzlement and a young, patriotic artist, who looked like a cartoon lion, tried to give us a newly-painted landscape. Quite a good one, by the way.

"This is it—Kiera Khan—the singing gazebo," Sasha majestically presented me to the local landmark. I bet Michelangelo used the same tone when he presented the Sistine Chapel to Pope Julius II.

"Well and all those," he nodded at the onlookers milling around, "are details of the landscape."

"It's astounding…" I whispered, examining the instrument from different angles. "I wonder if you cobble something like this together in Barliona, whether the wind will cause the strings to sound?"

"That's a question for the programmers," Pasha immediately recused himself from making any predictions.

"Yeah," Sasha agreed with his friend. "You know yourself it all depends on the little men in their closets pushing their magic buttons. The etherlords of the cyber, in a manner of speaking."

Pasha rolled up to the edge of the platform and stuck his face into the wind.

"Once upon a time, a young lieutenant named Mikhail Lermontov stood in the same spot where Pasha sits right now," Sasha intoned in the voice of a tour guide. "And took potshots at anyone who dared criticizes his poetry: Pushkin, Salieri and that, uh, Aesop fellow."

"Uh-huh," I nodded with an intelligent look. "And Homer…Simpson. I'm not as dumb as I seem, Snegov."

"Ah don't piss on my taking-the-piss-parade," he said indignantly. "Instead of backing me up with an account of Lermontov's tragic affair with Anna

Karenina, must you break my wings just as I am set to soar? Right at the root—at the very ass. Can you imagine my suffering?"

"You there, sufferer, did you bring the water?" Pasha spoke up.

Sasha sighed, and hollered: "Sir, yes, sir, Master Yoda sir!"

Like a crazed boar he tore past some tourists, causing them to start.

"In actual fact, Mr. Lermontov was a...peculiar individual," Sasha continued, returning. "Paradoxical, you could say. And, in a word, this place really was an observation post during that war. However, by the time Lieutenant Lermontov arrived for his service, the gazebo had been here several years already."

"The only people I know who aren't paradoxical are all assholes," I shrugged. "But at school, I remember, they told me that a great poet was exiled to these parts during wartime."

Pasha waved his hand, seeing someone from his acquaintances, and stepped away to say hello.

"Well, I think the epithet 'great' is arguable," Sasha disagreed, following his friend with a glance. "If you ask me, his verse is too sugary and pretentious. But the fact that his was a desperate kind of courage, that's without dispute. A daredevil if there ever was one. And a mouth fouler than mine, for which he paid dearly in the end."

I looked out over the stone railing: The hillside

was not particularly high, but still made me nervous.

"Come on, tell me more," I said, sitting down on one of the benches. "In school, they mostly focused on unrequited love, persecution by the powers that were and similar snot."

"Ugh, they do love their snot," Sasha crumpled his nose. "It's like with Vertinsky: All they talk about is how he was a great singer and artist of the Silver Age, blah, blah, blah—but try and find a single mention of the time he was saving lives on a hospital train during World War I. And Mr. Lermontov is no different—a classical officer of that era. A poet, an artist, and a master of slicing you face open with the saber. To his misfortune, he got too deep into politics, but that's a minor foible, as they say. Only the saints are spared those. Young Mikhail was feared and respected, even though he wasn't here long, less than a year. Courage sacks cities, as they say. And if it weren't for his cutting tongue, he could've made general or even field marshal."

"Speaking of cutting tongues," I remembered, "I have an order for another insult that will slip through the profanity filter. If only I had a larger client base—I would grow nice and rich of people's vim and spite."

"I don't understand," Sasha said, surprised. "What's the problem with using one's own unprintables?"

"Barliona has an abuse filter that includes a number of offensive words," I explained. "If a player doesn't want to encounter any cursing, he can just turn it on. Can you imagine how many people want to bypass it and tell their fellow man how they really feel about him? So my side gig is composing phrases that will pass the censor."

"Well, it couldn't take much work," snorted Sasha. "The good thing about any language is the wealth of options it offers. You can come up with such turns of phrase that no filter will keep up—even if you force a hundred programmers to update it day and night. Zoology alone can supply enough lampoons for generations to come, and there are other subject areas to explore after all. Like grammar, for instance. To wit: 'I'm about to conjugate all your roots and stick some choice suffixes and inflections so far up your coda that you'll spend the rest of your life speaking in the subjunctive.'"

"And what if we whip up something like that in game?" Pasha's voice suddenly boomed right into my ear.

I almost jumped over the railing from the shock, taking the bench with me.

"Sorry, I didn't mean to startle you," the pilot apologized.

I took a breath and mentally swore at the unknown engineers who had invented a silent electric wheelchair. Although what did that have to do with anything? I'm the one who'd gotten distracted.

"Whip what up?" I asked, puzzled. "An

advertisement that says: 'I'll let your haters have it so smoothly even the content filter won't notice? Find us in the Blighted Forest, third mob to the left?"

"Something like that," Pasha nodded.

On my other side, Sasha was all ears. I swear to FSM—he couldn't care less about making money as long as he got a chance to cause some grief.

"You've seen it yourself. The morally-upstanding, paying public will happily fall for any crap as long as it's original and useful," the pilot went on developing his idea. "So why don't we supplement our cartography enterprise by baking like fortune cookies but instead of a fortune they'll contain a choice phrase that'll slip through the filter unnoticed. Or something like that at any rate."

"Hah! There's an idea! So what can we cook up, without serious investment? Alchemy is not it. Jewelcrafting...too expensive. But cooking...Cooking!" I exclaimed. "We can bake some pies and muffins with insults on them. If you want, you can hurl it at someone's face, or if you like, you can send it by mail. We could engrave our best bits on weapons too."

"Too easy to rip off," Sasha said with a sigh. "And the trick here is the idea."

"While they're ripping it off, we'll come up with something new! And we can try and organize the entire venture around authorial recipes...or what are those scrolls called? I read that when creating an original item, you have to go through the registration procedure, which creates a recipe for you."

"Oh, there is an in-game patent office," Pasha said approvingly. "That's good to know. As the saying goes: One head is good, two is better, and three make it easier to think."

Sasha grimaced, his eyes narrowed, and he squeaked:

"You won't regret bringing old sea dog Billy Bones with you, you guys!"

* * *

THE ONLY PLACE we could use as a workshop was the training ground that Eben had sent Chip and me to. Most of it was covered with filth, but the inventory remained in place and looked undamaged.

"I will lead the parade," Chip proclaimed. "My ingenuity stat is high as hell and I've got a good smattering of professions I've picked up along the way—from drawing to engraving. They're not very high-level, but the hell with it. They'll do for a start."

"Sounds good," I nodded. "What are we going to craft?"

"I'm going to make some grub," Chip snapped his fingers in anticipation of the work ahead of him. He really was a Level 80 Glutton. With his enthusiasm, he'd be better off cooking than flying a chopper.

"Do it, Michelangelo," Bogart nodded

majestically. "I will keep things simple and tinker with my beloved toys…"

"You maniac," Chip said.

The orc responded by sticking his tongue out at him and went over to the machine. The work got underway. The pirq conjured over the fire like a wizard at work: measuring, weighing, mixing powders and substances burbling in pots. To my ear— uninitiated in the art of grub-o-mancy—even his muttering sounded like the recitation of spells.

Bogart meanwhile busied himself with planning, sawing and hammering together pieces of lumber into eerie contraptions that would have been fitting props for horror films.

"Kiera, hey, Kiera," he called to me, examining his newest creation—a ball of stakes. "Do you have friends with spells?"

"There is this one guy. Why?"

"I was just thinking…" He carved the inscription '*I, even I, am he who blots out your transgressions,*' into the stake and giggled. "Do you think you could help me put together something truly smashing? For example, Johnny falls into a pit and then whoosh— *immolated!* Could we me make something like that together?"

"I think 'immolated' might be out of my league," I sighed. "I just don't have that Wrath-of-the-Almighty edge to me. But we can experiment with my Shadow spells. They are pretty deadly."

"And you're just sitting there calmly?" The orc even sounded indignant. "I'm over here working up a sweat like a salt-of-the-earth proletarian, laboring for our common bright future—and she's just sitting there. Pasha, do you happen to know if biota are at times cats? Like maybe they can't help because they have paws instead of opposable thumbs? Although it's strange: You have paws but you're giving it all you got...Maybe you're not a cat?"

"Whatever it is, you talk too much," the pirq called from the fire. "You should use your tongue for good. Then we wouldn't need power-plants or other sources of energy."

"What's true is true," Bogart the Base stuck his knuckles into his hips. "I ams what I ams."

Meanwhile, I opened the manual to the cartography section. I still had never tried to master the creation of scrolls or songbooks. The songbooks that I received as a result of composing didn't count— the system had generated them automatically. But the process turned out to be fairly simple. Take a blank sheet from the cartographer's set, select the desired spell and start mapping. The only problem was that, instead of drawing a map, my hand produced mysterious symbols and runes, while my mana dipped twice as much as it should have for casting this spell.

You have created a scroll of Shadow

Transform Level 22.

"Not a bad outcome at all," I squinted, looking at the damage in the properties of the scroll, and then handed it to Bogart. "My spell's exact damage has been transferred to this scroll. It's fair to assume that the scroll will ignore level difference like the spell does too."

"Hell yeah," the orc's voice sounded beside my ear.

With his pleased mug, Bogart looked like a cat who'd just been let loose in a supermarket's poultry section. A special trait called Ingenuity allowed him to use a variety of skills—from carpentry to enchantment—to fashion elaborate traps. He used everything he could think of in the process: weapons dropped by monsters, logs, stones, nails, jewelry wire, scrolls with spells...Snegov knew how to turn any pile of random junk into devices of slaughter.

"Just what the doctor ordered," Bogart continued. "Custom made for someone like me! Straight slaughter in terms of power, and a level that's low enough for me to use it without having to run and ask my friend to help me. Especially since it's damn near impossible to run around here. Kiera Khan, you're a genius! I'd kiss you right here and now but I am already in my pajamas."

"First try to use the scroll. Who knows—maybe shadow spells don't work for non-Shadow players."

Bogart immediately snatched the scroll from my hands and darted over to his worktable like green lightning. A couple of minutes later he was already in full swing in a corner that had been given the dramatic title 'QC Department.' Having cobbled together something that resembled a rickety cobweb, he attached the scroll to it and ran off to find a target dummy.

"Kiera, let's get out of harm's way," Chip suggested, cautiously observing the orc's revelry. "He's dangerous to be around when he gets like this in meatspace—here, I wouldn't put it past him to slap together some nuclear warhead and then happily push the button. For the sake of shits and giggles."

At that moment, the object of discussion himself rushed past us with a joyful howl, and, yelling, "Fire in the hole!" hurled his contraption at the canvas dummy.

The device popped. A shade flashed and the mannequin burst into a cloud of rags and straw.

"I'll be a monkey's uncle," said Bogart and turned to us with a beaming face: "Did you see that?"

The orc was practically jumping for joy.

"All right, Kiera, start scribing. I'll make a whimsical little music box in the meantime."

He rushed to his workbench, which had been hastily assembled from some boards, and held up an eerie construction: A wooden frame, with two rollers of spikes inside of it.

"What the hell is..." I did not finish the question, struck dumb by the idea that came to me.

A musical...

Hmm... Why that's an idea. I can create musical spells. I can create songbooks. Could I also create a scroll with a spell that would also double as a songbook?

I tuned out Bogart, who was babbling as he worked, sat down and began to think, looking at my cartographer's set. How can I make a songbook instead of a scroll? How do you even create a songbook?

I dragged the Vengeful Flame spell I had created to the quick access panel and then cast it onto the blank sheet from the cartographer's set.

Would you like to create a scroll or a songbook?

Hmm. I didn't get the same prompt for Shadow Transform. Let it be a songbook.

My hand seemed to draw a sheet of music by itself and began to write down the song I composed.

You have created a songbook with the Vengeful Flame spell.

This songbook cannot be transferred to another player.

Yeah, we've been here before. A songbook is way to teach NPCs your tunes. But what if I make a scroll out of it now?

To create this scroll, additional resources are required.
Speak to the cartography instructor.

Well that's unexpected.

Okay, I think I get the gist. When inscribing a scroll with a spell, the magic incantations are incomprehensible, but when inscribing a songbook, good old notes still work fine. And if you combine the two?

I created a new scroll of Shadow Transform, turned it over and manually inscribed a musical staff onto it.

If manual charting works for maps, why shouldn't it work for a songbook? To begin with, I recorded a short musical phrase from Bach's famous requiem.

You must record a performance of the musical fragment.

I stared dumbly at the button labeled 'start recording' that had appeared, then picked up my eid, activated the recording and played the required passage in the bass clef.

The recording is complete. The performance corresponds to the notes. You have created a 'Musical Scroll of Shadow Transform (Level 22).'

New recipe created: 'Musical Scroll of Shadow Transform.'

"Saaasha," I called to the orc. "Look what I have for you!"

"What?" he jumped up over instantly. "Tell me!"

Instead of answering, I selected one of the training dummies as a target and activated the scroll. An impact shade went flying into the mannequin to the accompaniment of Bach's immortal music.

"Cool!" the orc rejoiced. "We need to figure out where we can stick it to make some fun happen. Maybe on a 'snake bite?'"

The orc fell into deep thought until Chip, whom we had forgotten about in our experiments, spoke up:

"Here's what I've cooked up," he boomed, showing us a cake made in the form of an ancient castle.

Bogart the Base whistled admiringly, while I merely asked, stunned:

"How high is your culinary skill?"

"Eh, over fifty now," Chip admitted. "Grinding without you was boring, and I can eat whatever I like in here without any restrictions."

He joyfully snapped at me with his powerful

jaw—large enough to snap the femur of medium size mammoth.

"Now we need an inscription that will get the people to buy it and send it to their enemies," Bogart grinned merrily. "Oh. Do you remember Sapkowski? Zoltan the dwarf with the inscription on his sword?"

"*'Death to the whoresons?'*" I recalled. "That's more fitting for weapons. And who knows whether the filter will let it slide. We need something about the razing of a castle or the ruin of a guild. We're trying to be personal here."

"*'Burn ye with the blue flame?'*" Bogart immediately suggested but encountered Chip's objection:

"This isn't a rum cake that you set alight! No, we need something...more epic. Something that invokes ruin and utter destruction."

"*Come tomorrow, the worms shall turn you into the shit you've always been?*"

"It's insulting, sure, but it won't get through the filter," I objected.

"*May all who you love transform to fetid cloaca?*"

"It's got a ring to it, but what's it got to do with a castle? What about...?" I walked around the castle-cake and proclaimed: "*'Now you can have your castle, and eat it too!'* It'll make a good double entendre if one guild is giving it to another."

"That's right!" Chip approached his masterpiece and began to administer the final touch with a piping bag. When he had finished, he stepped aside, giving us the opportunity to admire the inscription made of frosting.

"You're a mean one, Mr. Chip," Bogart summarized. "A real psycho chef from a horror flick. A half hour of your fussing will bring your customers a week's worth of despair. I want to be as good as you too."

"What's true is true," the pirq puffed up proudly. "By the way, I got a new recipe and without any registration process. Earlier it was a 'Holiday Cake,' but now it's a 'Funeral Cake.' And its list of buffs has changed too."

"I suppose variations on basic recipes don't require additional registration," Bogart reached the logical conclusion.

In the meantime, I opened my questlog and regarded my list of incomplete quests sullenly.

"Pasha, how's the seed quest going?"

"Why my head is full of holes!" Chip knocked on his forehead and reached into his bag. "I only have one so far. Those misers pile on a hell-full of quests for each one. Tomorrow, when I get back from the hospital, I'll come up with the second seed."

As soon as the fairly large seed, the size of a baseball, fell into my hand, a quest update popped up:

Quest updated: *Creating a Cicerone. Step 2.*

Read Cypro's Journal.

Damn it...I still had two days' cooldown on my soul summoning spell. How am I supposed to read the journal without Salamander's help?

"Thank you, Pasha."

I tossed the currently useless seed into my backpack and looked sadly at Geranika's kill count. It was where it had been and I only had a little more than three days to complete the quest. I wish more of Oto's hapless friends would come let me part them with their existences. I'd rather avoid fragging random players.

"All right, I'm glad you two are doing so well, but the Sith Lords don't take disciples just like that," I announced, getting ready to head out. "I'm going to go kill some young Padawans to prove my loyalty to the dark side. I still need a hell-full of frags, as you put it. I need to seize the moment, while we still have such a surplus in gear and lethal force. The big boys will come with the embassy and make a salad out of me."

"You hear that, Pasha?" Bogart started. "Our little sundew is growing up! She'll be a triffid before we know it!"

"Yup. Looks like progress," Chip nodded.

"Listen here, you dark apprentice," the orc shook the parchment in front of me. "How about postponing the genocide of the Jedi and doing a little to help your friends add to the heap of skulls at the foot of the throne of skulls?"

I sighed dramatically and picked up my cartographer's kit:

"What shall I play next?"

CHAPTER TEN

WHAT CAN YOU DO WHEN THERE ARE DOZENS OF ENRAGED PLAYERS from a powerful guild bent on hunting you down? Advertise your whereabouts as loudly as possible! I cast my Shadow Shield, and insolently, basking in my superiority, went straight to the border of the blighted ground. The players were leveling up somewhere nearby. And very soon they would have a new target.

The sound of an electric guitar—entirely out of place in this fantasy world—roared throughout the forest, kindly tipping off anyone who wished to find the Bard of Shadow.

The tempo gradually increased, the distortion grew stiffer and more aggressive, and anger waxed in the vocal part. A Forest Sentry appeared ponderously from among the trees and stopped as per custom at the border with the blight, incapable of overcoming the alien magic.

Not long thereafter, the curious faces of player biota appeared from behind the trees and yet not a single one bore a name familiar to me. Despite the nature of the quest, I did not want to be the one to attack first, so I continued to sing.

The nearby players gathered around for my impromptu concert and by the end of the song there were already a dozen of them. A few even started dancing, enjoying the unexpected entertainment. Then one particular clown named Tusken Radish took out his bow and began to make a porcupine out of me. Despite the ten levels that he had over me, Radish couldn't dish shit. Hardly had his arrow scratched my shield, when I, without interrupting my performance, one-shotted him with an impact shade.

Quest updated: *Way of the Apprentice*. Step 1.

14 of 30 biota killed.

This made an impression on my audience, though everyone reacted in their own way. Several immediately activated all the defensive spells and camouflage available to them, while others cheerfully whistled, hooted and clapped their hands.

There were no further would-be assailants and only the music lovers remained. It turned out that I could level up my Fame stat with players too. Thus, I had raised this stat to 32 when the PKers finally showed up.

"I see dead people..." someone whispered into my ear and the system notified me that I had been stunned. Immediately about two dozen players popped out of camo and fell upon me all at the same time.

I just grinned to myself. In five seconds I will send these jerks back to their grandmas' basements. But after the five seconds expired, a hunter shot an arrow at me, stunning me for another five seconds— and then again and again. The well-coordinated team of players just did not let me out of their control, negating my advantages of equipment and new spells.

It took them just under three minutes to kill me, without allowing me to shoot off a single shade. All I could to do was be angry at myself and my epic naïveté.

Consolation came from an unexpected source.

Like most people, I did not read the standard system messages, and just kept swiping them aside in irritation. Blah, blah, blah, you may reenter the game in 12 hours. Always the same.

But not this time. I found myself looking at two virtual buttons: "Yes" and "No." A bit stunned, I read the message:

You have died. You may continue playing in the Gray Lands. Do you wish to move to this location?

So that's the other way that a bard can enter the world of the dead! I could simply die!

My irritation gave way to curiosity. Yes, I wish to move to the new location.

The world faded, losing its colors, smells and sounds. My perspective skewed, the bright sunlight gave way the diffuse and lifeless glow of the dead sky. I was back in the Gray Lands.

Your time in the Gray Lands after dying in-game cannot exceed four hours. After this time period, you will be disconnected from the game for the standard time.

"You free citizens sure are a curious bunch," said Eid's voice.

The instrument's soul stood next to me in the same guise he had taken when I assigned him the role of tank.

"To visit the Gray Lands, Cypro had to make his way through the Intermundis. All you have to do is die in Barliona and wander around here until your revival."

"What can I say? I guess instead of a cereal killer, I'll have to live as a cereal suicide," I bowed theatrically. "Why haven't you shed your guise like last time?"

"You assigned my permanent appearance in Barliona and now I will shed it only in the Intermundis and only temporarily."

I nodded silently, taking note of the information,

sat down on the dusty earth of the world of the dead and took Cypro's journal out of my satchel. Since I've managed to 'survive' death, I had better keep working on my quest chain.

Vitus—vitality—life energy—flows throughout Barliona. In land and water, in plants and animals, in mortals and even in gods. I do not understand this subject deeply, but I have learned one thing—vitus is not homogeneous, it is different in properties and structure. And not all vitus is suitable for living beings. Plants and we, the biota, are nourished by the vitus of water and earth. Animals and sentients are nourished by the vitus of plants, other animals and other sentients. I do not have an understanding of what kind of vitus nourishes the gods, but I am certain that there is one. Sometimes it seems to me that memory and the feelings of sentients, capable of sustaining souls in the Gray Lands, are also a special kind of vitus. Someday I hope to penetrate the arcane knowledge of the true order of the world. But for now, I must impart something else on you.

Vitars are special plants related to the Tree itself. The vital force concealed in the vitar is not capable of accepting the soul of sentients, but under a number of conditions it can accommodate the souls of beasts. Summon the chosen soul into the vitar seed and sow the seed in the Land of the Hidden Forest. To bind the soul of the cicerone to yourself, nourish the seed with the sap flowing in your body. The power of your vitus will bind you with an unseen and inviolable thread.

But this is not enough. The cicerone is by nature a beast, and in you there is no animal essence. To help the vitar seed sustain an alien animal soul, it will require animal blood. You can ask for some blood from one of our pirq brethren, or representatives of other intelligent races who have a similar vitus. Do not dare use the blood of zombies or other undead! And remember that it is your vitus that the cicerone must know first.

Quest updated: *Creating a Cicerone. Step 2.* Summon the animal's soul to the vitar seed. Reward: Next quest in the chain.

I put away the journal, took the ghostly egg in my left hand, and the vitar seed in the other. I wonder whether uniting the two here and now will work...There are no restrictions in the quest description, but I realized that being in the Gray Lands was not a normal thing for the Tenth.

"Eid, did you see how Cypro created his guide?"

"No, Lorelei. At the time of my creation, the Tenth already had his cicerone."

"Do you know anything about the cicerone's creation or properties?"

"Alas, I do not know much about cicerones. They belong to two worlds at once and help the living find what they want in the world of the dead. The stronger and more experienced the cicerone, the more accurately it understands the purpose of the search. Some cicerones have special, sometimes unique properties."

"What determines the strength and experience of the cicerone?" I inquired.

"The cicerones are taught by special instructors," Eid explained. "They can be found both in Barliona and in the Gray Lands. Most often they are shamans and necromancers, but sometimes the most incredible creatures became mentors."

"And how can I find such a mentor?" I inquired.

"I'm afraid I cannot help you with this," Eid said apologetically.

"But I can," said an old, gravelly voice.

I shuddered and almost dropped the ghostly egg. And as I gawked around for the speaker, an insane question flashed through my mind: Can a phantom object break from falling?

"Do not be afraid, child," the stranger said again, and I finally noticed a hunched ash-gray silhouette, blended with the dusty gray of the environment.

Eid stepped silently between me and the stranger, and I had to crane my neck to get a look at him. The speaker wasn't merely old—he was ancient. The years had furrowed his face with folds and wrinkles. His bent back prevented me from estimating his height. Gaunt, knotty fingers gripped a staff whose shape I could not determine. It was fluid and changeable like the souls of the legendary objects I had seen earlier. The soul's name and level were hidden.

I replaced the vitar seed and egg in my satchel, got up and mechanically shook myself off. The omnipresent dust in this place made me feel dirty.

"Who are you?" I asked, stepping up abreast of Eid.

I did not feel any anxiety. Past experience suggested that the souls of the dead could do me no harm.

"My name is Nathan," the stranger introduced himself in the same old voice. "I'm one of those instructors your companion was talking about. Or rather, I was one of them when I was alive," he corrected himself.

"I assume you just happened to be here by sheer chance?" I proposed skeptically.

An unpleasant coughing laughter escaped the old man's throat.

"It would be a truly amazing coincidence," he answered, laughing. "No, I came here with a particular purpose. I sensed a future cicerone here and decided to offer my services for his training."

I paused to think. On the one hand, it is suspicious that an instructor suddenly shows up on a silver platter. On the other hand, maybe this is just like a tutorial to introduce me to guides? Maybe the game manual doesn't have an entry on this topic.

"I have a counter question. How can I train a cicerone that has not been created yet?"

"You cannot train it," Nathan agreed. "But I can augment the soul of your cicerone with an additional skill."

It sounded as interesting as it was suspicious.

"What kind of skill? What will I owe you for this service?"

The old man chewed his wrinkled lips and looked at me with faded, almost white eyes.

"An additional search ability. For this you must complete a task for me in the world of the living."

I looked at Eid inquisitively. The helmet with its lowered visor kept me from knowing how the spirit felt about this, but his voice sounded thoughtful:

"This is what the instructors do, Lorelei. They teach the cicerones to be better at searching."

"What kind of task do you need completed, Nathan?" I asked the spirit.

I expected anything: from vengeance against an old enemy to bringing the old man's soul back to Barliona, but Nathan surprised me.

"I need a family heirloom delivered to my descendant."

The old man laughed sadly and turned away, hiding his face from me.

"Once upon a time, I was an arrogant fool, concerned with the greatness of my family and kin. I wanted to give my daughter Maedzhan to a suitable suitor as if...as if she were some mare to be bred. She opposed me and fled with her beloved—a lowly beggar."

There was no anger in his words, only an immense weariness.

"Back then I deemed her flight a betrayal. I renounced my own daughter, calling her the shame of my family."

The old man was silent for a while and then sadly concluded his story:

"Only in very old age did I realize how wrong I was...I tried to make amends, to find her, but I no longer had the time. Death found me in the middle of my journey, preventing me from finishing what I had started. I wished to give Maedzhan the family ring that my father had given me. Now, probably, many years have passed. Maybe even centuries. But the fact that I have not passed on to Erebus yet, gives me hope that my family continues to exist. Maedzhan and her descendants remember me, despite the fact that it was I who betrayed them."

Quest available: *Family Relic*.

Description: Find the family ring at the site of Nathan's demise and deliver it to his descendant. Quest type: Unique chain. Reward for completion: Unlocks bonus skill for your cicerone. Penalty for failing/refusing the quest: None.

I read the quest description again and again, but I could see no cons to accepting. No penalties, no restrictions on time, and my guide would receive a bonus skill.

"I shall finish what you started," I promised Nathan, accepting the quest.

A smile crept across the ancient face.

"Let me mark my last route on your map. You will have to find the exact place of my death on your own. As well as locate Maedzhan and her descendants."

I unfolded the map and the ghost tapped his finger on an unexplored area somewhere in the Free Lands. A quest marker appeared on the map. Yeah...Finding a single ring in such a vast expanse will not be easy.

"How can I find the place of your death?" I asked in an attempt to narrow the search. "Do you remember any landmarks?"

The old man laughed hoarsely—a cold and cruel kind of mirth.

"Believe me, you will recognize the place. During my lifetime, I was not only a heartless fool but also a very skilled necromancer. Though I fell in my last battle, I managed to take all my assailants with me. I doubt that anything has grown there even if a thousand years have passed..."

Having finished laughing, he went on in his earlier tone:

"But you are right—finding the ring will not be easy...Perhaps I can offer you an advance, bard. The bonus skill I promised will be available to your cicerone from birth, though until you fulfill your promise, you will not be able to control it. From time to time, the cicerone himself will use the promised property, but not at your command. At least, this will help you in your search for the ring."

It sounded interesting. A bonus skill with a random chance of being triggered is better than no bonus skill, right? And necromancers should be well-versed in both pets and the interactions with the world of the dead.

"What do I need to do to get this advance?"

"Allow me touch the egg," the old man said. I hesitated, but then complied with his request.

The bony fingers reached for the ghostly egg and for a moment it was enveloped in purple light.

Item modified: 'Ghostly Egg' has acquired a new passive function ('detect cursed item').

"Heed an old man, bard," said Nathan. "Do not waste a single precious moment of life. Each one is irreplaceable."

As if in reply to his words, the capsule's warning icon began to blink in my interface. I waved goodbye to the spirit of the old necromancer and exited the game. The system reminded me that I had twelve hours before I could reenter the game.

"Kiera, you all right?" I heard Pasha's worried voice.

I peered cautiously out of my capsule. The pilot stood in the doorway, with his back turned politely to me.

"Everything's fine. Why?"

"We tried to contact you on the amulet," Pasha explained. "But you didn't answer. So I popped out and came here, and you were still in the capsule. So I got worried..."

"Eh. I got ganked. But it turned out that I can travel to the Gray Lands now after death. Wait outside. I have to get dressed."

"As you wish, Your Majesty," the pilot stood at attention. "Shall I order the chambermaids in, or will you continue to cleave to the vulgar etiquette of the hoi polloi and don your own dress?"

"Wha...? We have chambermaids?" I gaped, still not daring to leave my capsule.

"Well, there's Sarge. And Sarge has eight paws," Pasha reported with bravado. "That's worth at least three chambermaids. Do you wish me to summon him?"

"An upstanding bard does not treat with the descendants of the tarantulas!" I replied proudly. "Close the door and call Snegov. We have time to take a walk."

* * *

THE NEXT MORNING Pasha had to go to the hospital:
The doctors needed to run tests on his regenerators
and eye implant. The pilot explained that unlike with
other tissues, it was difficult to select and install an
artificial eyeball. The prosthesis had to be combined
with the implant, performing a number of functions.
What these were, however, he did not explain, and I
didn't want to pry knowing how little Pasha liked to
discuss his recovery.

At his request, Sasha and I were allowed to
accompany the pilot to a hospital in the neighboring
city of Kislovodsk. The pilot justified our presence by
the fact that after the inspection he wanted to take a
stroll through the city park, since the opportunity had
presented itself, and he would need someone to escort
him. The doctor in charge of Pasha's rehabilitation
gibed about the nobility and their servants, but he
still assented to our presence.

We were not allowed into the hospital itself
though. Seeing Sasha, the nurse on duty, turned pale
and aghast and threatened to call in orderlies, a
SWAT team and orbital lasers in that order, if (and I
quote) "that long-nosed log even thinks of setting foot
in my facility." Sasha immediately affected an
expression of pure integrity and innocence, took me
by the elbow and dragged me off with him to stroll
around the hospital's campus park.

"Am I to understand that you have been in this hospital before?" I asked a question that I already knew the answer to.

"Yes, there was a time," Sasha did not deny the obvious. "Who knew they were so spiteful here? No privacy to hear of in this place. And then these medical students reproach our boys for drilling too much. Meanwhile, they may as well hoist the Prussian flag in this panopticon. Oh, look, an empty bench..."

The view from the bench was a beautiful one: The hospital was located on a hill by the river, and it was possible to look out over the city's entire tourist area. Sasha reached into his pocket, took out a packet of sunflower seeds and handed it to me.

"The racketeers will show up any second now," he explained in response to my perplexed look. As if hearing him, a well-fed squirrel scurried down the tree and absolutely fearlessly clambered up onto our bench.

"Insolent piece of fluff," Sasha remarked about the rodent. "You're missing a fox in your life...Give the raider his share, Kiera Khan."

"I've never seen a feral animal act so comfortably around people," I said, trying to open the package without frightening the squirrel with my rustling. "Well, with the exception of Beast when he's lit. He gets terribly sociable when he drinks. And I do mean *terribly* sociable."

Contrary to my reservations, the squirrel jumped to my knees in a businesslike manner and thrust its muzzle into the barely open bag in the most boorish way. And not in vain—after hearing the rustling, another fluffy lover of handouts hurried to us along the trunk of the nearest tree.

"Better put the package on the ground," advised Sasha, watching as a couple more tailed raiders closed in on us along the branches.

In the meantime, the second squirrel tried to shove the first one from the grub and a brawl of rodents broke out over my knees. Sasha silently pushed them off to the ground, but they paid this bit of rudeness no attention, completely absorbed in their quarrel.

"It's too bad I didn't bring any peppers," Snegov complained.

I placed the package on the bench, further from myself: the hell with them, the lovely forest critters. They'd happily trample me to death if it were up to them.

"What are the peppers for?"

"I give it to them as a special treat whenever they step too out of line," Sasha explained. "There's this one brand called 'Fire & Flames': a small, red, sinister, little pepper. First you offer some seeds to the horde, then you watch the Hollywood brawl that breaks out, and finally the victor receives a whole handful of peppers for his own personal enjoyment..."

Sasha glanced at his watch, winced, took a flat flask from his pocket and took a few sips from it.

"Swill..." he said, putting the flask away.

"Polyjuice potion?" I asked, admiring the squirrel wrestling bout. "Do you really work for He-Who-Must-Not-Be-Named?"

"Nah—this is more of a Little Vanya scenario. Although, he was forbidden from drinking so he wouldn't become a goat, while I'm the opposite: I have to keep drinking until I turn into a goat," Sasha smirked. "Damn, I forgot my slingshot...And as luck would have it, there goes, the hospital's chief shrink."

He pointed at a well-fed military man, hurrying off somewhere along the nearby path.

"I'm afraid to imagine why it is when you see a doctor, you remember your slingshot."

"A shrink," Sasha reiterated, "not a doctor. He's scared of mice too..."

The expression on his face as he said this was both pensive and a little frightening. If only he could use all his energy for a good cause...That's right!

"Listen," I turned to Sasha, almost jumping from impatience. "Do you want to help me gank about three dozen jerks in Barliona?"

"Sure thing," Sasha agreed without hesitation. "As long as they're not furries. I like furries, there's something innocent about them."

"Nah. I mean Oto and his ragged band."

"Oh, my sweet, bloodthirsty darling," Sasha said

with emotion. And then added dramatically: "I knew I sensed a kindred spirit in you!"

The solemnity of the moment was spoiled by a squirrel scrambling onto Sasha's shoulder and thrusting a curious nose into his ear. Sasha cursed, and with the words, "but this squirrel on my shoulder is quite untimely," drove the rodent to the ground.

"Are they too much for you to handle on your own?" Sasha inquired, compensating the squirrel with sunflower seeds. "I thought you could handle a mob or two in your new form. What do you need me for?"

"Well, it turned out that even an imba can be rolled by teamwork," I confessed and related to Sasha the circumstances of my recent, shameful defeat.

"I still need a lot of frags," I concluded.

Sasha thought for a bit and then asked more himself than me:

"There's a forest all around there—a real thicket—right? Yeah...Nothing complicated. I'll set up a couple 'music boxes,' and a few other trifles. They'll have fun, I promise."

"The thing is, I have to be the one to kill them, not your toys," I reminded him and as I did so a very unpleasant smile broke on his face.

"Why you will, you will..." Sasha was obviously already in the woods, setting up his 'tricks.' "I'll make them 'less than lethal.' And you'll just land the coup de grace. A prick from the old misericorde. With the author's music as accompaniment. At the same time, we'll test out our invention."

"You do understand that they will come after you for this?" I asked Sasha.

"That's like asking a porcupine if he's scared of a bare ass," he snorted contemptuously. "Want some ice cream?" he abruptly changed the subject, spotting a white van that drove up to the square.

"Who doesn't want some ice cream?" I asked, a little surprised. "Get me a caramel cone."

Sasha perked up and headed for the truck, followed by the squirrel's thoughtful gaze. The fluffy racketeers were clearly reckoning how much of a cut to take from the second course.

"It's bupkis for you," I threatened the insolent creatures with a fist, stuck my earphones into my ears and turned on the player. Edilberto had shared the newest album of his beloved band and was now haranguing me for my judgment of 'this masterpiece.'

A young guy in hospital scrubs took a seat beside me.

"What are you listening to?" he asked loud enough for me to hear him over the roar in my headphones. It was evident from the nurse's debonair appearance that the purpose of striking up a conversation wasn't to expand his musical knowledge.

Instead of answering, I pulled out one earpiece and held it out to him. But as soon as he inserted the earpiece, the satisfied smile vanished from his face. For a few seconds he looked at me in silence, then without a word, he handed the earpiece back to me and left. I guess he didn't share my musical tastes. Well, to each his own.

"Weakling," Sasha snuffed in his wake, returning.

Solemnly handing me the caramel cone, he tossed a cookie to the squirrels, and, sitting down on the bench, pushed the earpiece into his ear without asking. I didn't mind.

CHAPTER ELEVEN

IT IS NICE TO SPEND TIME OUTDOORS. It is even better when you are in good company and have a guitar with you. And it is simply excellent when a crowd of butthurt, vengeful little nerds are after your hide. The mood was further improved by the sight of running water and a man working. Or rather, an orc: Bogart was digging pits, neatly collecting the dug-up earth into a bag. When the bag was full, the orc took it to the nearby creek and dumped it into the water. According to him, this was to destroy any traces of activity.

The pits themselves were small and shallow, but there were many of them, and the walls of each bristled with little stakes. They looked a bit like a brood of baby Sarlaccs to me.

"A foot goes in," Bogart explained, arming the next trap, "and when Johnny tries to yank it out, he gets spikes for his trouble. See how I'm setting them with their points downward? And just in case someone accuses me of having a poor imagination," he took a wooden jar from his shoulder bag and poured the contents into the pit trap, "this will increase the restraining effect and add debuffs, as you people like to say around here." The orc skillfully camouflaged the trap and set to work on a new one. "Learned how to make it just the other day. It's a nice touch, I made sure."

The sight of his thoughtful, businesslike face made a chill run down my back. From Pasha's tales, I knew that Bogart the Base's in-game exploits were a pale semblance of what he had done in meatspace. Sasha did not have to study trap-making in the game, he just made the same devices as he had in real life. Thanks to which, he received a rare trait—Ingenuity, which was similar to my Composition. It was just that his creative pursuit was very different from mine.

Bogart, meanwhile, completed the work and put on his shaggy cloak. It concealed his grotesque appearance and in doing so suddenly made him seem frighteningly real. My imagination immediately began to paint pictures of him hiding out somewhere in the forest, lying in ambush for some unsuspecting victim. Or did he have some other term for it? Target? Object?

"Yo, Kiera Khan, why are you just standing there?" Bogart's happy call snapped me back to the present.

"Oh I was just..." I drawled vaguely, driving away my anxiety.

"You better get ready," advised Bogart

sympathetically. "We have to do everything precisely here."

I nodded and cast my Shadow Shield.

"Daaang," the orc whistled. "Kiera Khan, you're like the Lord of Shadow around here—among us mere mortals. One, two...whoa...four. And three of them are like breakdancing or something. Where can I learn to do that?"

"You must join the dark side of the Force, young Padawan. We've got cookies for you too if you sign up now."

"I don't like sweets," he sighed. "I'll have to wait until you have some shishkabob or asado promotion. So, this looks like pretty much it..."

He looked me over meticulously once more, then examined the clearing and finally the thickets—as if the Yeti had just trundled into them. He was peering so intensely that I couldn't help but turn to look. Encountering nothing, I looked back at Bogart and encountered...nothing. The orc had vanished.

"Start your show," a voice sounded from the brush. "We need to draw an audience."

"I take requests," I announced, desperate to understand where Bogart was hiding. It was useless— he had disguised himself perfectly. "What should I play for you? What strikes your mood?"

"Hard to say," he said. "What's your favorite one?"

"Oh," the question puzzled me. "Hard to say.

Different songs for different moods. But, I can play the one that was my jam for many years."

"So play it," said Bogart.

"Only don't laugh too loudly, you'll give away your position," I warned and switched the eid into acoustic mode.

The primitive chords, more suitable for a beginning musician from a subway station than the future minstrel of the Empire of Shadow, resounded through the forest. And the vocals too were a bit more fitting for a local drunk. A sarcastic song sung by lazy booze-hound who dreamed of a special destiny and great achievements as he sipped his brew in a dirty dive bar.

Invisible in the thickets, Bogart snorted, holding back his laughter.

"Kiera, we hardly know ye," Bogart giggled softly. "After this song and your admission that for many years this was your jam, the question begs itself: Could this be the reason why you've joined the straight edge kids in leading a sober life? Or did your observations of Edilberto bring you to this? Tell the truth!"

"My observations of the entire world. The song is almost a hundred years old. And, it should be mentioned, it still sounds as relevant as ever."

"Well you've aged well," the orc whistled.

"Aren't you supposed to be sitting in ambush?" I squinted in the direction of Bogart the bush.

Despite all my efforts, I couldn't discern the orc among the blot of green.

"Aren't you supposed to be acting like a maiden in distress?" the bush reminded me in Bogart's voice. "Get to it!"

I merely hummed to myself, chuckled and sat down on the tree root sticking out of the ground. Then I began to arrange my sheet music around me. Just a lonely bard enthusiastically composing a new song. To make this picture seem more believable still, I really fell to my task—writing the song about Salamander. Progress creaked on slowly—my thoughts occupied with the forthcoming battle. But the loud sounds were sure to draw the biota of the Dark Legion to me sooner or later.

As for Bogart, he may as well have vanished entirely. I couldn't see or hear him while I tortured my strings.

He was like a true cat lying in ambush at the mouse hole—immobile, patient, occasionally twitching an ear. I didn't know a single player who would have had the patience to lie for hours without moving a muscle.

I was starting to think that no attack would be coming when my body ceased to obey my mind and the long-awaited system notification appeared before my eyes:

You have been stunned for 5 seconds!

Unlike last time, this was caused by an arrow from a biota hunter who emerged out of camouflage in the company of ten of his buddies. Someone beside me cursed elaborately. About a dozen rogues appeared one by one out of camouflage, stumbling into the small traps that Bogart had set in the clearing. The traps resembled small hedgehogs. Treated with poison, they saddled their victims with debuffs that would keep them from going into stealth again.

A second stunning arrow followed the second. The players quickly adjusted to their foiled plans and while the rogues began to steal towards me as cautiously as they could, the hunters worked to maintain my stun.

To my left, the thicket erupted in a roar—like a thunderstorm in May. The players reacted instantly to the potential threat. But as they searched for the new threat, they messed up their rotation, allowing me to leave stun. Taking advantage of this, I tore away from my attackers as quickly as I could. I needed to put some distance between us to avoid further stuns.

"After her! Use your pets to trigger the traps!" Otolaryngologist ordered his raiders.

It seems that everyone in the Dark Legion had already become acquainted with what Bogart the Base was capable of. Not so long ago, members of this particular guild helped Bogart organize a training ground with traps in order to repeatedly kill one brazen PKer.[1]

At that time, the tactic of neutralizing traps using pets proved themselves to a T and now, noting Bogart's hand in the location, and the scattered devices in the ground, Oto quickly made the right decision.

I ran through the forest as fast as I could, carefully jumping over the prepared pits and traps. A lengthy train of tamed wolves, foxes, cougars and other representatives of the local fauna chased at my heels. Behind them, with some lag, huffed a pair of demons summoned by the warlocks. The demons were in no rush—unlike the animals, they were relatively sentient and understood that in this race, it was the one who finished last that won.

Behind me, something popped with a loud bang. Unable to resist, I turned to look. Getting ahead of my other pursuers, a cougar had snagged the tripwire and set off a scroll of fireball that Bogart had set up. The primitive but powerful level 90 spell incinerated the animal where it stood. Immediately after this, another beast fell to Bogart's traps: A wolf landed in a disguised pit with stakes and tried unsuccessfully to free itself. The trap would not let it go, and with each jerk the beast pushed deeper into the pegs, howling as it lost the remnants of its health.

I continued to run along my pre-planned route,

---

[1] See "The Khaki-Colored Noob" by Vasily Mahanenko.

making unexpected turns and tacking like a hare. The pets behind me perished in the traps, one by one, creating a safe passage for the players, who ran behind me without losing sight of me but without taking the risk of leaving the 'swept' path.

A wise decision. Or so, no doubt, it seemed to them.

We tore around the forest like this for no less than ten minutes. A couple of sips was all that remained of the water in my flask when I reached the appointed place. It was located about fifty meters from the start of the chase. I even saw some of my score sheets scattered on the ground.

I dashed the last twenty steps with extreme care, exactly as Bogart had instructed me. And, no sooner had I reached the cross that marked spot, than I whipped out the eid and twanged an impact shade into one of my pursuers. I think I caught a puzzled expression on the hunter's face before he disappeared into thin air. That's right, bud. I too would be surprised by a spell with a radius of a hundred meters...

Quest updated: *Way of the Apprentice. Step 1.*

15 of 30 biota killed.

"Stun her!" Oto barked and vanished from sight along with the other rogues.

But I was not interested in them. The ranged fighters were quickly closing the distance, trying to get in range for their weapons and skills. One of them—a black-red pirq—yelped as he plunged into a disguised pit, from which a moment later a vicious series of curses followed. One of the dummy's comrades decided to help his friend—only to step into a snare of twisted vines. The noose drew tight around his ankle, jerked him to the ground and dragged him to the edge. After plowing a fair furrow, he disappeared into the bush, and once there soared up to the top of the tree which snapped upright, hoisting him. The player suspended by his foot fumbled absurdly, trying in vain to free himself.

"Get meee down!" he squealed.

Alas, the others had more important things to do. I managed to one-shot another hunter before his buddy struck me with a stunning arrow. The ranged fighters took up the best positions they could find—islands of greenery, which the blight had not yet filled in. Suspecting a trap, the warlocks sent forward the surviving demon. He calmly crossed two green spots and plummeted into the pit arranged in the third one. Delighted at the chance to avoid the blight's debuffs, the ranged fighters arranged themselves on the patches of safety and began to pour stunning arrows and spells on me. For a brief moment, I even felt flattered. So this is what a dungeon boss feels like. And, like any boss worth her salt, I was preparing for the battle's next phase.

The rogues were nowhere to be seen. There was no particular need to hurry so they were carefully choosing their path. The surviving hunters could keep me stunned for another half a minute, and the mages were methodically and implacably hammering my Shadow Shield. Each spell dealt monstrous damage, and I couldn't help but grow nervous, seeing my second materia shade's health start to grow thin.

The rogues' objective was simple: survive and get close enough to use their melee attacks and stunning spells. Experience had shown that stun was much more fearsome in PvP than the equipment and powers that Geranika had gifted me.

This time no one fell for the metal caltrops scattered on the ground. The players were watching where they stepped carefully, anticipating Bogart's tricks. They weren't wrong. But the tricks weren't only under their feet. A thin, barely-noticeable thread of spider silk, placed at chest level, stretched taut and tore. A doubled-over willow snapped upright, jerked the net after it and the players with it.

This knocked the others off their rhythm, making them nervous and forcing them to choose their footing even more carefully. Another rogue decided to be clever and stepped onto a trap that had already neutralized one of his unfortunate friends. He assumed reasonably that the place was now safe. In vain. Something like a rake popped out of the grass.

Only this rake's crossbar was studded with sharpened stakes which plunged right into the victim's groin. The glade erupted with a mournful howl of pain: I guess this player's pain filters were set to a lower value than my ninety percent. Poor guy...The new victim struggled to free himself, but only made things worse. I don't know what Bogart had devised here, but every new jerk only drove the spikes deeper in.

"Bogart you bitch!" one of the mages yelled angrily. "You can count yourself on the Legion's shit list! Do you understand, you bastard?"

I don't know whether the legionnaire's threat was real or just an attempt to unmask the smart-ass bounty hunter, but Bogart did not answer. Or, he answered in his own way: The sound of the orc's axe striking a trunk echoed from the woods and the 'safe area' under the feet of the mage and a couple of his comrades flipped, revealing a pit with stakes. The players dropped into the trap, and the lid rotated again to muffle their cries.

I watched all this from my 'front-row seats,' patiently waiting for the hunters to exhaust their stun spells. And the Seconds for their part seemed to understand that that moment was quickly approaching too. The rogues lost their cool and rushed me, trying desperately to close the distance. A fatal mistake. One of them finally got close enough to use his 'backstab' attack. But as soon as he appeared behind me, a big mossy log came whiffling through the tulgey wood and impaled the poor fellow along with several of his fellows to the nearest oak. I exhaled with relief. Until that moment, I wasn't sure that Bogart's calculations were correct and that terrifying ram wouldn't hit me instead.

The next moment, the latest stun expired and there was no longer anyone who could stun me again.

"Shall we dance?" I mimicked Plinto's smirk from the Legends of Barliona videos and strummed my strings.

The glade filled with the gloomy sounds of Chopin's funeral march, every four seconds generating a deadly shade. After the second one-shot, one of the surviving officers gave the command to retreat. The players who still had some mobility rushed back to the trodden path, which had brought them to this glade of horrors and death.

This was a further, fatal mistake. I hadn't wasted so much time jogging around the forest for nothing. Shadowing my pursuers, Bogart had armed the 'sleeper' traps and snares, generously scattered around the seemingly safe road. I could now periodically hear the riffs I had recorded at Bogart's request.

All I had to do was move along the truly safe path and one-shot my pursuers as they got caught in the traps.

"So what do you think, have the Chicago Bulls reached the playoffs or do we need to win another game?" asked Bogart, emerging out of nowhere and examining the trap in which Oto had been flailing only a few seconds ago—right before I put him out of his misery. "Mission Accomplished!"

Bogart held up his hand for me to high-five.

This was followed by a golfclap of approval. I jumped from surprise and turned my head. Geranika stood behind me, smiling and lazily clapping his hands.

"Bravo, Lorelei. You have a very resourceful friend."

He took a leisurely stroll around the clearing, setting off some of the traps. The deadly devices dissolved into dust as soon as they touched the Lord of Shadow.

"Hey, guy, did you build those? Then what are you breaking them for?" Bogart protested. "I labor my ass off, spill my dear orc sweat and then you show up—a real phenomenon, a real Travolta. I understand that you're like the top brass around here or whatever, but how about a little respect for another's work?"

Geranika froze for a moment. The imitator was processing the player's words.

"That's good. There's good. Just stand right there," Bogart went on, pointing his finger for emphasis. "Otherwise you'll ruin the rest of 'em. What is it you want anyway?"

Geranika frowned and snapped his fingers

irritably. The Lord of Shadow's gesture froze both Bogart and Merlin where they stood.

"Not very intelligent, but highly resourceful," Geranika went on, as if nothing had happened. "I am pleased with your work, my future apprentice. You have managed to learn that even the power I have granted you is not an excuse to underestimate your foes. You could have simply hunted your enemies piecemeal to complete my quest, yet you chose a different path. You took your past mistakes into account, and found a suitable ally for your purpose. More importantly, you achieved the desired result. You deceived your opponents, made them believe in victory, made them feel as if they were in control of the situation, and then you destroyed them. Excellent. I need an apprentice like you."

Quest complete: *Way of the Apprentice*. Step 1.

+1,000 Reputation with Geranika. Current status: Friendship.

The Lord of Shadow stepped forward, put his hand on my shoulder and the world disappeared, drowning in a leaden-gray fog. For a moment I thought that Geranika had sent me to the Gray Lands, but the fog cleared immediately and the world around me regained its colors. We stood at the edge of a precipice. A mountain range I had only ever seen from afar snaked all around us. A breathtaking valley unfurled below us: The Hidden Forest in all its grandeur. A teeming sea of green at the clouds' very fringe. And in the center of this roiling expanse of green stood the Tree.

I grew dizzy from the numbing height. Starting back abruptly from the edge, I slammed my back against the stone ledge behind me. My health bar dropped a bit, even despite my shield.

Geranika observed me silently. Curiosity and mockery played in his eyes. But the challenge in his look helped me regain my composure. The last thing I needed was an NPC laughing at me. I took a deep breath and managed to pry myself off the stone ledge and even took a couple of steps forward.

"This world is cruel, Lorelei," Geranika's dark eyes followed my every move. "It brooks neither weakness nor indecision. She who wishes to stand beside me must know how to harness her fear. Prove that you are capable of this."

And the Lord of Shadow politely stepped aside, clearing my way to the edge.

"Jump, Lorelei. Prove to me that you can follow me to the end. Prove to me that you are worthy of true power."

Quest available: *Way of the Apprentice. Step 2.*

Description: Take a leap of faith.

Reward: +500 Reputation with Geranika. Next quest in the chain. Penalty for declining the quest: Hostile status with Geranika.

My throat parched in an instant as my breathing quickened. I would never imagine that a game could do this to me...A game...What fun: Kill yourself for this NPC's amusement...and do it in the most terrifying way you can imagine...

I read mockery in Geranika's eyes. And superiority. Like he could see through me. Feel my fear. He despised my weakness. He despised me. *He.*

Rage kindled deep inside me, searing away my doubts and fears. I looked up at Geranika and our gazes crossed like two rapiers. I am a human. You—you're just part of a game. An illusion. Like this abyss with its scraps of clouds. And what kind of creator can I be if I cannot harness my own imagination?

Geranika's eyebrow rose slightly as I accepted the quest. Didn't expect that, did you, you arrogant prig?

"Hasta la vista, baby!" I grinned merrily, not caring at all whether the NPC understood me.

I exhaled sharply and took off. A short sprint, a jump and terrifying emptiness, at the sight of which my blood froze in my veins. My body plummeted like in a nightmare. The wind howled in my ears. No trace of the anger that had spurred me to do this remained. The thought of a monstrous blow against the ground vised my throat, stifling my scream. A game, it's a game, a game...The simple mantra did not help, and I forced myself to look only at my hands stretched out before me. No sight of approaching land. Only my fingers splayed taut. Green fingers covered in tiny thorns, but still my fingers. After this, I'm going to exit straight to meatspace and pick up a cup of hot tea with these same fingers. Maybe I'll even call up Sasha on my visor and we'll go for a walk. I'll tell Pasha about today's hunt for the Seconds and we'll have a laugh...

Thinking this allowed me to disconnect from what was happening around me. I stopped fretting about my fall and began making plans for the rest of my day. That is why I was very surprised to hear Geranika's voice right next to me:

"To tell you the truth, I am impressed, my future apprentice."

Only now did I realize that I wasn't falling. The air resistance and the whistling in my ears had vanished. I was suspended a meter from the surface of the very rock from which I had just jumped.

Geranika wiggled his fingers and an invisible force gently lowered me to my feet.

"I saw your fear, Lorelei. I did not think you had the heart to overcome it. And I could hardly imagine that you would remain so calm—you did not even scream."

I swallowed the lump in my throat and answered

as carelessly as possible:

"I was just thinking about the business I need to take care of in the Gray Lands."

The Lord of Shadow laughed.

"Excellent! I am sure now that you will be able to fulfill my next assignment."

Quest complete: *Way of the Apprentice. Step 2.*

I swiped away the system notification like an annoying fly.

"And what is this errand, master?"

"Future master," Geranium corrected mechanically.

He walked up to the edge of the cliff and pointed to the border of the Arras, where the lush greenery disappeared, as if cut with a sharp blade, and changed to a barren flatlands. I recognized the place without difficulty. It was unmistakable for the ugly crag that scarred the plain. The battlefield from my vision, the Stone Maw.

"This land has seen many wars. And it shall see many more still. There are those who will be able to penetrate the Arras. Peaceful life is an illusion. The strong always seeks to dominate the weak. Only those who are feared are given the luxury of enjoying peace."

I listened to the Lord of Shadow in silence,

wondering where he was going with all this.

"The races who now consider themselves part of the Kartoss Empire, have tried to conquer the Hidden Forest many times before. And each time they were defeated. But the races of the forest paid a terrible price too..."

Geranika paused dramatically.

"Now Kartoss seeks to form the First Alliance. An alliance against me. Astilba and a part of the Council are well aware of what this means. They shall simply be sacrificed to weaken my army. I, on the other hand, am proposing a true alliance. Indestructible. Eternal. I have never done any harm to the forest or its inhabitants. And I am able to help with more than mere words. Tell me, are you not happy with the transformation that gave you your new abilities? Does not the renewed earth make you stronger, your enemies weaker? Do you not wish to share this power with all your people?"

"I'm afraid that my people will not agree to the opportunity you offer until they understand its true significance."

"That is correct, Lorelei," Geranika nodded and turned his back to me, surveying the forest far below. "Astilba was the first who dared accept my gift. She thirsted for power. The chance to drive her old enemies from her native forest as they bring promises of peace she knows to be false. But, unlike you, she lacks the spirit to truly trust me. The past has Astilba in its grip. She has dreamed of bringing it back for so long that she forgot how to look to the future. Kartoss will not give up trying to conquer the Hidden Forest. And now, with the support of Malabar...I am afraid that without my help, the forest simply cannot survive."

I sincerely doubted that the newly formed alliance against Geranika would suddenly rush to conquer the Hidden Forest, but I didn't say anything. Let's assume that I am convinced of the impending catastrophe.

"Astilba refuses to recognize the obvious. She believes that those like you who accepted the power of Shadow will be enough to destroy the Kartossian embassy and foil the disastrous alliance. The Sixth refuses to allow the forest to change, to grow. She does not want to transform the Guardian, whose might alone would alter the balance of power this side of the Arras in an instant. She will only permit me to help imprison the Guardian for the time it takes to prepare the destruction of the Kartossian embassy. And the Guardian himself will never accept Shadow voluntarily because he does not understand it. He does not realize that with such power he will be able to protect the Hidden Forest from any encroachments."

Geranika turned and looked into my eyes.

"As you see, the Guardian requires our assistance."

"Our assistance?" I asked surprised, already understanding what my future potential teacher was driving at. "But how?"

"With this." A flickering orb appeared in Geranika's hand, with a small nondescript shard in its center.

"The power of this artifact is so great that without its protective shell it will be felt by all the powerful essences of this forest. It is capable of transforming the Forest Guardian, granting him unprecedented power. At the moment, my powers are maintaining the protective shell, but as soon as I give the shard to you, the shield will begin to deplete. You must reach the place of the Guardian's imprisonment before the protective shell wastes away and plunge the shard into the Guardian's body. If you tarry overmuch—the unrestrained power of the artifact will destroy everything around itself that is not Shadow. If you happen to be standing near the Guardian at that moment, he will perish. The forest will lose its defender, and we will lose a powerful ally. Thus, you must plunge in the shard before the shell depletes."

Quest available: *Way of the Apprentice. Step 3.*

Description: Plunge the materia shard into the body of the Guardian of the Hidden Forest, letting Shadow into him. Deadline for completion: 24 hours. Quest type: Unique scenario. Reward:

You will be initiated as Geranika's apprentice. Penalty for failing/refusing the quest: Hostile status with Geranika.

Good plan. I approve. Blight the Guardian, violating Astilba's direct orders, and even at someone else's order and with the excuse of 'it's for your benefit.'

"I'm flattered by your trust in me, but is it in my power to cope with a task that for some reason is beyond the power of such a powerful being as you, master?" I asked, taking my time in accepting the quest.

Geranika's eyes narrowed and his lips curved into a grin.

"You know how to ask the right questions, Lorelei," he said. "Astilba and her companions have encased the Shadow-bound Guardian within a miniature copy of the Arras. Only a forest inhabitant can pass through this barrier. One such as you."

I mentally applauded the Sixth's forethought. Astilba does not trust her ally and she has insured herself against any improvisation on his part. And it's a good thing she did! The Lord of Shadow is clearly not concerned for the well-being of the Hidden Forest, but for his own affairs. No wonder he's so obsessed with finding a student from among the locals...

"How can I find the Guardian?" I went on inquiring. "The forest is huge and full of perils for those like me. And the time for searching is limited."

"I shall mark the place on your map," Geranika shrugged off such a trifling objection. "As for the rest...I, of course, could escort you to the Guardian, protecting against any assailants. But that would be too easy. Who needs a student who cannot cope with a few hardships?"

"No one," I agreed, and squinted at the edge of the cliff. "Do you need me to descend from here with another leap of faith, or will you transport me to the ground yourself, master?"

Geranika looked at me thoughtfully, then down into the precipice and then back at me again...I swallowed with difficulty and took a deep breath. I'm not scared. I can do it.

"It would be damn amusing," the Lord of Shadow smiled, peering into me, "but we do not have much time."

Tongues of fog coiled from under my feet and in the next instant I was exactly where I had been when Geranika had transported me.

Bogart greeted me with a nod, occupied with scratching Merlin's belly. The sabretooth had already grown up to the orc's waist and weighed almost a hundred kilos. I tried to keep my distance from her: It wouldn't take her much more than an ill mood to send me to respawn. But that was just me—Bogart was entirely unconcerned with such trifles: Sitting on the ground, he went on scratching his pet's paunch as she purred with delight.

"How was your walk?" he asked, pausing his grooming.

Merlin raised her head in displeasure, wished me a fat minus to my karma, and climbed into her master's lap. Or rather, she placed her head and forelegs there, since no more of her would fit.

"Suicidal," I answered after a moment's thought. "At least I learned something interesting. I'll tell you later. For now we better engage in a bizarre combination of gardening and blood magic. But I need a donor..."

I made a terrible face and stared at Bogart meaningfully.

"And what part of my priceless body shall you require, oh Hannibal Lector of the flora phylum?" he replied with curiosity, scratching his blissfully squinting cat behind her ear.

"Blood," I whispered ominously. "Liters of it..."

"Are you trying to grow an alcoholic?" Bogart asked, astounded. "I'm not sure whether this world's ever seen a vampire with congenital alcoholism. My blood's 200 proof—to Edilberto's eternal envy."

"The only alternative is to wait for Pasha to return. FSM knows what's keeping him and how long it'll be before he gets here. And I have another quest with a tight deadline."

"As usual," the orc threw up his arms in despair. "Whenever anyone needs someone to bust his ass, it's up to trusty old Bogart the Base to wave his magic wand."

He rubbed the bridge of his nose pensively and added:

"That came out a little obscenely, don't you think?"

"I'm not going to discuss wands, especially in the context of eggs and seeds," I warned the orc.

"Hmmm...You're even more vulgar than I am, tender blossom of the jungle," Bogart said. Having cleared Merlin from his lap and ignoring her unhappy face, he got up, 'dusted off' his pants and asked: "Where shall we dig our vegetable patch then?" He flourished a small infantry shovel for comic effect. It was hard to believe that this merry fellow had just recently assembled some murderous devices. "We need to find some calm, secluded place. To keep all these Geranikas from our little cabbage patch kid."

"Let's just do it right here," I suggested. "There are still a bunch of traps around here, so the Seconds won't poke around. And a random wandering player will be unlikely to survive."

"Well, it is a good location," the orc agreed, looking around. "And we have already fertilized it quite a bit. Natural fertilizers brought to you by the Dark Legion Corp, with a trademark and a QA seal and all. Where do you want me to dig?"

"On those green patches. I'm not sure that blighted ground will nurture anything."

Bogart nodded and drove his spade into the ground. He dug a hole for the seed almost instantly.

"Sow away." The orc stepped aside, flicking Merlin's curious nose.

The cat pressed her ears to her head, but insisted on thrusting her face into the pit with an askance look at her master. Not finding anything interesting, she sniffled and flopped to her side over the orc's toes.

I took the vitar seed and the ghostly egg out of my satchel.

"It's too bad I can't summon Salamander for another day. The quest description says that a sentient can't be revived this way, but...What if it works anyway?"

"I think Pasha's already gotten his hands on another one," Sasha shrugged. "So there is room for experimentation."

I nodded and grew thoughtful. How do I summon the soul into the seed?

In Salamander's case, I would try to select the vitar seed and cast the soul summons on it. But in this case, I'm already holding my guide's soul here in my hand. I bet I needed to bind a song to it back when I was in the Gray Lands. Although...Maybe it's all much simpler than that?

Without truly believing it would work, I simply touched the egg and the seed to each other. The items rippled for a moment and then merged.

New item acquired: Ghostly Vitar Seed.
Quest complete: *Creating a Cicerone. Step 2.*

Quest available: *Creating a Cicerone. Step 3.*
Description: Grow a Cicerone from the seed.
...
Reward: A Cicerone of the Dead.

Encouraged by this success, I stuck the seed in a hole, took the dagger from its sheath and cut the palm of my hand. Ordinarily, avatars don't bleed in Barliona, but given the circumstances, my palm filled with a whitish, viscous sap.

"What do you think applies better here: Blood magic or fresh-squeezed juice magic?" I asked, generously watering the seed.

The seed immediately absorbed the liquid.

The Cicerone now knows its master.

"You'll end up hatching a two-ton dragon," Bogart prophesied, offering his paw. "My blood shall spawn nothing less! You'll be wandering around with a winged lizard circling around your head."

"So that every clown starts calling me the mother of dragons? Naaah."

The dagger blade slipped along Bogart's green palm and a thin stream of blood began to trickle onto the vitar seed.

The seed has acquired the ability to retain an animal spirit.

Bogart waved his shovel, covering the seed and turned to me awaiting further instructions. I shrugged. There were neither system notifications, nor further prompts.

"Maybe we need to perform like a seed dance or something?" asked the orc. "Read it a poem, sing a ditty?"

"No idea. As long as there aren't any further quests about caring for the plant, I don't care. Otherwise we'll be watering, weeding, fencing and warding off predators all summer."

"Here, lemme try something..." the orc cleared his throat and began jumping around the planted seed, hollering: "*It is the springtime of my loving! You are the sunlight in my growing! Flee from me, keepers of the gloom!*"

"Are...are you trying to sing 'The Rain Song?'"

"Yeah...what?"

"That's not how it goes..."

"Well what are you standing there for? Play the tune and the lyrics will come to me!"

While we were bickering, a sprout popped out of the earth. The sight of the green shoot made both of us shut up instantly.

"It grows," Bogart whispered, although I could see just as well as he could.

Merlin, catching our mood, immediately seated herself on her tail and also began staring at the rapidly growing stem. Within minutes, it had reached the height of my chin, and at its top appeared a blue bud with black veins.

"I told you it'd be a dragon," whispered the orc.

I had no idea why he was sure about this, but I didn't feel like arguing, completely absorbed by the spectacle.

The bud grew, its color growing more saturated until suddenly its petals opened revealing...a tiny owl. A little blue-and-black-colored owlet. When he saw us, he ruffled the little leaves that were his feathers. In general, he was more like a plant than a real bird. Looking closer, I noticed small thorns, similar to those that appeared all over me upon my joining the 'dark side.' It turns out that the contaminated blood had an effect on the vitar seed. I sincerely hope that my guide had not inherited anything from Bogart.

Quest complete: *Creating a Cicerone. Step 3.*

The owlet started, waggled awkwardly and jumped onto my shoulder. Having settled on his new perch, the birdie began to pick over his feathers.

You have acquired a cicerone to the Gray Lands.
Give your cicerone a name.

THE BARD FROM BARLIONA

"Ain't he the coolest dragon you've ever seen?" Bogart quipped with emotion. "Smaug's spitting image. Only, he's still little. Isn't that right, Merlin?"

The sabretooth regarded the owlet gloomily, snorted, expressing her contempt, and buried her face into her master's leg.

"That's a thought," I smiled and looked at the little owlet. "You will be Smaug."

You have selected a name for your cicerone: Smaug.

Smaug shook himself, sat down, twirled his head and went back to preening his feathers.

"Well, congratulations," the orc grunted. "You're now a real tree: Green and covered in birds."

"If you keep babbling," I warned, "I'll find him an instructor that'll teach him to crap on whosoever head I point to."

As if he understood what we were talking about, the owlet squeaked and stared at the orc with rounded eyes.

"Won't bother me," Bogart waved dismissively. "He and I are like Peter Quill and his daddy. Although no, that's a flawed analogy...Help me out here, Merlin..."

The cat glanced sideways at her owner and began to lick her paw with self-absorption.

"No, you just can't get good creative help these

days," said Bogart, aggrieved. "Kiera, you're more clever than me—help me think of something to defend my honor."

"You can talk less and defend your honor in the process," I winked at the orc, while Smaug hooted approvingly.

Bogart pulled a distraught face, but given the avatar's generally brutal and grotesque appearance, this looked more like the face of King Kong, constipated.

"By the way, thank you," I smiled sincerely at my friend. "Without you, I wouldn't have been able to handle that mob of Seconds. It seems that you have impressed Geranika. If you're interested, I could put in a kind word for you."

"Not until he learns to dress himself like a normal human," the orc snorted. "It's like he's some juggler in the Cirque du Soleil—instead of the chief villain of the most popular game in history. Why the hell do all the bad guys have such tacky fashion sense? Or are they all trying to look like members of M.A.V.O.? Black robes, business suits and idiotically pretentious armor? What kind of example do they set anyway—for the little, future villains of the world, I mean?"

He stuck his knuckles into his hips and stared at me with genuine indignation, as if the choice of Geranika's wardrobe was somehow my doing.

"Write a complaint to the Barliona art

department," I advised. "As for me, I need to deal with the Guardian's transfiguration, while my fan club is still resting in the Gray Lands."

"Try to do without platitudes, 'transfiguration,'" Bogart counseled. "Give him a Hawaiian shirt, Bermuda shorts and some Wayfarers. Otherwise, I'll be disappointed in you."

"It'll have to be the way it goes," I spread out my hands. "All I have is a single magic pill."

"In skillful hands, even a penis will do for a guitar, in a pinch, as it were" the orc parried. "Let's go, Merlin. We still have a world to save. I don't know when and from what, but we must be prepared."

The orc and the sabretooth both turned to me.

"Ah, well, there's one candidate, a future horsewoman of the Apocalypse," Bogart remarked casually. "Kiera Khan, if you decide to kick off Armageddon or Ragnarök or Y2K or whatever, make sure to let us know."

I bowed ceremoniously, waved at Bogart and studied the interface in search of a new function. Yeah, there it is—'Summon Cicerone.' The skill was active and I pushed the virtual button. Predictably, the owlet disappeared. How I love an intuitive UI.

My exploration of the guide's abilities will have to wait. Right now I was more worried about the limited time I had to do Geranika's quest. I fished an amulet out of my satchel to talk things over with Chip.

"I'm sending you coordinates, Pasha. You can

find your POW at that location. But make sure to go by yourself. I have my own plans for him..."

CHAPTER TWELVE

THIS TIME NO ONE PURSUED ME, nor tried to kill me, and in general, the journey was incredibly boring. Ordinary players shied away from the blighted parts of the forest, while the weird ones were currently raging about Bogart the Base on the fora, no doubt.

Thanks to the efforts of the Sixth & Co., the blighted ground now formed a labyrinth of paths mazing through the forest. A couple of times, in the renegades' labyrinth, I turned into dead ends but I caught myself in time and reached the designated point in a little over two hours. To tell the truth, I was afraid to see an honor guard of renegades, but I found nothing of the kind when I got there. In fact, there was nothing special here at all. No crude dungeon, no jailers, no Guardian. But according to the map, he should be here. Think, noggin, think...If you figure it out, I'll buy you a hat!

A survey of this ordinary swath of blighted forest did not yield any results. The hill, covered with the same sharp thorn-bushes, stood out only thanks to an old, gnarled tree. I'm not much for identifying tree species and when there's no foliage whatsoever and the branches are all black and twisted, well, there was no chance. In any case, the tree didn't seem like a Guardian. Crooked, withered, approximately fifteen meters tall, it did not stand out among the other vegetation around here, and it was clearly already blighted, whereas the Guardian should still be untainted.

Damn, I wish I knew what he looked like. What if he's just a flea, hopping somewhere around here in fancy shoes. Or a squirrel in the hollow of the tree. Or some bark beetle. A giant mole, or a hare...And there is nobody to ask...

Okay. I need to think logically. The renegades couldn't have simply dumped a cage with the revered Guardian in the middle of the forest. First of all, it seems disrespectful. And secondly, any passerby would find him. And that means that he is somehow hidden from random trespassers. The druids can't find the Guardian, so he is shielded magically. But since Chip was assigned to look for him and Geranika sent me without any additional instructions, ordinary players should be able to find him.

The first thing I did was pull the Shadow artifact from my inventory and walk in a circle with it. Nothing happened. So let the record reflect this—I'm not much of a psychic. My next experiment involved casting Shadow Haze. If the Guardian was sealed with the help of Geranika, could the use of Shadow will reveal the dungeon?

Nope. All I did was burn the spell for no reason. Hmm. With my intellect, maybe Sasha will give me a job digging holes...

The realization came suddenly. That's right! Pits! If the prison is here, but I can't see it, it must be under me!

While I was crawling on my knees searching for a manhole or hatch or some other entrance to the dungeon, I used the opportunity to collect some blighted earth into my empty flasks. I had been meaning to experiment with local recipes for a long time, and some of them required this ingredient. In addition to strategic reserves of mud, I managed to find the disguised hatch, behind which a rather wide, inclined passage descended into the ground.

"Follow the white rabbit," I muttered and climbed into the hole.

The passage bore an unpleasant resemblance to the throat of some outlandish monster. Slimy and thorny roots that formed a living carpet over the vaults and walls, intertwined on the earthen floor, making it difficult to walk. I spied movement in the murk of the underground passage ahead of me. Like a giant creature was trying to push me out of its throat and through the prickly grater of its jaws. Trying to keep as far as possible from the walls and now and then ducking under the thorny trellises hanging overhead, I cautiously made my way forward.

A Guardian devoured by the blighted forest...Sinister associations stubbornly crept into my head, causing goose bumps along my back. If I'm feeling this way at the entrance, what will happen when I get to the 'stomach?'

The answer did not take long in coming. The underground passage turned out to be fairly short and led me to a huge cave, which seemed to occupy the entire inside of the hill. The cave's vaulted walls and ceiling were also covered with trellises of roots, unpleasantly reminiscent of a ball of snakes. Along the walls, here and there, bunches of mushrooms, similar to luminous overgrown toadstools, protruded from the ground.

"If you cross a hedgehog with a snake, you'll get a meter and a half of barbed wire," I said, looking up at the tangle of spiked roots. The old joke I'd heard from Pasha helped drive off my unpleasant thoughts. It's not very comfortable here...not very comfortable at all.

An enormous cage occupied the center of the cave. Its bars were fashioned from the roots of the tree growing on top of the hill. Breaking through the vaulted ceiling, they snaked down like giant centipedes, straight through the entire cave and disappeared again underground. Thorny shoots filled the gaps between the thick bars—a cage of thorns that kept the captive imprisoned in his wooden prison. The free space between the improvised bars was occupied by a familiar, swirling fog. Its pale light hinted that the wooden spines were not the only obstacle to freedom.

There were enough gaps between the roots to discern the prisoner in the cage—the Guardian. He was mighty, smelly and hairy. And he was definitely no flea. In front of me stood a four-meter-tall pirq. Level 500.

Black, like the night, the mighty pirq drilled into me with his yellow eyes and vertical pupils. His fur bristled and his lips parted, revealing impressive fangs.

"WHAT DO YOU WANT, TRRAITOR TO YOUR BRREED?"

The roar filled everything around me, making my body tremble. My legs faltered and I collapsed to my knees, unable to bear the onslaught of the Guardian's voice. I wanted to curl up and cover my head with my hands, shutting off the overpowering roar. My head was spinning, debuff icons appearing and disappearing chaotically, but I did not even try to delve into the interface. Struggling with my sudden weakness, I slowly crawled to the exit of the huge hole. Every now and again stumbling over the tree roots, I finally managed to get out into the open.

I felt some relief. The pile of debuffs was gradually expiring and my mind was clearing. It was evident that I would not survive a conversation with the Guardian. That was one killer voice.

Sitting down at the entrance, I began to consider my options. How could I complete this quest? Maybe I can bean the Guardian with that orb from afar? I'll ask Sasha 'n' Pasha to fabricate a cannon or at least a slingshot and then I'll shoot the orb straight into the Guardian's maw when he starts to roar from a nice distance where it won't be so loud...Wait...Not so loud eh?

I grabbed the eid and cautiously tiptoed down the passage, hashing out my plan as I went. As soon as the cage of roots with its prisoner came into view, I touched the strings and cast Canopy of Silence. The spell covered the cage and its captive, muffling whatever noise the big pirq was bellowing up inside. Seeing me, the Guardian stirred, started and snapped open his mouth...yet not nothing followed. No debuffs, no nausea. I still wanted to get away from his menacing appearance, but that urge I could manage.

One of the protruding roots seemed quite comfortable so I sat down on it, without interrupting the classic Angra riff I was using to channel the spell. My fingers moved on their own, permitting me to concentrate on my surroundings.

Above all, I was interested in the sphere of fog that surrounded the Guardian. I did not believe for a second that some roots could contain a monster like this. It would take reinforced concrete at the very least. So he had definitely been fettered by some kind of magic. And how did get this giant into this hill anyway? It sure as hell wasn't the same way I'd come in from.

Looking closer at the foggy haze, I noticed a few shades, like the materia shades that danced under my feet. But if mine had a defensive function, then these it seems were like jailers. However, I could neither select them nor check their properties. Okay. Well what about the sphere itself? Can I step through it or what? And how am I supposed to stick the artifact into this irate NPC? Orally? And have my hand loped off? Why, this fellow could swallow me whole, artifact and all. Though what's the alternative? Build a slingshot?

Damn that Geranika...

For the sake of curiosity, I grazed the cage's foggy surface with one shoulder. The fog rippled with an iridescent effect, not unlike that of the Arras. Immediately after this, three shades flew out of the fog and began spinning around the Guardian's head. He growled silently, jerked and collapsed to the earthen floor. Then the cage's roots parted, forming a small passage.

Kewl. Protection from Geranika and a service for the renegades. So, in order to complete the quest, it is enough to enter the cage with the immobilized Guardian and, uh, administer the artifact. Now should I slice him open with a dagger, the way Geranika had done to the sentries, or thrust the orb into his mouth without trying to be fancy? Shouldn't be too hard considering that I can fit entirely into that overgrown pizza oven of a kisser. All I had to do was wait for Chip to show up.

I moved away from the cage and the wooden bars closed again. The shades immediately returned to their places, unpinning the Guardian. The pirq remained prone on the ground for a while, then staggered up to his feet, gave me a withering look, and sat down heavily on the floor. Channeling the Canopy of Silence was steadily eroding my mana so I finally decided to leave the cave and wait for Pasha outside.

He did not take long. No sooner had I started getting bored than a lump of white fur came tumbling out of the forest and seeing me, roared happily:

"Knock-knock-knocking on heaven's door..."

A blighted wolf burst from the thicket and immediately aggroed Chip. Chip, without pausing his singing, turned on his heels and met the beast with the tip of his halberd. Despite switching to the druid class, he did not want to change weapons. A psycho—what do you want?

"Why aren't you wearing your muzzle?" Chip dumped the aggressive beast to the ground and immediately impaled it with a coup de grace.

"And where the hell is animal control?!" the pirq asked rhetorically when the wolf disappeared.

"You *are* animal control," I deadpanned. "By the way, do you understand that you are playing a caster class?"

Pasha had already ascertained that 'caster' referred to any class that specialized in magic.

"Lady Luck smiles on all equally," he shrugged. "So there's no need getting hung up on my poor lot. Where is the patient?"

"In a damp cell below," I waved my hand at the entrance to the giant hole. "Only don't even think of springing him—I need to seduce him to the dark side of the Force first."

I took the Shadow artifact out of my inventory and showed it to Pasha.

"Astilba expressly forbade Geranika from getting his paws on the Guardian. She even enchanted the cell with a protective spell that only pirqs and biota can penetrate. She is sure that the locals would never hurt their Guardian. He's like a saint here or something. So the Lord of Shadow offered me an internship in exchange for desecrating the most precious creature of my race. When I insert orb A into slot B, the Guardian will become a part of our gloomy band," I explained.

"Kiera, you do understand, that this is your in-game Rubicon?" asked Chip.

"I understand very well and I'm not happy about it," I sighed sadly. "If Astilba learns of this, she will never forgive you. Nor anyone else in this place. You may as well kiss the Portulac quest goodbye. But there is not much choice. There's no place for me in the Hidden Forest. In a few days, high-level players from the Dark Legion will start showing up and then I'll have a hard time leaving the respawn area. Both empires already hate me, and my level isn't high enough to flee to the Free Lands. Some other time, I would say the hell with it, simply delete my character and roll a new one but now...with Eid and the souls I can summon...I'll lose Anica and Salamander if I delete my Lori. Geranika represents the possibility of playing on for the Shadow Empire."

"Yes..." drawled Chip. "That's one heck of a stew you're stirring up. Let me go and take a look at this Guardian fellow."

And, without waiting for my response, he darted down the passage. The funny part is that I heard no roar this time around. I guess the Guardian liked his pirq brethren more than me. Chip crawled out a couple of minutes later, looking surprisingly pensive.

"Don't transform him..." he asked softly.

"What? Why?"

"Just don't," Chip shot back, curtly, without a smile.

I stared at him blankly.

"What's wrong with you?"

"Nuthin'. Can we just not spoil things in here? Can we? Can we at least act better in VR than in real life?"

"Pasha," I reminded him, "it's just a game. This is a scenario. A scripted event in which some play heroes and others villains."

"Why that's all I ever hear—everywhere!" Chip barked unexpectedly. "Everything's a goddamn game. Only in some places when you die you sit out for twelve hours—and in others you die for good. And the one common denominator is the shitty things we do— whether here or there."

I listened to my friend's angry speech and tried to understand what had caused such a reaction. What did the Guardian tell him in there? Whatever it was, it had really gotten to him...

"My playing on the side of the villains didn't bother you earlier," I reminded him cautiously. "What's changed?"

"Earlier, you weren't about to kill a defenseless creature who's locked in a cage," Chip answered in a strangely changed voice.

He turned away without another word. I looked at my friend in bewilderment, unable to understand what was happening. And something was clearly eating him. Something bad. And this something hadn't started here and now but elsewhere and earlier. And it was much more real.

The pirq's shoulders sagged and for a moment the mighty beast looked powerless. It was like the sight of the helpless prisoner, awaiting his demise, had extinguished Chip's customary pep and enthusiasm.

I glanced at the entrance to the Guardian's

prison and rubbed my temples with my fingers. If I don't complete Geranika's quest, it's all over. No game empire will accept me. The Dark Legion will eat me alive. And in the Free Lands it will be the NPCs, whose minimum level was 100. The last thing I wanted was to lose this character with her ability of traveling to the Gray Lands and summoning the souls of the dead.

Yet something told me that if I blighted the Guardian, my friendship with Chip would come to an end. He won't make any scenes or kick me out of his place. But everything will change. He won't smile at me anymore.

No, losing a friend, this friend, would be far worse.

"How are we going to save him?" I could hardly believe I was saying this.

The pirq turned around, looking at me in disbelief.

"Are you serious?"

"It's just a game," I shrugged and looked up at the sky for some reason. Probably to avoid seeing Chip's face. "It's not real. You are real. You can even be killed in game because you don't care about it in reality. But if you do truly care about the fate of this NPC, I will do as you want, instead of what some poorly dressed fop tells me to do."

For a while Chip was silent, poring over what he had heard. Then his paw descended to my shoulder. I turned around and met his eyes.

"I'll remember this," he promised gravely.

I nodded and tried to sound carefree:

"Then go back to the Guardian and ask him not to yell at me. All those debuffs make me sick. We will come up with a way to help him."

Chip grunted, nodded, and disappeared again into the hill. I looked in his wake and for some reason found I had no qualms about the decision I'd taken.

This time around I had to wait for a long while. I even began to doubt that Pasha would be able to persuade the Guardian, but at last my hairy friend popped out of the hole and waved his paw.

"I have explained the concept of espionage and double agents to this relic, but he is still skeptical," Chip explained in a perfectly normal voice on our way to the Guardian's dungeon. "But he did promise not to yell at you, so that's something."

Almost nothing had changed since I had been here last. The Guardian still looked at me with suspicion but without the earlier hatred. More importantly, he remained silent.

"I tried to step through the fog, but it threw me against the wall and stunned me for a couple of minutes," Chip shared. "I have no idea what to do next."

"That's not the only problem..."

I pulled the sinister Shadow artifact out of my satchel and showed it to Chip.

The Guardian listened to our conversation in silence, but his yellow eyes gleaming in the twilight did not suggest anything good.

"What's that?" Chip nodded at the artifact with interest.

"That's the cookie I was talking about—the one you get for joining the dark side, young Jedi. All I have to do is feed the cookie to Master Yoda there and, ding, the Sith's ready."

"Well, so throw it away and that'll be that," Chip suggested instantly.

"Nah." I shook my head. "If I don't stick that thing in the Guardian, it'll go big-ba-da-boom in less than a day and spatter everything around it with blight. It's like a blighted bomb or something."

The Guardian bristled, his mighty body jerked towards me with the obvious intention of reaching through the bars of the cage and crushing me like a handful of dry leaves. Destroy the threat, even at the cost of his own life.

I jumped back from shock and slammed my head against the roots sticking out of the wall as hard as that was even possible. I really need to start taking something for my nerves.

Meanwhile, the jailer shades darted at my assailant. The ancient pirq helplessly floundered in the fog, plastered with shades and then slumped to the ground. His eyes burned with such impotent rage that I couldn't help feel uneasy. An ancient being, designed to protect this land from any enemies. Even now, captivated and helpless, he still inspired respect and fear.

Chip watched the Guardian with uncommon gravity. And I thought I caught a glimpse of comprehension in my friend's eyes.

"What do you think we should do with this junk?" he nodded at the artifact in my hands.

"I'll give it to someone who can figure it out. Like Astilba, for instance. I'm also thinking about telling her that Geranika decided to convert the Guardian while I'm at it. I could also hand it over to someone else from the Council. But they're pretty far away, and you'll be the one to take it anyway. They're not too keen on me back at the Tree."

"As it happens, this is resolvable," the pirq declared unexpectedly and, cheering up, grinned as usual. "We will summon Old Eben right this instant."

Chip began rummaging in one of his belt satchels for which Bogart had christened him 'Jurgen' for some reason.

"He's our boss, so he should know whether there are specialists of the right level here, or not..." the pirq continued, showing me a glowing golden flower bud. "It's like an emergency beacon. He gave it to me to use in a pinch."

Chip's paw crushed the bud, which crumbled into a flash of sparks, emitting a melodious ringing.

"Now we wait," Pasha announced laconically.

"Just don't tell him about our illegals," I said.

"Don't teach a cat to lick himself," the pirq winked at me and pushed me lightly: "Worry not, my young Padawan, the old Jedi will not let you fail."

"I expect your summons is truly important. Some outsiders have penetrated the Arras and I am very busy," I heard Eben's voice, accompanied by a faint flash and the smell of a spring meadow. The spymaster came out of the portal and was about to say something else, when his gaze swept across the foggy dungeon. "The Guardian!"

Eben stared in shock at the imprisoned forest custodian.

"Seventh," the black pirq rumbled in a dull voice and pointed a clawed finger at us with Chip. "Kill these traitors and remove the source of the bight!"

"But I'm willing to hand it over without any killing," I said instantly, to Eben's complete confusion. "Geranika told me that when the protective layer around the artifact deteriorates, Shadow will break forth. And according to his words, this will happen a little less than a day from now."

The spymaster's eyes narrowed and he carefully took the artifact from my hands.

"KILL THE TRRAITORS OF OUR RRACE NOW!" the Guardian roared so loudly that had I not been sitting down, I would've dropped instantly. The clamor filled my head, but this time it was not so overwhelming. Perhaps the Guardian did not want to hurt his allies at the same time.

"Will you listen to that...a voice from the depths of the centuries," Chip responded.

If it were not for his flattened ears and clenched fists, I would have thought that the voice of the Guardian had had no effect on him whatsoever. It seems that the ancient creature's desire to unscrew our heads had finally jarred Chip back to his customary rakish manner.

"Allow me to inquire, Comrade Gigantopithecus, when did you part with your memory? Only a few minutes ago, I was diligently explaining to you about our joint operation to enable our special agents to infiltrate the enemy camp! And now? You are again being disrespectful and unfriendly towards Lorelei, who has sacrificed," moving, patriotic notes sounded in the pirq's voice, "her very essence for the sake of saving our peoples! You should be ashamed of yourself, comrade! At your advanced age, with your life experience, it's high time you learned what deserves praise and what roaring! And instead, you just want to kill and punish...Tsk-tsk-tsk, a bad look..." he smiled ruefully, looking at the prisoner with reproach. "And you call yourself a Guardian..."

I watched in fascination as Chip, who had just saved the Guardian from me, now fervently defended me in front of the Guardian and the Seventh.

"Ahem," Eben cleared his throat, glaring at Chip indignantly. "Do not heed this young man's babble, oh Ancient One. "He is at times overly-talkative and disrespectful. Often he is completely incomprehensible..."

At these words from Eben, Chip raised his hat and bowed foolishly to the Seventh, grumbling: "Why thank you for the kind word and endorsement..."

There was some doubt in Eben's voice, but he continued: "Yet he is no traitor and neither is Lorelei. She joined our brothers who disagreed with the Council's decision, and gave Chip valuable information about Astilba's plans. The Sixth has decided to disrupt the alliance with Kartoss and contacted Geranika for the purpose."

At this point, I decided to enter the conversation:

"The Sixth commanded them not to harm the Guardian. It was Geranika, in secret from her, who ordered me to use this artifact to profane this mighty creature. If Astilba learns of this, their alliance shall end."

Eben's face took on a thoughtful expression and in the meantime Chip drew closer to the cage and with curiosity poked a finger among the bars.

"I wonder..." he scratched his head and returned to us. "Shouldn't the Guardian be like a powerful being, right?"

Chip turned to Eben as the most authoritative source of information in this matter.

"The power of the Guardian in his territory is immense indeed," the Seventh nodded.

"Then could you explain to a stupid old boot like me what it would take to capture the Guardian and then lock him up so that he can't get out?"

"THAT GERRANIKA," boomed the Guardian in reply. "HE WIELDS A POWER I HAVE NEVER ENCOUNTERED BEFORE. I STILL FAIL TO UNDERSTAND HOW MY PRRISON WAS CONSTRRUCTED."

"The forest is poisoned with something similar," Eben added. "And our druids have only just begun to understand the essence of this blight thanks to the seeds that Chip procured."

"Actually," said the pirq, "it was Lori who procured them. I was just the messenger. Or, err, the delivery boy. I merely brought them to the druids," he explained in response to Eben's puzzled look.

Eben turned and scrutinized me with a suspicious look.

"I will have the druids brought here under escort," the Seventh finally decided. "They must understand what is holding the Guardian."

"The shades," I said. "It is the shades that restrain him."

Three pairs of surprised eyes fixed on me.

"Explain," Eben demanded, "what these shades are and how you know this."

"As far as I understand, the shades are manifestations of the power that Geranika wields. I can see them surrounding the Guardian. There they are," I alternately poked my fingers at the jailer shades floating in the fog.

Eben looked carefully in the directions indicated by me, took out a strange flower and waved it in front of him. The flower dissolved into purple pollen that began to float in the air, but the Seventh's face did not clear up.

"I cannot see them," he said in a broken voice. "Can you destroy them, or drive them away, Lorelei?"

I shook my head.

"No. But, I believe I know those who can."

"The renegades?" The spymaster tensed.

"Not exactly," I glanced at Chip, but he only shrugged, leaving the decision up to me. "Those outsiders that crossed the Arras. They are free citizens and they have surely encountered Geranika's shades before."

I spoke without any certainty. After the continental scenario in the Dark Forest, when Mahan refused to become a disciple of Geranika, five classes were given the opportunity to destroy the shadows. I think I remember reading that the priests had devised a way to fight against the forces of Shadow. But I had no idea whether the raiders from the Day of Wrath had these powers. Who knew—maybe they weren't unlocked automatically and required some long quest chain to obtain...In any case, the Seventh knew about the invasion and was clearly going to take action, so it wouldn't do any harm.

Meanwhile, Eben's AI had crunched through the elephant in the room.

"You?!" His face twisted with rage. "Was it you who ushered them through the Arras? So this is why the druids could not determine which of us opened our border! Shadow veils you from their gaze."

"Yes, it was me." There was no sense in denying the obvious. "For obvious reasons, I did not have the opportunity to ask for permission. There was no one around to come to my aid and they did. These outsiders are not enemies to our forest."

"Not enemies?" The spymaster looked at me so fiercely that I involuntarily shivered. "They have already felled five Forest Sentries! Another dozen have gone missing—the druids no longer sense them. And you say that they are not enemies? You will pay for this, Lorelei!" he promised ominously.

"The sentries attacked them and the outsiders defended themselves," I said, without much confidence in my own argument. "As for the dozen missing sentries—that is Geranika's doing. He captured and blighted some of the sentries."

The Guardian growled mournfully, once again causing me to feel dizzy, but did not interfere in the conversation further.

"Fire and ice!" Judging by his tone, this was Eben's way of cursing. "What else do I not know?"

"Has Chip already informed you about Astilba's intention to ambush and destroy the embassy?"

"Yes." The Seventh began to measure the cavern with his steps.

"Then I have one last piece of news left. I'm going to help Astilba summon Portulac from the Gray Lands."

It was as if Eben had run into a wall. He froze, turned and stared at me in disbelief.

"You...you have mastered Cypro's spell?"

"I deciphered the songbook he left and learned the spell. And it seems that Astilba has found a way to embody the soul of a sentient."

"Impossible..." whispered the Seventh. "Inconceivable..."

"THE DEAD BELONG IN THE GRRAY LANDS!" the Guardian's roar plastered me against the wall. "NO ONE IS ALLOWED TO VIOLATE THE ORRDER AS CONCEIVED BY THE CRREATOR! SOULS MAY VISIT THE LIVING FOR BUT A SHORRT TIME. THEY MAY NOT RETURRN TO LIFE IN A NEW BODY!"

Now I had to agree with Astilba's decision to isolate this overly orthodox pirq. He is clearly capable of not only foiling the ambush of the embassy, but also interfering in the forthcoming summoning.

"We'll soon find out if it's possible or not." I rubbed my aching head. "I understand that I did a lot of things without asking permission, but you also received invaluable information. And that's not to mention the artifact that is now in your hands. I ask little as a reward: Allow the outsiders to try and free the Guardian and let me help Astilba bring Portulac back. After that, you can judge me, exile me, or kill me—it does not matter to me."

"YOU DARRE STAMMER OF A REWARRD?" barked the Guardian.

For his part, Eben scratched his chin thoughtfully. I could almost feel his ingrained distrust of the outsiders grapple with his desire to solve the problem. Either way, the imminent alliance would mean having to work with other races, so the current opportunity of a trial run was quite timely. It'd be a shame to miss this opportunity.

"As you see, you're out of options, you Onion Knight," Chip said, seeing the biota's vacillation. "All energy flows according to the whims of the Gitche Manitou. It's time to bury the hatchet between the Algonquin and the Iroquois."

The face of the Seventh grew pensive and he turned to me with genuine puzzlement:

"Tell me, Lorelei, are these free citizens as strange as he is?" The spymaster's dark finger pointed at Chip.

"No, the overwhelming majority of them are much more comprehensible and generally calmer," I reassured him.

"Oh don't you worry, you brambling rose," chuckled the subject of our discussion. "I'm crazy, but I'm not violent!"

Eben looked dubiously at Chip, his crossed eyes

and bulging chest, and sighed heavily:

"Very well. The time has come to learn to communicate with the free citizens and the races of the outside world. I will give them a chance to prove their good intentions. As for your request..."

A weighty pause ensued as I held my breath.

"Portulac has always been reasonable and constant," Eben continued. "Perhaps his return will help Astilba regain her clarity of thought. I would not like to fight our brothers and sisters. Summon his spirit, Lorelei, and tell him of all the madness that has swept over the Hidden Forest."

I exhaled in relief as Chip quipped:

"The voice of progress in the realm of obscurantism. Drill a buttonhole for that medal, Siguranța. And another question," he tossed his head in the direction of the prisoner, now without any of his former sympathy in his eyes. It seems that the thought of the Guardian's coming salvation had torn the invisible thread that had connected the NPC with something important to him out in reality. "What's to guarantee that this yeti doesn't bite off our heads in celebration of his release?"

In essence, the question was an excellent one, but its phrasing left much to be desired. I wonder what Chip's Attractiveness is with Eben? And whether Attractiveness can dip in the negatives?

"My word is your guarantee," the Guardian threatened. "If you manage to release me, you will in fact prove that you are working for the Seventh and the benefit of the forest. I will spare you and those outsiders who have trespassed across the Arras."

"Can you teach us your brand of negotiating as well?" Chip inquired, twiddling his whiskers. "I've always envied people like you: It's like you're up to your ears in it, yet somehow you insist that everyone dances to your tune and so confidently that there's no room to object."

"I DO NOT NEGOTIATE," growled the Guardian loud enough to shake the entire hill. "I COMMAND!"

"Why that's exactly what I'm talking about!" The pirq spread his arms. "There, do you see?" He turned to us, as if we were witnesses. "And there's nothing to object to...It's just like I'm back in boot camp, only this time it's scarier. So will you teach me?"

For a few seconds the Guardian silently drilled Chip with his eyes, and then, unexpectedly, burst into laughter and grinned with his entire impressive mouth:

"I shall teach you as soon as I am free," he said in an ordinary pirq voice.

Eben and I stared in amazement at the ancient pirq, while Chip cautiously clarified:

"Do I have your word?"

"You have my word," the Guardian nodded, still grinning.

"It's agreed then," Chip nodded in satisfaction, and turning to me, said with a touch of bitterness in his voice: "That's what our world's lacking these days, Lori. The fidelity to keep one's word."

"As well as keeping one's mouth shut," I muttered, pulling out my amulet to the raiding party. The time had come to set the Guardian free.

CHAPTER THIRTEEN

IRK RESPONDED ENTHUSIASTICALLY to the idea of naturalizing his merry band by helping the local authorities spring the Guardian. Due to the aggroing Forest Sentries, the raid had to stay together and the search for the new dungeon was going very slowly. Permission from the Council to stay in the forest would make it possible to spread out and search the territory far faster, and the Day of Wrath did not intend on missing out on such an opportunity.

So less than an hour later, the raiding party had surrounded the hill.

"Hell of a mug you got there," said Spiteful Chip, meeting Bogart the Base for the first time in-game.

And at this point a new problem came up: The orc and the pirq spoke completely different languages. Although I understood both friends due to my language pack, in an odd way, I knew exactly which language each one was speaking. In this respect, the in-game linguistics was much more convenient than real life. At one time, I had studied early modern

English and Russian, in order to expand my audience, but switching from one to another right in the middle of the conversation was not easy. There were no problems with this whatsoever here.

Luckily, the Seventh spared me from the dubious joy of having to relate the blather of my two friends by calling over Dirk to act as an interpreter. The raid leader managed to find out that it would not be possible to buy a biota or pirq language pack for his raiders—as it was simply not for sale, like all language packs for the hardcore races. One could only learn them through gameplay.

An invitation to join the raid party appeared in my interface. As soon as I accepted it, a torrent of incoming data transfixed my eyes. Without further ado, I concealed all this wealth, leaving only the raid chat.

"I welcome the representative of the Council and sincerely apologize for the invasion of your lands," Dirk bowed respectfully to Eben, waited until I finished the translation, and continued: "My guild arrived in the Hidden Forest with the intention of preventing Geranika from destroying the Dark Lord of Kartoss. Geranika has plunged his dagger into the throne of the Dark Lord, and if we do not find a way to neutralize it, our liege shall perish. According to a document we found, there might be an artifact on the territory of the Hidden Forest that is capable of destroying the accursed dagger."

I ogled Dirk with astonishment, but translated everything. The words of the raid leader surprised not only me; the raid chat exploded with questions:

"*Whaaaa...??*"

"*We found a way to save the Dark Lord?*"

"*Why didn't you tell us?*"

Finally, Dirk lost his patience and began twiddling his fingers barely noticeably, typing a reply on the virtual keyboard:

"*Everybody calm down. It's the best excuse I could think of. Anyway, it *could* be true. We don't know, they don't know.*"

"I have heard about the Dark Lord's unfortunate predicament," the Seventh answered thoughtfully after a long pause, "but this is the first time I hear that the item of his salvation is hidden in our lands."

"This is only an assumption," the priest hastily explained. "The instructions in the document are very vague."

"And because of, as you put it, such vague instructions, you dared to invade the Hidden Forest, fell several Forest Sentries and scour our lands without the Council's permission?"

Eben had not raised his voice, but his words sounded ominous. A debuff called 'The Displeasure of the Seventh' appeared on Dirk, temporarily reducing his crit chance by 90%.

"Would you not yourself have gone to extreme measures in order to save the Guardian?" Dirk said, unflapped. "The demise of the Dark Lord risks granting victory to Geranika, who seeks to destroy all of Barliona. Even a fleeting chance to stop Shadow is worth a minor violation of the borders. I guarantee and swear that none of my people wish evil to the people of the Hidden Forest."

"You're right, free citizen," Eben said after listening to my translation. "Shadow must be stopped, but for the sake of the Guardian's salvation, I am prepared to accept the help of outsiders. However, if you fail, I will destroy everyone and make sure that none of you cross the Arras ever again."

A strange discrepancy caught my attention. Despite the gravity of the negotiations that would decide the fate of the raid, many players were grinning and, every now and again glancing somewhere off to the side. Looking over, I saw my two pocket clowns trying to have a conversation in pantomime. At that moment, Bogart was portraying some episode of his adventure: Stamping on the spot, he put his fists to his temples with his index fingers stuck out (I think these were supposed to be the tauren's horns), bulged out his eyes and stared in front of himself with the dull stubbornness of a bull who'd noticed the moon for the first time. The impression was so funny that even Pops, whom Bogart was aping, snorted with delight, stamped the ground with his hoof, and wiped his eyes. Qupip had already turned his back on Dirk and Eben entirely to watch the spectacle, giggling into his fist.

Finally, the negotiations were completed, the raid received the quest and we moved to free the Guardian.

"No more than six can fit in that hole," Dirk announced, assessing the situation. "Pops, Fro, Elk, Soul, Huron and Lipo—you destroy the shades. Everyone else, remain at full readiness. Experience shows that it's never simple with Geranika."

How right he was...

Entering the cavern with the cage and the Guardian, the players set up some artifact that broadcast what was happening underground to the surface in the manner of a holoprojector, so that the raid could watch the first phase of the battle in real time.

A dazzling radiance began to pour forth from the paladin's hands, at once throwing the light and the shadows in the cave into sharp contrast. But when the aura faded and the dungeon again plunged into gloom, not all of the shadows were gone. The shades circling around the Guardian acquired density and volume, becoming vulnerable to the players' attacks— which the players immediately took advantage of. Now the rogue's daggers and warrior's broadsword destroyed the embodied shades in a matter of seconds. My ears filled with the Guardian's triumphant roar and I could hardly hear the words of Dirk beside me:

"Seems too easy."

In the next instant the tree roots that permeated the entire hill came to life, entangling the players in a suffocating grip. Health bars began plummeting, but the immobilized players were unable to do anything. New shades grew from the roots ensnaring the Guardian who was just dashing to freedom. To top it off, the blighted tree on the hilltop twitched its twisted branches and, with a heart-rending creak, began to pull its own roots out of the hill. At the same time, the tree received a name and characteristics: 'Blighted Ironwood.'

"*Nieta, get into the hill. You have to sever those roots,*" Dirk reacted immediately. "*Sylvan, try to draw the tree's aggro. Everyone, spread out, so that the roots can't do splash damage.*"

The players immediately scattered all over the hillside, shooting arrows and spells at the living tree. But in the cave, things were going quite poorly. Casting a bubble, Fro freed himself from the roots strangling him and was now hastily casting healing spells, restoring the health of his comrades. But he simply could not push through to the exit—there was no room. All that remained for the paladin was to wield his sword, freeing Huron, the druid beside him.

"*I'm caught!*" Nieta reported suddenly, stuck in the corridor. Her little figure was rooted so tightly that even the top of her head wasn't visible.

"*The wood is resistant to physical attacks,*" Fro's

message flew through the chat. *"The roots don't have a lot of HP, but their armor blocks 99% of the damage dealt. I used an AoE scroll. But 99% of the damage was also absorbed. We have to focus each root with magic."*

"Statimania, can you reach Nieta without having to enter the lair?" Dirk asked a mage in the chat.

"I'll try," she replied.

"Cut her free and pull her out. Fro, forget the roots and just heal the guys. It'll be faster to kill the tree up here than to set you free. Sylvan, what have you got?"

"The boss won't aggro individual players, he's just whipping the entire raid with his roots and branches. If they hit, it's a one-shot. The trunk is still invulnerable, we're working on the limbs."

Everything happening around me, seemed like a light show. The air buzzed with spells and flying arrows, the creaking of twigs and the dull thumps of the roots against the ground. It was completely unrealistic to follow everything at once, but Dirk seemed to be coping with his duties just fine. All that I could do was already done: I buffed the raid and debuffed the enemy. My impact shades did no damage to the tree—they simply soaked into the blighted plant. Our common Shadow alignment made all of my better spells useless, so all I could do was stand and watch the high-level raiders ply their trade.

At some moment the earth disappeared from under my feet, I was jerked somewhere, and a branch of the rabid tree whistled right past my ear.

"Use your eyes," advised Chip.

He held me by the collar, like a kitten.

"If you keep this up, you won't be long for this game. And then you'll have to sit in the kitchen waiting for us in anguish and anxiety. You should be more cautious, like for example this..."

Bogart swept past us hollering joyfully and began to weave between the whipping branches, loping them asunder with his battle axe. For some unknown reasons, the strange hunter preferred his 'Croaker' to his crossbow.

"...unfortunate example," Chip finished his thought, dragging me to a safe distance.

"*I got Nieta out,*" Statimania announced in the chat. "*She tried to move forward, but the roots got her after a couple of steps. Fro's caught again too. The roots come back after we move a meter or so.*"

"*Forget the cavern and focus on the tree,*" Dirk ordered, continuing to heal his raiders.

"I'll try to go enter the cave," I told the occupied priest.

"You'll die, minnow."

"I am a creature of Shadow. Maybe the roots won't aggro me."

"Try it then," decided Dirk and I, trying not to lose sight of the branches that flashed here and there, ran for the familiar entrance.

My assumption turned out to be correct: My

shades didn't do damage to the tree and in return the tree didn't perceive me as an enemy. I ducked into the passageway and moved as fast as I could into the depths of the hill. Straight in front of me, blocking the passage, hung Pops' immense body—immobile in the thorns of his coiled straitjacket.

Machine gun
Tearing my body all apart
Machine gun
Tearing my body all apart...

The magic missiles slammed into the wooden fetters, blasting them with spectacular effect. Since I was still on blighted ground, one volley knocked 5% off the root's HP, so I hoped to release the tauren in just twenty shots. As it turned out, seventeen was enough. Three of the magic missiles were fire and therefore dealt critical hits to the wood.

"Move at least half a meter," I asked the tank, and the tank squeezed himself against the wall as best he could, allowing me to squeeze through to the next cocoon. Fortunately, it contained Huron the druid who helped me cut through the roots.

"What are we going to do?" Elk asked, when all the players in the cave had been freed.

"I would try and kill those shadows," suggested Pops and immediately echoed his idea in the raid chat.

"*Give it a shot.*" Dirk granted the go-ahead after a few seconds of meditation.

The cave's earthen walls began trembling so violently that I involuntarily stuck my head into my shoulders and waited for the whole place to collapse at any moment. At least, the seasoned raiders were hardly affected. They again embodied the shadows and then artfully dealt with them, freeing the Guardian.

The Guardian straightened himself to all his mighty height, squared his shoulders, raised his paw and began to bulldoze aside whatever pathetic little obstacle blocked his path. From somewhere above, apparently from the trunk of a tree, shadows appeared yet again, coiling around the ancient pirq. New roots shot from where the destroyed ones lay, punching through the earth, weaving upwards. And in short order, the players found themselves bound all over again.

"*I don't know what you guys are up to down there, but I need you to keep doing it,*" Dirk wrote in the raid chat. "*Two of the roots plunged into the ground, leaving the trunk vulnerable. We've whittled it down by 20%.*"

For a moment I pondered whom to release first—Huron or Fro—but the latter again cast his paladin's bubble dispelling both the roots and my deliberation. After that, we found our rhythm and began acting more or less in sync: The liberated druid destroyed the roots of the other fighters, they embodied another shade, the Guardian busted though his prison, wreaked havoc for a few seconds, and then everyone was restrained all over again. I had no idea what was going on upstairs, but judging by the cries of 'second phase!' and Dirk's incessant commands—it was fun.

At some point, once more freed from the shadows, the Guardian went completely berserk, smashed his cage to smithereens and with a wild growl surged up like a geyser through the soil and the tree trunk.

"I AM FRREE!" he roared, smashing the blighted tree, which had by then been stripped of most of its branches.

From his roar, I not only flattened my ears, but also received a bouquet of temporary debuffs ranging from stun to disorientation. If you ask me, the entire forest had heard that triumphant bellow and Geranika was no doubt aware that I had failed in my assignment.

"Kiera!" Two mugs appeared in the newly-formed hole—one white and fluffy, the other green and bald.

Remarkably, my name sounded the same in both languages. After making sure that I was all right, the friends exchanged glances and the shaggy one said reproachfully:

"Nope, I just can't take you anywhere without supervision. What have you done to make this ancient behemoth," Chip pointed to the Guardian, "...croon like the rockers of old? If he keeps this up you'll have no choice but to schlep him around with you on your concert tour."

"I would lose my mind from a vocalist like that," I snorted, but the end of my sentence was again drowned out by the Guardian's roar.

"YOU OUTSIDERS HAVE PRROVEN THE WORRTH OF YOUR WORRD. I ALLOW YOU TO REMAIN IN MY FOREST, BUT I WILL WATCH EACH STEP YOU MAKE. DO NOT DISPLEASE ME!"

While the Day of Wrath raiders were climbing out of the collapsed lair, Bogart tossed me a rope and as soon as I grabbed it, the guys hauled me up and out of the destroyed hill.

"Listen," said Bogart pensively, assessing the destruction caused by the Guardian, "maybe we can use him as an engineer? I don't know about digging, but this boy can smash any bunker we set him on—why he's got more effect than a good old Paveway."

The raiders, meanwhile, hastily resurrected the dead fighters, and the chat was already in full swing.

"*Manitou, what the hell did you stand in front of that whipping branch for?*"

"*I was gonna jump it...you know, like a jump rope...*"

I didn't keep reading and replied to Bogart instead:

"Why don't you shut up for like ten minutes? Otherwise your engineer there might bust your bunker."

The next moment I wanted to squint: One after another, blinding auras of light burst from Bogart the Base, announcing his new levels. Some of the raiders also began blinking like tiny supernovae. I guess they had earned a good deal of XP for this quest. Alas, Chip and I went unrewarded: Not being outsiders, the quest was unavailable to us.

"YOU," the Guardian's meaty finger pointed at Chip. "DESPITE YOUR YOUTH, YOU HAVE PRROVEN YOURRSELF A COURRAGEOUS DEFENDER OF YOUR NATIVE FORREST. AND AS A DRRUID-DEFENDER YOU DESERRVE THE OPPORTUNITY TO CHANGE YOUR APPEARANCE."

"I serve! My native! Forest!" yelled the pirq, saluting with his paw at his temple.

Standing next to him, Bogart naturally didn't understand a damn thing without my translation, but either by reflex or from sheer tomfoolery, he also snapped to attention beside his friend, thrusting out his chest and raising his chin. He did not salute, however. And yet, it was the strangest thing: Despite the absurdity of all this, the sight really was a solemn one. I guess, there's a lot of time to practice this kind of thing in the army.

Judging by the approving grin on the Guardian's face, he liked it. The black pirq threw up his paw and his smaller, albino cousin (the three really looked like Yin, Yang and Wasabi) was enveloped in the familiar aura that signified that he had received some new trait.

"*Look for the bare necessities...*" Chip suddenly began to sing and turned...into a bear. A big blond-brown grizzly bear stood in the pirq's place, jumping and chortling cheerfully:

"*The simple bare necessities,*

Forget about your worries and your strife..."

Bogart stared at a friend for a couple of seconds, and then, recognizing the melody, chimed in, in Kartossian:

"*I mean, the bare necessities*

Old Mother Nature's recipes

That brings the bare necessities of life..."

The entire raid, the Seventh and the Guardian watched with astonishment as the pair began hollering a song from an old children's cartoon, dancing around the pit that remained where the prison had been.

"*The bees are buzzin' in the tree...*"

"*To make some honey just for me...*" bumping their heads and butts, the two sang incoherently, in two languages, loud enough for the forest to hear.

"Are they clowns in meatspace or something?" Dirk asked me quietly, without taking his eyes off the wild dance. "I'll pay one gold for a recording of this show."

"I think this dance is an example of a group concussion. And a contagious one," I added, glancing at Qupip who had joined the dancers. "Should we quarantine them?"

"If I'm given the ability to turn into an animal, which druids can only get by doing a long quest chain that's only unlocked at Level 100, I'll dance naked in quarantine with them."

The Guardian, who had been watching the wild dance with a grin, again began to boom:

"MY WORRD IS INVIOLABLE. THERREFORE, RECEIVE NOW THE PRROMISED SKILL...BARRTERING."

Another radiant aura enveloped the dancing bear and then the bear's face broke into an eerie smile. I scratched my head, puzzled. Strange, I thought Chip already had the bartering skill...

"AS FOR YOU, MINION OF SHADOW..." The black's pirq's muzzle turned in my direction and lost all trace of gaiety. "YOU SHALL NOT BE DESTRROYED WITHOUT THE POSSIBILITY OF REVIVAL. I SHALL ALLOW YOU TO FINISH WHAT YOU STARRTED BEFORRE YOU ARRE EXILED FRROM THE HIDDEN FORREST. SHADOW SHALL HAVE NO PLACE IN MY LAND!"

Oh how generous. If you think about it, it's not such a bad reward. Especially if you remember the video of the trial of Mahan after the scenario of the Dark Forest. He almost had his avatar deleted for his shenanigans with Geranika. The heck with it, exile. The main thing is that I will keep Lorelei and have time to finish the scenario.

"I thank you for your mercy, Guardian," I answered with all possible respect.

"If you want to deceive Geranika about the reason you failed his quest, I can help," said Eben who had been silent until now. "Tell him that you encountered me under the hill and I sent you to the Gray Lands. I can do more than kill you. I can also leave a special mark on you which will deceive Geranika into thinking that I killed you. There is a chance that you will be forgiven, you will not lose his trust and will be able to reveal his plan to us later. Do you agree?"

Quest available: _A Friend among the Outsiders_. Description: Eben wishes you to learn Geranika's plans and tell him about them. Quest type: Unique scenario. Reward: Variable. Penalty for failing/refusing the quest: Eben will no longer consider you his agent.

"Yes, oh Seventh," I answered after a moment's hesitation.

I won't be any worse of for accepting this quest.

"Here is an amulet to contact me. Good luck to you, Lorelei," Eben said very gravely and the next instant, a blow from his dagger sent me to respawn.

You have died. You may continue playing in

the Gray Lands. Do you wish to move to this location?

The 'No' option beckoned me to take a break and relax a little. After such an eventful game session, I could use some rest, especially taking into account today's scheduled band practice. But the Gray Lands also represented an opportunity to read a new entry in Cypro's journal...

"I'll just read the entry," I promised myself, pushing 'Yes.'

The colorless, lifeless world resembled an old film. A silent movie from the beginning of the twentieth century. I wonder if I get Chip in here, will he start imitating Charlie Chaplin?

Such delirious thoughts really did point to the need to take a break, and I hastily opened the Tenth's tattered journal. Instead of a new entry on the blank page, however, I encountered the following notification:

Bardic Inspiration 15 required to read the next entry.

I sighed in disappointment and exited the game.

The apartment was still and empty. The capsule in Pasha's room hummed steadily. I bet he hasn't yet completed his business with the Guardian and the druids' quest. Sasha, most likely, will continue to hang around for a long time with the raid. Great. The most important thing is to snatch a couple of hours of sleep—that's all I had before Pasha's cartridges had to be swapped again.

But by the appointed time, Pasha had still not emerged from his cocoon, though Sasha had and was now puttering around the kitchen. I was already used to the fact that the kitchen was like Pasha and Sasha's joint estate, in which I acted the part of the guest and the court taster. I cannot say that I was very upset by this state of affairs. Sasha, who seemed to have his own electronic key for the apartment, was chopping vegetables with a hefty cleaver, slightly smaller than Bogart's Croaker.

"I'm going to make ratatouille," he announced. "Would you like some tea?"

"Do me the favor," I did not refuse, sitting down on an empty stool. "And where is the second behemoth?"

"Pasha's stayed in the game," Sasha replied, conjuring over a teapot. "Your Eben has taken him away on some kind of mission."

"I'll go press the call of the meatspace button, or that evil doctor will come and take his undisciplined patient back to the hospital."

"There is still time," Sasha nodded at his watch. "You'll have time to have some tea."

"Good idea," I agreed, making a ham and cheese sandwich. "How did the whole thing end in there?"

"Ah with nothing," Sasha waved his hand. "The raid went on about its business. That spy-root of yours to Pasha with him and then I got eaten by dinosaurs."

I popped out my eyes and choked on my sandwich. Sasha immediately began hammering me between the shoulder blades, catapulting the bit of sandwich out of my throat and onto the table in an appetizing still-life.

"Huh?" I asked when I'd done coughing. "What dinosaur?"

"Who the hell knows?" Sasha shrugged, laying his knife aside and picking up the sponge. "They were like velociraptors or some-other raptors...dromaeosaurids, in other words. I was walking along, minding my own business and a pack of these prehistoric feathered creatures burst out of the forest and fell upon me." He began to wipe my arts and crafts from the table. "And I had a brain fart. Instead of thinning them out with my crossbow, I chose hand-to-claw combat...And was punished for my short-sightedness with a series of crits."

"Where did dinosaurs come from in there?"

"Pasha told me that the pirqs raise them like cats, dogs and other cattle. They're found closer to the mountains," Sasha happily shared his knowledge of the matter.

"What will the devs cook up next..." I wondered. "We'll need to interrogate Pasha about the pirq starting location. It doesn't look like I'll be able to go there anymore."

"Could be, could be," Sasha tossed the sponge in the sink and then started to rummage in an obscure corner of the kitchen cupboard and produced...a bib.

"Here." He dangled the bib in front of me. "Baby Sinclair..."

"Oh but I couldn't possibly presume to use yours," I declined such a generous gift. "And where'd you get that anyway? Don't tell me it's your patrimony or something...Even taking into account Pasha's problems with the jaw, it's not his size."

"Why we ordered it for you," Sasha gibed back. "You're a musician, a cultural persona. In other words...a savage. I'm sure you'll like it. It's a nice pink and it's got these kitties all over it." He stuck the bib right up to my nose, eager I see the kitties.

"Nope. Not my style," I concluded after carefully trying on the bib. "And you didn't get my size right."

"Have it your way, you bib snob," Sasha snorted, putting the bib away. "Just don't tell Pasha. It might piss him off," he warned.

"Why?"

"He doesn't like it when people touch his daughter's things. Or remind him about that whole thing in general," Sasha said after a brief pause and returned to his cooking.

I was stunned. Pasha had of course mentioned his divorce to me, but he somehow kept silent about having a child. Now, however, his overzealous care towards Anica began to make sense. It seems the NPC somehow reminded him of his daughter.

"He never said he has children. And there isn't a single photo in the apartment," I said, stating the obvious.

Sasha quietly made me a new sandwich and only then replied:

"He does not like to remember that episode of his life."

And he returned to shredding the defenseless vegetables with the knife. I pilfered a slice of an innocently-killed tomato from him, crowned my sandwich with it and began to chew pensively, considering this new bit of information.

"Oh, the intelligentsia!" Pasha's voice boomed behind me.

The pilot staggered to the table, studied the activities of his friend and flopped down beside him. His eyes gleamed, his face shone with delight. It was clear that the game had succeeded in really capturing him.

"Guys!" The tone in which this word was uttered, fully confirmed my assumptions. "You're about to turn into a pack of wild horses, neighing and stomping your hooves, but I'll tell you anyway: Being a bear is the bomb! Hey you long-nosed log, where is my juice?"

"In the fridge, oh avatar of Baloo," the long-nosed log replied humbly, without looking up from his work. "Lend me a paw and pass it over here. The juice, I mean, not your paw."

"What poor manners," Pasha reproached his friend and reached for the juice.

"Tell me more about the bear," I said. "What skills, traits and particularities does he have? I'm curious."

"Um..." Pasha sucked on the straw and only once the juicebox began to cave in, he exhaled loudly and only then attended to my curiosity. "I have not fully understood yet—there wasn't much time—but I found out that my stamina is doubled. There's a bonus to strength too, something to do with level. And we need to earn more money, 'cause the grizzly has his own gear. Or something like that."

"And how do you do damage? With your teeth and claws?" I grew even more interested, vividly imagining Pasha in his grizzly form, phlegmatically chewing up the enemy.

"Uh-huh," my companion nodded. "But that's also full of various details like levels and buffs and stuff. We'll figure it out in due time, basically. All right there, Bogart, what do we have for our barbecue tomorrow?"

Sasha scratched the tip of his nose with his knife, rolled his eyes to the ceiling, calculating something, and reported:

"It's all almost ready, I just need to buy some

meat and marinate it. I already told Butcher Bob to save us a pig neck in advance. Well, and we're also waiting for Wallace and Morgana to show up."

"WALL-E? Where's he bouncing around these days?" Pasha asked.

"Still with my brigade. You know those combat engineers. They're either building a bridge or blowing one up. Here's what I think I'll do: I'm going to get everything ready right now and stop by the bar for a drink. After that way I'll pop into the super—maybe the whiskey will remind me of what else I need to buy."

"Fine, we'll change the cartridges while you're out," I approved the plan.

"No one asks me a damn thing as usual," sighed Pasha, playing the victim of some dictatorship.

The replacement of the cartridges passed by in the habitual order, except that we had to use the last cartridge on the face regenerator, the one restoring Pasha's lower jaw.

"Listen, I was just wondering, is it about time that I head home?" I asked Pasha, after the procedure was done. "Snegov is here almost all the time, so I don't think I'm that necessary anymore."

"What's with you?"" Pasha propped himself up on his elbows. "Did we do something wrong, Kiera?"

"No, everything is great," I even laughed. "But I have my own house, rehearsals, concerts..."

"Well, you're not having any problems with your

practices," reasoned Pasha. "And you said yourself that you guys don't have any shows scheduled. On top of that, they're sure to send our long-nosed log to Africa soon, and then I'll be left here alone—with Sarge."

"How soon?" I asked, baffled. "Wasn't he complaining that his vacation was too long and he didn't know what to do, except 'languish in his VR sarcophagus?' Doesn't he have another month or two on his break?"

"Oh didn't he tell you?" Pasha asked, surprised. "He finally made lieutenant. He's going to the big time. They've given him a platoon."

"I won't pretend that I understand what that has to do with his vacation ending early."

"They're calling him up," Pasha explained patiently. "There's no one there to command the platoon. For now, it's assigned to garrison duty, the deputy CO is in charge, but it's not the same thing. So they're calling up our beloved Lieutenant Snegov— he's going to be issuing orders."

"Mmmyeah..." I drawled. "Fun life you guys lead. All right, in that case I'll hang around a little longer. But keep in mind, as soon as I gain worldwide renown, I'm off on my world tour!"

"Agreed," Pasha said and picked up his T-shirt. "Let's go down to the street. I don't want to miss the sight of Sasha fleeing the supermarket in a shopping cart again."

CHAPTER FOURTEEN

A T LAST THE MOMENTOUS DAY ARRIVED—Pasha's jaw regenerator was coming off and he would be able to eat solid food again. The pilot's ecstasy knew no bounds. He was glowing so much that at any moment now, I expected sun specks to go running along the walls turning the place into a disco.

For the occasion, Sasha arranged a picnic with a barbecue and other treats. Two more joined our small company—Wallace, who came literally the day before, and whose nickname was WALL-E and an old friend of Sasha's named Eugenia. Wallace served as an engineer-sapper, in the same peacekeeping brigade as Sasha. All three of them had been friends since childhood—or as Sasha put it, 'we shared one pot in pre-K.' Wallace also had the reputation of being the only respectable person in their trio, as he was married and already had two children.

On the other hand, respectability did not get in the way of his fooling around.

As for Eugenia, who liked to go by Morgana—we had quite a lot in common. She was the only one who like me had no relationship whatsoever with the armed forces and also played Barliona—but she also worked in there as an in-game lawyer. She had never actually met Pasha before and only knew of him because of Sasha's tales and so for once I did not feel like I was the only newcomer in this company.

Mount Mashuk was chosen as the location for the picnic. Pasha insisted that this was the only place worthy of entertaining such a respectable audience. Now I can't speak for the venerable public, but the plain at the foot of the mountain seemed perfectly fine to me. Still, here we were. Overgrown with forests and fragrant grasses, the mountain's slopes curved fancifully in places, forming level meadows suitable for camping.

The first thing the guys did when we reached our camping ground was pull out bags and latex gloves and started picking up the refuse left behind by the previous campers. Pleasantly surprised, I joined the cleaning without objection.

"I have a special poster for them, for the pigs," Wallace huffed spitefully, stuffing the gathered garbage into a green bag with an alphanumeric combination on its side. "Help me out Pasha—not as a fellow grunt but as a friend—there's another bag in the trunk."

The pilot looked into the beaten up SUV, which had hauled us up here, and fished out a frame with a solar panel battery. A hoop large enough to fit around a tree trunk was mounted to the frame.

After fiddling around for a couple of minutes, Pasha attached the device to a tree and turned it on with interest. Three dirty piglets appeared on the neon screen with the inscription 'Only *you* can prevent the three little pigs from littering in the forest!'

"Verily," Sasha approved, brandishing his shovel with such menace that it seemed he was about to bash in some littering piglets. "Is that enough?"

He straightened out, standing in a hole dug for garbage disposal and wiped the sweat from his bald spot with a handkerchief.

"More than enough," Wallace nodded. "Step aside..."

Sasha climbed out and the first plastic bag went flying into the pit. In general, these bags intrigued me quite a bit: In addition to the incomprehensible alphanumeric combination on the side, they were equipped with a vacuum clasp and a fishing line with a ringlet.

"Fire in the hole!" Wallace yelled cheerfully and pulled the little ring.

A wave of heat erupted from the pit accompanied by a tiny mushroom cloud of ash. And that was that. Nothing remained of the bag filled with empty bottles, beer cans and other litter.

"That's how we recycle out there," the sapper explained to me, throwing the next bag into the pit. I figured by 'there' he was referring to Africa.

"Want to try to yank it?" he asked, offering me the ringlet.

"Will it blow my hands off?" I asked just in case.

"Well, you're not going to hold the package in your hands, are you? So go ahead and pull away, no need to be afraid," Wallace encouraged me and walked to his SUV for the next package, of which he had a box in his trunk.

I looked at the ring in my hand doubtfully, took a deep breath and, following Sasha's example, hollered, "Fire in the hole!" and pulled. A hot blast blew into my face, ruffled my hair, and...that's it. Nothing to be afraid of—if you don't hug the package to yourself, that is.

"You look like Medusa," Pasha giggled. In view of his limited mobility, he had been tasked with uncorking the beer bottles.

"Yes, there is a resemblance," Sasha agreed with him and clarified, "Medusa after surviving an explosion in a fireworks factory."

"It's a pity that I'm missing my ability to turn you clowns into stone," I complained. "You lot would make a nice group sculpture. The Burghers of the Nuthouse."

"Oh what fine black bile," Sasha quipped, quickly thrust a ring into my hand from the next demo package and stepped aside. Here was my second chance to cremate 'the artifacts of a civilized society,' as Wallace had dramatically dubbed the garbage. Meanwhile, the author of this bon mot was watching the fire, periodically prodding it with a long branch and filling in the loss of liquid with the help of a bottle of beer.

"Kiera!" Two voices shouted indignantly behind my back. "Bogart's eating raw meet again!"

Turning around, I saw Sasha, scurrying for the forest with a piece of meat between his teeth. He didn't go far though—right up to the treeline, where he stopped and began to collect more firewood as if nothing had happened.

"He's a ranger after all. A born savage," Pasha chided me. "If you only knew what kind of crap they eat when they're behind enemy lines. Sometimes I was even afraid to extract them: They spend two weeks in the jungle, subsisting on god knows what, sleeping in lean-tos made of their own shit, and then when they hear my bird chopping the air, they come running out like...like an undiscovered tribe, only one that's armed with AKs and Dragunovs instead of clubs and spears. So just make sure you eat your fill because this one leaves no grub behind."

Hearing that we were talking about him, the object of our conversation hid behind a tree, popped out and stuck out his tongue.

"There, do you see!" the pilot pointed an accusing finger at him. "Like I said: Sa-vage!"

It was a little strange to see grown men who were almost forty fooling around like utter children.

Strange, but pleasant all the same. To be honest, I'm sick and tired of people who act like the masters of the universe, slick businessmen and brutish alpha types. My opinion of people, of course, is pretty spoiled by all the corporate offices I've worked in, where everyone tries to outdo the next guy. Often the achievements are completely trivial or utterly fictitious. Chattering about some new luxury car, or a new addition to some collection of items the collector doesn't even know how to use, arrogant discussions of how someone rose through the ranks normally...All that always caused me sincere bewilderment. What is the pleasure of building yourself up into someone who you really are not? Wasting your life in trying to live like someone else? This is probably why I've always felt more comfortable in the company of careless friends. They may be goofballs, but at least they're true to themselves.

Pasha and his friends were like this. And even though their fun-loving carelessness, at times betrayed something else, something dark, gloomy and unkind lurking beneath the surface, they rushed to live life, eagerly enjoying any trifle that came across their way and utterly unafraid of seeming ridiculous to someone else.

When the meat was ready, everyone sat down by the fire and the conversation somehow wound its way to the topic of Barliona. Pasha and I relived our adventures in the Hidden Forest and began to discuss my negative reputation with both gaming empires.

"Damn. That's a hell of a way to lose a character," Morgana said, impressed. "You barely learned to walk and you've already borked your Rep. That takes talent! How hard is it to get to the Hidden Forest anyway? It would be interesting to see the botanical wonderland."

"As I understand it, the scenario will have the biota and pirqs form an alliance with Kartoss. And then they should open the border. And in the meantime, it's no easy feat at all. The Arras is surrounded by nasty aggros and crossing the border illegally means hatred status with the locals. Anyway, the embassy is due to arrive any day now, so there is no point in hurrying. Wait a week or two and go visit your new allies formally."

"Do you have a map on the tablet?" Morgana asked. "I want to estimate how much a teleport will cost."

I had my tablet with me and as it happened, I had just downloaded my map from the game in order to share it with Sloe, so there were no problems with this. Thanks to the Day of Wrath cartographers, the map on the tablet was much more detailed than my version. To my surprise, not only Morgana became interested in the map, but Wallace too.

"Will you look at these smart-asses," the sapper snickered. He prodded a point on the map with his finger: "They've made a corridor here with a bend in it."

"Well, yeah," Sasha entered the conversation and, sniffing with concentration, turned the tablet. "Someone's planning ambushes here and here—I'll bet a case of beer on it. They'll hit the column here and cut off a part of it. After that, depending on how things go, they can retreat or call up some reserves and finish the job. And if anyone tries to relieve the target, they'll be stopped here and here."

He returned the tablet to me and summarized:

"I'll wager my tail that one of our boys is helping the corp with this scenario. What it lacks is fantasy, imagination. I guess he's decided that since it's for gamers, the bare minimum will do. But it is clear that the guy's got some experience under his belt."

"You should risk your tail less," Morgana deadpanned amid the general laughter. "And could you explain for us special needs types, what are you looking at there so intently and who is going to be doing the hitting, the cutting and the relieving?"

"All right." Sasha took the tablet from me again and turned on the three-dimensional holographic projection, shamelessly burning my battery.

"Look here..." The blighted areas of the forest filled with red, outlining a convoluted labyrinth that for some reason reminded me of a map of urban catacombs I had seen once. "The renegades have an advantage on the blighted ground, which allows them among other things to quickly transfer resources from sector to sector, making the best use of their small numbers. Here and here..." Sasha drew some blue circles and labeled the locations he was talking about, "...they hem the road in from both sides and make a sharp turn at a right angle. These are the spots to set up an ambush—the renegades will let the vanguard pass or whatever part of the column they're not interested in, and then they can strike the target. And any help coming will be cut off. This way, they can easily destroy a fairly large formation piecemeal, unless there's air support of course."

"I'd mine the corridor too," added Wallace. "You know—to ensure that life doesn't always seem as sweet as honey. And here..." He pointed to an area that resembled a town square: the narrow road widened, forming a kind of circus arena and then narrowed again to a bottleneck. "...here I would mine the entrances. And more mines around the open area. And when the enemy enters—I'd hammer him from all sides with everything I had, periodically setting off the mines to keep him disorganized."

"Well, and the cherry on top," said Pasha "is that the passage from the border also passes through the blighted areas. Heck, even without landmines and other modern amenities, those renegades have really prepared very well and stand a good chance of winning."

Everyone stared at the map pensively, contemplating the conclusion the 'true blockheads' had just come to.

"Okay, ladies and gentlemen," Pasha suddenly said, tearing the company away from its meditations.

In his hand, Pasha held a cut glass tumbler—an incredible anachronism that remained quite popular in our time. It was not entirely clear to me why he would bring such a fragile item on a camping trip. My puzzlement was immediately cleared up, however: Two golden stars fell to the bottom of the tumbler with a quiet ring, and then the helicopter pilot filled the glass to the rim with vodka.

"Here." He handed the tumbler to Sasha.

Sasha took the tumbler, stood up, cleared his throat, and rattled off:

"I hereby present myself with my newly-assigned rank of Lieutenant." And to the approving roar of his friends, he dumped the vodka down his throat.

Having emptied the tumbler, he kissed the stars and placed them into a case that Pasha held for him.

"Well, finally," Wallace clapped Sasha on the shoulder. "It's for sure?"

"Uh-huh."

"That was quick," hummed the sapper. "I figured it would take another half a year. So what now? A cushy desk post in the Pentagon?"

"Nothing doing," Sasha grinned like a tomcat that had just cornered a carton of half and half. "It's back to the Congo next Saturday, this time at the head of a platoon."

"To the Congo?" To my surprise, the warriors grew gloomy.

"That's where Mtoro is up to his usual again..." Wallace spread his arms. "What are you, incapable of sitting in place, calmly on your ass? Is that stick that's up your butt bothering you again?"

"Something like that..." Sasha filled the glasses.

"Let's drink to your return," said Pasha, taking his glass.

"Ah come on. Without the purple stuff, please," Sasha replied dismissively. "It's just another day on the job."

"Sure. Just another day. Just a bunch of scumbags who've managed to raise and recruit three combat ready battalions," Pasha concluded for him. "With all the materiel and all. Transport, armor, artillery."

"I have an idea," Wallace winked. "Let's break his legs. Then they won't send him anywhere."

"Let's break his neck," said Morgana ominously.

"If there's anything I value about people—it's their willingness to help a fellow human out of a difficult situation," said the 'explosives master' with emotion. "By the way, Snegov, shouldn't Diver get a promotion now that you've taken his place?"

"No." Sasha frowned unexpectedly and from his suddenly sullen demeanor, as well as the sullen looks that appeared on the other soldiers' faces, I understood that the vacancy and subsequent promotion had come at a terrible price.

"And so," Sasha changed the topic. "The base is still equipped with capsules, so you won't get rid of me that easily!"

"You're going to keep playing?" Wallace asked, surprised. "How come? You used to hate all that crap."

"Well, at least I'll be able to see you guys," smiled Sasha and cast a quick glance in my direction.

"That's it!" Morgana approved. "At least you won't vanish for weeks at a time because you're too lazy to charge your visor. By the way, I have an idea! We should implant a generator in you. The rotational speed of that crowbar that's stuck up your ass will allow you to recharge not only your comm, but the VR capsule too."

This uncomplicated joke finally broke up the lingering gloom. And we went on laughing, joking and belting out songs to my guitar's accompaniment into the early morning.

CHAPTER FIFTEEN

I RETURNED TO BARLIONA RELUCTANTLY. I wanted to hang out and have fun instead of fermenting in that VR capsule, and yet less than two days remained before the First Bulbs Festival and the arrival of the embassy. After that, I couldn't imagine what would happen with the renegades' camp, and therefore I wanted to finish my business and prepare for the scenario finale. Sasha was shipping out that night and I had to complete my in-game business before the sending away party began.

Alas, my plans were dashed in the very first seconds upon entering the game. Geranika appeared in front of me right there in spawn. The Lord of Shadow's pursed lips and scornful glance suggested that he was not happy to see me.

"You failed to cope with a simple task," he said after a brief silence. "The Guardian is free. I do not need such worthless students."

Quest failed: *Way of the Apprentice.*
Current Reputation status with Geranika the

Lord of Shadow: Hostility.

"The task turned out more complicated than expected," I tried to justify myself without much enthusiasm. "Eben freed the Guardian with the help of free citizens from beyond the Arras and then he killed me. Am I expected to handle a member of the Council?"

Geranika fixed me so intently that I involuntarily shivered and a chill ran down my spine. In the next instant, a flash of light formed around me.

"You speak the truth," Geranika said with some surprise. "And I see the mark of the Seventh on you. Do you know that he can track your movement thereby?"

"That bastard!" My exclamation was sincere. That damn spymaster. He could have warned that his mark would track me. Although, maybe he doesn't trust me and wants to know my every step?

"It's okay. I know how to take advantage of this opportunity," Geranika smiled mysteriously and a shadow flew from his hand and rushed towards me.

In the next instant, it was like I had been wrapped from head to toe in dark translucent matter: My vision blurred and I felt a cool touch on my skin. And when the shadow pulled away—I stared at a shadowy clone of myself standing before me.

"Your shadow clone now bears Eben's mark," Geranika explained.

At the wave of his hand, the shadow biota sprinted from the camp, and the Lord of Shadow's gaze turned back to me again. An oppressive silence followed.

"Perhaps I shall grant you a second chance, after all. In the future," he added and disappeared, leaving me alone with a system notification.

Current Reputation status with Geranika Lord of Darkness: Neutral.

I exhaled and hurried away from the respawn point. Who knows, maybe my gig as a Shadow court minstrel might work out after all.

Completing the second step of the *Help the Renegades* quest immediately took me from Level 22 to Level 26 and raised my reputation with the renegades a little more. I didn't receive any items as a reward; most likely my 'losing' the two seeds was to blame for this. I was just about to ask the legate about the skills that he had gained by adopting Shadow when a very agitated Vex came rushing into the tent.

"Lorelei! The Sixth wishes to see you. This instant!"

"What happened?"

"The time of the embassy's arrival! It has been moved. The ambassadors are already on their way to the Arras! We must start right now!"

As if in confirmation of his words, the sound of a horn echoed through the camp. Hearing him, Signifier Lotos instantly jumped out of the tent and began to bark orders. Vex grabbed my arm and dragged me to headquarters. Throughout the entire camp, NPCs were springing to action, putting in motion a plan developed long ago. Voices were booming even in the renegade HQ, a pirq commander roaring orders and directives. In the process he almost stepped on me with his huge paw. I managed to check his properties and mentally sympathized with the embassy from Kartoss.

Kodiak. Shadow Pirq. Level 400.

By the way, I wonder why the biota became 'blighted biota,' while the pirqs became 'shadow pirqs?' What's the difference? Vex interrupted my further contemplation of this issue. He pulled me out from under the paw of Kodiak and confidently dragged me along an unfamiliar corridor.

Strange, I had imagined that the ritual would be held in Astilba's laboratory...

The goal of the trip turned out to be another cave, resembling the one where the captive Forest Sentries had been kept. The resemblance was reinforced by two blighted sentries, standing dutifully by the earthen wall.

An enormous bulb was growing in the center of

the cave—almost an identical copy of the ones that biota spawned from on the Tree. The difference was the familiar fog, twining about its black petals.

My recent experience of growing a guide for the world of the dead came to mind.

"A Bulb of Shadow," announced the Sixth in a ringing, triumphant voice. "Geranika helped grow a bulb from a piece of the Tree and the power of Shadow. When you summon Portulac's soul, I will furnish him with a vessel for his new body. It is a pity, of course, that we only have two vitas available, but time does not permit us to do more. Commence the summons, Lorelei."

With difficulty, I tore away my mesmerized eyes from the Bulb of Shadow, blinked and quickly cast the Detect Currents of Vitality spell on myself.

My magical vision revealed inky umbilical cords between me and the blighted sentries. The vitality channels pulsed unpleasantly, resembling feeding leeches. Three more channels, translucent and very thin, ran into the wall of the cave.

The other blighted sentries were out there somewhere.

"Do not delay!" Astilba snapped angrily.

I shuddered and touched the eid's strings. Hundreds of years of waiting have not mellowed the Sixth.

Music and song intertwined, filling the cave, and an invisible fabric descended over all of us: Vex standing mutely, Astilba frozen in expectation and the bulb with its slowly winding wisps of fog. This time there was no transition to the Intermundis. Simply, the game world faded and lost its colors. The air in front of me swirled, gradually condensing, and formed a portal through which I could see the familiar surreal landscape of the world of the dead.

The earthen floor underfoot of the Sixth began shining blindingly, a magical seal appeared, and the necromancer's voice filled the cave, intricately intertwining with my song.

"Do not interrupt the summons!" Vex yelled.

In the next instant the umbilical cords that connected me with the sentries flared brightly and disappeared, while the elementals themselves crumbled to the floor in a heap of dry twigs and branches.

New scenario event: You have been endowed with the powers of a Level 300 Blighted Forest Sentry. Your current level has increased to Level 326. The respective stat points have been automatically distributed among your base stats.

You have been endowed with the powers of a Level 300 Blighted Forest Sentry. Your current level has increased to Level 626. The respective stat points have been automatically distributed among your base stats.

You are unable to cope with such power and are losing your strength. Level loss rate: 1 level per minute.

Attention! An increase in levels caused by a scenario event does not unlock any relevant achievements.

The portal gained clarity and grew in size. Landscapes and faces succeeded each other until the detached face of the biota from my vision appeared before me. As I played my ballad, his face acquired a meaningful expression, until by the final chords, it had become completely clear.

Portulac stepped through the portal into Barliona.

You have summoned a soul from the Gray Lands at the cost of half of your vitality.

Attention! Summoned souls cannot exist in Barliona without an external supply of vitality. Every 505 minutes, you will lose 29% of your maximum HP. The upkeep for summoned creatures ignores all skills and spells of damage absorption or reduction.

In the event of your death, a summoned creature will return to its original plane of existence, unless it finds another source of vitality.

You have summoned the soul of Portulac, the Fifth of the Biota Council. The level of the summoned soul is Level 400.

This is a scenario event: You cannot unlock achievements related to summoning this soul.

A torrent of accessible skills and spells from the summoned creature streamed through my log. While I was sweeping aside a bunch of system notifications, the Sixth moved to the next stage of the ritual. The Bulb of Shadow drew Portulac's spirit as if it was a giant magnet and the vitality channel connecting me with the summoned soul flared up and disappeared.

You have transferred your vitality to your summoned soul. Your level has been reduced to 26. Due to the instability in the channel, some of the vitality has been wasted.

The level of the summoned soul has risen to Level 500.

Portulac's soul has gained a body and no longer needs to be nourished by your vitality. You are no longer bound to the soul of Portulac.

The petals of the bulb unfurled, revealing a new Level 500 Shadow Biota to the world. His coal-black epidermis seemed to absorb the light, turning it into a misty haze around his body. Fog seeped from the eyes of the Fifth, giving the biota's face the unpleasant resemblance of a frightening mask.

Portulac looked over himself with fascination, brought his hand to his face and froze studying his new body.

"What has happened to me?" the Fifth's voice was full of reverb as if his words were resounding in both worlds at the same time.

"You have received a new body, new strength, a new life, my love."

Despite the inherently warm words, Astilba's husky voice remained as cold and detached as before. She did not rush to embrace her revived beloved. There was neither triumph nor happiness on her face. The necromancer simply stood there, looking at the revived Fifth, and I thought I spied emptiness in her eyes. Hatred and the thirst for revenge, which had sustained Astilba for hundreds of years, burned in her soul, forcing her to strive for her goal at any cost. And now that the goal had been finally achieved, the Sixth's hardened heart was no longer capable of the same feeling.

Hearing the familiar voice, the Fifth turned his head and looked at Astilba. The face of the oldest biota mage, which had been so tense and focused, smoothed out, and an incredulous and simultaneously happy smile appeared on his lips.

"Astilba?" he asked for some reason, observing the Shadow-altered Sixth.

The next instant Portulac disappeared,

appearing again next to his beloved. He embraced her and pressed her to himself. Astilba did not resist. She remained standing like a stone statue, peering into Portulac's face. She looked like she wanted to cross out the centuries of separation by some effort of will and return to the past. Back to the time when she still knew how to love.

Alas, this was beyond the power of the mighty necromancer.

The confusion in Portulac's eyes gave way to determination. He pressed Astilba tightly to him and quietly whispered a few words in her ear.

"Now the time has come for me to revive you," I heard him say, before the couple was enveloped in a foggy sphere that concealed their further conversation from outsiders.

Vex and I exchanged glances and silently left the cave. Turning around at the very exit, I saw the silhouette of Astilba as quiescent as a broken doll in the mage's arms.

I do not remember how I got out of the renegades' camp. Maybe Vex helped me. The odd, morbid and utterly unhappy reunion lingered in my mind's eye. Damn, that was not at all what I had expected. Beautiful and tragic.

Around me, the renegades' camp teemed like an anthill. The renegades were preparing for the last battle for the forest. I suppose Chip or Bogart would find this activity mundane, but I felt like I was in the way. Orders were sounding everywhere around me, messengers and senior officers were darting about. As far as I understood from the snatches of conversation I overheard, Pasha and his friends had accurately divined the tactics of the upcoming battle.

It looked like this was it—the last chapter, the scenario finale. A handful of renegades would ambush the superior forces of Kartoss and its guard of high-level players. They would attack and die in a desperate attempt to foil the alliance. The Hidden Forest would become a part of Kartoss, while the surviving renegades along with their leadership would retreat to the HQ—a dungeon, which would be raided day after day by players seeking to grind loot and experience. Both Astilba and Portulac would die again and again, losing each other until the next rebirth, which itself would promise nothing but a new death.

And, it seemed like this is a game and this was all just a matter of design...And still, I felt a deep sadness. It is a pity that nothing can be changed. A sad conclusion to a sad story. A new dungeon for the delight of the players. And all I can do is watch the show until its end. I only need to decide whether to join the renegades' mass suicide attack or to contact the Seventh and watch them die from the other side of the battle lines. Only the second option seemed reasonable, but for some reason I wanted to choose the first one. It was stupid, senseless, but seemingly the only right thing to do.

The flip side of creativity is that you begin to care about the stories and characters you create.

"The time has come, Lorelei," Vex called me. "Go ask Legate Ulver how you can help in the upcoming battle."

"Okay," I nodded and took a few steps towards the exit from the dungeon, before stopping. "Hey Vex! With the ritual and all, I completely forgot about an important message I have for Astilba."

"Is it so important that you wish to distract her at such a moment?" he frowned. "Right before the decisive battle?"

"Geranika! He betrayed us and tried to desecrate the Guardian despite Astilba's direct orders!"

"How do you know this?" Vex drilled me with his eyes.

"He wanted me to do it."

"And you?"

"But I didn't," I replied, not lying.

Vex grabbed my arm and dragged me back to HQ.

"You must report this to the command," he said without stopping. "The Second and Kodiak planned the attack with Geranika's support."

The brain center of the renegades was a huge cave. A hefty stone table with a map occupied the center. Around it stood a crowd of renegade biota and pirqs. Tribune Kodiak—a red-white pirq in black armor with golden highlights—was indicating the positions of the units to the commanders with a pointer. Wisps of fog whorled amid his fur, as was usual for Shadow creatures.

"The second and third maniples of the Aquila century," he growled, "shall develop our initiative by striking the enemy's rearguard. At the same time, the Prima century shall cut off any attempts at relief..."

Here the tribune noticed our presence and snapped:

"Get out!"

The next moment, the entire stabbing-hacking arsenal of the guards was aimed at us, and the tribune turned back to his map, having already forgotten about us. At the moment he had more important tasks to deal with. Despite the commanders' concentrated looks, I had the distinct impression that they all understood the futility of their efforts. There was some kind of doom about them, mixed with the determination to see it all through to the bitter end. Although, what's the point of guessing? I still vividly remembered the Guardian's reaction to me, which saved him from a dark fate literally. The extent of his generosity was not to exile me right that moment, but a little later. The same fate awaited the renegades, even if they survive. Shadow had no place in the Hidden Forest.

"We bear important news, tribune," said Vex, entirely unfazed by this reception.

The pirq looked up and gestured to the guards,

who were already getting ready to grab us and toss us out of the situation cave.

"Get on with it," he ordered.

The other officers also stared at us with expressions ranging from discontent to curiosity.

"Geranika ordered me to blight the Guardian of the forest," I uttered a phrase that had the effect of a bombshell. The pirqs snarled threateningly, the Second cursed angrily, the others began to roar in indignation as they digested the perfidy of the Lord of Shadow.

"I will tear that pitiful shaman to tatters with my own paws!" Kodiak's roar pressed me into the wall. "How dare he encroach on the very heart of our land?!"

The pirq placed his paw on the hilt of his sword, straightened his shoulders and looked around, as if he was looking for Geranika, who was cunningly hiding among the crowd.

"As I understand it, you did not fulfill this order?" the Second, who seemed more tranquil, inquired.

The oldest warrior of the biota made quite the impression. Tall and unusually massive for a member of his race, he radiated menace. The body of the general was clad in the same ornamental wooden armor I remembered from my visions.

"No," I said, without going into details. "But I wanted to see the Guardian, and I went to his dungeon. The Seventh was there along with outsiders from beyond the Arras. They freed the Guardian, and then Eben...the Seventh sent me to the Gray Lands."

"The Guardian is free..." gloomily summed up the biota warlord. "This changes everything."

"What changes everything?" asked an inappropriately-cheerful, yet no less strange voice.

A smiling Portulac entered the room in the company of the cold and collected Astilba. The face of the Second twisted in shock. He looked incredulously at his long-lost friend and exhaled quietly:

"You..? But how? Astilba?"

The Sixth nodded with dignity and in a demanding tone returned those present to the original topic of the conversation:

"So what changes everything? And what are Vex and Lorelei doing here?"

This, however, did not prevent Portulac from tightly hugging his still-bewildered friend and shaking Kodiak's mighty paw.

"Lorelei, repeat for Astilba what you have just told us," asked the Second.

Having heard me out, the Sixth twisted a lip and hissed maliciously:

"I swear that foggy fool shall pay for his treachery!"

"Undoubtedly," agreed the Second. "But right now we need to make a decision. The embassy is about to cross the Arras."

"We have to attack them!" Kodiak rumbled confidently. "We shall tear off the Master's head and the alliance will be consigned to oblivion. With or without Geranika, the Kartossians cannot be permitted onto our territory!"

"But the Guardian!" the Second objected. "As soon as we attack, he will interfere. He, the Seventh, the First, the rest. Are you prepared to raise your paw against the Guardian? To risk the lives of our brothers and sisters?"

"We have no choice!" Astilba barked angrily. "We've gone too far and sacrificed too much to retreat now. Geranika betrayed us, but the powers bestowed by him are still with us. Portulac has returned, his power renewed to heights unparalleled. Neither the First nor the Guardian can oppose the might of Shadow. We only need to hold them, slay the Master of Kartoss and retreat. If we act quickly, we will get away with few casualties."

Hearing this, the Fifth took a step toward the table and angrily swept the figures depicting the order of battle from its surface.

"Listen to yourselves, madmen!" he exclaimed and, it seems, the whole dungeon shook with the power of his voice. "How calmly you speak of killing your own...You are ready to wield arms against the First herself! Against the Guardian! Against your own people! Few casualties..."

He smirked darkly and looked over his audience.

"You have already sacrificed too much. Look at us. We are all altered. We have torn our bond with Sylvyn. We are repellant to the forest itself. We dare not appear in this guise before the Guardian. The earth itself suffers from the blight that has penetrated our lands. Yes, the outsiders have brought us a lot of grief. But no outsider has invited such evil as you did. The schism in the Council, is the schism of our own people. Shadow stalks Sylvyn's lands. The Guardian imprisoned. The land suffering. And now you want a civil war? Do you understand that Nigella will defend the embassy and, if necessary, will join the fight personally? Which one of you wants to meet her in battle? Which one of you *can*?"

His words had an effect. Everyone silently pondered what they had heard.

"*You* can," Astilba's voice broke the silence. "Your new power can do more than that."

The Fifth shook his head.

"This is an alien strength that I have not had time to master yet. I cannot be sure that I will not destroy my own forest with this power that I do not understand. I cannot guarantee that I will not harm our people. But I am well aware that we cannot do without casualties. What is better? A questionable alliance with outsiders that might betray us and shed our blood or our own betrayal and the blood of our brothers and sisters on our hands? We will forever shatter the unity of our people."

"Forever," echoed the tribune, and his growling bass gave this simple word a special weight.

Kodiak bowed his head and lowered his ears, realizing the full weight of the latest developments.

"Between a possible misfortune and an imminent catastrophe, I will choose the first," having finished speaking, the Fifth looked searchingly from one council member to another.

"The red orcs that once killed you, are now part of Kartoss," said the Sixth, haltingly. "You suggest we simply permit them onto our lands?"

"I suggest we speak with the First, and reconcile with the Council," Portulac answered. "And then jointly negotiate with the embassy to enter an alliance in which our borders will be open only to those who deserve the respect of the races of the forest. We will limit our assistance to the Empire, consolidate the advantage of our own laws on our territory. This is why we must participate in the negotiations—to protect our land with words, not arms. Even if this must be as a part of the Kartossian Empire, if indeed the Council ratifies such a decision."

Tribune Kodiak leaned heavily on the table, staring at the map as if he was seeing it for the first time.

"I, Kodiak," he roared suddenly, "joining the ranks of the Legion..."

"...do swear," Ulver joined in, "not to tarnish the honor of a warrior..."

"...and to protect our people and our forest until my final breath," the rest of the pirqs echoed the oath in a chorus.

Another silence followed and again it was broken by Kodiak.

"Portulac is right, Sixth," he said, looking at Astilba. "Times change. Our strategy was calculated for a surprise attack. Now that the Guardian is free and the Seventh knows too much, we cannot follow our original plan. The war will bring only death, grief, and..." he trailed off, before resuming reluctantly in a lower voice: "It's not that we will be defeated—we could lose everything. The forest and the Tree and the Lair. We are not only those who are with you, Astilba. We represent all those who live here. Do you understand?"

He locked eyes with the Sixth. The necromancer's eerie eyes narrowed maliciously:

"We all, every one of us, sacrificed ourselves. We adopted Shadow to become stronger—to be able to protect the forest from outsiders. We knew that we would be exiled. And now you tell me that the outsiders will have more right to our land than we—in exile?!"

Anger seethed in her voice, her eyes gleamed fiercely, and her fingers flexed convulsively, like the talons of a bird of prey. Portulac took her hands in his and said quietly:

"There have been enough sacrifices."

The necromancer's wrathful, contorted face slowly smoothed out, her anger ebbing.

"The words of the Fifth have always been wise," said the Second. "I am glad that the Gray Lands have not changed this. We must restore the Council and we must force Kartoss to accept our terms for the alliance. As for the exile...Nothing is in vain. We can settle on the other side of the Arras and guard the borders of our forest."

Kodiak nodded in agreement.

"I'm glad to hear this, old friend," he rumbled. "Wrath is a poor counselor."

It was odd to hear these words from the hot-tempered pirq, but Kodiak seemed to have changed entirely. Looking at him, it was hard to believe that this was the very same tribune that had threatened to destroy Geranika but a few minutes ago.

"All right," Astilba finally said. "Vex, you should contact your mentor, the Seventh. Let him relay our words to the Council. The Tree will not accept us, so we will meet here."

She indicated a point on the map between the camp and the Tree, on the border of the blighted lands.

"We want to speak with the Council and the outsiders before the alliance is made," Astilba said. "If the Council refuses, we will destroy the embassy at any cost."

Vex nodded in agreement and left the cave.

"We need someone who speaks Kartossian," the Second reminded. "Is there anyone among our warriors?"

"I learned the language of the dark empire and will be glad to help," I said.

"Very well, Lorelei," Astilba nodded. "You are a bard, a master of the word, which means you will be able to relay our speech accurately."

Quest available: *Common Tongue.* Description: ... Reward: Variable improvement in reputation with the parties to the negotiations.

"And what about Geranika?" Kodiak sneered. "We dare not leave that villain live."

The pirq struck his left palm with the fist of his right paw.

"We shall send scouts to track him down. And when we find him, we will destroy him." Astilba's face again adopted a predatory expression. "As soon as Portulac has mastered his new powers, he will be able to destroy the shaman with his own power."

Kodiak grinned, pleased, and turned to his subordinates:

"Until we complete the negotiations with the Council, our troops will remain in these positions, in full combat readiness," he ordered.

The officers in unison banged their fists against their breastplates and hurried out to rouse their troops.

"It's up to the Council now..." Kodiak took a cape from an orderly and fastened it with an ornate fibula at his throat. "Well then, shall we go?"

And without waiting for a reply, he left the hall to the salute of the guards' pikes and halberds, thumping the floor.

CHAPTER SIXTEEN

THE LOCATION SELECTED FOR THE PEACE TALKS resembled one of those fantasy paintings that strives to depict the opposition of light and dark. It was as though this was the precise place where the primordial force of nature encountered its distorted reflection in Shadow. The black intricacies of the thorny labyrinth, through which the tendrils of fog moved as if grazing herds, seemed alien here amid this ancient forest. The outsiders' embassy, surrounded by biota and pirq guards seemed just as out of place. In spite of their transformation, the Shadow pirqs and blighted biota nevertheless looked much more at home than the motley group of NPCs and players from Kartoss.

Almost all the players who accompanied the embassy bore the guild sigil of the Dark Legion, but about half a dozen were freelancers or members of guilds I did not know. The embassy consisted of a Level 450 Master and four Level 400 Magisters.

But everyone paled next to the First. The Level 500 head of the Council dazzled with her exotic beauty. The tender green of her epidermis was emphasized by the amaranth petals of her vestments. The druid held a living branch that glowed faintly in her hand, and Nigella's gaze bore the age-old wisdom of the forest itself.

The Seventh stood like a somber shadow on her left, while on her right stood the Third—Fresia the Paladin of Sylvyn. The Third did not look menacing in the least but I remembered how, in one of my visions of the past battles, this seemingly delicate biota mercilessly slew enemies with her faithful sword.

Off to the side, the pirq chiefs loomed amid their guards. Clad in heavy armor, reddish-colored Speleus clutched a two-handed flame-bladed sword in his paws and glowered at the outsiders. A golden-colored pirq named Conquolor propped up a tree with his shoulder, cradling in his paws an intimidating device, similar to a hefty gun with a thick barrel which bristled with six arrowheads. All of the pirq's gear gleamed with gold and his thick mane reminded me of a character from my childhood reading—he looked none other than Aslan himself.

There was neither hatred nor anger in the parties' eyes—only confusion and surprise and the bitter sympathy for the renegades from the unblighted creatures. Yet the outsiders from beyond the Arras all squinted with suspicion.

The former allies, members of the Council, were now standing in silence opposite each other. Suddenly the renegades' ranks parted and the Fifth stepped forward. The heretofore imperturbable eyes of the First grew wide; the Seventh shook his head in amazement; the Third mumbled some kind of oath and ran her hand over her eyes. Portulac took a few steps forward and knelt before the First.

"We are the fruits of one Tree," he said softly. Nigella, hesitated, but then laid a hand on his shoulder:

"One Branch, one duty, one fate."

She gestured for the Fifth to stand up and then warmly embraced her old friend.

"I cannot believe you are really alive, Portulac. I do not understand the power that fills your body. But I am happy to see you again, brother."

"It was a dark hour when I went to the Gray Lands and it is in a dark hour that I have returned," said the Fifth sadly. "I do not know much of what happened in my absence, but I know one thing for sure—our unity is our strength. There can be no schism between us."

"It was not I who opposed the will of the Council," said the First after a heavy silence. "It was not I who left the Tree, leading away a part of our people. It was not I who ushered the blight into our forest."

"But it was you who allowed the outsiders in!" the Sixth yelled, her voice brimming with the pain of her sister's betrayal.

"So ruled the Council," the First reminded her.

"The Council was wrong!" Kodiak roared fiercely. The pirq of Shadow stepped forward, his fur bristling. "The outsiders wish to use us in their war. After that they will destroy what is left of us and seize the forest!"

"It was not the outsiders who abandoned our Father Sylvyn," Fresia spoke up. The paladin's eyes sparkled with righteous anger. "No outsiders brought blight to our lands, sowed it!"

"We accepted the help of Shadow only to protect the forest!" the Second objected angrily.

"Shadow does not help anyone," the Master of Kartoss did not raise his voice, but everyone heard him. It turned out that the ambassador was fluent in the languages of the Hidden Forest. "Everything that Geranika does, he does only for his own benefit. Kartoss knows this from its own bitter experience."

"You were not permitted to speak, outsider!" There was enough hatred in the Sixth's voice to speak for the entire army of the forest.

"He is our guest and has come to speak to us," Speleus growled. He approached the First and stopped behind her. "The better question is why you're here. You were the one who left the Council, split our people and desecrated our forest."

Astilba's eyes narrowed angrily, Kodiak's fur bristled, but Portulac raised his hands in a conciliatory gesture.

"We have all been wrong about something or other," he said, stepping between the sides. "But this does not mean that the Schism should continue. We too have come to talk. The time has come to reunite the Council and find the right solution together. To correct the mistakes that have already been made and prevent those that await us ahead."

"An alliance with Shadow is out of the question!" the Kartossian ambassador said harshly, but was stopped by an imperious gesture from the First. Her gaze wandered over the faces of the former members of the Council.

"We are not discussing an alliance with Shadow," she said. "We are discussing the reunification of our family and the resolution of past mistakes. Am I correct?"

"Yes, oh First," Portulac tilted his head.

After a pause, the rest of the renegades repeated his gesture.

"But they are Shadow!" exclaimed the Master and the Kartossians behind him mumbled their agreement. "No minion of Geranika may be trusted! They will betray us!"

"Shall I list to you how many times your people have invaded our forest, Ambassador?" asked the First, quietly but with a perceptible threat in her voice, turning to the outsiders. "Shall I recount to you how much grief and suffering you brought us? Do you need me to explain to you why my brothers and sisters have so little faith in this alliance?"

Unable to maintain Nigella's gaze, the Master of Kartoss looked away.

"The Council split as a result of the distrust and the gravity of what we suffered in the past," she continued sadly. "None of us was wise enough to maintain our unity. It is time to learn to forgive the wounds of the past and create a new future together. A better future."

She looked over the renegades and solemnly proclaimed:

"I hereby restore the Council and offer clemency to all those who left us. Together we will go to the Guardian, we will call on Sylvyn and find a way to mend what has been done and expel the blight and the Shadow from our lands. Perhaps not today or tomorrow, but you will be able to return to the Tree and to the Lair once again!"

Jubilant exclamations filled the forest and then all the biota and all the pirqs present knelt before the reunited Council. Yielding to the solemnity of the moment, I too knelt down and bowed my head respectfully.

And doing so—missed Geranika's entrance.

"Why wasn't I invited for the reunion party?" came the familiar voice of the Lord of Shadow.

Looking up I saw him standing beneath a blighted oak near the renegades. Seeing him, all present jumped to their feet and grabbed their weapons.

"Because you betrayed us!" roared Kodiak loudly and rushed at Geranika clearly intending to tear him to pieces.

Geranika lazily raised his hand and the mighty pirq stopped as if he had encountered an invisible wall.

"Tsk, tsk, tsk. Is this any way to speak with the Lord of Shadow after you have accepted Shadow into yourself and become one of my minions?"

He snapped his fingers and I felt like I was losing power over my own body. Beside me, Vex's eyes filled with fog and his body jerked several times, like a puppet in the hands of a novice puppeteer.

Scenario event: Geranika the Lord of Shadow has taken control of your avatar temporarily.

Obeying his will, my avatar turned to the Lord of Shadow and knelt before him. The renegades around me did the same thing, and only at the edge of my vision, could I see the Second and the Sixth, with visible effort struggling to keep their feet. Gradually, the fog trickled into their eyes.

"The trouble with you spawn of Sylvyn," complained Geranika, "is that your bodies cannot fully merge with Shadow. Fortunately, there are others who do not suffer from this malady."

Another lazy wave of the hand and Kodiak and

the Fifth approached the renegade leaders and shoved them to their knees.

"Release our brethren this instant, shaman!" the First's angry voice resounded throughout the forest and was reflected from the mountains.

"Or what?" asked Geranika with genuine interest.

"We will destroy you even at the cost of our lives," Fresia replied, drawing her sword.

"You can try," Geranika chuckled merrily. "Kill anyone who is not Shadow!"

The army of Shadow rose harmoniously to its feet, turned to its brethren, unsheathed its arms and took one mutual, thundering step forward.

CHAPTER SEVENTEEN

SHADOW HAD TRANSFORMED THE RENEGADES. Hundreds of blighted biota turned their empty, expressionless faces to face their kindred. The eyes, veiled with the magic fog, were like tears in the very fabric of Barliona. Punctures through which you could see the alien inside of the world.

Meanwhile, the pirqs of Shadow not only remained as ferocious as they had been—they grew even more so. Savage anger filled their scowling faces as saliva dripped from their exposed fangs. Now more than ever they resembled wild beasts, no longer sentient creatures.

The renegades remained silent. For now, they remained silent.

Like a tide, Geranika's newly-minted minions moved to attack, reorganizing themselves into battle formations as they marched. The renegades' bodies streamed with fog as if it was their blood, the mist from them settling on the tormented, blighted ground. For a moment it seemed to me that I was knee-deep in their blood. The blood of the forest itself.

But even more frightening was the silence of it all. There were no commanders shouting orders, not a single word was spoken. The fog muffled the sounds of footsteps and the clatter of armor, which gave the whole scene a dreamy quality. Even the forest went quiet as if it were holding its breath, waiting for the outcome.

The oppressive silence was interrupted by music. Dark, full of unspeakable power, it seemed to seep under the skin, causing the body to tremble in anticipation of the battle. It was only by accident, glancing down at my hands, that I realized where the music was coming from. My fingers moved against my will, forcing me to perform an unfamiliar composition and cast the Song of Encouragement. The small hillock, atop which my unruly legs carried me, stood as an island amidst the living current of the army of Shadow.

Stepping out to the clearing, the archers, mages and healers fanned out into a single rank with the formidable columns of the heavily armored pirqs following in their wake. The sight reminded me of a flood when a river overflowed its banks and flooded the lowlands, forcing people to climb higher and higher to escape from the inexorably rising water.

The enemy did not wait with folded arms. The forest's defenders began to maneuver to meet the threat: groups of warriors congealed around their leaders, forming a battle formation and retreating orderly from the edge of the blighted ground.

"Master, retreat to the Arras!" the amplified voice of a player named Evolett made me wince in surprise. He seemed alien, out of place amid this solemn tide of inexorable death. "Beyond the Arras, you will be able to teleport to the Nameless City. The Dark Legion will buy you time!"

"We will not leave, Evolett," the Master of Kartoss sounded strange, his voice trembling with growling notes. The hood thrown over the ambassador's head did not allow me to discern his face. "An alliance is not mere ink on a parchment. An alliance is an oath. Kartoss will perform its duty, even if its words have not been written down. Geranika shall not conquer the Hidden Forest!"

The eyes of the First and the Master of the Dark Empire met for an instant, silently ratifying the new alliance. Fresia and the pirq chiefs briefly saluted with their weapons, joining the covenant.

This was like a signal: Both groups opposed to Shadow, who had previously stood in separate columns, moved towards each other until they merged and formed a united front of bristling steel.

"Geranika is the enemy," the First said to her new allies. "Our brethren have been stupefied. They must be stopped, not killed."

The players grumbled, and their leader asked bluntly:

"And if we have no choice?""

"You have answered your own question, Evolett. The Hidden Forest shall not fall to Shadow!"

The minions of Shadow meanwhile were not concerned with having to murder their kindred. To the hum of twanging strings, the air filled with bolts and arrows hurling from the bows and crossbows as from the wings of death. They were echoed by the roar of numerous magical missiles and the full-throated roar of the pirqs of Shadow rising to the sky.

But now a wall of flame flared between the two armies and incinerated most of the incoming arrows and ice missiles. And those spells that did reach the ranks of the allies broke powerlessly against a magic shield conjured by the magisters of Kartoss. The enchanted flame destroyed the flying arrows and spells, harming neither the grass nor the trees growing nearby.

The blighted biota parted silently, unleashing an irrepressible torrent of Shadow pirqs. The beast-like figures rolled like an avalanche onto the wall of flame, without the slightest fear of fire. A moment before they leaped through the inferno, the furry figures faded a little, as if a shadow had covered them. Protected by a temporary invulnerability to the element, the pirqs painlessly passed through the fiery barrier. The magical traps that the Kartossians managed to set up flashed and vanished. A roaring, scowling wave of Shadow pirqs crashed against the allied tanks.

My throat contorted with pain. I—as well as all the blighted biota casters around me—doubled over in a severe fit of coughing. Out of the corner of my eye, I spied the figure of a biota rogue hurling a flask of bubbling liquid at the detachment next to mine. The barely noticeable mist from the fragments made the next group of healers fall into a fit of coughing.

You have been exposed to a choking cloud. You are unable to make sounds and cast spells until you leave the suffocating cloud.

It was not immediately possible to get out of the affected area. The Seventh's rogues were popping up here and there, tossing flagons of chemicals into our ranks. The Seventh and his adepts knocked out most of the mages of Shadow, but there seemed to be no concern about this turn of events. With the dull indifference of brainless homunculi, the blighted biota simply wandered in search of places free from poison. The only problem was that it wasn't much easier in the places with fresh air. The coughing fit did not let up, and the system blessed me with a debuff that maintained the effects of asphyxiation for five minutes. And then, without my participation, I cast the only spell that was not covered by the debuff: Summon Instrument Soul.

Eid's ghostly figure appeared next to me. The instrument's soul looked neither surprised nor confused, which suggested that even when he wasn't summoned, he could observe what was happening to me. Having assessed the situation, Eid pushed me into the nearest poisoned cloud, and then did the same with all the nearby renegade mages, renewing the debuff. He was in no hurry to kill the biota controlled by Geranika. And, given his low level and specialization, doing so would probably be a bit complicated. The renegades did not try to kill Eid either. They looked on with their eerie, fogged-over eyes and dutifully waited for their ability to conjure to return to them. Whatever way Geranika ruled the blighted biota, it all seemed careless and very predictable. All of the rogues that he sent against the enemy's rear became ensnared in numerous traps, prudently placed there by a roving band of healers and mages.

The Shadow pirqs however were another matter. They had been deprived of free will and the spark of Sylvyn, but not of reason. The pirqs of Shadow jumped deftly over the pits that opened beneath them, clambered over the ranks of the tanks and smashed into the soft archers, mages and healers behind them. For a moment it seemed to me that the avalanche of shaggy bodies would crack the allies' defenses, but the forest itself, heeding the summons of the First, came to the aid of its children.

The roots and stalks of the plants wound around the feet of the renegades, clutching them in a death grip, slowing their movement, knocking them to their feet, fettering them in place. Branches wound around the limbs of the pirqs that had broken through the defenders' ranks. Snarling with impotent rage, the pirqs of Shadow struggled within their cocoons of branches and leaves even as they were hoisted up to the tops of the trees. Those who remained below made incredible efforts to avoid the fate of their less fortunate brethren.

Kodiak's immense figure was swaddled in thick branches from head to toe and yet even the forest could not budge him. The pirq general roared and fought in his chains and the wood cracked and creaked like living armor around him.

Geranika's offensive had bogged down. Stopped by their own forest, the renegades fought in snares and bonds. Those who were still free tarried on the blighted ground soaked in Shadow, where the First did not have power over the plants.

"Focus Geranika!" Amplified with magic, the voice of the Dark Legion leader, cut through the clamor of battle. "Mahan took his immortality. We can kill him!"

All those who could reach Geranika with an arrow or a spell directed their arsenal at the Lord of Shadow. The damage from a few players, for whom distance had not been an obstacle, was similar to mosquito bites. However, the magic crossbow bolts of the gold-maned Conquolor, the spells of the First and the ambassadors of Kartoss forced Geranika to falter and frown slightly. The shaman's elegant suit became stained with the blood oozing from his wounds.

Jubilant cries erupted from the raiders and for a moment I believed that they would succeed in forcing the Lord of Shadow to flee. But at this point the Fifth joined the battle.

And the flames flared...

A tsunami of fire—in comparison to which the recent wall of flame was as an ember beside a blazing bonfire—surged from the blighted ground like an unstoppable tide. The insatiable, magical flames devoured everything in their path, sparing neither foe nor ally. Ancient trees blazed, writhing in agony and releasing from their arms the Shadow pirqs remained immune to magic. The grass and bushes, which clung to the feet of the renegades to the last, were covered with ash. The traps and snares that had bound Geranika's minions evaporated in the blaze.

Even the minions themselves perished in this hell: Those that did not have time to hide under the protection of shadows, those that failed in time to get out from under the onslaught. The earth itself burnt out, turning to a barren crust. The flames lapped at the barrier erected by the Kartossians but could not pass through the magical aura. But the fire consumed all the oxygen in the area, threatening to suffocate the sentients who were trapped within.

The army of Shadow ebbed back, returning to

the blighted ground to heal its wounds. Hundreds of pairs of fogged-over eyes watched pitilessly as the fire struggled to devour their kinsmen.

It did not succeed. There were enough powerful fire mages among the defenders who knew how to dampen the fire. And yet on the newly scorched battlefield, the forest could no longer help its children. The miserable patch of greenery was rapidly disappearing, trampled by the boots of those who were hiding under a magical shield. Wounded by the fire, the trees crackled plaintively, threatening to collapse in burned embers to the ground, without any distinction of who was beneath them. Charred bodies lay like grim reminders on the still-smoking earth. And there was no way to tell whose side the casualties belonged to anymore. Death, as ever the great equalizer, reigned over the field.

The Fifth, who had created this conflagration, slowly moved towards the defending army, already charging a new spell.

"Rally our forces!" the Master of Kartoss ordered the magisters around him. "Together we can hold off the Shadow host. Meanwhile, try to slay Geranika!"

Alas, it was not so easy. The army of Shadow, which had restored its strength, rushed again to the attack, but this time there were no branches, nor roots, nor traps, nor snares to stop them. The two hosts clashed, Kodiak and Speleus coming together in their midst.

Blood sloshed onto the dead, scorched earth.

Not far from Geranika, Astilba was drawing a complex pattern with a luminous powder on the ground with a frightful indifference to what was happening around her. Suddenly she froze and the fog flowed like a cataract from the eyes of the Sixth, giving way at last to her customary green. The Lord of Shadow turned to look at Astilba and frowned. The gray fog again filled the necromancer's eyes and the necromancer returned to her task.

Geranika, meanwhile, examined his blood-stained suit with an annoyed expression. Ugly black roots stretched to the feet of the Lord of Shadow and wrapped around his legs like a nasty tangle of snakes. The pulsating, predatory tendrils absorbed the blood oozing through his clothes. Geranika's health began to decrease bit by bit and I involuntarily looked at the First. The magical radiance of the channeled spell poured from the hands of the druid. For a moment, I decided that Nigella had the power to command even blighted plants, but soon I realized my mistake. Soaking in Geranika's blood, the blight surged, rapidly covering more and more areas of the forest and promising the Lord of Shadow an easy victory. It was clear that as soon as the blight reached the defenders, they would be swept from the field of battle.

Fresia too understood this. Embroiled in a duel with the Second, the paladin strained, shoved her enemy away from herself, knelt down and plunged her sword into the ground, inevitably opening herself to the countering blow. And it came. The Second's hand did not flinch as he brought his sword down on the defenseless Fresia. But the blade did not reach the body of Sylvyn's warrior. A dagger hurled by Eben ricocheted of the blade, deflecting its trajectory and the Second's sword powerlessly tore the air next to the kneeling paladin. The spymaster did not permit him the luxury of a second strike. He threw a handful of powder in his eyes, deftly dodged the answering lunge and enveloped the blinded enemy in an intricate dance of blades.

And meanwhile, from the spot where the Third's blade had pierced the ground, Sylvyn's grace flowed like the circles of water radiating from where a stone plunges into a lake. The blessed ground encountered the sprawling blight and stopped it. Foggy tongues helplessly crawled along the border, unable to overcome the holy barrier. Caught on the blessed ground, the blighted biota began to change: the fog of oblivion gave way to alert, lucid green looks.

"Eben?" the Second whispered in amazement, coming to. His green eyes widened and he lowered his weapon. "What is happening, brother?"

"Retreat!" sounded Geranika's order.

The Lord of Shadow knit his brows; his face contorted in tension. The biota who had begun to recover—again lost all their emotions. Like clumsy puppets, the renegades slowly lumbered back toward the blighted ground nearby. The Second's eyes once more fogged over and, step by step, he retreated from the bewildered Eben.

A few scarlet drops of blood appeared from Geranika's nose, and he casually wiped it with a cambric white handkerchief.

I didn't get a chance to see what happened after that. Eid understood what was going on, grabbed me, hoisted me onto his shoulder and dragged me towards the blessed ground.

"I still need her for one important piece of business," Geranika said politely, noticing this maneuver.

A lone shade flew from his hand and rushed toward Eid. At its slightest touch, the disembodied soul returned to its instrument. And I...And I again limply rose to my feet and touched the strings. The first minor chords of an ominous hymn sounded across the battlefield. The Hymn to Shadow.

At the same time, the world clouded over with darkness. Not even darkness, but something far more frightening. A massive version of the Shadow Haze spell descended on a part of the forest like a black and white film, blinding all who did not bear Geranika's 'gift.' Alien to Barliona itself, the spell's power blocked even the gaze of the gods. Sylvyn's blessing was losing strength and slowly, centimeter by centimeter, the blight was creeping forward, again threatening to devour the entire battlefield.

The pirqs of Shadow rushed to the attack, easily sweeping away their blinded foes. A lively band of them rushed onto Fresia, who was still somehow holding back the implacably advancing blight around her. The Third, the most ancient paladin of the forest, could not see through the viscous gloom, but she could hear the battle drawing inexorably closer to her. And although she heard it, she didn't dare halt her appeal to Sylvyn.

Disoriented and blinded, the defenders of the forest could not stop the onslaught. Here the pirq chieftain Speleus missed Kodiak's powerful blow and slumped heavily to the ground. But the commander of the renegades did not waste his time on a wounded opponent. He continued his advance towards the kneeling Fresia and now there was no obstacle that could stop the pirq of Shadow. Kodiak loomed over Sylvyn's warrior, raised his sword, intending to solve the problem of the blessed ground with one powerful blow, yet his blade did not reach its target. In some unthinkable way, the Seventh again appeared next to Fresia, deflecting the blow. The eyes of the spymaster were closed and his movement resembled an intricate dance of blades more than anything else. It seems that his inability to see did not hinder the rogue one bit. He danced around Kodiak, dodging his blows and all the while screening him from the Third.

This did not however alter the larger course of

the battle. Supported by Geranika, the Shadow Haze turned the defenders into easy targets for the renegades. Even I was about to make my contribution to the fall of the Hidden Forest. All I had to do was complete the Hymn to Shadow and not only would the whole army grow stronger, but Geranika himself—and he was no weakling as it stood. And that's to say nothing of the Fifth or of Astilba...

The latter had not been standing around idly and had just completed her enigmatic ritual. She threw up her hands in a strange gesture, and a portal of flaming fire flashed before her. Drained by the spell, Astilba collapsed weakly to the thorny grass—while a Level 350 Archdemon stepped through the portal's blazing threshold. Immense, no less than three meters tall, he looked around dully and grimaced. Belonging to another plane, the demon was just as helpless in the face of Shadow as the other creatures. But this did not prevent him from opening five more portals, from which a variety of smaller demons began appearing, ranging in levels from two hundred to three hundred. Anthropomorphic and beast-like, small and large, beautiful and ugly—they poured from the portals in jumbled masses, unsure of how to fight in complete darkness. Only a few beastlike creatures sniffed the air, grinned predatorily, and rushed in the direction of the barely holding raiding party. There was no doubt that as soon as the Shadow Haze expired, the other demons would join their fellows.

But I sincerely doubted that there would be anything living left to feast on. The retinue of the First has already suffered serious losses, barely half of the players survived, and meanwhile my fingers fluttered along the strings, playing the Hymn's last, brooding arpeggios.

And then something huge and impetuous knocked me down, pressed me to the ground and interrupted my song...

You failed to complete the Hymn to Shadow.
−22% to all Shadow creatures' base stats for 7 hours.

A familiar sabretooth tiger sat on top of me, resting her paws on my shoulders. I wonder how she had found me in the pitch dark cover? By smell, like the demons?

"For Kartoss!" sounded the battle cry, and right after it Bogart's cry from somewhere far beyond the battle:

"To me, Merlin!"

The hefty cat released me and rushed to her owner. I got up and looked around. The Day of Wrath raiders had maneuvered to our rear, right on the blighted ground where the Shadow Haze had no effect, and attacked Geranika. And still, they stood no chance of victory or even causing serious damage: The boss of the latest expansion just jerked a cheek in irritation, not even deigning to utter a word to the annoying players. Weakened by the blight under their feet, they posed no threat.

The players also understood this and acted accordingly. They resorted to a mysterious artifact of local invention. As soon as Cranton hurled it at Geranika, a light cloud of pollen enveloped the villain. The effect remained a mystery to me exactly until the moment when one of the pirq elders, the golden Conquolor, threw up his crossbow and shot a bolt directly into the Lord of Shadow, despite being blind like everyone else. The powerful blow to his shoulder spun Geranika around and threw him back. He did not wait for the second shot. The Shadow Haze dissipated, and a foggy shield bloomed around the wounded Lord of Shadow.

There were cheers from the players as their sight returned to them, but these were immediately replaced by cries of panic. The demons, who had been lying in wait, now rushed to the attack.

"Revive the tanks!" a voice cried from the ranks of the Dark Legion.

"Protect the Council and the Embassy!" Dirk ordered.

"For the Horde!" Bogart echoed, pulling his crossbow taut.

Lipo swept past me dual-wielding two morning stars and scattering the renegades like a bowling ball. The entire raid followed him into the breach, pitilessly slaughtering anyone who got in their way.

"Ah do declare! Here you are again, out strolling without your dear governess!" Bogart slowed down beside me, twisting his head in all directions like an epileptic owl. "Permit me to be so bold as to accompany you," he went on. "These damn Yankees have no sense of proper, etiquette..."

I was still puzzling over how Bogart managed to survive among all the high-level enemies, when he heaved me onto his shoulder like Eid had done earlier and carried me toward the blessed ground.

"Like a steppe horseman abducting a bride," he sighed along the way. "Although, I didn't roll you into a rug and there is no horse, but we will put all that down to force majeure."

Encouraged by the reinforcements and their returning eyesight, the defenders of the forest managed to throw the enemy back and reorganize their defense. Bogart slipped through the tanks' ranks and gently placed me on the ground.

You have entered ground blessed by Sylvyn. −20% to all Shadow creatures' base stats.
You have regained control of your avatar.

"Oy, Kiera Khan," a fat green finger flicked my nose, drawing my attention, "are you with us or what?"

"I think so...That was good timing on your part. I

had almost finished playing the hymn."

"Just like at the parade," Bogart smiled broadly. "A hymn answered by a march..."

Merlin appeared beside him and greeted her master's hand with her forehead, nagging for affection. The orc tussled her ear and the sabretooth began to purr contently, almost drowning out the sounds of battle.

In the next instant, a fireball slammed into me, causing me to recoil. The system notified me that my materia shade had absorbed some ridiculous amount of damage as Dirk yelled:

"These are friendlies! Hold your fire!"

"So add her to your raid or we'll wipe her out," grumbled one of the player mages.

Not having the slightest desire to tempt fate, I accepted the invitation to the raiding party, waved away the avalanche of ensuing information and hid the raid interface. I left only the chat open, since that would be the only useful channel. At my level, my contribution would be minimal anyway and I don't need to see the others' frames in order to buff people. Which is what I began doing.

"Well, how shall we deal with this jerk?" Bogart got down to business, cradling his crossbow which was useless against enemies of this level.

Who "this jerk" was, did not require clarification—Bogart's thoughtful gaze was turned to Geranika, who was calmly directing his troops.

"No idea," I admitted. "Neither you nor I can do anything. At our level, all we can do is stand here and watch the show."

"I can't help but feel like Gunga Din: *''E would skip with our attack, an' watch us till the bugles made 'Retire,'*" Bogart quoted his beloved Kipling. "Too bad there's no beer and nuts..."

Sitting down, Bogart drew Merlin to himself and began to scratch her belly, watching the battle unfold.

Despite the unexpected reinforcements, things were very bad. The blighted biota still held their lines outside the blessed land, but the Shadow pirqs and the demons were thrashing the worn out allies.

"Portals! We have to destroy their portals, or they'll overrun us!" boomed Evolett's amplified voice. "Dirk, will you lot be able to break through?"

"We'll try," the leader of the other guild replied. "But it is better to combine our raids!"

"Go ahead and disband. I'm sending you invitations now."

Dirk disbanded the raid and in a second I received an invitation from Evolett. The frames from my new companions blotted out my entire field of view, and I again hid the raid interface.

Meanwhile, something had changed in the protracted confrontation between the Fifth and the Embassy of Kartoss. The exchange of spells and shields waned to a trickle as a hedge of foggy tentacles began to grow from Portulac's body. They stretched and thinned and as soon as one of them reached its target, the tentacle coiled around the victim causing his HP to plummet.

"*Shoot the tentacles!*"

"*They're invulnerable!*"

"*So embody them first! He is a minion of Shadow!*"

Before the players figured out how to cope with this new onslaught, they lost six of their number.

"*He has three hidden abilities. We're all gonna get slaughtered here before we even figure out what he's capable of.*"

It was like the idea that occurred to me all of a sudden illuminated everything in my head. I burrowed into my logs, looking for the necessary passage. Uh-huh, here it is. Copying a part of the log, I pasted it into the raid chat. As Dirk and Evolett read the text, their faces stretched in unison. I too would be surprised if some low-level noob offloaded all the abilities of a previously-unknown boss on me.

"Where'd you get this?" Dirk asked in shock.

"The short version of it is that he was my pet for a few seconds," I explained, without going into the details.

"When this is over," said Evolett, "you and I will have a long chat."

And at this point, I was blinded by a bright flash. Just for a moment, but it was enough for everything to change. The demons and Shadow pirqs who were attacking us were cast back by a mysterious force, and a surprisingly familiar shimmering dome covered the allies' thinned out army. The First, who had been charging some spell this entire time, had completed her incantation. We were surrounded by a miniature Arras, at the borders of which the bighted pirqs and summoned demons flailed helplessly.

"Well, I'll be a goblin's orcish uncle," Bogart drawled.

Tearing his ass from the ground, he walked over to the dome, tapped it with his finger, kicked it a couple of times, and then made a face at the rabid pirq on the other side. The pirq almost burst from rage, and Bogart, grumbling in satisfaction, returned to his seat.

"Now I understand the thrill that a cat gets, licking his balls in front of the dog pound."

"What is everyone standing around for?" Evolett roused the players out of their stupor. "Shoot the portals that are in range and after that focus the demons. They're lined up like in a shooting gallery. Anyone who can, revive the tanks and healers. Healers, regenerate your mana, you'll still need it."

Aided by the NPCs, the players began to systematically thin out the demons surrounding the dome. The exhausted healers collapsed to the grass. Some hastily gobbled exotic foods; others lounged on the grass and meditated.

The First remained standing with a look of

concentration on her face. An iridescent sphere sloshed around her hands, the core of the spell that shielded us from the minions of Shadow.

"How long can you maintain the Arras, Nigella?" Eben asked anxiously.

"Five hours, no longer," came the tense voice of the First. "If they succeed in hitting me, the spell channel will collapse."

"Make sure to keep Nigella's safe," Evolett immediately ordered into the raid chat. *"Paladins, keep two bubbles on her at all time. If the Arras goes down, they'll rout us in an instant."*

But the First had already seen to her own safety. Sprouts appeared on the trampled earth, growing and forming an impassable hedge of stalks and branches around Nigella. A myriad flowers opened their buds. Some exhaled useful auras, others snapped with bristling maws.

Without hesitation, Bogart and I hid among these thickets, sincerely hoping that the Piranha Plants would deal with the occasional demons that aggroed us. For some reason, the renegades ignored my person. I suppose this was due to my Shadow alignment but it could also be that they simply did not perceive me as a serious threat.

"Eben, where are the reinforcements?" The First asked her spymaster. "Where are the other members of the Council?"

"They will not be coming," he answered quietly.

"I contacted the Fourth. Soon after we left the Tree, disturbing news came from the Lair. It is under attack by hordes of blighted animals. The remnants of the Council went to relieve the Lair and are now defending the Lair, the Fourth is preparing for a possible attack on the Tree."

"So, there will be no help."

"But this is no problem now," remarked one of the players, pointing to the soothing glow of the mini-Arras. "We are safe and can gather our strength, and perhaps reinforcements will arrive later."

"I don't think so," Dirk joined in, pointing his finger at me. "She recently led us through the same Arras. And that means that other blighted biota can pass through it."

"So let them," Lipo shrugged. "Geranika has no control over them on blessed ground."

"That's true too."

It was too bad that (virtual) reality foiled all expectations. One of the blighted biota approached the Arras where it intersected the blighted ground, stood at the border and extended his hand to a demon beside him. As soon as their fingers touched, the demon passed through the Arras. He was immediately greeted with arrows and spells, but similar 'passages' began popping up all over the section of blighted ground that lay beneath the mini-Arras.

"*Tanks, close those passages! Mages, splinter the earth, set fire to it, place ice walls—do whatever you must to keep the blighted biota from approaching the Arras."*

The players did everything they could, but the enemy still filtered through the gaps in the defense. And if the small fry did not pose any particular problems, then the appearance of the Archdemon in the company of Kodiak and the Fifth again upset the battle's delicate balance.

Carelessly brushing off the blows of the players, the raid bosses rushed toward Fresia, who was still praying to Sylvyn and maintaining the blessed ground. The magisters of Kartoss managed to occupy the Fifth in battle, but Kodiak and the Archdemon continued toward their target. The latter, in passing, opened up four more portals right in the midst of the players' ranks, forcing them to meet the new threat.

Speleus, as always, took on Kodiak, tying down his brother in battle. And it was Eben who met the archdemon. The spymaster whirled near the red giant, fluttering like a butterfly and stinging like a bee. The First helped as much as she could, summoning flowers to bloom throughout the blessed ground. Some opened predatory jaws and tore at the Archdemon's flesh, others buffed the Seventh and still others hung various debuffs on his opponent.

"I will never make fun of the nerds ever again," Bogart solemnly put his hand to his chest, admiring the fight with the air of a fan was getting a chance to see his favorite band free. "Hell, I'll even let off trolling them."

"Why, did you used to do that?" I looked at him in surprise and almost missed the moment when the dead stirred and began to rise from the ground.

During ordinary gameplay, corpses in Barliona vanished once the loot had been pilfered, but for some reason this was different in the Hidden Forest. The tattered, burned and mangled bodies of the dead now rose to their feet like broken puppets and set upon their still-living friends. Screams of horror sounded here and there, as well as curses directed at the Sixth. Astilba, with her customary indifference, went on raising more and more undead to join the battle on the side of Shadow. Those who returned to non-life outside of the Arras were unable to cross it, but there were plenty of zombies on our side too. The dead, demons, Shadow pirqs—it was getting pretty claustrophobic under the mini-Arras—when the Forest Sentries that Geranika had corrupted came trudging from the direction of the renegades' camp. Five sluggish, ponderous giants walked past the parting minions of Shadow and calmly crossed the Arras.

"*We're fucked*," someone remarked in the chat.

And I was in complete agreement. We were being crushed by numbers and it was only the two major debuffs that were weakening the minions of Shadow that allowed us to somehow hold on.

I looked around for a path to salvation. And my

eyes encountered the eyes of the Sixth. She stood again, frozen at the very border of the Arras, and once again the fog in her eye sockets cleared and revealed her natural green. A moment. For a mere moment, Geranika lost control of Astilba, but that was enough for her. She took a step forward—and set foot onto the blessed ground. The remnants of the fog cleared from Astilba's eyes and she sang a vaguely familiar incantation. Three of the five blighted sentries crumbled in a heap of dry, blackened branches.

Scenario event: You have been endowed with the powers of a Level 300 Blighted Forest Sentry. The vitality channel has not been stabilized and as a result a significant portion of vitality was lost during transmission.

Your level has grown to Level 176. The respective stat points have been automatically distributed among your base stats.

Scenario event: You have been endowed with the powers...
Scenario event: You have been endowed with the powers...

Your level has grown to Level 476.

You are unable to cope with such power and are losing your strength. Level loss rate: 1 level

per minute.

Scenario event: The cooldown time of all skills and spells has been reduced to 1 minute. This change does not apply to skills and spells whose cooldown time does not exceed 1 minute.

"Look at how they've fertilized our cactus…" Qupip quipped, shielding his eyes from the unbearably bright flashes that accompanied my new levels.

"Yah," Bogart nodded eagerly. "May as well patent this new type of shit and go sell it to the farmers. We'll solve a crop failure in China and famine in Africa in one fell swoop."

Merlin wriggled from under his arm, which Bogart had used to shield the eyes of his beloved, sneezed and sat down to lick herself, blowing off her accumulated stress. It did not work. A ghoul hacked into two halves somehow crawled past the predatory flowers and latched onto the tail of the sabretooth. She barked with fright, kicked with her hind legs and turned to gnaw off the insolent zombie's hand—but the zombie simply expired. Emanating from the Sixth, the magic fueling the living dead had dried up and the corpses began returning to the ground.

"What a stubborn lady," said Geranika, with a mixture of annoyance and respect.

He spoke calmly, but somehow his voice

resonated through the entire battlefield. Meanwhile, the shaman himself stared at the Sixth. She staggered and cast him a hateful look. A meaningful look.

Geranika extended his arms and thin tendrils of fog began to stream from the dead bodies of the renegades to his fingers. The Lord of Shadow began reabsorbing particles of the power he had once granted and the dead began transforming, returning to their original appearance. As the Lord of Shadow accumulated power, he regained his former sheen and luster. His foppish suit no longer bore traces of blood or burns.

Unfortunately, the changes were not limited to this: Once more, fog poured from Astilba's eyes and she retreated away from the blessed ground. Those few who tried to restrain her were instantly rooted with horror as soon as they touched the necromancer.

I cast about looking for some way of being useful. My incredibly high level came without the appropriate gear; when you factored in the debuffs on me, I was like a Level 200 mage in the best case scenario.

A mage with an impoverished arsenal of spells. Small help in battle...

Help? Help!

I strummed Asus2 and then Asus#4 and the ghostly figure of Eid (Level 400) materialized over my shoulder to the classic and eerie Tristram theme. So this is the maximum level of the Tenth's instrument...

"Stay awhile and listen!" Eid greeted me cheerfully. He adjusted the shield in his hands and added, "I didn't think that I would get a chance to fight at my full power before I met Cypro again!"

Uttering a warlike cry, he buffed the entire raiding party—and immediately aggroed Kodiak. Now unengaged, Speleus immediately hurried to the aid of the players, who were having difficulties with the archdemon and the remaining two blighted sentries.

You are unable to cope with your newfound powers and lose a level!
Your level has fallen to Level 475.

"Lorelei!" Geranika's icy voice came with a shiver. "You have the chance to atone for your failure and take your place as minstrel at the throne of the new Emperor! Take my side, or the Empire of Shadow will forever close to you. Then you shall be an outsider everywhere you go!"

All at once, I felt the allies' wary eyes on me. Eid's appearance had impressed them, and Geranika's temptation now worried them.

"I don't think I much feel like singing of your deeds, Geranika," I replied, hesitating only a moment. "I would prefer to preserve the memory of worthy heroes."

Em9 to Em9b6 to Em6add9 back to Em9b6 and an ancient tune sounded amid the drone of battle...

The rusted chains of prison moons
Are shattered by the sun.
I walk a road, horizons change;
The tournament's begun...

"You have lost much, my failed student," said Geranika with a disappointed look.

Reputation status with the Geranika the Lord of Shadow changed to Hatred.

The blighted biota standing beyond the mini-Arras collapsed to the grass, losing consciousness, and the Sixth and the Second stepped through the shimmering Arras. Though they were now on blessed ground, Geranika did not lose his grip on them.

Numerous portals began to pop open again and a new wave of demons washed over the battlefield. The new reinforcements could not boast of high levels, but there were so many of them that the combined raid was simply mobbed.

Taking advantage of this, the Second and the Sixth reached the kneeling Fresia and her defender, the Seventh. Eben adjusted the bloodied daggers in his hands and rushed to the attack, but his body froze, paralyzed by fear. With all her magical power, Astilba inspired an inexpressible horror in the spymaster.

The Second raised his sword, intending to cut off

the head of his immobilized foe, but instead of the pliable flesh, the blade of the Second was parried by Fresia's sword, yanked from the ground and raised just in time to protect her brother. Sylvyn's warrior emanated an aura of purification that allowed Eben to cope with Astilba's mental attack, but the irrevocable has already come to pass—the land, deprived of Sylvyn's blessing, succumbed to the blight.

> *...The black queen chants*
> *The funeral march,*
> *The cracked brass bells will ring;*
> *To summon back the fire witch...*

You have stepped onto blighted ground and gained Blighted Strength (+50% to all stats. +1% HP for every minute spent on blighted ground).

The air around me seemed to turn into a viscous jelly. Every motion of the hand, every touch of the strings demanded willpower. Unnecessary, meaningless concentration. Why exert all this effort, when you can just relax and allow someone else to do the mundane things? I wanted to close my eyes and fall asleep, to plunge into foggy dreams. My eyelids grew heavy and sank, cutting off the fuss of the outside world. Only darkness, peace and music remained. My body went on performing the song I had started on autopilot, but someone else's insinuating whisper urged me to leave even this task to him.

And then something in me that had been silent all this time rebelled. I was ready to forget about the game because it was just a game. I was ready to allow someone else's will to take possession of my body—it wasn't even really mine—it belonged to my avatar—a virtual doll, no more. None of this was real, after all. None of this was that important. But the music...As soon as some stranger tried to take away the only gift I had in this life, my soul resisted, rebelled, fought back and dashed the illusion.

Telepathic control failed. You have gained immunity to Geranika's telepathy for 1 hour.

The gardener plants an evergreen,
Whilst trampling on a flower.
I chase the wind of a prism ship,
To taste the sweet and sour...

The air lost its viscosity, the sly whisper disappeared and my consciousness ceased to float. Opening my eyes, I could clearly see everything going on around me. The reinforced renegades had already sent a dozen weakened players and NPCs to the Gray Lands. The blighted biota who had recently been unconscious were again among the renegades' ranks, inexorably marching to the mini-Arras. Geranika himself marched in their midst. His hand touched one of the blighted biota, the Lord of Shadow stepped into the shimmering shroud and...stopped, as if he had encountered a wall.

The First's spell did not permit such a powerful concentration of an alien power through itself, and even an usher who contained a piece of Sylvyn would not allow Geranika to overcome the magical barrier. The Lord of Shadow jerked his cheek with irritation and folded his arms across his chest, defiantly waiting for his army to solve the problem.

And, it seemed, he had not long left to wait.

Here, one of the magisters of Kartoss faltered and collapsed, struck down by the Fifth. Weakened by the blight's debuff, the embassy could no longer restrain Portulac the Champion of Shadow and was now forced to think only of its survival.

Eid cast some kind of massive ability and the renegades engaging the raiders turned and piled onto the ghostly knight. The strip of life above his head was falling at a catastrophic rate, but I could not help my companion. The traditional healing spells of the raid's healers did not work on the instrument soul, and I could not cancel the summons and start channeling my own HP to Eid.

"*The wise men share a coke...*" Bogart lampooned somewhere behind me. "You sure picked a long one there, Kiera Crimson. Might last long enough to double for our funeral march."

With an academic's interest, the orc looked on as

a pack of beastly demons chewed their way through the First's thickets of predatory flowers. He dispelled Merlin, unwilling to risk her death, and began taking potshots at the frenzied mobs, marking each hit with a joyful, "Get some!" But this did not make anything better. Another minute or two and we would be eaten, appetizers before the main course which would be none other than the First.

All this occurred to me almost subconsciously, without interrupting my performance. My attention meanwhile was drawn to the portal growing into focus before me, through which I could see the already-familiar, surreal landscape of the Gray Lands. No one else reacted to this strange phenomenon, which suggested that only I could see this portal.

Eid's icon blinked and disappeared, but in the meantime the priests of Kartoss managed to revive three tanks, who somehow held back the renegades' latest onslaught. Everyone already understood that the battle was lost and was doing everything possible to make the foe pay dearly for his victory.

> *The yellow jester does not play*
> *But gentle pulls the strings*
> *And smiles as the puppets dance*
> *In the court of the crimson king...*

For a moment, the space separating Barliona and the Gray Lands wasted to a thin line—and snapped, ushering a long-dead soul into the land of the living.

You have summoned the soul of the Salamander King (Level 357).

Skill increase:
+5 to Summoner. Total: 7.

I was expecting some changes, but Salamander looked the same as the last time I summoned him, when he was only Level 23.

"It seems that Barliona will never be rid of evil," he observed, unsheathing his sword and, in the same motion, slicing in half a demon that had broken through to us.

"Another fan of yours?" Bogart asked, looking on as the crimson king began to dispatch our foes. "You should make him your head bodyguard, heed my advice..."

"For Barliona!" Salamander's war cry echoed over the battlefield, casting all sorts of buffs on the allied raiders.

The legendary king of the past did not have unimaginable power, but he was still a strong leader who could rally the army behind him. And the army did rally. The already well-worn Archdemon fell to the players' onslaught and his remaining minions followed closely on his heels.

But there were still too many enemies left and there was no longer any force capable of stopping Astilba and Kodiak as they advanced toward the First. Thanks to the help of the pirq chieftains—Conquolor and Speleus—the Fifth had not yet destroyed the embassy. Eben, engaged in his duel with the Second, was unable to help anyone either. Only Fresia stood at the right hand of the First and cast healing auras on her allies. When the enemies approached, the Third raised her sword and attacked Kodiak.

"The time has come to punish those who dare oppose the will of the new Emperor," Geranika announced with a triumphant grin. "As punishment for your insubordination, you, Astilba, will crush the holdouts with your own hands."

Amid a whorl of fog, a black dagger with a wooden handle materialized in Geranika's hand. The weapon traced an arc through the air to the Sixth, easily passing the Arras.

"Mages, archers, destroy the dagger!" Evollet immediately reacted and dozens of arrows and spells immediately flew at the strange weapon.

The attack did not have any effect: the invincible dagger continued on its way and landed right in Astilba's hand. Fresia rushed to her in an attempt to disarm her, but Kodiak stepped in the way. Meanwhile, the Sixth used her ghostly fetters to immobilize Salamander who had also rushed to help.

Suddenly, a blurry gray shadow darted to

intercept the Sixth, seeking to snatch the weapon of Shadow from her hands. A moment was all that was lacking. Geranika waved his hand and an invisible force threw the creature away, pressing it into the interlacing of the stalks near the First. I recognized the Master of Kartoss only by his characteristic attire, now rather battered and more reminiscent of rags. His hood had slipped down, exposing the vagren's fur-covered face.

"What an honor!" smiled Geranika, flattered. "The son of the Emperor of Malabar and the brother of the Lord of Kartoss in person. You would make a good addition to my host."

The wounded vagren snarled something angrily in a language unfamiliar to me. His HP dropped into the red and his attempt to rise to his feet ended in failure.

"Tsk, tsk, tsk," Geranika clicked his tongue condescendingly. "Words like that are unbecoming of your exalted station, sire."

The Sixth did not participate in the conversation. She moved forward inexorably, stifling all resistance. When it came to Bogart and me, she cast us an apathetic, blank look. We were not even worthy of her recognition, it seemed.

Too bad that.

Asus2 gave way to Asus#4 again and Eid reappeared in Barliona. Due to the increased levels, his summon had cooled down a lot faster.

"Stop Kodiak," I commanded, not wanting the spirit to encounter the same fate as Salamander.

He nodded and rushed forward, distracting the pirq of Shadow from the Third, who had managed to suffer a serious wound. As for me, not thinking of anything better than to keep playing, I began to summon another soul from the Gray Lands and watched the battle in the meantime...

Geranika's dagger cut through the stems and branches protecting Nigella like a hot knife through butter. Slowly and inevitably, the necromancer advanced towards her goal, in the process destroying the protective barriers. And when the last one fell, time seemed to stop.

The First and Sixth looked at each other in silence and there was no fear in the eyes of the head of the Council. Having lived many millennia, Nigella looked at her sister with sympathy and inexplicable tenderness. Even now, the First did not cancel the Arras spell, maintaining Geranika at arm's length from the battle and us.

Astilba raised the dagger over the defenseless First and froze as Fresia's hand gently alighted on her shoulder. The wounded paladin, whose right arm sagged like a limp whip, spoke a prayer to Sylvyn and a warm greenish glow emanated from her palm. It forced the fog out of the Sixth's eyes and a look of recognition washed over the necromancer's face.

"You...shall...do...as...I...command..." Geranika

spat haltingly and a chill ran down my back from the tone of his voice.

Clouds of fog exploded around the Sixth. Tendrils of the stuff wrapped around her arm, driving it down to strike the fatal blow. The eyes of the necromancer glittered, her lips twisted for an instant into an evil grin, and the hand holding the dagger obediently sank, plunging an obsidian-black blade into the body. Her own body. Within a moment, the mighty weapon of Shadow sucked the life from the Sixth, but she managed to look me in the eyes and, quietly, mouth two words...

"You just can't find competent help these days," Geranika deadpanned and turned to the Fifth: "Portulac, will you kill the First finally."

Obeying the order, the Shadow biota let off tormenting what remained of the embassy and headed straight for us.

"Now I understand how the Roman legionnaires felt when Hannibal sicced his elephants on them," Bogart remarked and added hopefully: "You don't have a 2x4 and some nails lying around, do you? We could toss it under his hooves to slow him down like a little." He shouldered his crossbow—useless against an enemy of such a level—and took aim.

I didn't have a board with nails, but there was something better. Ignoring another notification about my level loss, I completed my next summons. The Paladin General's ghostly foot stepped into Barliona.

Obviously he wouldn't slay the Fifth or anything but he could buy us some time.

You have summoned the soul of a paladin general (Level 372).
Skill increase:
+5 to Summoner. Total: 12.

"In the name of Eluna, I shall punish you, spawn of Shadow!" the paladin hollered and brought his shining sword down on my head.

I even jumped from surprise. A notification popped up explaining that a materia shade had absorbed the lethal dose of damage.

"Have you lost your damn mind?!" I hollered back, reflexively shielding myself from the next blow, again absorbed by another materia shade—my last one.

"Minions of Shadow shall be swept from Barliona's blessed visage!" the holy warrior yelled dramatically and again swung his sword at me.

This time Bogart took the blow, pushing me aside. His avatar blinked and vanished—Bogart had been sent to the Gray Lands. And it looked like I would be following hot on his heels.

"Well, why don't you go and kill the actual foe himself. He's standing right there—in the flesh!" Without much hope, I pointed my finger in the direction of Geranika—who, by the way, looked like he was having a ball.

"He shall be next," the paladin promised and again raised his sword to strike.

I no longer had any protection, so I involuntarily closed my eyes, waiting for the notification that I had died. But it failed to appear and finally, I carefully opened my eyes. Fresia loomed over me, her blade crossed with the paladin-general's. Their eyes met and Sylvyn's champion shook her head. I got the impression that the divine warriors were having a chat that no one else could hear. After a few long moments, Eluna's zealot bowed his head and withdrew his sword.

I could not believe what happened next. The paladins brought their blades together again and they began to shine. Fresia's sword glowed with spring verdure and its ghostly fellow with the gold of the summer sun. The light born of the two twined, formed a beam and struck the chest of the oncoming Portulac. The Shadow biota staggered from this blow, barely keeping his feet. He tried to spawn his shadow tentacles with which he had practically wiped out the Kartossian embassy earlier, but they disintegrated in the divine beam cast by the paladins. The Fifth's HP dropped into the yellow and kept going until it hit the red.

I hastily regenerated the health that the summoned souls were draining from me, while absent-mindedly strumming the eid. Astilba remained in my mind's eye, standing as she died. Though she had died, she had not succumbed to another's will. Her moving lips, emitting no sound, had uttered her last request. And I intended on fulfilling it.

My fingers found the frets I wanted and a new melody sounded amid the cacophony of battle.

Chaos reigned all around me and if it were not for the Salamander King's protection, I would have been trampled into the landfill forming underfoot. I sang and watched Eid fall and dissolve into the air. I watched Kodiak rush forward with a triumphant roar and send my ghostly paladin back to the Gray Lands. I watched the Fifth, no longer constrained, reach his shadow tentacles for Nigella. I watched the First scream from her pain as the tentacles touched her. I watched the Arras fall. I sang and understood that I would not have time to complete what I had begun.

"HOW DARRE YOU ENTER MY FORREST?"

I almost went deaf from the monstrous roar that rolled over the battleground. Had it not been for my wealth of experience playing shows where all kinds of things could happen, the noise would have interrupted my playing. But by some miracle I maintained my composure and continued to play, looking around for the source of the infernal voice. A familiar, infernal voice.

At the very edge of the blighted ground, stood a colorful couple. Against the background of the colossal, ebony black Guardian, snow-white Chip seemed quite small and inconspicuous, like a bear cub next to his Grizzly dad.

Seeing me, he raised his paw in greeting, and then turned to smash a demon that had scurried up on the skull with his halberd. It did absolutely nothing, since the demon had a hundred levels on him, but I had already studied my friend well enough to understand that standing around and letting someone else take care of the problem was not Pasha's style.

"HOW DARRE YOU DEFILE MY LANDS?!"

A familiar sphere appeared in the Guardian's paw, with a shard of white stone inside of it, and the Guardian squashed the demon Chip had attacked with one paw while slamming the shard into the ground with the other. Foggy tendrils emanating from the blight that permeated the soil reached for the inconspicuous shard, swirled in a whirlpool around it and began to flow into the artifact. The blighted ground began to dissolve, revealing scorched, but quite ordinary soil. The artifact that was supposed to spread Shadow was now absorbing it, clearing the ground.

Having received this unexpected bit of help and finding their debuffs dispelled, the players exulted. At once, the weakened minions of Shadow began to lose ground, and the outcome of the battle no longer seemed so obvious. But contrary to my expectations, the appearance of the Guardian did not frighten

Geranika. He gave him a mocking look and asked:

"Do you really think this little trick will save your forest? You have managed to temporarily redirect the currents of power in my artifact and now you've decided that you've won? What naïveté..."

Obeying the will of Geranika, the artifact soared into the air and moved to the open palm of the Fifth. The fifth squeezed his fingers, crushing the protective sphere like an eggshell, and the white shard entered his inky flesh. But instead of absorbing Shadow from Portulac, the artifact released all its accumulated power *into* him.

"Behold the true power of Shadow!" It sounded like Geranika's voice resounded throughout the forest, echoing even from the mountain range at its limits.

A grim aura enveloped the Shadow biota until Portulac resembled some malevolent deity. The life bar above his head instantly recovered and hundreds of shadow tentacles burst from him and reached for the players and NPCs. They wrapped around their targets, depriving them of the opportunity to resist, and leeching their vitality to Portulac. The Sixth's max HP began to soar, turning the already-formidable raid boss into a completely unkillable monster.

Even the Guardian, with all his might, was powerless against such an alien force. Wrapped head to toe in the tendrils of fog, he was slowly dying, unable to do anything. Judging by the fact that everyone's health bars diminished at the same speed, the spell caused damage as a percentage of maximum hit points. At this rate, in a minute or two, only the minions of Shadow would remain standing. And I among them. Feeling a kindred power, the spell of the Fifth ignored me, allowing me to finish my ballad.

"Soon the Hidden Forest will become part of the Empire of Shadow," said Geranika with a satisfied smile. "And it is all thanks to you, Lorelei. You returned the Fifth to Barliona, furnishing my host with a worthy general."

"And she shall take him from you too!" said a woman's wrathful voice.

Beside me stood another soul summoned from the Gray Lands, while the system notified me that another +5 had been added to my Summoner trait.

"You?!"

Geranika stared in disbelief at the incorporeal, but no less formidable Astilba. Inspired by her love and revenge, the ballad allowed the soul of the necromancer to return, fulfilling her last request: "Summon me."

"That's right, love, it's me again," the soul smirked, approaching the Fifth and plunging her disembodied hand directly into his body.

The Shadow biota shuddered, convulsed and collapsed to the scorched earth.

The Fifth was dead.

"Impossible!" Anger and surprise sounded in Geranika's voice. "He was invincible!"

Seeing his beloved's altered, lifeless body, the Sixth looked up at the Lord of Shadow.

"You forgot that it was I who bound his summoned soul to its new body. And I know how to break that bond. Portulac is now free from your power, traitor! I have redeemed my guilt."

"NOW IT IS YOUR TURRN TO PAY YOUR DEBTS!" rumbled the Guardian, unchained.

Waves of heat emanated from him, quickly restoring health to all those who were still alive and were not infected by Shadow. "YOU SHALL DIE FOR YOUR CRRIMES, GERRANIKA!"

There was little doubting his words. The balance of power has changed and it no longer favored the Lord of Shadow. The Guardian, the First, the Third, the Seventh, Conquolor, the spirit of the Sixth and by some miracle the still-alive Master of Kartoss with a lone magister stepped forth to face Geranika, a wounded Kodiak and the Second.

Geranika was no fool and quickly oriented himself in the situation. Threads of Shadow weaved towards him from the bodies of the fallen renegades, restoring the power he had loaned them. And as Shadow fled the dead, they changed right there where they had fallen, returning to their original appearance. And now it was impossible to tell who of the deceased was an ally and who an enemy. The glade had turned into a mass grave. Only the body of Portulac crumbled to ashes, immediately carried away by a gust of wind erupting from somewhere deep in the forest.

The returned shadows surrounded Geranika with a shield, and the new hazy threads reached out to him from the surviving blighted biota. A sharp splinter twitched somewhere in my chest and I rejoiced that my sensory filter only allowed a faint glimmer of the true pain to reach my brain. My body was paralyzed as an unknown force lifted me and other blighted biota around me above the ground, suspending us like marionettes.

"The time has come for you to solve a delicate conundrum," Geranika smiled politely at the First. "If you insist on continuing this battle, then I will be forced to reclaim my powers from these sentients. Unfortunately, doing so will kill them. The alternative is allowing me to depart with my new vassals here," he nodded at the surviving Shadow pirqs, "in which case your brethren will retain their lives and freedom of will."

"You shall release all our brethren," the First said in a steely voice. "And you shall be banished forever from the Hidden Forest."

"Alas, this is beyond my powers. Pirqs of Shadow cannot be returned to their original state. They are devoted to me and will become part of my empire. Or die. I am powerless to change anything. But they..." A slight motion from his brows caused the blighted biota, including myself, to levitate even higher. "They will keep their will and will be able to choose on their own. What do you decide, Nigella? Shall you earn your revenge through the sacrifice of those you can save?"

Nigella exchanged glances with the other Council members and then said slowly:

"We must save our brothers. But this does not mean that Geranika shall escape justice. We shall march to the walls of his castle with the army of Kartoss and we shall raze them. We shall wipe his damned empire from the face of Barliona and before his death he will hear the name of everyone he has killed today."

All of the members of the Council bowed their heads in agreement, and the First appealed to the Guardian:

"Do you agree with the decision of the Council, oh Ancient One?"

The immense, black pirq looked at the imperturbable Geranika and hate smoldered in his eyes. The Guardian was silent for a long time before making his decision.

"YOU ARE RRIGHT. WE WILL HAVE THE OPPORTUNITY TO TAKE THIS TRRAITOR'S LIFE AT A LATER DATE. NO ONE CAN RETURRN THE FALLEN. BUT AS THE RRENEGADES STILL BEARR SHADOW WITHIN THEMSELVES, THERE SHALL BE NO PLACE FOR THEM IN MY FORREST. MY FORREST SHALL BE FRREE OF ALL THE BLIGHT."

The First sighed heavily but did not argue with this decision. Instead, she turned again to Geranika.

"We will grant you and the pirqs of Shadow free passage to the Arras, but here and now you will swear on the spirit of Barliona that you will not subvert the will of these blighted biota ever again. Nor will you intentionally harm them."

"Unless they force me into doing so by attacking me," added Geranika and nodded, "I swear on the spirit of Barliona."

A bright glow surrounded the Lord of Shadow. The spirit of Barliona had confirmed his oath.

"Go now," the First spat and I felt the invisible hand that had gripped my heart unclench itself.

I collapsed but, contrary to expectations, I didn't hit the ground. Instead, I found myself in the arms of Chip who had appeared out of nowhere beside me.

"Look, I found the magical glade where girls rain from the sky!" the clown quipped, cradling me comfortably.

Geranika winked at me slyly, turned away, and strode leisurely toward the border of the Hidden Forest, surrounded by fifty or so Shadow pirqs. He was followed by more than one unkind look.

The current scenario has completed and your level has been restored to its base value.

Your current level is Level 26.

You have gained a level!

...

Your current level is Level 37.

Unallocated stat points: 75.

Training points: 9.

Oh boy. I sure did earn a lot of XP with this raiding party.

"Listen, are there any more girls? Up there, I mean..." Qupip approached us and gawked at the sky above us.

"Lemme check," Chip tossed me up in his arms: "You see anyone of the fair sex up there, Kiera? There are people down here who want to know. They're taking numbers and forming queues."

"Stop that. Stop that. I'm not a flapjack in a pan! There aren't any other chicks up here!"

"Throw her a little higher so she gets a better look, you flea-bitten cat," the jolly priest advised.

"I don't have any fleas," Chip replied defensively. "I've gassed them all..."

And the bastard tossed me up again, much higher now.

"Put me down where I grew!" I demanded and seeing no sympathy on the pirq's face, I decided to bribe him. "I'll write you a song about some legendary beauty and summon her spirit."

"Will that do?" Chip asked Qupip.

He shook his head: "Nah, necrophilia ain't my thing."

"Hear that? Your offer's no good."

And again I soared into the air, making plans for revenge.

"You should revive Bogart," I reproached, "instead of sorting out your love life by means of up and down motions."

"That's true too," Chip dug a hole with his foot, stuck me into the resulting pit and poured water on my head from a flask.

"It's like she really is growing here," said Qupip examining Chip's latest jest.

"You two aren't relatives, by any chance?"

"Twins, actually," Qupip confessed.

"But from different parents," added Chip. "Okay. Let's revive our blockhead or he'll grow bored out there in beerspace and go to my house and drink all my beer."

"Here he is, as good as new!" declared the priest as a hale and healthy orc rose from the ground next to him.

"Where's that little goody two-shoes?" asked Bogart brandishing his 'Croaker' fiercely in his hand.

"He died in the battle with Geranika."

"Oh no. I'm so saddened by this loss," the orc mocked. "In what Mesozoic did you dig up that hyper-aggressive fossil, you musical cryptozoologist? A goddamn ghostly T-Rex, may a pterodactyl crap on his head..."

"I didn't have time to learn the proper epoch and

history of that fanatic, and I didn't have much choice but to summon him at that moment. But if you really want to, I can summon him again when the ability cools down. He won't be higher than Level 50, so you should be able to handle him."

"Nah. It's not interesting that way," Bogart refused my generous offer. "I don't beat up on the small fry."

"By the way, why have you lost all your levels?" Qupip asked me. "And how did you get them to begin with?"

"It was a scenario event. I lost a level per minute and when Geranika left, the scenario ended and my level returned to what it had been before the battle.

"Oh..." he drawled with some disappointment. "But still, that was cool."

"All right—what happened around here while I was gone?" Bogart demanded and Qupip, periodically interrupted by Chip, launched into a colorful and utterly exaggerated retelling of the battle's conclusion. Bogart listened without interrupting and only enviously sighed at especially intense moments.

Meanwhile, I looked around, trying to understand why the battlefield looked so unusual: The bodies had not dissolved in an airy haze and the wounded had not been automatically restored to full health. The survivors were coming to their senses around me and mourning their dead.

The battlefield, strewn with hundreds of dead

bodies, was depressing. A single glance at the grief in the eyes of the living was enough to forget that all of this was just a game. The developers had done their utmost to convey the violence and destruction of war.

The Sixth stood over her own body with a devastated, deadened look. I approached her.

"In the pursuit of my obsession I committed a great evil," she said quietly without turning around. "Revenge blinded me. My strength engendered pride and arrogance that made me reject Sylvyn's divine order. I rebelled against the will of the Council, thinking that I knew better. All these deaths are my fault."

I didn't say anything. Astilba was not the type who would take well to words of comfort or assurances that others were to blame. Of course, there were others who had contributed to the current outcome, but this did not diminish her guilt.

The First approached us silently. The Seventh followed her like a shadow. Wounded, exhausted by the fight, with mourning faces—they did not at all resemble the victors they were. And anyway, it was hard to call all this a victory.

"Yes," Nigella said, looking with sadness at the Sixth's ghostly figure. "These deaths are your fault. As these lives are your merit."

She gestured at the survivors around us. The surviving members of the Council approached us. Fresia, whose wounded arm rested in a sling of vines across her breast was helping Conquolor who was limping. The Guardian stood a little to the side, but his eyes rested on the First and I had no doubt that he could hear every word.

Neither the Kartossians nor the players risked joining this conversation. I was just looking around for a way to retreat, when Eben took me by my shoulder, restraining me.

"You have made a terrible mistake," the First went on. "And we allowed you to make it. But today you did everything you could to amend for your deeds. And you paid a high price. You managed to defend your people. You have done your duty. You are forgiven."

The Sixth raised her head, looked into the eyes of the First, and then each of her brothers and sisters. Relief, gratitude, remorse, and regret all swirled in the summoned soul's eyes.

"If I could forgive myself, Nigella…"

No one replied to this. No one broke the silence. Even the sounds of the surrounding world subsided, as if we were surrounded by a magical barrier.

"My soul will know no rest until I fulfil my debt to the Forest. In the name of Sylvyn!" she proclaimed and a sudden gust of wind stirred the canopy around the glade. "I swear to protect my people from now and as long as I exist!"

A green glow surrounded the necromancer. The forest god had heeded her oath.

"Lorelei," the Sixth said to me, when the glow faded away, "give Nigella the songbook that you created. The First will decide which bards deserve to receive it. I will respond to the summons and come to fight for my people!"

Nigella took from my hands the songbook I had created with a slight bow.

"We will call on you when the need comes, sister," she promised the Sixth and then turned to me.

"You have been invaluable, Lorelei. Despite the fact that Shadow dwells in you, you still remained faithful to your people. You warned Eben of Geranika and the plans you knew of. With your help, we managed to free the Guardian and received new allies from among the free inhabitants of Kartoss. You managed to resist the will of Geranika and fought on our side. You gave Astilba a chance to correct her mistakes. I thank you, Lorelei."

Reputation status with the Biota raised to Esteem.

Reputation status with the Biota Council raised to Esteem.

"Unfortunately, I cannot rescind your exile from the Hidden Forest," continued the First. "As long as there is a piece of Shadow in you and our brothers, you are fraught with danger."

I sighed and bowed my head in acquiescence. Who knows how else Geranika can control us? The Lord of Shadow is full of surprises.

"But I cannot let you go without a reward either," Nigella continued. "Tell me what you need more: Items that will help you in your adventures or new knowledge?"

"Knowledge," I answered without hesitation.

Items can be bought or created, whereas knowledge imparted by the High Druid of the Biota is a truly rare gift.

"You do not possess the knowledge of the druids, and therefore I will not be able to teach you much, but this should help you on your journey..."

Nigella has taught you 'Prairie Grass I.'

Spent 1 training point. 8 training points remaining.

Nigella has taught you 'Summon Animal.'

Spent 1 training point. 7 training points remaining.

Attention! You may choose the path of the Wild Bard, forever linking your life with natural magic (+100% to druidic spells). However, you will lose the ability to learn the spells of other schools. All previously learned spells for other classes will be forgotten.

Do you wish to accept the Wild Bard specialization?

"Thank you for these gifts, First," I said quite sincerely after I had declined the system's offer.

"That's not all," Eben smiled a little sadly. "You kept your word and fulfilled the assignment I gave you."

> **Quest complete:** *A Friend among Outsiders.*
> **Experience earned: +30,000 XP.**
> **You have gained a level!**
> **Current level: 38.**
> **1,677 XP remaining until next level.**
> **Unallocated stat points: 80.**
> **Training points remaining: 8.**
> **200 gold earned.**

"As long as you belong to Shadow, you will be hated and persecuted," said the spymaster. "I will teach you a few tricks that allow you to hide from any unwanted attention."

> **Eben has taught you 'Soft Step I.'**
> **Spent 1 training point. 7 training points remaining.**
> **Eben has taught you 'Hide I.'**
> **Spent 1 training point. 6 training points remaining.**

Eben has taught you 'Conceal Essence I.'

Spent 1 training point. 5 training points remaining.

Attention! You can choose the path of the Spy, forever linking your life with the masters of the cloak and dagger (+100% to Rogue skills). However, you will lose the ability to learn the spells of other schools. All previously learned spells for other classes will be forgotten.

Accept the Spy specialization?

I only had time to scan the descriptions of my new skills but it was enough to understand that the spymaster had made my in-game life a lot easier. I was even tempted to accept the specialization, but losing the spells of the other schools seemed too much.

"Thank you for this knowledge, Seventh," I said, refusing the spy specialization.

It was even a little disappointing that neither Fresia, nor Conquolor, nor the Guardian taught me anything. Either the First had rewarded me for everyone or they did not find my actions worthy of rewards. But then the Sixth unexpectedly joined the award ceremony...

"You already know how to see the currents of vitality, Lorelei. The time has come to teach you how to manipulate them. I will start by teaching you how to sever them."

Astilba has taught you 'Sever Current of Vitality I.'

Spent 1 training point. 4 training points remaining.

"I have to talk to the surviving renegades before I go to the Gray Lands," Astilba said and without awaiting any response from me, stepped aside to the rest of the blighted biota.

The Seventh followed her with his gaze, then hesitated over the slumped figure of the Second and at last picked up the lifeless body of the Sixth.

"We will return to the Tree and announce what has happened to the races of the forest," he said. "After that we shall say farewell to the dead. The Tree will not accept minions of Shadow and therefore neither you, Lorelei, nor the other renegades will be able to attend the ceremony. Today you will return to your camp and make ready to depart. Tomorrow you must leave the Hidden Forest. If you wish to say goodbye to someone, you don't have much time."

One after the other, the bodies of the fallen began rising into the air and streaming into a portal to the Tree. Speleus' broken body looked so terrible that I involuntarily looked away. The developers overdid it, trying to impress the players...boy did they overdo it.

The guild leaders had no time for me. They were speaking with the ambassador of Kartoss, apparently receiving their rewards for the scenario. Even the First stepped over to them, so I didn't see much sense in waiting around. Chip was listening to the Guardian, whose loud voice, this time, could be heard by no one but the pirq. Bogart had wandered off somewhere. The right thing to do was to head over to the renegades' camp and then exit the game but it was too far to plod there on foot. It looked like either I had to wait to get a ride or ask someone to fix Roach's bridle.

Having nothing to do, I moseyed over to the barely visible border with the blighted ground. The black stain was slowly shrinking. I guess the Guardian was restoring his forest, expelling Shadow from its boundaries. And if so, I didn't have much time to amass my strategic reserve of blighted earth for my subsequent alchemical experiments. Geranika is unlikely to help me in this, so I won't be able to find this ingredient anywhere else.

Shaking up the meagre supply of alchemical flasks in my backpack, I wondered how to gather the earth more conveniently. The dagger Palisandro had given me seemed quite suitable, although it'd be nice to scrounge up a nice little infantry shovel like the one Bogart had.

I managed to fill a dozen flasks when a voice sounded above my head:

"Welly, welly, welly, welly, welly, welly, well! Fancy seeing you here!"

The sinister greeting made me reflexively squeeze the useless dagger. Right before me appeared a pair of boots I already recognized. They belonged to none other than my old droog—Otolaryngologist. As calmly as I could, I straightened, shook off my hands and looked around. Over Oto's shoulder, an unfamiliar biota priest was grinning unkindly, but my sixth sense told me that he had several more rogue friends hiding around here somewhere. He was just too confident, especially considering the outcome of our last PVP encounter. I'd wager that his whole gang of hoodlums was hiding in the bushes...

My first thought was to grab an amulet and call for help from the Day of Wrath or the Dark Legion. Of course, we were not extremely close friends, but I had promised to tell them in detail about the completed scenario and the bards' ability to summon souls. They'd save me from being sent to spawn for that alone. I even opened my inventory, looking for the right amulet, when a better idea occurred to me.

"Listen, let's stop this stupid back and forth," I suggested to Oto's bewilderment. "You won't let me play normally, I am well aware of this. But I can offer something interesting to you in exchange for a truce."

The rogue looked skeptical.

"I can't even imagine what it could be," he drawled doubtfully, playing with his dagger. "I don't find you very interesting—you're a bit too ugly."

I could hear a few muffled guffaws.

"How about the coordinates to that dungeon you were looking for?" I asked, trying my best to ignore the insult. If all goes well, the cat will cry the mouse's tears.

Oto's face stretched for an instant but he immediately put on his gameface.

"Oh, don't make me laugh. How would someone like you know the coordinates of the dungeon?"

"Well that's my business. I call on the Guardian of this forest to witness that I know the exact coordinates of the dungeon and, as far as I know, no player has completed it yet."

A bright green glow enveloped me. The Guardian confirmed that I was telling the truth. Morgana had told me about this trick during our picnic. She was simply brimming with interesting factoids about the intricacies of legal relationships within the game, funny anecdotes and common types of fraud.

The rogue's eyes flashed eagerly and trying to make his voice sound as indifferent as possible, he suggested:

"So be it. In exchange for the coordinates of the dungeon, I promise that neither I nor my friends will ever touch you again."

I even admired such arrogance. Morgana had explained to me that the coordinates to new dungeons sold for very, very good money. Even the seediest cellar, a Level 1 Dungeon, could bring in a million in a second. Being the first to complete a dungeon granted a guild such nice bonuses that passing on the opportunity was out of the question. A Level 300+ dungeon, where you could actually find loot that was useful, was many times more valuable. The final price depended on the various bonuses, chances of rare quest items dropping, et cetera.

"Why you're a cunning one!" I objected, actually annoyed now. "Do you think I'm a noob who doesn't know anything about the game? Forget it. This kind of info costs a good penny and you know it. Two hundred thousand!"

I stared at Otolaryngologist defiantly, while inwardly straining to hold off the smile that kept stubbornly trying to creep onto my face. Come on, buddy, make up your mind. It's a considerable amount for one player, but crumbs for a guild. Even if you buy it for 200K right now, the reward you'll get from your guild will be much higher. And if you don't buy it, your friends in the bushes there sure won't pass up the opportunity.

It seems that similar thoughts were bouncing around the rogue's head. He cast a sidelong glance at the suddenly pensive priest next to him and blurted out:

"Deal! Here, take this purchase agreement. Sign it and give it back to me to sign. The only hitch, is I will pay you the money within two days. I simply don't have that amount on this character."

These words once again confirmed Sloe's

assumption that Oto and his friends were using the peculiarities of the hardcore races to search for the dungeon. The Barliona admins did not allow players to have more than one character, with one exception. Those who wanted to try out the new hardcore races were allowed to temporarily suspend their main character and create a new, hardcore one. If the player decided that he had had enough, he simply deleted the hardcore and the main character was automatically enabled. Obviously, Oto was one of those who had temporarily 'moved to another character.'

A contract appeared before me. I really didn't feel like reading all the fine print and delving into the details. Especially since I'd just made friends with an in-game lawyer.

"Nothing personal, but I don't trust your legalese much," I said to the robber, with a hint of uncertainty in my voice. "Wait ten minutes. I'll download a standard purchase agreement from the web. We can sign that. Who knows what you've slipped into the fine print here."

Oto only sniffed irritably and nodded. I left full immersion and quickly dashed off an email to Morgana's work address. She had told me that she works inside the game and all her mail is redirected to her game inbox.

I was lucky. Morgana replied less than a minute later. I briefly outlined the situation and soon received a boilerplate contract, in which all the terms of the sale were outlined in the most neutral way possible: Namely, that I would provide information about the dungeon that was accurate at the time of my last visit and that I was not responsible for any changes that had occurred to it since then. Because ten hours had not passed since the visit and, at the insistence of Morgana, I indicated in the contract the levels of the opponents I had seen there, I had no doubt that Oto would bite.

And he did. He read the contract, nodded, agreeing with the condition of not intentionally causing me direct and indirect harm, and we signed the contract. With a clear conscience, I conveyed to him the coordinates of the renegades' HQ, which after today's scenario, would be completely abandoned. Had Geranika won, the renegades would have once again returned to their camp and become a constantly respawning source of loot and experience for the players. But Geranika had been defeated and the dungeon was empty, a useless network of caves.

Oto and I parted almost on friendly terms. Fortunately, he did not start openly gloating and trying to cast the stupidity of what I had done in my face. I'm afraid my acting talents might not have been enough to affect an adequate response. It was only once he'd moved some distance away from me that he cheerfully said to one of his hidden friends: "Suckers ain't mammoths—suckers don't go extinct."

"Amen," I thought, and pretended that I hadn't heard anything.

I did not feel remorse. Oto wasn't my friend by any stretch of the imagination and he had effectively screwed me in this deal, paying at least 800K less than what the dungeon was actually worth. Perhaps more. Were I to arrange an auction between the Day of Wrath and the Dark Legion, the amount could grow significantly. But I was not suicidal. To punish the insolence and greed of one player by exacting a small amount was one thing. To defraud a powerful guild for a good amount of money is another. Strictly speaking, Oto never told me that he was in the Dark Legion. In fact I still couldn't be sure that this was the case. So this little prank is exclusively between me and one over-confident rogue.

I did not dare continue to collect the blighted earth. A deal is a deal, but when has a piece of paper ever stopped an irate, inventive person? And it wasn't like his friends, whom I'd sent to spawn with Bogart's help, had promise me my safety.

Out of harm's way, I rejoined the gathering of players.

Neither party hurried to leave the battlefield. The players were picking up loot, reviving the last of their fallen comrades and sharing their impressions of the scenario.

"Ah! Lorelei!" exclaimed the leader of the Dark Legion, who had been talking with Dirk, and waved me over with a friendly gesture.

Otolaryngologist was already back too. He was spinning around nearby, glowing. Upon seeing me, his smile grew so wide that its corners risked circumnavigating his skull. Chip and Bogart were speaking quietly off to the side, both unusually serious and quiet. Hearing my name, they stopped and looked at Evolett.

"I have a lot of questions regarding the scenario that just ended," the leader of the Dark Legion said when I approached. "But first, I want to invite you to join our guild. You have potential."

"The Day of Wrath will also be glad to see you in our guild," said Dirk, glancing at Evolett with irritation. "Especially since you've already managed to meet some members of our guild."

Urgh. What is everyone on my case for suddenly? Glancing at Bogart, who was scowling for some reason, I shook my head.

"Thank you, of course, but I'd like to play this character without joining a guild yet. Imagine if I created trouble for your guild by switching to Shadow? It's more appropriate to play solo in my case. I can get myself into whatever trouble I feel like without having to worry about the consequences. No responsibilities, no mandatory online time, no enemy guilds that could spoil my game. The organizations you guys are running aren't a game for me. And I prefer to work in another area."

"And what would that be, if it's no secret?" inquired Dirk.

"Music. Now, if you're planning a party or some corporate, err, guild event or something like that—you should call me. The guys and I will make it a real smash."

Evolett grunted thoughtfully, rubbed his chin and nodded:

"I have always valued the ability to prioritize. And now, my esteemed colleague Dirk and I would like to hear your detailed account of everything related to this scenario."

I had no idea where to begin. In the end, too many minor and seemingly insignificant episodes had merged into a single story. Dirk interpreted my silence in his own way:

"Name the price."

I sighed involuntarily. I still have to get used to the fact that in Barliona everything had a price.

"I started playing only recently and do not particularly understand the intricacies. Let's do it an easier way: I will tell you everything that happened to me, and you can decide how much that info costs on your own. You know better what can be useful to a player of my level who has borked her reputation with all the empires to hatred status."

The guild leaders nodded simultaneously and I began my story with my first vision of the Schism. At the mention of the dungeon beneath the renegades' camp, Dirk squinted at Evolett, but he only waved his hand, urging me to go on.

"It seems to me that the scenario did not end exactly the way the developers planned," said the leader of the Dark Legion when I had finished. "Stop staring at me, Dirk. My people are checking the dungeon right now and judging by the messages in the guild chat, it is completely empty. You saw all the bosses with your own eyes and none of them, obviously, will be going back there."

Evolett smiled cheerfully in reply to Dirk's unvoiced question:

"Less than an hour ago, this nice lady sold the coordinates of an empty dungeon to a dimwitted player from my guild."

Hearing this, Dirk grunted while Qupip and Lipo, who were standing nearby, burst out in loud, merry laughter, making fun of the loser.

"Since you, Lorelei, did not grow greedy and try to earn millions from a dummy, I don't have any complaints about this little deception," said Evolett to my relief. "Wiegraf was trying to scam you for several million and this will be a good lesson for him."

This was a great relief. If the guild leadership is not offended, then everything is in order. Meanwhile, the name Wiegraf, which obviously belonged to Oto's main character, is worth remembering. Judging by the way Pasha and Sasha exchanged glances, it was not just me who came to this conclusion.

"So as I understand it, you only have the Free Lands available to you?" asked Dirk. "That place isn't too friendly for players of your level. If you want, we will give you access to the guild training ground to level you up faster. If you grow a bit, you'll have better chances of surviving in difficult conditions."

"And what will I owe in exchange for this service?" I asked, remembering that everything in Barliona came with a price tag.

"Nothing," Dirk shrugged. "I promised to thank you for the story. The next time you come across an interesting quest, feel free to invite my players. It seems to me that in the coming months bards will often encounter non-standard quests."

"We, too, would be grateful for an invitation to participate in the scenarios you encounter," Evolett did not lag behind his rival. "And since we are talking about expressing gratitude, do you have any idea about a suitable reward for your story?"

I paused to think. A guild's assistance in leveling up sounded pretty good. I had read a couple accounts of the Free Lands and had understood one simple thing: There was no point going there until I hit Level 100. But decent gear would also be useful, since auctions and most of the traders were now off limits to me. As for the rest...I didn't know enough about the game in order to immediately understand what exactly I needed. Alchemical ingredients? I haven't even decided yet, whether I wanted to grind that. As far as cartography went, I already had everything I needed. Although...

"Could you give me some uncommon or even rare maps? Just any scrap you have lying around. They could be for locations that are completely useless."

The guild leaders looked at each other in puzzlement.

"And why do you need maps and not even any specific ones?"

"I have this cartography quest. Chip and I are charting a map for our cartography instructor and he promised me some kind of bonus if we brought him some rare maps."

"Minions of Shadow may not enter the Tree," Dirk reminded me.

"Well, if I can't go, I'll send Chip to do it. Maybe we'll get some cool gear out of it."

"Why not?" said Evolett after a little thought. "Hang on, I'll send you a contract."

A few minutes later, a few dozen maps came crashing down on Chip from Evolett and another dozen or so from Dirk. The attached contracts prohibited me from giving or selling these maps to anyone other than the cartography instructor.

"I still can't get used to calling these tapestries maps," Chip muttered as he approached me, examining the presents. "And I can already sense with the tip of my tail who will have to verify all these tapestries…"

"If you happen to be in the Celestial Empire or in Astrum, be sure to verify them," Dirk grunted.

"Big deal," Chip shrugged, carefully furling the scrolls and placing them in a tube hanging from his shoulder. "A hundred leagues is not too out of the way for us. We'll take a detour to the Celestial Empire, if necessary."

"Yeah, we'll pacify the Boxer Rebellion while we're at it," Bogart nodded. "Or help out the Yellow Turbans. Pasha, let's grab our cactus and go already. The hell are we hanging around here for—I have a night flight and we aren't ready yet."

"I am going to ask for a ride to the renegades' camp and then I'll exit too. It'll take me too long to get there on my own. By the way, Pasha!" I fished out Roach's bridle from my bag. "Can you fix my horse for me, what do you say?"

"No problem," the pirq nodded, taking the item. "And now run along so we can wrap things up out in beerspace!"

EPILOGUE

I JOINED SNEGOV'S GOING AWAY PARTY exactly in time for Wallace's arrival. More precisely, I arrived at the very moment when Sasha needed a hand and he shamelessly tasked me with setting the table.

"I'm an officer now," he explained self-importantly, loading me with platters of snacks. "So I get to order my subordinates around. Onward, recruit!"

"Now I understand why your subordinates prefer to hide in the jungle," remarked Wallace, taking bottles from the refrigerator. "Come on, you newly-minted noble you. Finish your cookery so we can eat already."

"Yah, five minutes," Sasha stuck his nose in the oven, inspected the state of the chicken and potatoes and concluded with satisfaction: "She looks good boys."

At the table, the conversation naturally turned to the game. Sasha's departure was not mentioned at all as if doing so was some kind of taboo, and so we began discussing the day's main event—the battle with Geranika. To be fair, I did most of the talking as Sasha had missed the finale and Pasha arrived only at the denouement. As a result, their participation in my retelling of the epic battle was limited mainly to incidental comments.

"There's just one thing I don't understand," I brought up the one detail that wouldn't stop nagging me. "Why Geranika wanted to kill the ambassadors is understandable. Spoil relations between the neighbors, destroy the alliance, enrage two emperors at once...The ambassador is their mutual relative, after all. But why was Geranika so eager to kill the First? It makes no sense. If she dies, all that happens is an eclipse and then the Tree simply spawns a new leader. It makes no difference to Geranika whatsoever. Every creature of the Tree is devoted to Sylvyn and will never have anything to do with Shadow."

"What about seizing the opportunity presented by the ensuing power vacuum to strike the Tree when its defenders had no one to command them?" Wallace suggested with a shrug.

"But there already wasn't anyone to command them," I disagreed. "Their top commander, the Second, went over to the side of Geranika. As far as I understand, one of the pirq elders, who was also there, assumed his duties. And the new First would appear almost immediately and on the Tree in safety. If his true aim was to decapitate the biota and paralyze the Council, it would make more sense to capture the First alive. But, again, minions of Shadow cannot approach the Tree. Neither Geranika nor his army would be able to attack it physically."

"Are you really sure that there even should be a point in all this?" Sasha asked with genuine surprise. "When was the last time you saw a holo-flick? Logic has long been sacrificed for the sake of entertainment and tragedy. And Barliona is pure entertainment. To kill the leader is a standard cliché. The solemn state funeral that follows, the tragedy of it all, is supposed to wring tears from the players."

"Well, yes," I had to agree with this assumption. "That would also explain why the bodies didn't vanish at that location, like they do everywhere else in the game. For the sake of a beautiful solemn funeral. It seems like those who came out of the Tree are returning to the Tree again. Symbolism, the cycle of life..."

"Hang on," Wallace intervened. "A funeral? That is, they're collected in one place and then a farewell ceremony is held? Is that right?"

"Something like that," I nodded, putting food on the plate. "Why?"

"Eh no reason..." He began to thoughtfully chew his lip. "I remembered something...But from actual history...I doubt it applies here. Snegov, do you remember how in Kouilou once..."

"Let's not remember that at the table," said Sasha. "Found something to remember, damn it. Pour the next round, you're punished."

"What if we remember it but without details?" I asked. "Short and to the point. What's it have to do with the game?"

Wallace froze with the bottle in his hand and looked inquiringly at Sasha.

"All right, come on, get on with it, now that you've brought it up." Sasha granted his permission with a wave of his hand. "Our Lady of the Cactus is already all ears."

Wallace sniffled guiltily and began:

"You see, there is this old and very vile tactic of booby-trapping corpses. We came across it in Idiofa for the first time: After a wave of ethnic cleansing, the rebels there would booby-trap the dead civilians. Typically, they'd rig an unpinned grenade under a corpse or else make an incision and..."

Here, Wallace encountered Snegov's cold glare and trailed off mid-sentence.

"Nah. That's not an option in the game," I shook my head. "The NPCs sent all of their dead through the portal to be buried on the Tree..."

I did not finish my thought. Something clicked in my brain and all the pieces of the puzzle fell into place.

"I have to go do something for a couple of minutes!" I said, jumping up from the table and dashing to the capsule.

"It's that urgent?" I heard Sasha call after me.

"Okay, okay, flutter away Batman, save the world..."

Activating short-term immersion mode, I climbed into the cocoon right in my clothes. As soon as the system connected me to Barliona, I whipped out Sloe's amulet from my inventory and made a call. After a few painful seconds, he answered in a quiet whisper:

"I'm at the farewell ceremony. Call me later..."

"STOP!" I yelled as loud as the Guardian. "The body of the Sixth contains Geranika's dagger. When the body is submerged into the Tree, the dagger will blight it! It will blight the Tree!"

"Are you sure?" Sloe asked quietly, after a pause.

"Dead certain! Imagine what will happen if I'm right!"

"Should I give the amulet to someone on the Council? If you are right—the reward should be insane."

I thought for a couple of seconds. The reward will be princely but they'll hold on to me for a while to. And Sasha will leave for a hot spot in a few hours. What kind of person would I be if I spent those hours in VR?

"It's all you," I told Sloe. "I have more important business in meatspace."

"I'll call you back."

"I'm exiting. If anything, call me on my visor irl."

Ignoring the astonished looks of the renegades around me, I exited the game.

"And? Has the world been saved then?" Pasha asked me, sitting at the table in regal isolation.

I could hear Wallace's voice in the bathroom and figured that the rest of the duet was discussing the wine list, examining the bottles that were being chilled in the ice bath.

"It seems so," I replied uncertainly. "Sloe will call me back and tell me for sure."

"*We will...we will...rock you!*" a voice roared behind my back and the couple of winos tumbled into the kitchen together.

"Like a bunch of Queen groupies," Pasha quipped. "Although, why groupies? It's Mercury and May in the flesh."

"You just wish you had our vocal chords," Wallace retorted, squeezing into his seat. "Kiera, why don't you sing something, huh?"

"Yeah, Kiera Khan, play us a tune," Pasha joined him.

Sasha didn't say anything for the giant bite of an apple in his mouth, but he actively supported his friends with gestures.

"What'll it be?" I picked up the guitar synth and waved my hand.

* * *

SLOE CALLED BACK an hour or so later, chipper and cheerful. My guess had been confirmed, and our prickly friend managed to become the hero of the entire Hidden Forest, which came with some incredible rewards. When he called me, he was already basking in his unexpected fortune.

"Geranika's plan was a cunning one indeed," I related to my friends after Sloe hung up. "He did not want to simply kill the First, he was going to leave his dagger in her body and then let her corpse be solemnly buried. During the funeral ceremony, the Tree absorbs the dead. Thus it would absorb the dagger with the corpse. After that, it's simple—the dagger blights the Tree and it spawns a new leader—the Blighted First. But a further consequence would be that all newborn biota would be born blighted too. It's like a Trojan dagger, you see. Thus Geranika's Empire grows in territory and warriors and the remaining unchanged biota are sent to Kartoss. I am even sure that they have some kind of sacred seed of the Tree, which they will solemnly plant, so that players can still play as vanilla biota for Kartoss."

"That is," Wallace clarified, "since he couldn't get rid of the First, he secreted his dagger in the body of the Sixth."

"Uh-huh." Pasha poured himself a beer. "She stuck it into herself when she did the hara-kiri. And after that, everyone forgot about the dagger, while Geranika's weapon remained in the corpse waiting for its moment. Like a biological bomb or something."

"Are you sure that Geranika of yours isn't a

descendant of Shiro Ishii?" Wallace wondered. "He's like a master of biological warfare."

"You should ask the game designers who his ancestors were. Sloe pulled out the dagger at the last moment like a classic action movie hero," I giggled, remembering the player's enthusiastic, drunk voice. "So he was not only rewarded royally, but the reputation of his entire guild increased to Respect status."

"Hooray for the hero." Sasha looked at his watch and sighed. "The taxi will be here soon. Let's go wait for it downstairs, eh?"

"Indeed, let's," Pasha answered for everyone and lumbered up from the table.

"Well, and what did you get as a reward? You're the one who figured it out," the sapper asked.

"Who knows," I admitted honestly, pulling on my jacket. "I think Sloe mentioned who warned him, so I should get something out of it."

"Ah the customary fate of recon," Sasha chuckled from the hall. "Take care of the entire business and the hell with the guy who gets the credit. As long as you don't get punished, you're good."

"I wouldn't go that far," I replied. "I'm still getting exiled."

The spring night was surprisingly still and warm. We stood at the building's entryway, waiting for the car and talking quietly. At times our conversation was punctuated by the clinking of glasses which Pasha had brought down for the occasion. The guys told jokes, stories from their tours and doggedly avoiding any mention of Sasha's departure. I got the impression that this trip would be...not a quiet one, to put it mildly.

"And don't eat any of the green bananas," Wallace instructed his friend.

Sasha nodded intently, refilling the glasses.

A car arrived and Pasha asked:

"Well...Shall we be coming back alive?"

"We shall come back alive," Sasha nodded and raised his glass.

"We shall come back alive!" Wallace echoed.

They clinked glasses and were silent for a couple of seconds, then tipped the glasses into their mouths.

Sasha tossed his knapsack in the trunk and turned to us.

"Until we meet again then?"

"Take care, Snegov," the guys took turns hugging Sasha.

Sasha turned to me:

"Keep an eye on my boy, huh?" He playfully poked Pasha in the belly.

"Don't I get a hug?" I asked indignantly, squeezing Sasha who suddenly grew flustered. "You be careful out there."

"A true alley cat can handle himself anywhere," he smiled.

"Ah-ha look at his ears, his ears are blazing!" yelled Wallace ecstatically.

"Oh go to hell, you talking dumpster," muttered Sasha, embarrassed, and slipped into the taxi before his friend could return the favor.

The engine revved quietly and the taxi dove into the night, carrying our friend into the unknown.

END OF BOOK TWO

FROM THE AUTHORS

Dear Readers,

We are very pleased that you have read our work. For both authors this was the first time writing collaboratively: The work was very arduous and we constantly had to argue with one another, defending our points of view. We hope that the outcome was successful and you enjoyed it. If not, we will continue to work in order to make the next books better and more interesting. Please leave your comments about the work. It's important for us to receive feedback from our readers.

We have a nice surprise for all of our readers! A story we wrote which we wish to give you for free. Go to www.Mako-books.com, register and received an extra story for free. Share the news with your friends and make them happy. Pleasant reading!

Want to be the first to know about our latest LitRPG, sci fi and fantasy titles from your favorite authors?

Subscribe to our NEW RELEASES newsletter:
http://eepurl.com/b7niIL

Thank you for reading *A Song of Shadow!*
If you like what you've read, check out other LitRPG
novels published by Magic Dome Books:

An NPC's Path LitRPG series by Pavel Kornev:
The Dead Rogue
Kingdom of the Dead

Level Up series by Dan Sugralinov:
Re-Start
Hero

**The Way of the Shaman LitRPG series
by Vasily Mahanenko:**
Survival Quest
The Kartoss Gambit
The Secret of the Dark Forest
The Phantom Castle
The Karmadont Chess Set
Shaman's Revenge
Clans War

Dark Paladin LitRPG series by Vasily Mahanenko:
The Beginning
The Quest
Restart

Galactogon LitRPG series by Vasily Mahanenko:
Start the Game!

**The Bard from Barliona LitRPG series
by Eugenia Dmitrieva and Vasily Mahanenko:**
The Renegades
A Song of Shadow

The Neuro LitRPG series by Andrei Livadny:
The Crystal Sphere
The Curse of Rion Castle
The Reapers

**The Expansion (The History of the Galaxy) series
by A. Livadny:**
Blind Punch
The Shadow of Earth
Servobattalion

Point Apocalypse *(a near-future action thriller)*
by Alex Bobl

The Sublime Electricity series by Pavel Kornev
The Illustrious
The Heartless
The Fallen
The Dormant

You're in Game!
(LitRPG Stories from Bestselling Authors)

You're in Game-2!
(More LitRPG stories set in your favorite worlds)

**The Game Master series by A. Bobl and A.
Levitsky:**
The Lag

Moskau by G. Zotov
(a dystopian thriller)

El Diablo by G.Zotov
(a supernatural thriller)

More books and series are coming out soon!

In order to have new books of the series translated faster, we need your help and support! Please consider leaving a review or spread the word by recommending *A Song of Shadow* to your friends and posting the link on social media. The more people buy the book, the sooner we'll be able to make new translations available. Thank you!

Till next time!